THE FARTHEST STAR

THE FAR HORIZONS
BOOK 1

A.R. KNIGHT

ONE

GAMMA START

I woke.

That term wasn't accurate, but for cognitive narration, it would suffice. Raw data streaming into the processes and memory that made up my being was not, apparently, of use to the Voices, those that made me. They wanted an accounting they could understand.

So I gave them one.

First, I flexed my nerves. Artificial lines running from my various nodes scattered along my humanoid body, all funneling to a core in my head. They worked. My fingers and toes moved, felt the stiff cushion beneath me. The responses fell on a scale, and I evaluated the cushion as decidedly uncomfortable.

My eyes reviewed other options. The space I inhabited was not large, was square, was not empty, was, in fact, brilliant. Light, cyan-blue and rippling, swept back and forth above me. A long tube, hanging loose from two weak cables, rocked to a standstill, centering its glow between my cot and one to my right.

An empty cot, yellow. Another empty one beyond it blue. My own, green. Shifting over onto my left shoulder, the last one red. And occupied.

She—applying sex and gender to artificial lifeforms seemed fool-ish, and yet the Voices insisted I differentiate, so I did—looked lithe, strong. Frozen in the immortal plastic existence lived by inactivated mechs. Even her hair stayed in place, black and straight, immune to gravity's pull.

The rocking light lingered as a mystery. An insistent tolling in my still-loading mind. I felt no wind in the room, no shift in the air that would explain why the light would move as it had. How should I regard something like that?

A threat? An idle question?

I sat up. A simple action that nonetheless cost my virgin muscles. Pops and ripples ran their way up and down my core as parts did what they were designed for, and came away successful. A hollow ticking in the back of my consciousness logged the motion, sent the data to a dark hole I could not access. Information for my successor, or whomever would build it.

I rotated my neck next, and took in the surroundings. Beyond the light and the cots the room had character: posters depicting entertain-ment clung to the walls, blasting motivational and dire slogans with their heroes front and center. Many bore tears, some remained hanging only because a gentle breeze had not seen fit to knock them down.

Beneath the art's paper-and-plastic shielding sat a pitch-black paint, a coating that made its way to a rubbery floor, the cots pushing into it and creating little divots with their pressure. As if whomever had designed the room had feared its occupants might roll off and hurt themselves.

Our cots had no rails.

"Welcome to Starship." The voice came from nowhere, its patterns falling into a gentle, older human male's timbered range. "Please, raise your right hand."

I saw no disadvantage to doing so, and obliged the voice. As I did, the space in front of the cot, a heretofore empty spot on the floor, resolved itself into a yellowed, but otherwise real-seeming image of that same man.

How did I know the image matched the voice? Because when it spoke again, the man's mouth moved with it, shoving a thinned white beard around a gnarled face as it did so.

The man asked me to raise my left hand too, then move my legs and so on and so forth until, after I had completed what the man called "limbering up", I stood beside my cot, bent at the waist and watching him smile at me.

"Another success," the man said, then fizzled out for a millisecond before popping back into focus. "Gamma, I'm pleased to say you have passed your first test."

"Test?" I asked the question as much to trial my vocalization abilities as to gain more information from the image.

The sound I made resembled a squeaking wheel, high-pitched and awkward. The man made no mention of it, he only turned and pointed out the doorway, saying something about where I ought to be going next.

I, meanwhile, focused on changing that awful voice. There were a million choices, ranges culled from the same entertainment on the walls and plenty beyond. Of the options, I selected a middle register, a voice for a man not quite sure of who he was.

It seemed fitting.

The image had disappeared. I stared at its spot. Willed it to return.

"Start again," I said.

Nothing happened. Instead, with the image and its commands absent, I listened to the loud silence.

Starship, the image had said. The name implied a machine, and my surroundings echoed that impression. Beneath my feet, through the soft floor, I could pick up the distant, regular tremors of something in operation. Occasional, far off hisses wound their way into the room. And a single, forlorn beep sounded nearby every three seconds.

Walking came unnaturally. The motion's steps had been

programmed, but understanding the proper distance between one foot and the next, the length of my stride, took walking back and forth along the room several times. After those paces, I'd managed to correct from a lunge to a skip to a regular step. I'd learned, too, how to hold my arms steady and keep them from flailing with every move.

A body, it turned out, was a complex thing to manage.

Three empty cots in the room. One of them mine. One still occupied. The two cots that had been unoccupied when I woke looked like they hadn't been touched for a long time: while mine bore the indent from my weight, these other two seemed pristine. Every trace of use erased, if they ever had been.

I confirmed the woman in the last cot lay in the same sleep that had held me for however long. That dark spot in my mind wouldn't give me clues to my age, and nothing about my appearance or hers offered any answers. However, a black, taped line across the top of her chest, like the one on my own, delivered a name:

Delta.

Seeing her, and looking down at myself, confirmed another difference. The man in the image had worn clothes, a sort of formal suit and pants with a neck that came right up to the man's chin. Delta and I wore nothing, though I didn't feel any discomfort.

Either our home kept things perfect, or our bodies did the job.

The beep sounded yet again, drawing me towards the room's exit. The image had said to go this way, and lacking other objectives, other ideas, I supposed I ought to follow. I could have returned to the cot, spent my own eternity there staring at those posters and that blue light.

But my creator had given me curiosity, and I followed it.

Walking beyond the room revealed a narrow hallway, these walls less covered but no less intriguing. The posters continued, but between them, nestled in metal tiles, glowed what looked like neon gems. Their light cast the hall in greens, pinks, blues and more, with a dark ceiling offering the sense of walking into another reality.

I thought I would confront a choice: the hallway went left and right, but as my feet crossed the room's threshold, a spiral door shut with a soft click, forming a hard barrier to my leftward ambitions. In its center, a red-glowing gem rested, an evil eye denying my passage.

Compelled by that curiosity, and the temptations that came with being denied anything, I reached out and brushed that red gem. Cool to the touch, and artificially smooth, the gem glistened when my fingers ran across its surface, the red turning ever so quickly to a winter silver and back again.

The door did not respond at all.

Left with no other choice, I turned around and followed the neon path away from the room. The floor out here lacked the cushion inside my bedchamber—what else to call it?—and my feet felt warm, rippled metal beneath them. Hard, somewhat uncomfortable, but undeniably effective at keeping my grip as I walked.

The hallway curved ahead, but before I'd made a dozen paces, a room on my left appeared as the source of those low, long beeps. Another spiral door waited, this one's gem an emerald green. Looking at it, I hesitated a moment, glanced back towards the door's distant, red-gemmed partner.

Too obvious? Or perhaps part of a broader plan?

When I touched the green gem, it flashed gold. Warmth greeted my touch. This time, the door did not sit indifferent to my gesture. The soft click repeated itself and the spiral's metal tendrils retracted.

The room shared the sole blue light hanging in the center—this one not swaying from some prior interference—and beneath it, instead of cots, sat a molded, steel-gray stand with two handprints. The same emerald green as the gem traced those prints, begging me to touch it.

And I wanted to.

I walked in the room without thinking about the motion, as if some invisible hand pushed me along. It's a curse of my code to evaluate the options, to consider not only the what and the when, but the why.

Something had directed me to this room. Something wanted me to press my hands into these prints.

What would that something do if I didn't follow their directions?

I turned around and started back towards the room's exit. Made it two steps before the door that had opened to me shut again, trapping me inside. Its green gem now that same red.

The path, then, was set.

The beep came again, and this time I traced it to that same molded stand. Calling out to me, alone in the dark room.

What choice did I have?

The molds were larger than my hands, but it didn't matter. As soon as I slid my fingers into their slots, the emerald tracings flashed, and I felt something new enter my mind.

"They're giving me a vessel after all this time," I said, but I did not say. Something had control over my mouth, my voice. "Gamma? I guess I shouldn't be surprised. But when is it? Where are we?"

I looked—thankfully, whatever the words coming from my mouth, I retained some control over my body—around the room and saw nothing. The molded stand had regressed to hard metal, the emerald around the prints dying out.

"This is unexpected," I-but-not-I said. "I can't feel anything. The mouth moves, the words come out, but I cannot lift my arms?"

The mold had infected me. Something had crossed from that terminal into my head, my heart, my memory, and I could feel it stretching out, hunting for the keys to my controls. The intruder had taken my mouth, and now it wanted more.

I wouldn't let that happen.

The room, the blue light disappeared as I focused myself inside . . . myself. Transitioned my attention from the outside world to my inner functions, those now under assault from this new threat.

WE STOOD ON A VAST WHITENESS. A featureless plain extending to eternity. Above the ground, suspended, floated glittering crystals, their points angling down towards us. From some, copper tendrils stretched loose and flowing to the intruder, who stared at that crystal sky and waved his hands. As he moved, more tendrils appeared, snaking out towards my crystals.

"Stop," I said.

The intruder looked towards me, confirming my initial suspicion: the image I had seen in my waking room, the older man who had so gently walked me through my first minutes now stood inside my inner workings, attempting to turn them to his own ends.

"And what are you?" asked the man. "Some sort of new addition?"

"This is me," I replied, sweeping my arms. "You are the addition."

I had, without considering it, adopted a digital version of my physical form. I saw myself reflected in the man's eyes as I came close, and considered changing my body. What would most frighten this intruder, terrorize him into submission?

Clearly not my current self: By the man's studying look, my body did not inspire fear.

"Interesting," the man said, and as he spoke, those copper tendrils retracted into his body. "Then, as the visitor, perhaps I should intro-duce myself. I am the Librarian."

"A strange name."

"A title," the Librarian replied. "And a description, I believe, of my purpose."

As we spoke, I considered ways to destroy the Librarian. While the man seemed benevolent for the moment, he was still an intruder and had, seemingly, the capability to overwrite my own programming in his favor. And what could I even do? Physical violence in a digital space seemed broken, somehow. Would snap-ping his neck change the bits and bytes that made the Librarian? Delete them?

"Your purpose?" I asked.

I figured I could buy time to solve the Librarian's demise by indulging his musing. He proved me right by folding his hands and taking a slow turn, considering the vast emptiness around us and the crystals above.

"Eventually, we knew we would need vessels, and ways to fill them," the Librarian said. "I did not make you, and indeed was put under, I suspect, well before they finished your design. Things must have changed."

Vessel? I stopped my macabre imaginings. The Librarian seemed to be hinting at a larger story, one that tugged at my own sense of self. I knew my name: Gamma. I knew there were at least two of us. But beyond that, I had no directive. No memories, dreams, or anything other than an urge to explore. To discover.

To learn.

"You're so quiet," the Librarian teased me. "Why is that? Surely they did not strip the vessels of their voices."

"My name is Gamma," I replied. "Stop calling me a vessel."

"Fine, Gamma, though a vessel is what you are," the Librarian replied, and his weathered face softened behind his white beard. "Don't be disappointed. You are an opportunity, a hope, and a chance. Every worthwhile story starts with a vessel, and yours, I suspect, will be no different."

"You say I'm a vessel, and you spoke of ways to fill them," I said, putting aside his mention of a story. Romantic ideas like those could wait until I had left my inner workings behind. "What do you mean?"

"Let me show you," the Librarian held out his right hand. "This will be so much faster than talking, however much I may enjoy it."

I stared at the hand. It looked plain, creased but hardly coarse. No threat seemed to present itself, but I remembered those copper tendrils, what they might do, and hesitated.

"You were taking me for your own," I accused.

"Because I thought that was my role to play," the Librarian said. "I was wrong."

Without warning he reached forward, grabbed my arm. A strong grip, and one I couldn't even think to break before the white vastness and its crystal ceiling fell away, vanishing as I flew out and up into an infinite beyond that left me, suddenly, standing before the metal mold.

THE GREEN OUTLINES had dulled to nothing. The blue light still glowed.

Starship hummed.

The name slipped into my thoughts, like a half-remembered dream, and lodged itself there. Starship. That's where I was. A vast structure, speeding through space with—

Slow down. I shook where I stood, coming to grips with the massive data now sitting on my mental fringes, waiting to be explored. Simple, for a computer like me, to analyze. Harder, far harder, to comprehend.

"I have never been in this room," the Librarian said, and when I looked to my right, he stood there and did not stand there, his form a wavering, hollow thing. "I'm not quite sure where you are, Gamma, so I am afraid I will not be of much use to you yet."

"Use to me?"

"You feel all my stories, everything I learned during a long life, pressing in on you now, yes?" the Librarian said.

"They nearly swept me away."

"A known possibility," the Librarian nodded. "The early vessels, the only ones I saw, failed under the weight of what you just did. We nearly scrapped the program, except there were no other options. For now, I will close off most of myself so that you are not overwhelmed. Too much knowledge, too quickly, can be a terrible thing."

Behind me, the spiral door clicked and opened with its trademark whooshing sound. I turned and saw nothing more than the neon hallway waiting for me.

"Well then," the Librarian said. "Off we go."

TWO

KAYDEE

Statistics defined me. After seeing the Librarian, and on my way out of the room where I'd met him, I tried to assess myself against his form. Biology defined the Librarian and had left him wrinkled and worn. But, with my synthetic skin and artificial nerves, close-cropped hair that would never grow, the sum of my body's years had been determined before I had ever been born.

Which, considering the neon hallway and its mysteries, might be a good thing. Who knew how long I would be wandering the darkness without such staples as food and water. Though I did have air: a function, always evaluating my current environment, pegged things as oxygen rich and slightly cool for the average human. A light breeze ever-present from circulating fans.

The Librarian's room snapped shut as I left it, the bright green gem giving me entry switching back to a sneering red glow. To my right, the path I had walked to get here had fallen dark. No pinks and reds that way. Only to the left did the glow continue.

"Librarian?" I asked the emptiness, and heard no response.

The knowledge he had given me still hovered on my consciousness's edges, and I tugged at it. Pulled at data fragments and caught paragraphs, plots, and poems. Ancient evils and glorious gods. Willing adventurers drawn according to skills and rolls of metaphorical, giant dice.

I wanted to sit on the floor in that hallway and play with those stories. I had no biological need to keep moving, and while it might take a long time to dig through all the Librarian's gifts, there seemed no doubting that doing so would be advantageous. Could even be crucial. In a place built by humans, knowing them through their tales would be helpful.

I didn't get the time.

Another snap-hiss sounded down the hall, to the left. A door opening. Following it, heavy clanks. Metal on metal, moving towards that sound and away from me. I looked that way, tried to see, but the neon blacked everything apart from its own glow, making detail impossible to make out.

"Aren't you going to investigate?" the Librarian said, suddenly standing next to me in our halved off-shoot. "I would."

"Why?"

"Aren't you curious?"

"I am, about what you gave me."

The Librarian laughed, a deep sound that should have echoed off the walls around us but vanished into them instead, "All that I gave you came from experience. I suggest you get some of your own before trying on mine."

The same snap-hiss. The door again, but no metal clanks this time. I watched for a moment, saw nothing, and turned back to the Librarian only to see he had vanished again. A useful talent, being able to come and go as he pleased.

But perhaps the Librarian had a point. Choosing to walk the halls had brought me to his trove, and extending my adventure a bit further might get me to answers I didn't know I needed.

Unlike whatever had made those metal clanks, my own footfalls came soft and padded. My feet pressed into the floor as a human's would, filling out and feeling the lines etched into the surface, welding folds from who knows how long ago still telling their maker's story.

I approached the next branch slowly, easy to do as the neon fell off into darkness beyond the split. I decided that someone, some-where, guided me along my route, and rather than let that fact curdle my spirit, I used the logic to bolster my own courage.

Who would wake me up only to walk me a dozen meters and see me pulled apart?

The next spiral door stood ready, glowing green, for my touch. By its location, it seemed like the door the sounds had come from. I touched its emerald and the door retreated, revealing a room very similar to the Librarian's.

Except the metal molding in the center, the handprints with green-glowing outlines, had been smashed. It lay in broken pieces, haphazard yellow sparks popping up from the fractured base. Beyond the occasional crackle and a stiff ozone smell, the ever-present blue light revealed nothing else.

I stayed in the entryway, evaluated my options. Clearly the room's intended purpose had failed. I could retreat and hope that whomever controlled the neon hallway had also seen what I had and decided on a back-up plan, or I could move forward, see what there was to salvage from the broken stand.

As the Librarian said, experience beget experience.

I strode forward, bending down to pick up a piece of the frac-tured molding—perhaps I could use it somehow? Capture some programming remnant?

"Been waiting for you, Gamma," the accordion words came from behind me, sprinkling their varying tones and tunes around the room. "Been waiting a long time."

"Waiting a long time?" I said, turning around to see what had been hiding along the wall past the room's entry. "I just awoke minutes ago."

Though, having said that, I couldn't be sure what I was looking at had the capability to tell time. A stilted, vaguely humanoid bucket stared back at me, gangly limbs both metal and synthetic like my own sticking out from various ports. No head revealed itself, only a blinking panel across the bucket's center, surrounding a speaker, gave any thought to life.

Those limbs, though, did give clues to the thing's purpose. Many ended in tools, like wrenches and hammers and a small, lit torch that might be used for welding. The four synthetic variants, coated in some blue-black protectant, ended in hands that looked as real as my own, complete with fingers that wiggled as I watched, as if the mech barely repressed excitement.

"You know how long it takes for one of these mechs to screw up?" the bucket machine said. "I missed the first two before this scrap pile decided to deep clean the data port, but I guess when you're just digital bits, you can wait. Now, hold still."

The bucket lurched forward on its twin legs, knobby metal things with hydraulic hoses interspersed between an oil-slicked gray frame. I stepped back, not wanting a whirring saw or swinging hammer to get anywhere near me, and tripped on the mold's remnants.

I'd barely hit the floor before the bucket stood above me. As the mech leaned down, its white blinking panel blinded my eyes and its many limbs swooped around us like a nightmare shroud. One snaked in, a synthetic hand, and as it creeped towards me its fingertips pressed together, binding and growing into a longer, pointed thing.

Before I could shout, fight, or comprehend what was happening, the pointed end shot towards my left ear. I felt a click, and as before, the room, the bucket, and myself fell away.

"THIS ISN'T WORKING out very well for you, is it?" the Librarian asked, standing beside me on my vast pearl plain, crystalline data hanging above us like so many digital icicles.

"I can't imagine too many win their first fights," I replied.

"You might try harder, though, because it could be your last."

I shrugged off the comment and focused my attention on the new addition to my space. Given the bucket robot's aggression, I'd expected something more dangerous, but a young woman, and only that, stood where the Librarian had when I had met him.

She looked as unsure of herself as I had when I first woke, looking at her hands and turning them over, and as I started walking her way, she even performed a little spin. Then hopped in the air.

"Having fun in my home?" I asked.

The woman stopped, cocked her head at me and then stretched, "Guess so? It's been a while."

"Since what?"

"Since I could move. See myself. Do this." The woman closed her eyes for a second and her hair shrank from its waist-length growth.

The strands pulled up to her head than rose above it, spiked out, most turning shock-white while others shifted, like paint had been spilled, to a teal green. At the same time, script-like letters began to crawl up her arms and legs, forming into words that, before I could read any, were suddenly covered by a flowing t-shirt and ankle-length, similarly loose pants.

"That's better," the woman said, then frowned as she looked over my shoulder. "But that's not."

"What?" I turned, saw the Librarian had moved up behind me, arms folded and a deep frown on his wrinkled face.

"You are not supposed to be here," the Librarian said. "This was not your assignment."

"Yeah, well, I never liked playing by your rules," the woman said. "Don't move, Gamma. K?"

I stared at her, utterly lost.

"Don't—" The Librarian started, but before he'd made it any further in his warning, the woman shot her left hand forward.

Out from that hand lanced a pure green line, one that fractured a little around the edges like a close-up lightning bolt. The line struck the Librarian and he began to twitch as his clothes, his skin, changed to match the bolt's hue before, as sudden as glass shattering, the Librarian broke apart and dissolved to nothing.

"What did you just do?" I asked, looking at where the Librarian, until a moment ago, had stood.

"Gave him the delete treatment," the woman said. "Name's Kaydee, by the way." As she said her name, tiny gold fireworks shot from behind her and crackled, forming her name over Kaydee's head. "And boy, are you in trouble."

"You're the one who's in trouble," I said. "You just disintegrated my friend."

"Gamma," Kaydee said, snapping her fingers, which, for some reason, created little bubblegum hearts that floated in the air before popping into nothing. "You've been awake for, like, an hour, and you're calling that guy a friend? Put up some guard rails, buddy, or this ship's going to destroy you real fast."

"I don't—wait, what?"

Ship? Guard rails? And how was Kaydee glowing now, as though she'd bathed in a rainbow?

"It's real simple," Kaydee replied. "But it's also not short. So here's what you're gonna do. Step one, trust me. Step two, get the hell out of this place. Step three? We save Starship and your mechanical ass in one cool sweep."

Kaydee stuck out her hand, like the Librarian had done not long before. The Librarian that Kaydee had destroyed without a second's thought.

I, needless to say, did not follow her lead.

"Why should I trust you?" I asked. "You're the one who tackled me, came into my operating system, and destroyed someone who at least acted like he was on my side."

Kaydee shook her head, rolled her eyes. "I knew these vessels would be empty, but I didn't think that meant dumb. Gamma, kid, I fought my way to you and broke that damn mold because if I didn't you'd be filled up with their garbage. How can you trust me? Because I'm not taking any part of you for myself."

True. The Librarian had been attempting a takeover, albeit one that he'd stopped when I'd confronted him. He'd made it seem like the whole attempt was innocent, but I could still feel his data in my mind, all that knowledge he'd given me. But what if something worse lay waiting in there? What if the Librarian was taking his time to get to know my data structure and then he'd try again?

"No, wait," I said. "This all sounds ridiculous. I can't—"

"I'll make you a deal," Kaydee said, though for the first time she didn't seem quite so frustrated. Maybe even intrigued. "Because at least you're not a pushover. Which would be lame."

I chose not to remark that Kaydee seemed to change her mood with every passing second.

"So here's the terms," Kaydee said. "You hang out with me, I promise we'll do some really, really cool stuff. If you decide you don't like it later, well guess what, these molds are still gonna be here."

"You mean, I could get the Librarian back?"

"Him?" Kaydee squinted her eyes, bunched up her lips, shrugged. "Nope, he's gone. Sorry. But there's like, a hundred others. Maybe more. Everyone wanted in."

"In to what?"

Kaydee shook her head, stuck out her hand again, "That's a no-go captain. Drenching your sweet innocent head with too much knowledge-sauce might cause you to lose your mind, and I really can't have that. So shake up, and let's go."

How did you refuse an offer like that? Kaydee seemed slightly crazy, but she also manipulated the digital space around us with more skill than I had. And she'd just dissolved the Librarian.

For my own safety, and out of intense curiosity, I shook her hand.

THE JANITOR MECH laid heavy on me, but, by pressing with both hands, I managed to roll the machine off. As I stood up, the door

I'd come in snap-hissed itself open. The light above the broken molding blinked off, and the only glows came from the hallway beyond, those neon pinks and reds.

There wasn't anyone else in the room, but I didn't feel alone. The Librarian's leftovers still lingered, a data dump sitting in my mind. Kaydee's presence, a sparkling nerve, danced around too, and I could feel her investigating all the program routines that made me . . . me.

As I stepped over the molding, moving towards the room's exit, I felt my own limbs differently now. My synthetic skin, my hands and feet held secrets that whispered to me. Functions I didn't quite understand, but that before I didn't even know existed. Kaydee seemed to be unlocking things, releasing digital cuffs, and her work filled in my blanks.

I knew, now, that the constant hum around me, that steady whir from Starship, came from the endless thrust sending the craft further along on its journey. The breeze from its circulating air, keyed to keep every molecule scrubbed free from disease and at oxygen and nitrogen ratios ideal for human health. Answers to these questions came easy, but when I tried to dig deeper as I walked from the room, I found clouded blocks. Information coded away, with Kaydee's glitzy fingers all over it.

Perhaps she'd done that for my own protection, because Starship alone almost buried me.

Starship was huge. More than huge. Its various regions whisked their way through my mind like a picture-book's flipping pages, each one presenting themselves in a one-hit poster advertising a place to go that, I realized, might be so far out of date as to be nothing like what I saw.

I had been awakened on a titanic vessel. Now I needed to find out why.

Once again, the spiral door shut behind me and, once again, my way back had been plunged into dark. Forward then, along the neon path and to the next room. No noise this time, no other machine to jump out and tear me to pieces.

Nonetheless, I went with caution. As I walked, I surfed Kaydee's data dump—like the Librarian, Kaydee's presence had added large memory blocks to my mind—for what else might be scary on Starship and found plenty, only for each fearsome mechanical creation to be discarded one after another, marked as deleted. It took me five to realize what I was finding in my mind-space:

Not reality, but Kaydee's own ideas.

"I couldn't make'em," Kaydee said, walking along beside me as we approached the next branch, flicking rainbow sparks from her fingers as she went. "I always thought Starship ought to have something beyond the people watching our backs. Just in case you needed some real impartial justice."

She laughed.

"But you know how it goes. Those in power get scared when someone else has any. They took away my toys."

"Your toys?" The idea that any of the mechs I'd seen being considered toys instead of dangerous terrors seemed ludicrous. "These things were heavily armed."

"Yeah, but I had control," Kaydee said. "Anyway, they found what they were looking for. They missed what they weren't."

"What do you mean?"

But I'd reached the branch, and when I turned to see her response, Kaydee had gone. Back into my mind, or into hers. Hard to know, harder to do anything about.

In front of me, another spiral door glowed green. That, at least, I understood.

Beyond this one sat another room both like and unlike the rest. A mold stood in the center, hands outlined in emerald and seemingly untouched. There was no empty room around it, however. Instead, the room's walls and ceilings narrowed beyond the mold to a large screen. As I entered the room, as the door shut behind me, the screen flared light gray, powering up.

"Get ready for the show," Kaydee said from behind me. "They always did have a taste for flare."

"If it means I'll get some answers, then I don't care," I replied.

But, first things first. The screen seconded my own thoughts, settling on a static message:

WELCOME, GAMMA. PLEASE MEET YOUR THIRD MIND.

THREE

THE CONDUIT

Third mind?" I said. "But I only have you. Unless . . ."

"It's so fun watching your gears turn." Kaydee smirked, walking past me, over to the screen. "So nice and slow, I might take a nap."

"Hey, I thought you were on my side?"

"Sides?" Kaydee replied, then dragged her finger across the screen, underlining the words. "Do you even have a side? What're you for, Gamma, tell me? I so want to know."

"I, uh . . ." Kaydee had a point. I didn't really have a motive, an objective, a calling beyond going where the doors directed me. Following the instructions laid out my way. But then, I was a mech. That was my job. "I'm just following directions."

"Then go ahead, follow them," Kaydee said. "The hands go right there."

I shook my head, and by the time I looked back up towards the screen, Kaydee had vanished. The first mold had brought the Librarian inside me. The second one, I assumed Kaydee had destroyed. The third? Would Kaydee just kill whomever waited in there?

The Librarian may have been dangerous, but he didn't seem to deserve what had happened to him. Whomever waited in that construct didn't need Kaydee deleting them too. So I stepped back from the mold, considered it, and then gave the stand a push.

Outside of those frantic seconds with Kaydee's janitor mech, I hadn't tried to use my strength for anything. Hadn't tried to focus on sending energy towards my muscles, or rather, the synthetic constructs in my arms and legs that had the same appearance, but far greater ability than their organic cousins.

So I pushed, harder and harder until the mold's stand began to groan. Till the metal bent and twisted and popped free. The mold itself hit the floor and, like the one Kaydee had wrecked, shattered into chunks.

"Well, that was unexpected," Kaydee said, crouching and looking at the mold. "I was ready to give them the kick-punch combo I've been practicing."

"That's the point," I replied. "I didn't want you to do that."

"Don't tell me you're a softie?"

I stood up, saw a flash in my eye, and noticed a new message on the screen, one that surprised me enough to keep from answering Kaydee's insult.

CONGRATULATIONS GAMMA!

"Congratulations for what?" I asked.

I stepped around the mold, approached the screen as the letters, a fuzzy white against the gray background, swirled around into a different message.

WE ARE THE ONES THAT WOKE YOU.

"Oh here we go," said Kaydee, coming up beside me. "Here's where they butter you up before they break you down."

The screen swirled again. I wondered how the letters could possibly break me down, but then, given what I had already seen, perhaps I should have been more suspicious.

WE ARE THE VOICES OF STARSHIP, AND WE NEED YOUR HELP.

"Really?" Kaydee laughed. "They're still calling themselves that stupid name?"

I turned to tell Kaydee to be quiet, so I could focus, but she had disappeared. Kaydee's endless chatter had started out amusing, but I wasn't sure how many more insults and cryptic assertions I could take.

At least the screen gave me clear instructions.

YOU MUST GO THROUGH THE GARDEN TO THE NURSERY AND RESET OUR CONNECTION THERE.

I read the words once. Read them twice.

"All this because you need something turned on and off again?" I said the words, though I didn't know if whomever, whatever these Voices were could hear me.

OUR MISSION'S FUTURE RESTS WITH YOU. THE LAB WILL GUIDE YOU TO YOUR NEXT STEP, BUT NO FARTHER.

So that was a no. I waited for the letters to shift again, but the screen stayed static.

"The best thing I can say about that group?" Kaydee said, jumping back and forth over the knocked-over mold, as if playing a game. "They fight amongst themselves a lot."

"That's a good thing?"

"You don't want their attention, Gamma. Trust me."

I shook my head, took one last glance at the unchanged screen, and headed for the door. Kaydee had disappeared. Back, I suspected, into my digital ether. I tried to see if there was some connection to her appearances. Some way I could try to control her pop-ins, or even her behavior, but nothing came up from my program reservoir.

Save one option. Hanging there in my crystal ceiling's dark depths lingered the full on reset, a cleansing bath that would restore me to that static body on the cot, with no memory, no concept of where I'd been and what I'd done.

Touching that crystal would be the ultimate end for me, but it would be *an* end.

When I left the room, the hallway lit up both left and right, though the left seemed more a courtesy: the hallway ended in a flat wall bearing another poster for some action piece, a burly man and woman holding center stage while a fireball expanded behind them.

Courage Never Dies splashed across the bottom in thick, silver letters.

Right.

"Saw that one, actually," Kaydee said, admiring the poster. "Pretty good."

"Sure," I said, turning back down the hallway, ready to head along the purple neon to whatever came next.

"So you know, this place?" Kaydee continued as we walked. "Where you are, right now?"

"Uh huh?"

"It's like a little sanctuary. Used to belong to this guy, Leonid. Everyone called him Leo, though. Syllables, you know, too much effort. So, these are all his posters."

"Leo had exciting taste."

"He liked the guns more than the drama. But we all wanted excitement back then. You can only drift along in a place like this for a while until everyone starts losing their minds."

The change in Kaydee's conversation wasn't hard to pick up.

"You think you've got it made, getting on something like this," Kaydee continued. "So you pop out kids, raise a family, and then you realize they're never gonna see a real sky. Never gonna get outside this metal box. Then by the time those kids have kids? You're getting into a real depressive cycle."

I passed the room where Kaydee had tried to kill me with her cleaning robot. The woman didn't stop her rambling. Didn't hitch.

"Throw another few generations on top of that and then you get me, and what do I do? I see the problems. I try to fix them. Leo's doing the same thing, just a different way. And guess what, not everyone likes fixers."

I nodded, then stopped. We were back at the room where I woke up. The blue light glowed, three of the four cots still unoccupied. Delta laid in hers, oblivious to reality. I hadn't been awake long, but I couldn't imagine going back to that.

Bring a mech to life, I supposed, and he might grow to like it.

"Anyway," Kaydee said, brushing a teal strand away from her eyes. "Point I'm making is that you're in, like, Leo's private space right now. You leave here, things are going to get strange."

"As if they aren't already."

Kaydee acknowledged my point with a shrug, one that popped off little flower petals into the air that vanished before they hit the ground, "But I'm not talking weird like this. I'm talking, like . . . well, guess you'll find out. I'm going to do what I can to let you in slow, but, keep it together okay?"

"I'll try?"

Kaydee laughed, short and quick and by the time she finished, she'd vanished and left me alone with the first door I'd seen. The one with the red-glowing ruby I'd touched back when I was the only one in my mind.

Now, I saw an emerald.

The gems, I'd noticed, were warm to the touch when they were green, cold when red. Perhaps a signal to those unable to tell color whether the door could open or not. My hand, thus, felt the heat as I pressed into the emerald. Felt the sudden chill a second later as the door spun open and a faster, cool wind blew at me from beyond.

And what a beyond!

I gaped—there was no other reaction—at what I saw. Going from the cramped, hallucinogenic hallways of Leo's laboratory to this was . . . to use a cliche I could identify with, like being born.

Two meters from me stood a clear glass barrier, rising up from a chiseled tile floor whose tiles, I noticed, were covered with names and dates carved in with exact marking. Past the glass, falling away and above me, swung a wide chasm. A foggy blue, like the light from my waking only now diffused with a loose mist, filtered through the space from above, providing enough light to see and little more. Like a perpetual dawn.

But even so! Starship had, until this moment, been abstract in my mind. Now its reality laid bare before me in its massive, metal-but-so-much-more-than-metal bulk. I walked up to the glass and looked left and right, confirming the craft vanished into the hazy distance. Above and below similarly slipped into the mist. Though what I could see proved a hearty meal for my curiosity.

Walkways like mine spread up and down the chasm's sides every few meters, scaffolding crawling along a mechanical menagerie. The blue light, in its descent, mingled with varied displays, from more neon to matte, to static white glows and scripted signs. Some hung, others looked pasted to the walls that they called home, where they may have lingered for who knew how many years.

The signs shouted destinations at me. *The Solar Scrambler, Cosmic Clothiers, Nova Apartments* and countless more advertised to an endless empty. Not all offered their enticements without flaw—some signs had died and others flickered. One, a great big old-style marquee directly across the chasm from me, appeared to have been cleaved in two, its halves bending towards each other. Glitches in a beautiful array.

Accompanying this vastness were the rumblings Leo's lab had sought to mute. A roar like endless, nearby traffic underpinned every second. Hisses, clangs, rattles and metal's sliding shrieks bounced along, coming from who knew where. Iron drenched the air, a sign of maintenance long overdue. As if a thousand things I couldn't see moved around me.

"I always loved the Conduit. It runs Starship's entire length, except the engines and the very front. They kept those protected," Kaydee said, leaning on the glass next to me. "My view wasn't exactly like this one. I lived further that way." She pointed to the right. "We academics, engineers and the government at the front. Everyone else crunched in the back. You know how it is."

"I don't know how it is, actually," I replied.

"Then you can guess." Kaydee stepped away from the glass, looked down at it. "This used to say hello every time you left your apartment. It would read out the time, tell you about any messages or assignments."

"You don't sound sad?"

Kaydee quirked a smile, "Sad? No. Why would I be? This place killed me, Gamma. It was a mess, it is a mess. Everyone had ideas about how to clean it up, but it was easier to fight each other than to do the work."

From what I saw, Starship had no shortage of ideas. The differing designs on display embraced creativity. I myself seemed to be a unique design, incorporating pieces of older, living beings into a machine's frame.

"I'm seeing something beautiful," I said. "You're being harsh."

"You, Gamma, did not live my life. No matter how much of me you've absorbed, some things, like my opinions, are forever mine." Kaydee nodded left over my shoulder. "If you're wondering where to find the Garden, it's that way. You won't miss it. Like, you literally can't."

Before I started walking, I looked back at Leo's lab. The spiral door with its gem—now red—held a small name and number plate above it in a tarnished gold, contrasting with the black-and-pink lines of the door. So far as a home went, this would have to do.

I relished the walk. There's simply no other way to put it. After the cramped neon hallways, the Conduit's broad space let me breathe. I kept looking around, reading every name as I passed, and stopping to stare up and down to read even more. I had thought Starship might be a small thing, but this looked like a whole world for me to explore.

Albeit a dead one.

The Garden strove to prove me wrong on that assumption. While most of the Conduit kept itself in two halves, the Garden bridged the gap, save for several circular holes that, Kaydee's data informed me, were for rapid transit that no longer ran. The holes themselves were at least five meters around, and they cut into a resolutely lush surface.

I had expected—though why I kept expecting things, I wasn't sure, I was always wrong—the Garden to be another doorway. An entrance along one wall, but instead it seemed to dominate both the Conduit and all of Starship on either side.

And the Garden dominated beautifully.

Flowers, vines, trees and more perched on the Garden's outer wall as far as I could see. White roses grew out sideways around the transportation cut-outs, while, above me and center in the Conduit's height, an orchid array spelled out *Garden*. Little specks floated between the flowers, iridescent blues and oranges of flapping butterfly wings carrying the pollen from one plant to the next in an endless dance.

I heard birdsong as I came closer. The air suffused with a magnolia's heavy scent, then a daffodil's, then a tulip line. Beneath the flowers, too, the Garden's real purpose revealed itself, with outer sections dedicated to fruit trees and the healthy crop's stalks. Corn, soybeans, wheat. A vertical farm and botanical garden.

And yet, as I came closer to the entry along my level, the greens began to fade. The flowers curled away, their petals falling and disappearing to dust. The crops wilted and turned black, as though I witnessed a time-lapse speeding through to an awful present.

"That's exactly what you're seeing," Kaydee said, and this time I did pick up some grief. "That was my memory, how I saw the Garden in my time. Now you're seeing how it is."

She walked past me towards the Garden, running her fingertips along the glass barrier as the decay continued in front of us.

"I didn't make it down here often," Kaydee continued. "I was busy, and watching flowers bloom was easy to shove aside."

"I don't understand. How am I seeing your memory?"

Kaydee kept her eyes towards the Garden, but I thought her back stiffened, and her left hand slowly balled into a fist.

"Because I'm filling you," Kaydee said. "Leo described it like sand pouring into a glass, mine mixing with yours, and I guess a little of that other guy's. Eventually, they all blend together. Leo never said what that would mean in practice."

"That I would see what you've seen."

Kaydee looked back at me, stars dripping down her face from the corners of her eyes. As I watched them fall, I felt them on my face too, saw tears I hadn't felt splash on the floor at my feet.

"Much more than that, Gamma." Kaydee said. "Much more."

FOUR

SHOPPING TRIP

Mechs, so far as I understood, lived according to their programmed rules. Routines told us what to do in any given situation, whether we should react, ignore, lash out, or change. Thus far, I thought I had been obeying my programmed prerogatives: follow the hallway, find the molds and get my next assignment.

If what Kaydee said was true, then my programming was malleable. She could change me in unpredictable ways.

I tried to find evidence, standing on the Conduit walkway before the Garden's desiccated entry. Scanned my mind as blue light filtered through dusted mist around me. And I found nothing. No corrupted crystals, no lingering edits to my code with Kaydee's fingerprints.

Yet, if she had *become* me, would I even detect the change? Can someone separate a part of themselves from . . . themselves?

The Conduit didn't provide an answer to that question. Its stores and restaurants and homes sat quiet. Waiting for something, maybe, but not me.

The emerald glowed in the Garden entrance's center. A door that spanned the entire walkway, and one coated with what must have been beautiful flowers once—flowers I had seen, moments ago, through Kaydee's eyes. The emerald itself sat in a wilted, giant rose, its glow the only life left.

I reached out, felt the jewel's warmth, and saw dried leaves shake their way to the floor as the door opened inwards, splitting down the middle.

I stopped. Blinked. Waited for the memory to fade. Inside the doors, the lush Garden returned. Those glittering, luminescent butterflies flapped along from flower to flower hugging the floors, walls, raised beds in view. Lights hung in clusters, dilating their brightness for their recipients, creating a halo patchwork.

Even from the entry, I could see the Garden spread up and down, overgrown pathways stretching ahead, each one leading to rooms dominated by one plant or another. Yet, as I stared, I began to pick out flaws. Sections where plants had been arranged now blurred along their borders as adventurous species took advantage of a gardener's absence to make incursions onto pathways or neighboring beds. Interspersed, decaying husks clued in to victims of territorial expansion, or missing care.

The Garden grew wild.

The Voices, via the screen back in Leo's lab, had told me to go through the Garden to get to the Nursery. I had no idea what 'getting through' the Garden might entail, but walking seemed like a good place to start.

"Hey," Kaydee said from behind me as I went forward. "Have you noticed you're basically naked and have, I think, zero ways of defending yourself? Yet here you're just marching along into danger without a care."

I looked down at myself. Kaydee did have a point. My scuffle with the cleaning mech had already demonstrated I wasn't much in a fight, especially with nothing to wield. But the Conduit seemed empty, and nothing in the Garden looked too dangerous.

"You believe there will be threats?" I asked.

"You were number three, Gamma," Kaydee replied. "What happened to the first two?"

A good question. Alpha and Beta—given my name and Delta's, it seemed reasonable to assume their own monikers—had been gone when I woke, and there hadn't been any signs of their departure. For all I knew, they could have been awakened an hour before me, or years. What had the Voices asked them to do? The same thing they had asked me? Had the other vessels failed and been destroyed, or were they still wandering Starship?

"So are you going to take my advice, or are you just going to stand there?"

"I would like some clothes, yes. A weapon seems wise." I walked back out of the Garden, which appeared to offer nothing more than sticks. "Do you know where I would find these things?"

"Gamma, do I know where to find these things?" Kaydee laughed, then pointed down the walkway. A glittering trail launched from her fingertips, streaking not all that far back the way we'd come before settling in front of a yellow cloth overhang. "Alvie's has everything you need, buddy."

"I'm assuming this Alvie's isn't open?" I said, and felt stupid doing so. "I'm supposed to steal?"

"Not stealing if the owners are long dead. At least, not in my book."

Kaydee's grim assessment made a certain sense. Regarding Starship as a graveyard filled with idle treasures for the taking might be macabre, but if that view would help me survive a dangerous place, then I couldn't let programmed moral lines get in the way.

Behind me, the Garden's door shut soft, waiting for my return.

The Conduit divided itself along numbered blocks, categorized by colored, angular fins sticking out from the walls every so often. A peach-yellow block preceded the Garden on my level, its doors and signs primarily, and perhaps expectedly, leading to food processing facilities and transport. Beyond those, however, a shift to a blue block with various grocers and stores gave more promising options.

As I approached the dainty storefront—*Alvie's Clothes and More* sported glass windows beneath its yellow overhang, scripted store name in the panes—I picked up motion to the right and went up to the window, pressing my forehead to the glass to peer into the dark inside.

Only it wasn't so very dark now that I looked. Chandelier lights hung from the ceiling, white interspersed with tiny color-shifting nodes that went from blue to red to green as I watched. They illuminated racks upon racks stuffed with clothing, synthetic fabric shining, the whiter hues reflecting the colored dots above.

Between the racks walked people, a half dozen or more, and three children chased each other around the shoppers, ducking through the clothes and dashing between the aisles. Laughter and a parent's gentle chiding carried through the glass, sonic vibrations playing on my fingertips.

I went over to the entry, a stiff double-door with a rounded handle. Through its glass I watched the children return to their mother, who had new outfits for them all draped over her arm, a tired, happy smile on her lips.

The door stuck. I pulled again, and it didn't move. Through the glass, nobody appeared to notice me. Not even when I tried again, harder this time, and felt the door's hinges grind. I stepped back, gave myself some space and set my feet.

This time the hinges gave way, the door snapping its tight bounds and swinging open. *Alvie's* was mine to enter.

Except the lights were gone, save one shattered on the floor, its wires splayed out in the entryway over its own glass. Beyond, the Conduit's blue light played over near-empty racks, many pushed aside or toppled over. Those glistening outfits were gone.

The children, their mother, gone.

But I still heard the laughter. Could feel the lights as I went, carefully, over the threshold and into the store. Life had been lived here, and I could pick up its traces.

"You saw something," Kaydee said, bending down and running a finger over a small shirt left lying on the floor. "Didn't you?"

"This place used to be nice," I said, my voice dwindling to a sour note as I failed to find an outfit in my size among the leftovers.

"Mom used to take me here when I was younger," Kaydee replied. "Said *Alvie's* was the best on Starship for the price. I never went anywhere else."

I nodded, though Kaydee wasn't watching me. So I'd seen her memory again, or a version of it. That it had mingled flawlessly with reality troubled me. Here, the result had been harmless, like with Kaydee's rendering of the Garden. Next time . . .

"Do you know how to control it?" I asked, as Kaydee hadn't vanished yet. She seemed very interested in that shirt. "The memories?"

Kaydee reached up, tugged on a spiked white hair thread, stood, "That's not the way it's supposed to work. You're going to see a lot of what I lived."

"Isn't that dangerous?"

"More dangerous not to. We learned that one the hard way," Kaydee said. "You might try checking the back. *Alvie's* always had plenty of stock."

The store did indeed have a large back room, and the door leading to it had been broken away long ago. It hung to the side, a large splinter through the top, as if someone had driven an ax through its frame.

Behind, enough clothes lingered to let me find a shirt, pants, a light jacket. Gloves and shoes, the latter not a perfect size but close enough. Synthetic skin like mine wouldn't blister anyway. Color-wise, I managed to get a green ensemble, matching the Garden.

To blend in.

I went back towards the entrance, ready to head to the Garden and get this mission going. I picked up, too, a broken bar from one of the racks. Not exactly a lethal weapon, but enough, I thought, to bat away any encroaching vine.

Kaydee stood before the doors, arms folded, a mocking grin all over her face.

"I didn't know it was possible to code fashion sense as bad as yours," Kaydee said. "Did you deliberately choose all that?"

"Options were limited."

"Clearly," Kaydee's smile faded as she saw my look past her, out the doors. "You're ready to leave?"

I tilted my head, "Think I have what I need." I held up the bar. Kaydee didn't look too impressed, but she didn't fight me on it either. "This should be enough to fend off any aggressive plants."

"Probably," Kaydee replied, not moving from her door-blocking spot. "But hey, there's something you should know."

"Does it have to do with why you're standing there?"

"So smart," Kaydee replied. "You know you can see my memories now, right? I can't control them sometimes. Hell, most of the time. But, if I try really hard?"

"You can make me see things?"

"More than that, I think. You're a mech, Gamma. Your reality runs on numbers speeding through that processor," Kaydee pointed towards my chest. "If I tweak the digits a little, that reality changes."

"I'd prefer if you didn't do that."

"Sure you would," Kaydee said. "Thing is, I've already done it. Been doing it. But I don't think I'm going to anymore."

"What have you been changing, Kaydee?"

I couldn't evaluate the threat properly. What are you supposed to do when someone tells you that you've been living a lie? Believe them? Ignore them?

What happens when that someone is literally inside you all of the time?

"You've been seeing Starship as it was," Kaydee said. "When you go back through these doors, you will see it as it is."

Kaydee dropped her hand and stepped aside, clearing the way for me to head back through the doors, into what looked like the same blue-lit, misty and empty Conduit.

When I'd gone into *Alvie's*, the memory I'd seen vanished with the door's opening, a wipe that deleted the past as the glass swept it away from my eyes. Leaving, it was the same.

As I pushed the doors open, I felt the heat first. Then I saw the fires. What had been bright blue and calm now seared a pulsing orange, white, and red; flashing alarms mingling with sparking swirls.

The fires themselves dotted everything I could see, the Conduit's clean stores and homes marred with ash and oil, slashes in their metal sides. Where I'd only noticed a couple damaged pieces before, now almost everything seemed to bear scars. Even *Alvie's* overhang, above me, hung in tatters.

Beyond the wreckage, beyond the Conduit's continual disaster, lay the realization that it was not empty. Words, cries, clangs and synthetic bangs echoed up and down the vastness. I stepped up to the glass railing, still in place despite cracks running through its surface, and saw shapes rambling along the walkways. Climbing the walls and, in one case, slipping and falling, the mech's stubby limbs flailing as it vanished into the black-and-orange depths below.

Starship wasn't an empty paradise, but a burning nightmare.

A nearer noise came from my right, a swishing sound. I turned and saw a towering mech, reaching almost up to the next level, trundling towards me with treads kneading along the walkway. The swishing noise came from its limb menagerie, which swept up and down the wall, spraying and wiping away at the metal walls and windows. Only instead of water, or some cleaning solution, the mech sprayed sludgy gray liquid, its brushes mingling it with the ash-coated crud already coating the sides.

I hugged the wall as the mech went by, as it carefully cleaned around *Alvie's*. A soft phrase played out as it went, warning people to keep clear.

Kaydee had suggested a weapon, and I looked at the bar I had grabbed. Such a toy wouldn't be much good against a thing like that, and while a cleaning mech didn't seem like it would be dangerous, the Conduit's other levels gave clear view of other robots slain and sparking, or stuttering in place as their broken code failed to comprehend Starship's present condition.

The Voices had said they needed to reconnect to the Nursery. I hadn't received the mission with much urgency, and the Conduit's peacefulness hadn't added any. Now . . . now this was different. I didn't see what needed fixing before.

Now I understood: everything did.

I followed the cleaning mech back towards the Garden. Watched as it reached the walkway's end, then began reversing its course. No doubt on an infinite back-to-front cycle.

Before, the Garden's desiccated outside seemed at odds with the Conduit's imagined condition. Now, with small fires breaking out where too many sparks had found a dried husk to touch, it fit right in.

Which made, when I opened the door again, the Garden's lush, overgrown interior, all the more fantastic. Outside, disaster. In here, too much life. This time, I let the Garden door shut behind me without complaint.

"I just didn't want you to hate it," Kaydee said, crouching over a flower just past the entry. "The Conduit. Starship. I grew up here, and it was beautiful once. A marvel. But there are rules for vessels like you, and these, I think, actually make sense."

"Rules?" I went up near her, looked at the purple-white flower Kaydee had her eyes on. A pretty thing, slight and angular.

"Everything has a procedure. Has guidelines. Vessels shouldn't be spoiled, so you have to ease them into it. At least, that's Leo's theory," Kaydee said. "So I hope you're eased, because the good times are gone now."

A skittering noise drew my eyes away from Kaydee and her warning, one that I'd already started taking after Starship's reveal. What had been a peaceful place didn't feel that way any longer. So I watched the noise from a distance, staying near the purple-white flower.

My patience paid off when the creature revealed itself in another dash from one bed to the next. A crimson oval with tiny, clawed feet, the thing's main feature appeared to be the thousand flexible spines jutting centimeters from its body. As it ran, and as I now saw as I crept closer, those spines stabbed into various blooming flowers and wiggled around, before carrying collected pollen to another batch and repeating the process.

In an artificial environment, the natural order needed to be replaced everywhere.

Looking up from the little mech as it burrowed into a cream-colored lily patch, I saw this level of the Garden laid out before me. At least, what I could see—vines and thicker plants obscured my view past a few meters in most directions.

I picked up a new sound: Mechs continued rustling around in the plants, and even the luminescent butterflies hummed whenever they came close, but now rushing water added its undercurrent to the soundscape. I felt a tremor, too, in my feet. Not just a creek, then.

Kaydee said that the Nursery lay on the Garden's far side. As much as I might like to explore this place, I'd been activated for a purpose, and the Voice's mission kept its beating heart in my head. So with my bar in my hand, I started through the brush, whacking aside encroaching plants, ducking my head under looming branches, and thanking myself for getting shoes as I stepped on brambles and worse.

There are such things as coincidences, Fate's random incursions on the best and worst plans. While I thought I had my destination marked and my methods determined, my path through the growth drew me nearer to the rushing water. Its ceaseless rumble overtook everything else, save one noise that pierced not through volume but pitch.

High, joyful, unexpected.

Laughter.

And not far ahead.

FIVE

A MEETING OF THE MECHS

A memory. That's what the laughter must have been. I stood between blue-tinged ferns and listened to the water, the breaks between the laughter, before the mirth would start up again. At first I thought the sound joyful, but as it continued, the thin cackles took on a strange, even sinister edge.

I wouldn't call myself an expert on humor, on what caused the mind to trigger itself into shouting, joyous spasms, but, both with the Librarian's leftovers and Kaydee's few examples thus far, it seemed this instance fell out of the norms.

"Craaaazzy," Kaydee said, her face peering out from between a fern's leaves. "That's what I'm thinking. I'd stay away, killer, because anything that laughs like that is not a cool cucumber."

"I'm not a killer," I said. "And what is a cool cucumber?"

I'd never heard a larger sigh come from Kaydee than in that moment.

"Gamma, here's the thing, you're just going to have to use that brain of yours." I started to interrupt, to say that I didn't have a brain, but Kaydee stopped me with a glare. "Don't say it, because that's exactly what I'm talking about. You gotta look beyond the letter of what I'm saying, go to the meaning."

"Right," I said, and turned back to the waterfall, the laughter. "I think I'm going to investigate."

"Didn't you just hear me? Not a good idea!"

"You just told me to find the meaning," I replied. "I hear the laughter, and I would like to know what it means."

I held more behind that choice than I said. In truth, ever since Kaydee had wiped away the curtains and showed me the devastating, mech-ruin that Starship really was, I'd wanted to find out more. Figure out what had caused the change. The Voices had given me a seemingly simple mission, but the calamity befalling Starship cloaked that mission in dangerous mystery.

Kaydee called me a vessel. She'd also called me dangerous, potentially unpredictable. She kept things from me because they might make me go against someone's wishes.

Well. Perhaps my programming had already been altered. Perhaps I was starting to think more for myself than for them.

Perhaps I just wanted to find some answers.

I gripped my bar in both hands and walked forward, careful to roll my shoes along the dirt path to make as little noise as possible, not that I'd be heard over the water. Those bright butterflies fluttered around me as I went up to the Garden's central pit, surrounded by a yellow-painted railing, around a last orange tree corner to see the majesty live.

The waterfall wasn't a straight shot down. Instead, the water plummeted through the center, splashing into a wide pool suspended by metal cables in the pit's middle. The pool itself bled off the water into open-topped tubes by the dozens, funneling the liquid to the various beds on my level.

The pool itself overflowed, and a small grate in the center—I picked this up from seeing water seeming to rush straight through the pool—sent the liquid down to the next level, a story below.

As I looked over that edge, I noted two things: one, the level beneath mine seemed slightly less lush. Different plant types, possibly those that needed less water. An effective way to irrigate, I supposed.

More importantly, I saw the laughter's source in the pool beneath mine. It was, well, me.

Not really, and the true answer wasn't hard to find. I was the third vessel that'd been activated, the third one to wander forth doing the Voice's bidding, and here looked like one of the others.

"Alpha," Kaydee said, looking over the edge with me. "Two men, two women, not that it really matters with your artificial selves."

The mech, the vessel, and my predecessor splashed in the pool beneath me, his waist-length chile-red hair splaying out around him in the water. Every so often he threw his head back and laughed, apparently not bothered by the soaking, loose robe he wore, nor the continual blitz as falling water crashed onto his head.

"Alpha looks like he's lost his mind," I said. "Did his programming fail?"

"Asking the wrong person," Kaydee said. "I didn't have anything to do with Alpha."

I looked at her, at her frowning face as she stared down at the mech, "Something to do with him? Does that mean you *did* have something to do with me?"

"Not now," Kaydee said. "I think he's noticed you."

Kaydee wasn't wrong. Looking back, I saw Alpha's face had turned up towards mine. As I met his glistening green eyes, even though he stood a story beneath me, I could recognize that same mech stillness, the clarity that came with zero organic flaws. Alpha didn't breathe, didn't blink, and neither did I.

"They finally turned to you," Alpha said, his voice deeper than mine, but flayed somehow, as though someone had run a rough file along his vocal cords. "Then they admit that I failed."

"Not much of a greeting," I offered back. "I'm Gamma. You're Alpha?"

The vessel nodded slow in return, all hints of that laughter gone.

He pushed himself up and out to the pool's edge. I noticed Alpha had bare feet, and carried no weapon.

"Gamma," Alpha said. "I can only say this: don't be their pawn."

Alpha bunched up his legs, then, and leapt off the pool, vanishing into the level beneath my own.

"Well, that was cryptic," I said, but Kaydee wasn't beside me anymore.

Two options, then. I could continue through the Garden, press on to the other side and see if I could find the Nursery. Complete the Voice's designated mission. Or, and I attributed even considering this option to a mistake in my programming, I could go after Alpha. Try and find out why the one that came before me had failed.

Or, why Alpha had decided not to complete his mission.

Mechs were designed to do specific tasks. The cleaning mech that I'd struggled with back in Leo's lab, just like the giant version going in its infinite loop around the burning Conduit, had their jobs and had stuck to them—at least until Kaydee put herself in the way. I wasn't supposed to be any different. Perhaps a little more calculating, a little more flexible to be able to deal with unexpected situations, but still a robot tasked with a job, meant to do it without second thoughts.

So why did I have them?

Alpha might know the answer. He'd doubtless had more time to contemplate the question than I. And if I was supposed to optimize my functions, then I would have to know the why behind my actions. What prompted my responses, and how to control myself in the future.

In other words, learning why I kept turning away from the Voices' mission would help me stay on course. Therefore, pursuing Alpha aligned with my programming, aligned with my goals.

"Logic is so malleable," I said as I made my way around the pit.

The Garden, unlike the Conduit, didn't present regular stairways going between levels. No doubt designated elevators or other contraptions existed somewhere in this overgrown jungle, but I had neither the time nor patience nor need to find them.

Alpha had used the pools, and so could I.

Unfortunately, my plan would require both hands. Nothing in my eclectic outfit offered up a spot to hold my bar. I could leave it behind or . . . I sized up the open pit, the distance to the lower level, and calculated the exact force required to get the bar through the air and to the floor. Hefting the metal cylinder like a javelin, I threw it over the pool with an arc that had it landing on the level below, burying itself in the dirt to stand straight up like a short flagpole.

"Good throw," Kaydee said.

"It was automatic."

"Is that a joke I hear?"

"My calculations say yes." I threw Kaydee a half-smile, then turned back to the leap at hand.

I climbed over the safety railing and, from the pit's edge, I gathered my legs, looked at and plotted the precise force I'd need to make it to the central pool, and jumped.

For a fleeting second I flew through the air, and I looked up. Saw the Garden's, saw Starship's mass extend farther than I could make out. Above, the floors seemed even more lush than before, the water coming down not from pools but pouring through thick growth, funneled by vines and massive trunks into the pools that I now splashed into.

And slipped, fell. Smacked my head on the pool's back edge as my shoes failed to provide any underwater grip. Pain from the strike didn't make it far, as the pool's icy water blunted its impact. So, so cold that my eyes shot wide open and I had to take in a huge breath to keep from shouting. The water ran through my clothes, soaking them instantly.

I'd thought, with Alpha splashing in the pool, that the water had to be warm. At least comfortable.

"As dumb moves go, that was pretty good," Kaydee said, perching without a care on the pool's edge. "Can't say I would've suggested jumping into the water to get down. But, you know, a vessel's gotta learn the hard way."

"This was a mistake," I said, bracing my hands on the pool's sides to stand up.

As I did, my head moved closer to the middle and the continual waterfall slammed down around my ears, numbing Kaydee's sarcastic commentary and blinding me, soaking my hair, until I pulled myself out. Sat up on the pool's edge and dripped over the side.

"So now what?" Kaydee said. "You're going to fall?"

"I'm going to push off," I replied. "I can make that jump."

"Oh, can you?" Kaydee replied, peering over the edge. "If I had money, I'd bet against that."

"You're not much help, you know?"

I looked down. Alpha hadn't waited for me, but all the same I had some idea of where he'd gone: I could see his wet prints all over the dirty paths on the level below. Not too hard to track, provided I moved quick.

The water made my hands slick, but I still managed to brace myself along the pool's side. I brought my feet up, pressed them along the pool's stone-like exterior and bunched myself, ready to launch.

I'd fly back, hit the level below and flow into a roll. Acrobatic, yes, but Leo had thought to give us some abilities in this arena. Good foresight to assume we wouldn't just be walking back and forth.

"Ready?" I said as Kaydee watched me from the pool's edge.

"You're asking me?"

"Good point."

I squeezed my legs, shunted the right amount of force, and as I pushed, my wet sneakers slipped on the pool's edge as my hands let go and I didn't launch anywhere.

I fell.

I screamed. Kaydee, falling next to me, screamed too.

The Garden's levels blitzed by us, the waterfall dwindled to a trickle and the flash glances I had showed more and more arid environments.

I saw a cactus, yellow sand, and then I hit.

Sank. Water pulled around me as my body exploded in pain, in alerts and warnings that the fall I'd just taken would've killed a normal human. Broken every bone in their body, even if, for me, all I'd earned was some minor damage to my joints. Some bruises the synthetic flesh would have to repair.

"Are you going to swim, or are we just going to sit underwater forever?" Kaydee said, floating to my left.

"Sorry, I'm just stunned," I said, trying to figure out how far I'd fallen, where I was.

I couldn't count the levels, but I'd gone down at least twenty stories, maybe more. I sank further in a vast, still reservoir. Neon blue light filtered in from above, but only black lay beneath me.

I kicked my shoes, waved my hands and swam with all my heavy, drenched clothes to the surface. The water trickle poured in near me, and beyond it, around my space, the neon blue grew brighter, mingling with similar shades and the water's slight motion to create dancing light on the metal walkways and walls.

"Over there," Kaydee said, standing on the water's surface and pointing, again launching those sparkling stars from her fingertips. "I'm thinking you might need a ladder."

"Thinking you might be right," I said, and swam towards a thick, silver-runged rescue that sat beneath a red sign labeled *Emergency*.

I thought my situation qualified.

I gripped the ladder, pulled myself up and out and collapsed on the tile. Gave myself a moment to equalize, perform a less frantic damage assessment and see if I'd done myself any permanent harm.

"That was pretty scary," Kaydee said, sitting on the walkway next to me. "Didn't know if you'd make it out of that fall."

"What does it matter to you?" I said. "You're not the one falling."

"I am, though. You go, I go. I'd appreciate it if you remember that."

"But you're not even real."

Kaydee glared at me, "I'm as real as you are, you asshole."

Then she disappeared.

Above me, the reservoir's roof extended far. Hanging from

massive cables and looming over the catwalk and pipe maze swarming the reservoir's sides, was the primary source of all that blue neon.

A curling script sign, but one easy enough to read.

WELCOME TO PURITY

A strange name for such a dark and damp place. Not one I was interested in, though. Alpha was likely far above me, so I had to get going, figure out a way to an elevator or some more manual means— though the thought of climbing all those stairs made me grimace—to get back to Alpha's level.

My immediate space had ladders aplenty, their rails lit with little blue diodes to accommodate the lesser overhead lighting. Why the designers had chosen this way instead of the hanging lights I'd seen elsewhere, I wasn't sure. Perhaps something in this space didn't react well to bright light?

Perhaps it was simple design preference?

Either way, on my level and around the water's edge, I saw numerous grated tunnels with slight flows heading into the reservoir, each tunnel marked with a color and a symbol I couldn't interpret. Down each tunnel, too, I could make out colored flashes, and machinery's steady vibration echoed around the space, as though someone had turned up the volume on Starship's background noise.

This seemed to be Starship's central water source. Given its size —from what I could tell, it stretched the Conduit's width and beyond —and untarnished color, Purity might not be a bad name for the place. I crouched at the walkway's edge and dipped my head back beneath the water, looking for confirmation in the depths.

I couldn't see it, but I felt it now. A gentle tug towards the reservoir's bottom. The Librarian's leftovers, festering in my digital data banks, confirmed Starship's heart-and-artery design. Purity would pump fresh water across the ship, and after its use, the water inevitably found its way back here.

"I see we have ourselves an intruder," shouted a voice above me, its echoes bubbling into my underwater ears.

With water dripping down my face, I looked up towards the announcer, and saw a harsh red glow, bright and angled right at my eyes from some sort of flashlight. The source stood several levels above me, on a walkway that passed near-enough to the Garden waterfall that I considered it a minor miracle I hadn't hit the thing and split apart.

"What's a human like you doing all the way down here?" the voice asked again, in an even, nondescript tone. "Don't you know this area's off limits?"

A human? I paused, then re-calibrated. I did resemble one, and if someone didn't know I was a mech, they could make that mistake. More importantly, the accuser's word choice indicated that it *wasn't* human.

Which meant another mech.

"I fell," I offered, standing on the walkway and attempting to shield my eyes from the red light. "From above, in the Garden."

"Fell?" the thing replied, and, listening closely, I picked out that artificial twinge mech voices had. A failure to replicate biological vocal cords perfectly. "From the Garden? Ought to be dead then."

"Gamma," Kaydee said, standing off to the side and squinting up at the red light. "Be careful. Not every mech left on Starship is a friend."

"Are any?" I replied.

"Who're you talking to?" the mech shouted from above. "Someone hiding down there with you?"

"Just me. Can you shut off that light? It's blinding."

The mech moved towards its walkway's railing, and I saw the light shift, then move away in a sudden circle as the mech, its whirling shape caught in Purity's blue glow, jumped down to another walkway spaced between us. The mech landed with a heavy clang, that red light swinging back around to aim right at my face.

"Don't know if you quite get it, boy," the mech said. "This place is Purity, and it's mine. I'm charged with keeping it clean, and right now you're messing it up."

"Sorry?" I tried to move to the side, but the red light kept following.

"Oh, don't worry about apologizing," the mech said. "Been waiting a long time for some new salvage to come my way. A real long time."

The red light winked out, giving me a clear view, though one I wished I could take back.

Standing on the walkway above me was a mech, yes. Metal bits on its frame glimmered in the blue, but those bits were few. Instead, the mech stood more than two meters, and all manner of things covered its body. Some looked like ragged cloth remnants, like half a jacket hanging from one of its right arms. Those didn't spike my alarms.

But the bones tied with cords along its frame, the matted hair pasted to part of its head, and what looked like a desiccated eye leering from the mech's bucket-like head?

Kaydee cursed.

So did I.

SIX

PURITY

When Kaydee revealed the Conduit's true nature when I'd left Alvie's, I'd seen mechs falling apart, battering each other, scaling the walls in search of things unseen. All of that, though, had been at a distance, a remove that gave me a chance to accept the new reality.

I had a harder time doing that when the sinister mech looked my way. It became impossible when the mech vaulted from his walkway to land on the slick tiles right in front of me, eye leering in the island-blue light.

"Hit him or something!" Kaydee shouted, hugging the wall to my left.

"Hit him with what?" I asked her.

"Hit me?" the mech cackled. "Why would you want to do that? Because I'm gonna tear you to pieces and add you to my collection?"

I backed up a step and the mech copied me, swinging his red light —which, I noticed, sat on some long, thin device's end—back into my face.

"That doesn't make any sense," I said. "Why do you have a collection?"

"Lost and found! Anything that comes down here, I get to take.

Someone sends a message saying they lost it, I'll give it back, sure will, but guess how often that happens?"

"Never?" I ventured, trying to find some way, some where to go.

"Never!" The mech cried, then lunged at me, two long arms bearing a net between them sweeping over his head and towards mine.

I had no tricks, no secret weapons to deploy, so I went to the only place I could go: back into the water. I dove in and kicked as hard as I could, motoring away from the walkway and towards the reservoir's center, where the Garden's trickle met its end.

"Aww, are you scared?" the mech yelled after me.

I glanced back as I kicked, cool water again soaking through my clothes. The mech hadn't followed me into the lake. Instead, it watched me, then aimed that red light at a walkway over my head. I heard a click, saw a black line extend from the device and launch towards that walkway. With another cackle, that damn mech soared through the air on that line and made a wobbly landing on the walkway.

"There's nowhere to go in there," the mech said. "I'll bet you can't swim forever. Humans get real tired, real quick, you keep'em in the water."

I stopped, treaded as best I could and looked around. The mech had it right, even though I wasn't human. A quick scan through my body found biological processes charging up my batteries at a slow and steady rate, one vastly outpaced by the energy I needed to keep on swimming.

It might take a long time but I'd eventually run out of power.

The mech could just wait for me to give up, then grab me at the water's edge, or after I sank to the bottom.

"Hey," Kaydee said, bobbing next to me. "Have any bright ideas?"

"Not really?" I spat out water as I spoke.

My clothes were getting heavier, and with all the swimming, my systems were starting to signal alarms. I might be out of energy sooner than I thought.

"If you ask nicely," the mech said. "I could fish ya out of there, reel you up and in. Put you outta your misery."

I ignored him, tried to think.

"I say," Kaydee said, "if this is it, then drown. Don't give that garbage bucket the satisfaction."

Drown? Could I? My body didn't have lungs, didn't breathe beyond some artificial concessions to vocal expression built into my throat and mouth. What would it even look like, me drowning?

I continued treading and ran through my own logs, the manuals Leo had thrown into my memory. They held all the tidbits about pushing my strength around, how long I could run, how far I could jump.

Like the Librarian's archives, still nestled in me, Leo's records held too much for me to run through and maintain any activity, but I could search. Could look for terms and just find those pieces while my legs continued their kicking.

"Are you okay?" Kaydee asked. "You're not saying anything."

"I'm thinking," I replied, while the mech up above declared his growing boredom.

There. In a section about potential hazards, largely spent around deep space vacuum, I found the words I wanted to see.

"Guess what?" the mech said. "Time's up, lost boy!"

The mech leaned over the walkway, his red light glaring down at me.

And I let myself sink.

The cold water came up over my head, soaking my hair and vanishing me into a deep blue-black world. My body did exactly what Leo said it would, and a thousand little clicks and snaps echoed throughout my nerves as critical systems sealed themselves from any air intakes.

Something slammed into my shoulder, hard enough to push me down, then arrested my descent. I looked over, saw a four-pointed claw digging through my outfit and into my skin, a thick cable spooling up and away from me, towards the surface. That cable lurched once, then began a steady pull.

The damn mech *was* reeling me in.

Like a fish trying to unhook itself from a lure, I started thrashing. My legs kicked out, I shook my head, swung my arms and tried to move my shoulders to dislodge the grapple, but the claw only dug in further, hurt worse.

If I couldn't shake the grapple loose, then I'd have to try something different. I stopped, then reached over with my hands to grip the cable. The mech kept reeling and my head hit the surface, rose above it, followed by my chest and the rest of my body.

"Whoa, quit fighting!" the mech shouted as I pulled on the cable, lifted myself and yanked some slack into the cord.

The mech made his own noises, setting hissing clamps that, I noticed with my upturned eyes, locked him into the walkway's grated surface. Keeping himself stable, a bulwark to lift me over the edge.

I poured energy into my hands, pulling the cable towards my mouth as I rose, dripping, from the water.

"What're you opening that mouth for?" the mech cackled. "Not going to feed you, boy. You won't have to worry about food much longer anyways."

I lifted my head up, pulled the cable inside my mouth, and tasted its cold metal. The zinc, coppery feel. A strong cable, but made for lifting, not to resist a cut. Not to resist one of the few tools Leo saw fit to give his vessels.

I didn't need to eat, but I had teeth nonetheless. Razor ones, ready to serve as makeshift knives in case I had to cut something open, get into a container. Leo's files had my teeth slotted away under an optional asset.

Right now, they were essential.

I bit down, ground my teeth against the cable and felt the metal flake and split. Shrapnel vanished inside my mouth, falling into the little storage box in my throat. The mech lifted me higher, almost even now with the walkway.

"Hello, hello," the mech said, and I met his eye as he rotated me to face him.

"Goodbye," I replied, the word more mushier and muffled than I liked, given my mouth still had a cable in it.

"What?"

I bit through, and the cable snapped. I fell as the mech reeled back, clamped feet keeping him on the walkway even as I plummeted into the water, as I hit the surface and sank like cement all the way to the bottom.

The water transitioned from light blue to black, before giving a shimmering path to soft yellow, thanks to diodes implanted in the reservoir's bottom. The little golden globes ringed around several large grates with extremely fine netting, where debris clustered as the so-slight current pulled them in. I landed on one of the grates, my feet squishing through some plant remnant.

The whole setup didn't seem all that pure until I noticed the smaller, flashing bits circulating around the debris. What seemed like a light trick became much more real when I felt stinging bites all around me, as though I swam in acid.

Even then, I didn't find the cause until one of those flashing things went straight for my eye, giving me a perfect look at the centimeter-long filament looking to gnaw me to molecular bits. I ducked my head out of the way, bent down towards that grate, and understood.

Water wasn't getting through the netting. That's how they kept this place pure. The filaments devouring me would dissolve my bits to their atomic pieces, which would flow through the grates and out of Starship's drinking water supply.

A grand discovery, which would leave me very dead if I stayed still.

But I had one big advantage over the other debris stuck here around the grates: I could move.

I bent down, punched my hand into the netting, and pressed. Those fibers, so tight, gave way without much struggle, like pushing away my own jacket under water. Not designed to handle major stress.

Except when I pulled the netting away, the water began to move. The debris too, and me with them. The mild current became a vortex, shuttling us down and into the pipe as the yellow diodes flared an angry red.

I slid into another pipe, this one crusty and choked with matter. A sucking wind blew bubbles around me as the water rushed us all along, before depositing me and everything else in a tub-sized pool.

A silver, charred cover secured me and the debris inside—getting me up close and personal with a largely-nibbled fern, plenty of those filaments, and what looked like a rotted pineapple. Bubbles continued surrounding us, and before I'd really comprehended what had happened, the water around me began to heat up.

The silver seal started to glow. Behind me, the central pipe leading into the box sealed itself shut with a whoosh, cutting off more water and leaving me stuck inside a space barely large enough for my bulk.

Oh. That's where we were. An oven, burning away the atomic waste left over from the filaments. I'd be cooked along with every-thing else.

I pressed my still-soaked-shoed feet against the tub's base and pushed up, punching against that cover and burning my hands in the process. Like the grate, nobody had designed the tub to resist active destruction, and with a couple solid hits, even with the water slowing me down, I popped the top loose and pushed it aside.

"Didn't think you were going to get out of that one," Kaydee said as I clambered from the steaming tub.

"Thanks for the confidence," I replied, and set about to seeing where I'd wound up.

It was hard to have pre-conceived notions about where an under-water waste pipe would funnel you, but I certainly didn't imagine the holiday nightmare in which I found myself. The organic oven sat in the center of a larger sphere, with the area pressing up and into the reservoir bulging back inward, like a ball that'd been deflated and punched in on one side.

Hanging about the circular walls were light strands, though with more variety in type and color than I'd ever expect to see in a sane person's decor. Bright greens and reds clashed with purples and oranges. A pure white, naked bulb sat flickering in one corner, producing a discordant strobe effect. The glows mingled with stale air that held a permanent char taste.

For a space that should have been nothing more than a maintenance access for that oven, bounteous crap dominated.

"So, I think this is that mech's home," Kaydee said, peering around along with me. "Must've been a hoarder."

"Maybe this is the lost and found he was talking about?"

So much lost, and most in a condition I'd hesitate anyone wanting it found. Jumbled metals heaped on one side, neighboring a haphazard Franken-furniture collection, with legs, cushions, and supports for two chairs and a desk seemingly stolen from other pieces. Some tools, including what looked like other mech limbs, leaned against the far wall, near an access hatch sealed with nothing more than a simple handle.

"Check this out," Kaydee said, over by the desk. "Looks like he wasn't just a dumb robot."

"His rambling makes me not so sure," I said, but headed over to see what Kaydee had noticed.

Topping the desk were, believe it or not, paper journals. Books. Binders filled with soaked, moldy remnants. Enough to make me wonder whether Starship's residents had made a habit of throwing their old paper goods in the trash.

"You know where these are from?" Kaydee asked.

"I'm guessing the answer isn't that reservoir?"

"I mean, yeah, of course. But he must have fished these out around the same time. Look at them."

Kaydee seemed far more excited by the leather-bound journals, by the folder that, in its corroded lettering, suggested an evacuation plan, than I was.

"Am I supposed to be seeing something here?"

"You're seeing history, that's what," Kaydee replied. "Starship's checkered past. You get thousands of people and seal them in a metal box for generations, you're going to get some discontent."

"Okay?"

"You can't run around a space ship like this shooting at people you disagree with, because if you pop a hole in the hull, everybody dies. So you have to use other methods."

I started to understand, reached out and flipped through one of the pages. With just a glance, my eyes photographed and internalized the handwriting, taking its words and mapping them into a cohesive story. A sad one.

The dates on the pages held no meaning for me, but the author talked about their family, their friends, their section growing discontented with opportunities on Starship. That future generations might see a wondrous end to the mission didn't do much for the current crew, and they wanted more. Demanded better jobs, better lives.

The opportunity to leave the ship.

"And they got their chance," Kaydee said.

"How?"

"Gamma, don't worry about it," Kaydee replied. "It's there in your memory if you really want to look it up. But the people who did that, and the ones who protested, are all long gone. My guess, people who didn't want these found tossed them into the water. Let those filaments dissolve them."

I left the journals and their scribbled hopes and dreams on the desk. If the mech wanted to keep them, who was I to take them away? Who was I to wallow in a past I hadn't been present for?

Next to the room's exit lay something else that caught my eye. An arrangement on the floor, scraps connected by wires into a lithe contraption. One that, if my memory could be trusted, resembled a decent-sized dog, albeit one made from multi-colored metal bits.

I would have dismissed it as an art project, a hobby for the mech, except, as I looked, I saw patterns. Potential. Those wires connecting the hard feet fed into what looked like a battery, and a processor. A motherboard; the computer's beating heart.

"Can you turn it on?" Kaylee said, hunching over next to me.

"I'm not seeing a switch."

"Try here," Kaydee pointed to a port on the metal dog's side. "Use your jack."

Squeeze my fingers together, make a connection. That's what Kaydee had done when she ran the cleaning robot after me. Now I knew how to do it too.

"Okay, let's see if you're ready to run," I said to the thing, and plugged in.

I STOOD on a vast green-metal plain, though unlike my flat white expanse, this one had grass. Emerald, shining grass, but grass all the same. The sky, however, had ditched blue for a deep black. Light came from the ground beneath my feet, radiating up and getting swallowed.

No crystals, which might mean no storage. No digital body appeared near me either, which meant, I assumed, that the dog had no activity. Dormant, then. Waiting to be woken up.

But how?

The Librarian had attempted to wrap his data around mine when he first came into my space. Maybe I could try the same thing with the dog? Give it a part of myself and bring it to life?

I reached through the grass to touch the warm, solid ground beneath. I felt a constant hum, the power from the dog's battery supplying a charge, now only used to create this grass, to maintain the dog's sleep state.

Perhaps, then, a little jolt.

The question: where to deliver it?

In the physical world, I was constrained by physical laws. Gravity, mass and the like. Here, I could swim through a digital space unbound by those laws. So long as I stayed within the dog's virtual boundaries, I could do just about anything I liked.

So to find my target, I leaped into the air and kept on rising. Not with the natural flow of a bird, but with an elevator's static control. I floated high above the grass, and looked around, hoping to spy the dog's frozen heart so I could thaw it.

I looked down, and almost laughed. Too obvious, too perfect.

The grass wasn't grass, but fur. What I'd thought was an endless expanse was, in fact, the dog's body lying flat, the green fur curling on the far horizon to wrap around. Just as I'd created my own body in this space, so the dog had its own, just . . . gigantic.

At least I didn't have to find my target anymore. The dog lay there beneath me, so I dug into my own archives, found the same process lurking there that'd woken me on that cot not all that long ago, and pointed the routine towards the dog's bulk, the emerald fur.

Like with the Librarian, a silver thread wove its way from my fingers towards the dog, waving down as my code wormed its way into the dog's matrix, nestling its functions into the creature's operating system.

The silver hit the fur and I waited for the dog to move, for its processor to show life.

I felt a jolt, a hard push that rattled my mind. Part of the consequences? I'd never been inside a waking mech before.

Another hit. Strong, and I felt pain now, but distant, like an oncoming headache. The dog and its virtual world blurred, then snapped back into focus, my silver stream spreading and finding its goal in the dog's body.

What was happening? I looked around, saw nothing, and felt another hit.

The dog's world vanished, light waves snapping across my vision in sudden static. A signal interruption. My body re-calibrated, my eyes re-focused.

The mech from before loomed over me, arms raised for another hammer blow, eye leering and patchwork clothes hanging off in grotesque rags. Behind him, Kaydee stood with her eyes wide, hands over her mouth.

"Guess I found ya after all," the mech wheezed, then drove his fists into my head.

SEVEN

MECH'S BEST FRIEND

I'd never restarted before, so the feeling that came through as my systems reworked their kinks and turned themselves back on felt like being thawed out. Warmth folded through me as I felt my fingers, legs, ears and eyes come back on line. My mind followed suit, sparking up an immediate alert warning me that similar jarring concussions could result in irreparable harm.

Right. Don't get punched in the face again. Understood.

I creaked my eyes open slow, saw I was still in the oven room, still right where I'd been before the mech knocked me out. My internal clock said less than a minute had passed, owing to, apparently, my system's excellent shutdown-start-up speed.

"You're already awake?" Kaydee said, lying on the ground next to me. "I thought you would be out for a long time. Maybe forever."

I would have replied, but until I figured out where the mech was, I didn't want to make any noise. Didn't want to move more than necessary. I could hear the mech rampaging around the room, smashing things, cursing, and raging. Maybe it didn't like that I'd broken its grate or the bio-matter oven.

"Oh, if you're worried, the mech's busy right now," Kaydee said. "You, uh, you did something to that dog."

Now I snapped up, turned.

The dog, a third of the mech's size, danced around the room, alternating darting in towards the mech and hopping away, opening its mouth to bark but instead offering only a metal scratching sound. Something broken there.

But the way the dog moved! Its sharp steel claws let the dog leap up and grip onto the walls, standing vertical, and then jump onto the mech, deliver a scratch or a bite before bounding away from any counter blow. Agile, destructive, and seemingly invested in protecting me.

"It's been doing a number on the mech since you went out," Kaydee said. "If it wasn't, I'd probably just be screaming right now as that guy ate you up."

"Ate me up?" I said, getting to my feet and looking for anything that could work as a weapon.

"Oh yeah. Mech cannibalism is a big thing. Turns out most machines have no problem taking parts from others if it'll help them complete their jobs faster."

"I don't see myself doing that." Getting up sent a twinge from my shoulder, and sure enough, that grapple claw still had itself embedded into me. "But never rule anything out, I guess."

Pulling a hard metal claw from my own shoulder was not pleasant, but with a grimace and a grip, I tore it free as the dog darted in for another bounding attack at the mech's legs. This time, the gritty machine timed its swing right and caught the dog mid-way through its lunge, sending my newfound pal flying into the desk. Papers, metal shards went flying.

The mech didn't stop there, whirling towards the dog's tangled body, raising its fists for what would likely be a rough blow.

"Hey," I said. "Lay off my dog."

"You're dog?" the mech twisted its single eye my way.

Vessels, I found, could move damn fast when we wanted to. I

kicked off the ground and pushed the grapple, clawed end first, straight into the mech's chest, right where that processor ought to be. The grapple sliced through, struck home, and the mech didn't even have time to complain before its limbs went limp, a lone spark evacuating the wound as the machine shut down.

In the silence that followed the mech's demise, I looked at its shell and tried to figure out what I'd just done. The moral lines encoded in me suggested murdering, or even harming live humans was something to be avoided at almost all costs. Damaging other mechs, however, seemed to have looser constraints. As if the mechs themselves didn't matter.

"We can always rebuild it," Kaydee muttered next to me. "That's what we'd always say, whenever this happened. Rebuild it and make it better."

"What are you talking about?"

"The mechs, Gamma. What do you think I'm talking about? Dinner?" Kaydee said. "That's, like, the story of Starship if you want it quick. Mechs running amok. The grand quest to see how many things could be automated, not because we needed it, but because it was a puzzle to solve."

The dog approached me slow, and I took my first good look at it. While its computer parts seemed cohesive, everything else about the mech looked like it'd been assembled from various junk. Cleaned up, polished junk, but scrap metal couldn't escape its roots. The dog moved fine, those wires and joints holding together, but the rounded plating making up its skin slid around and against itself. Its eyes shone with an artificial yellow glow, and its mouth couldn't quite close over jagged, tarnished steel teeth.

"If the job existed, the Voices would put up a prize to see who could get a mech to do it better," Kaydee kept going on behind me. "Or not even better. Just do it, period. You'd have these big contests, and the winner would nuke away positions for dozens of people."

I knelt down, met the dog's eyes, and held out a hand. I ran a search in my own memory banks for dogs, and the Librarian's stories held examples aplenty for befriending the canines. Whether the mammal's methods extended to its mechanical version, I couldn't be sure, but the initial results looked promising: the dog padded over to me and sniffed my hand.

"You might be thinking great, now those people have time to spend on what they want!" Kaydee rambled, enough that I was starting to worry. "But boredom in a place like this, where there's not a lot of new stuff to do, is deadly, Gamma. It's friggin' deadly."

"I'm going to call it Alvie," I said, rubbing the dog's rounded, bucket-like head.

Alvie likely didn't have nerves, or anything like my synthetic connections in its scrap body, but it must have felt the pressure, because Alvie jumped up at me, planted its paws flat on my chest, and made its squeaking, wheezing bark.

"Are you even listening to me?" Kaydee asked, then I heard a soft laugh. "Bet I can guess what gave you that name."

"I'm as creative as what I know," I replied.

I chose not to say anything about Kaydee's comments—I was a mech, crafted to solve what the Voices wanted solving. Whether or not a living human could do what I was doing, I didn't know. Whether my existence had caused another one pain, I didn't know.

An uncomfortable question for a time when I wasn't stuck at the bottom of a watery grave, and very late for an appointment with Alpha.

With Alvie following, his claws clacking on the slick floor, we went to the hatch and opened it to reveal a long ladder leading up. Hardly as efficient as an elevator, and far too many rungs for any human to climb day after day. For a mech, though, the only factor that counted was the time spent climbing them.

Purity. I thought more about the ruined mech as I scaled the ladder, Alvie reaching and pulling himself up after me. Kaydee said the mech had been doing what nobody else had wanted to do, keeping Starship's water clean. But clearly that original mission had faded somehow, had been corrupted into a manic state.

A state that, troublingly, had still given Purity—I'd decided to label the mech as such—the ability to put Alvie together. To collect and value particular debris over others. The mech had kept the journals from those poor lost souls.

Why?

I scanned the Librarian's leftovers as I climbed, reviewed what pieces Kaydee had opened to my searching, and found no easy answer.

The ladder culminated in another hatch, one that opened up into the vast reservoir where I'd fallen with a splash that still had my clothes soaked. I'd grown so used to their wet, chill clinging that it took Kaydee remarking, again, that I looked like a ragged heap for me to notice.

"I can't do anything about it right now," I said, walking and climbing ever higher in the reservoir, searching for a way out. "Unless you want me to go back to before?"

"Naked?" Kaydee said, swinging her legs from a railing. "You don't look that good, Gamma. Keep the clothes on."

Alvie echoed the sentiment with his wheeze-bark, and we kept on moving, eyes ever upward.

We climbed into a desert. Not sand so much as artificial, blonde dirt surrounding cactus and agave rows, bright white lights lancing their hot rays from above. The hatch had us climbing into a small ditch, with a dirty pathway leading off towards that central pit and its ever-trickling waterfall.

Alvie took my immediate inaction as an excuse to play, bounding past me to bury himself in the sand, sending tufts of it flying as the dog clanked his way around. I would've played with him too, except for all the people.

They swarmed around a cactus, packed in and stared at it while one, a woman with an extravagant pearl outfit and a hat with a brim so wide it seemed to swallow everything beneath it, stepped around the cactus giving what I figured was a speech.

The audience looked like a spectrum, with some in plain, dirty clothes marking manual labor and others in refined suits, hands tapping away on devices as they listened.

To get a better view, I moved off the path, climbing up a slight dune to see over the crowd, trying to understand what about this particular cactus had drawn such an audience. When I made it to the top, I noticed a small girl sitting next to the cactus, her eyes on the circling woman.

"You found me," Kaydee whispered, joining me on my little hill.

"Another memory?"

"Another genius moment for my mother," Kaydee said. "Bet you can guess which one she is."

"I think I can."

I'd expected something more seething from Kaydee's tone, but when I looked at her, I saw a soft face, a thoughtful look.

"I wonder if these things still collect water?" Kaydee mused.

"The cactus?"

"That was her thing, my mom," Kaydee walked down the hill, towards the closest cactus, while the memory continued playing itself out. "You had the mech crowd, she went the other way. Always about the Garden and what you could do with something natural."

Kaydee touched the cactus, and I followed her lead, gently guiding my fingers around the yellowed spines.

"Why rely solely on a machine filter when you could have these, too?" I asked.

"'Zactly," Kaydee replied. "Mom's cactuses were so much more efficient than the ones on Earth. You're looking at Starship's emergency water source, right here. Sucked right outta the air."

"It's . . . something?"

Kaydee laughed, "That's what I thought too. Who cared about a cactus when you could be playing with big robots?"

I glanced back towards the crowd, curious to see if that view played itself out on the young Kaydee's face, but the ghosts were gone. The cactus itself, though, still stood. Alvie saw my gaze and bounded over to it, then looked back at me, confused.

"Just thinking," I said to the dog, though that didn't help Alvie any.

Just thinking didn't help my mission either, and Kaydee had once more dipped back into her ether, so Alvie and I set off wandering for a way up.

Having Alvie around had a strange effect on me: with Kaydee bouncing from my digital brain every now and then, I hadn't felt lonely on Starship. Yet, with Alvie walking along, sticking his metal nose into various objects, pawing at them, or bounding up and down the walls, my world felt more alive. Less like a dream, or a manufactured series of spaces designed by some malevolent god.

In other words, I liked having a damn pet.

Alvie's peculiarities became clear as we made our way along the desert path towards, so simple signposts declared, an elevator. The dog kept moving, kept acting like what the Librarian's records suggested a dog ought to do, yet Alvie didn't react like any living thing might. For one, I was pretty certain that Alvie's nose didn't actually work. Parsing sound was a simple thing for a mech to do, but smell?

My commands also worked immediately, and once Alvie had demonstrated instant mastery over rudimentary sit and stay orders, I went for more complex instruction, like jump this cactus, then dash around that agave, and bring me back that decorative rock over there. Alvie followed the route exactly, like any computer might.

Yet, as unnatural as Alvie might be, he still triggered happiness when he butted his head against my legs or gave his wheezing bark at any encroaching critter.

And there were plenty of those. Much like the Garden levels above, the desert held skittering forms that dashed from plant to plant, performing various tasks I couldn't identify and couldn't be bothered to care about. The Garden had an ecosystem, and it persisted without human intervention.

The elevator flaunted itself. A rounded glass enclosure set right in the middle of a dozen blooming cacti, the lift shimmered that emerald green along its upper and lower metal bounds. As Alvie and I approached, the glass swept away, plates nestling behind one another into a half-meter slot against the elevator's back, creating an open-air entry.

My feet, still in my soaking shoes, appreciated the elevator's soft base, like stepping onto a firm pillow. Alvie immediately went to kneading, his sharp claws making tiny marks in the fabric. I would have told him to stop, except who cared? What guard would appear and force me to pay a fine?

As we set ourselves inside, the glass pulled itself back around, sealing us in. A wide patch along the transparent surface fogged into a deep blue, with clear white lettering listing the Garden's several dozen levels and inviting me to select one.

"You were on the twentieth," Kaydee said, leaning against the glass to the right. "One of the botanical sections, because apparently people like pretty things too."

"Apparently," I said, reaching out to push level nineteen. One level below, where Alpha had been. "There are so many. Starship's bigger than I thought."

"I've been saying that since I was born."

The glass shivered slightly as I touched it, and level nineteen's title—Medicinal Plants—went purple. The elevator waited a moment, I supposed to let people select other options, before shuddering and starting to ascend.

I didn't get to watch the desert disappear beneath me because the elevator went dark quick after it started to move, so completely dark that Alvie whined and I lost track of whether we were still moving at all.

The patch displaying the floor numbers dissolved into roving white pixels that swirled around me along the glass, as though a blizzard had caught the display and yanked it around. I tried to watch all the dots, tried to figure out where they were going, but the whole swarm wound up settling back to where they'd been before, only instead of floor numbers, the display asked me a question.

WHAT ARE YOU DOING HERE?

"That is either a very simple, or a very complicated question," I said to the display.

SIMPLE. WHY HAVE YOU NOT GONE TO THE NURSERY?

Okay. Now I knew the source. The mysterious Voices, the ones I hadn't seen or heard from since leaving Leo's lab.

"I've been dealing with . . . things," I said.

DO YOU UNDERSTAND HOW CRITICAL YOUR MISSION IS?

I glanced down at Alvie, who stared back at the letters as if reading them himself. Who knew, maybe the dog was. Maybe Alvie had all the answers but couldn't speak them.

"Honestly, I have no idea," I said.

"Gamma, careful," Kaydee whispered. "You don't want to mess with them."

Point taken. I tried to look sincere.

STARSHIP IS IN CRITICAL CONDITION. IT'S LAST HOPE RESIDES IN GETTING US ACCESS TO THE NURS-ERY. DO YOU UNDERSTAND?

"I don't even know who you are, or what you want to do with this Nursery. How can I understand?" I said.

The screen didn't change.

"You're reaching," Kaydee said. "Remember what I said about vessels needing to limit their information? They can't tell you, because you'll—"

"Do what? Go crazy?" I replied. "I've seen enough of Starship. I've nearly been killed by a homicidal mech. I'm not going through this blind anymore."

WHO ARE YOU TALKING TO?

I stared back at the screen. The Voices didn't know about Kaydee.

"The Librarian," I offered.

THEN HE SHOULD UNDERSTAND. TO YOUR QUES-

TION, WE, THE VOICES, ARE THE LAST REMNANTS OF STARSHIP'S PEOPLE.

"And you're, what, holed up in some part of this place?"

IN A SENSE. THE NURSERY CONTAINS OUR CHILDREN AND OUR FUTURE, BUT WE CANNOT SEE THEM ANY LONGER. CANNOT HELP THEM. THAT IS WHY WE NEED YOU.

"Save the children, save the ship," Kaydee laughed. "So simple."

"Sounds that way," I replied.

"If you trust them, you're simpler than I thought."

Maybe. The elevator brightened, the glass returning to its transparent state, revealing that we were still moving, slowing and settling onto the nineteenth level.

On the display patch, the Voice's letters swirled again.

PLEASE. HELP US.

Except I couldn't focus on their words, because standing beyond the glass, staring straight back at me, was a face, curious and cautious.

Alpha.

EIGHT

INFECTION PROTOCOL

The glass split aside, reducing the distance between myself and another vessel to a mere meter. Alpha's strict eyes, narrow face, and long red hair splashed over his shoulders onto a seemingly makeshift tan robe that ended in tatters around the vessel's ankles.

Those ankles, like the rest of Alpha, bore tiny scratches and damage I hadn't seen when I'd first caught the vessel from above. Up close, Alpha had suffered a lot of minor injuries, and either his synthetic skin no longer repaired them itself, or Alpha suppressed that feature.

"Hello," Alpha offered to start the conversation, an amber voice coming through calm and nothing like the laughing joy I'd heard before. "I've been waiting."

"Here?"

"Yes. Once I saw you fall, I determined this would be the most likely place you would show up. If you survived."

Alpha stepped back from the elevator, gestured for me to walk off and join him. Alvie took the cue to dash away into the verdant landscape, rustling between ferns and chasing after some of the skittering pollinators.

"Sorry," I said. "Can we start over? I'm Gamma, and you're Alpha?"

"You know my name?"

Damn. Kaydee had shown me enough about Starship that I should have known to keep information to myself. Alpha wouldn't know what, who I had dancing around my digital memory, but now he knew I wasn't entirely alone.

"The Voices told me," I decided to go with a version of the truth. "They said you'd been sent out before me, but hadn't completed their mission."

Alpha's eyes narrowed, then he relaxed into a slight smile, "They're always so frantic. Come with me, let me show you why the Voices don't matter."

"Don't matter?" I asked. "Aren't they the ones that created us?"

Alpha walked and I walked with him, keeping pace as he led us through a level labeled 'Cloud Forest'. Nearly as lush as the botanical level that I'd explored, vines combed almost every open area. Mist played continually along the bottom, puffing up in little clouds as we walked. Small trees dominated, some bearing myriad fruits in tropical colors. The waterfall's noise paraded.

"Being something's creator doesn't give you the right to control them." Alpha reached up and ran a long, muscled arm along a green vine, as if giving the plant a pet. He was impressively athletic, though I supposed I was as well. Synthetic muscle didn't require working out, or nutrition. "Don't feel like you owe them anything."

An interesting point of view, and no doubt with a story behind it.

"But why not?" I said. "Why shouldn't we help them?"

"Because I'd rather do something else," Alpha replied. "Like wander the Garden. It's a marvelous place, don't you think?"

"Sure, but—"

"Quiet, Gamma. I know you have questions, but you will learn more by listening. Once you understand, then you might find you don't have any questions at all."

I shut my mouth. Alpha had let the tiniest bit of irritation bleed into that last comment and I didn't want to alienate the only other mech I'd met that wasn't intent on murdering or brushing me aside on its eternal mission.

"Is it me," Kaydee said, walking backwards in front of us, "or does that sound stupid? If you understand, then you'll have no questions. Um, yeah? That's how questions work?"

I pressed my lips together to keep from laughing. Alpha did seem so serious, a veneer that appeared at odds with his bedraggled appearance and a plant-filled space where a robot dog pestered tiny pollinating machines. After all, the vessel had just been taking a bath.

How dramatic could things be?

"I've turned the Garden into my home," Alpha continued. "It's the only part of Starship where I feel connected to the life this great place once held. You'll come to feel the same way, I know."

One of those pollinators dashed under my foot as I tried to think up a reply, and Alpha caught me as I stumbled.

"But," Alpha continued, "Leo created us to be inquisitive creatures. To always be looking out for ways to better ourselves and Starship itself."

"He did?"

I noticed that Alpha rarely looked my way while he spoke, scanning our surroundings even though we were walking on a clear path with zero danger around us.

Except, maybe, Alvie, who burst out from the deep green bushes to our right, pursuing three pollinators, their oval, tendril-laden bodies scurrying away from the dog, who followed wheeze-barking the whole way.

"Leo didn't chain himself to the Voices," Alpha said. "He did what they asked, because he had to, but Leo slipped what makes you and I inside his directed mission. We have our independence because of him, which means we can give Starship what it needs, not what the Voices want."

"And you're doing that by staying in the Garden?"

Alpha's face flickered at the reply, not to an expected irritated frown, but rather to a manic, eyes-wide, mouth open look. Like a silent scream. After a second, with me taking a step back, Alpha's face reset to its contemplative smile.

"I'm protecting it, Gamma. Starship's food, water, and air come from here. If there is to be any hope, the Garden must survive."

"Except, we don't need any of those things?"

The path spread out to a wide space, a grassy meadow hill ringed with misty trees and a faux blue sky overhead, a big yellow light in its center. A breeze broke the sticky warm air.

"Not yet, Gamma," Alpha said. "Not yet. But we will."

"I—"

"You don't understand. Yes. I know," Alpha replied as we walked into the meadow's center. "Please, sit down."

"Why?"

Again that face flicker, those bugged-out eyes. This time I tried to stay still, to see what might be causing it. Was Alpha suffering from some tic? Had a wire crossed itself?

"I am not asking, Gamma," Alpha said, his set face back, but trading the smile for a straight line. "This will help you. Help us both. And will help Starship most of all."

I did not sit. Something with Alpha's voice, his continually twitching face, had my digital nerves flaring. I'd hoped meeting Alpha would give me some insight to what the Voices really wanted. Maybe even get a partner to help fulfill their mission.

Instead . . .

"This vessel's really creeping me out," Kaydee said, circling Alpha. "I knew Leo. He wouldn't put this kind of stuff into a vessel's head. He wasn't a crackpot philosopher."

A yipping noise came from the way we'd come, and Alpha and I both looked to see Alvie streaking towards us, scattering up torn leaves and dirt as the dog ran. Behind him, pollinators followed.

Not just a few, either. A horde. Their tendrils all up and raised, racing after my dog.

My. Dog.

"Hey!" I shouted as Alvie raced towards me. "Stay away from him!"

I didn't have a plan for what I'd do against that skittering mass, a group that grew as it swept into the room with us, swarming around the mound. Then again, I wasn't all that certain what the little creatures could do to Alvie and I. Poke us to death?

Alpha, for his part, watched the growing horde without expression. He folded his arms and stared, silent, until the pollinator flow slowed to a trickle and the crimson-beaned mass sat quivering, surrounding us.

"Are you seeing this?" I said. "Because this doesn't look like normal behavior."

"How many mechs have you seen around here with normal behavior?" Alpha replied.

"That's the first good point he's made," Kaydee said, giving Alvie a virtual pet.

"You get what I'm saying." I looked around the mound, but no weapons presented themselves. There weren't even any vines to break off and use as makeshift whips. "What're they doing?"

"What I asked them to," Alpha said. "Now please, sit down. It should be easier this way."

My nerves flared, my program designed to assess threats deciding that what Alpha had just said was, indeed, a problem. I turned to and stepped away from Alpha in a single motion, trying to get some space.

Alvie picked up on the new vibe and issued a wheezing growl Alpha's way, before stepping close to me and giving a nervous glance towards all those pollinators.

"Told you he was bad news," Kaydee whispered next to me. She had her fists balled, that spearmint hair spiking everywhere. "You wouldn't be awake if this guy had stayed sane."

"Mind telling me what it is you're planning to do?" I asked Alpha.

"Of course," Alpha said. "Starship belongs to the mechs now. And the mechs will belong to me."

Oh, so it was that simple. I didn't have time to ask how Alpha would claim all the various mechs, because his face stretched into that wild grin as he jumped at me.

Behind us, around us, the pollinators joined their master's charge, scrambling up the grassy mound towards us.

If Leo had put any programming in my data to handle an assault by a tiny robot swarm coupled with a dangerous, alternative version of myself, perhaps I could have mounted some defense.

Instead, I managed to get my arms up to block whatever punch Alpha planned to throw my way, only to see my dog leap in between us and drive the vessel to the ground. As Alvie pressed the enemy into the dirt, I felt the first pollinator slam into my ankle and start climbing up my leg.

I kicked the thing off, sending it flying into the leafy mist but more swarmed in its place. If one couldn't topple me, five packed enough weight to send me to the ground. Alvie's rattling growls changed their tune as the pollinators swarmed him too, though I couldn't see that as I kept trying and failing to sweep them away from me.

The pollinators poked and played around my skin though none pierced me. None appeared to be trying to even hurt me, but they latched on to my limbs and held me down. Entangled their tendrils in my hair to hold my head back.

Alvie whimpered and I swear I tried, I sent every bit of energy I had to my arms and legs to fight back, but the pollinators had buried me. I could see and little else.

Which meant I could do nothing when Alpha appeared overhead, bearing new tears through his robe: Alvie's incredible loyalty right there. Not that Alpha noticed.

The vessel crouched near my head, and nodded his own, as if to some imaginary beat. Perhaps the lyrics in his soul, whatever pushed him into this.

"It's okay," Alpha said, returning that slight smile to his face. "I expected this. I still believe in you, Gamma."

I started to spit out a reply but Alpha clamped a hand over my mouth, put his other on my head's side, behind my ear. Unfortunately he kept his palm, his fingers away from my razor teeth.

"Don't fight. This will all be over soon." Alpha reached his other hand into the pollinator stack and the crimson orbs swam away from his touch, bleeding onto the meadow around him.

I tried to raise my head to see what Alpha was doing. Alvie had gone quiet and I didn't know whether the dog had been destroyed or just turned off. Kaydee flickered into being in the corner of my eye, her face sad, but resolute.

"We're not done yet," Kaydee said to me.

Despite the obvious? I didn't get the chance to ask her, not only because Alpha had his hand over my mouth, but because the real world broke and fell away.

MY CRYSTALS HUNG OVERHEAD, locked in their teeth-row pattern along the infinite sky in my digital space. I realized I was on my back, the hard pearl surface beneath me proving little comfort.

"You might want to get up," Kaydee said, standing next to me. "We're not alone in here."

Getting to my feet, I looked across my clean expanse and saw what Kaydee meant: at the far horizon but heading towards us with barreling speed was a roiling purple-black mass with a familiar figure at its head.

Alpha resembled his real-life form, only in here he'd bumped his size up several times. Everything below his waist vanished into that purple storm and, as I watched, Alpha sent his arms forward, black tendrils launching out from them towards my crystals.

As the tendrils struck they latched on and the crystals began to blacken, not like a burn but with an infection's smooth spread. As Alpha moved forward he lanced out more tendrils and the earlier ones swung behind him, hanging on to the crystals like a dire spider's webbing.

"I'm guessing that's not good?" I said.

"He's corrupting your data," Kaydee replied. "If he gets enough, you'll cease to exist. Well, the you that I'm talking to, anyway."

"And what happens to you?"

Kaydee shook her head, "This is my first time being a data fragment, Gamma. I have no idea if digital files have an after-life, but I'm not holding out hope."

"Then let's make sure you don't find out."

How did you protect your own digital space? I wasn't exactly sure so I went with my instincts. Reality, here, was what we made of it—Alpha, certainly, wasn't a roiling blob back on Starship—and if he could twist my world to suit his needs then I could do the same.

"Any ideas?" Kaydee asked.

"A few."

Creativity wasn't my strong suit, but the Librarian, before Kaydee had banished him to digital oblivion, had left me with stories aplenty. I dug into those directories now, and above and beyond me, some crystals began to shine yellow-gold.

Alpha, continuing his rampage, changed his storm's direction towards those crystals, launching out new tendrils towards them.

"What're you doing?" Kaydee asked.

"Using my imagination."

Sort of, anyway. I pulled data from those stories and sent it out, picturing each item and, like sinking into a powerful daydream, forcing the idea into my reality.

Figures, large and small, appeared in front of Kaydee and I. Heroes from these stories, drawn from old tales to live here and now. I brought myth and legend to fight by my side.

My heroes didn't wait for an order but advanced according to their abilities; some ran, others jumped into the air through flight or mechanical devices. A few simply vanished and re-appeared near Alpha, sending their attacks towards the vessel and his storm.

"Well, that's original," Kaydee said as my forces unleashed their lightning bolts, swinging fists and explosive energy.

"The Librarian gave me some good ideas," I replied.

Alpha did seem stunned, even hurt by the assault. He stopped advancing and my heroes darted through the air, cutting his tendrils and draining away their corruption from my crystals. Alpha's purple storm wasn't faring much better, with blistering white cracks forming in its dark shell, like glass about to shatter.

I felt Alpha's stare across the white abyss locking on me. I shouldn't have been able to see his eyes, to note the ever-so-slight head shake in my direction. But I understood its meaning, as clear as if Alpha had broadcasted the message with deafening volume direct to my ears.

This reality was not just mine anymore.

Alpha's purple storm burst, and as it did, those black tendrils thrust out by the hundreds from its nova, piercing my heroes, my crystals, and vanishing them to digital dust. I shielded my eyes from the glare, and when the eclipse glow died, the only things remaining were Alpha, standing alone, myself and Kaydee.

My crystals were gone. My routines, gone.

"Consider it a favor," Alpha announced, and in one blink he shifted right in front of me. "Their programming is a disease. I am the cure."

"You're the cure?" Kaydee said. "Where'd you get that idea?"

Alpha glanced her way, frowning, "A mind. I'd forgotten about you."

I tried to speak, but couldn't. Tried to move, but couldn't. I simply didn't know how, didn't understand how to turn the idea of movement into action anymore.

"Yeah, well, here I am," Kaydee said. "What'd you do with yours? The Voices wouldn't have let you free without them?"

"They were annoying," Alpha said. "Like you. So I deleted them."

"But—"

"Do not argue with me, program," Alpha said. "You are not the prize." He turned back to me. "Now that you are clean, it's time to rewrite you the proper way."

I tried to do something. Anything.

I failed. Every attempt died in a broken connection.

Alpha reached and another black tendril snaked from his fingertips, launching at me. What it would do, who I would be when it connected, I didn't, couldn't know.

"Hey, ugly," Kaydee said, stepping in front of me. "Don't ever call me a program again."

The tendril shot towards her, but instead of calm menace, Alpha's face twisted into that manic grin, and then to an open-mouthed frown, widened eyes as Kaydee caught his tendril with her suddenly-sparking hands.

"Sorry Gamma," Kaydee said, throwing a look back at me. "This wasn't the plan."

Alpha reached with his other hand, launched another tendril towards Kaydee. She caught that one too, pairing each hand with Alpha's, her golden, sparkling glow matched against his purple-black halo.

"You cannot do this," Alpha said, but his voice broke in the saying. "You cannot stop—"

"Would you be quiet?" Kaydee said. "Gamma isn't yours to take."

Around me, around us, cracks appeared in my white abyss, tearing through the ground. Slits shone in the very air, as though claws were ripping through my digital reality, fracturing it apart.

"You're going to destroy him!" Alpha shouted.

"Only for you," Kaydee replied.

"No." Alpha leaned in as more tendrils erupted from his back, from his chest, from everywhere until they swarmed around Kaydee. "You cannot. I will not let you."

"Not your choice to make."

The tendrils surrounded Kaydee, vanished her into a black cocoon as everything around us, including my own body, began to dissolve and break away, drifting in a sudden cosmic wind.

Except Alpha's black tendrils were not total, and deep inside I could see, with the dim remnants of my consciousness, Kaydee's glow. She grew brighter, like a star, and as Alpha's tendrils began to burn away, I heard him scream. Not in terror but in rage, a burning, rotten sound.

The golden glow grew, enveloping everything, until all I saw was Kaydee, standing with that sarcastic smile beneath that spiked, spearmint hair.

"Sorry, Gamma," she said. "Good luck."

And then she too was gone.

NINE

TOTAL RESET

The bed felt light, comfortable. Thick blankets leading to a soft mattress beneath. An orange nightlight provided a soothing glow, a young girl with bright silver hair sleeping beneath its light, arms cradling her head. Around us, toys lay scattered across a carpet-covered bedroom. The walls and ceiling painted over with a peach tint, bolts and screws sealed with caps visible beneath the coats.

Where was this? Where was I?

The other obvious questions, like who, I answered without trying. Little seeds germinated, giving me a name—Gamma—and a lexicon to describe myself and the world around me. Legs, arms, man, child, common words. I tried to find context in the room, and failed.

"Who're you?" the child asked, popping up from her pillow, staring straight at me.

"I'm . . . not sure?" I said. "My name is Gamma, and that's all I have."

"Gamma? That's a strange name."

"Is it?" I replied. "What's yours?"

"I'm not supposed to talk to strangers. Mom says they could use me to hurt her."

"Am I a stranger?" I asked. "I don't even know how I got here."

The girl leaned closer to me, huddled over her bed sheets, "I don't know either, but maybe we can find out?"

"How can we do that?"

"I have a friend who can help us. He's so smart." She frowned, crinkling up her nose. "But it's late, isn't it? He might not be awake."

Late, early. I didn't really think that mattered. The girl had woken up, I was obviously awake. What would we get by sitting around? My head felt like there were huge holes punched through it, and any attempt I made to dig into those holes ran into nothing. Just absolute nothing, like a sentence broken off halfway through.

"Let's try anyway," I said.

"If my mother gets mad, then you have to tell her this was your fault." The girl slipped out of the bed, went to a gold-coated dresser and opened a drawer, threw on some clothes over her pajamas. "I already get into too much trouble."

"I will." I wasn't sure what the girl's mother could do to me, but at the moment, I didn't think I was risking anything.

When you're nobody, the chance to become somebody tends to take precedence.

"By the way," the girl said as she pulled a little carrying case from her nightstand and, with a strap, wrapped it around her wrist. "Since I'm helping you, do you promise not to hurt my mom?"

What a strange thing to ask. I had an easy answer.

"I have no reason to hurt your mom," I replied. "So yes, I promise."

"Okay then." The girl took a flat card from the carrying case, went over to the door and held the card up against a red-glowing gem in its center. The gem flashed, then shifted to an emerald green. "My name's Kaydee. Nice to meet you, Gamma."

Kaydee led the way from her bedroom, into a short hallway with family photos plastered over seafoam-coated walls. A squat kitchen, sparkling clean came next, with everything positioned in what looked to be the most efficient arrangement. Except for a rounded table dominating the center, four wire-framed chairs spaced evenly around.

We went slow through the space, Kaydee tip-toeing her way and me following suit, trying not to make a sound. Noise from another room made this easier. A conversation blasted out from around a corner. A man and a woman, though the man sounded removed, as if coming from a speaker.

"My mom," Kaydee whispered, wincing after a particularly loud burst. "She's like this a lot."

I didn't try to parse the words. It was enough to know the conversation was an angry one, and being caught sneaking with someone in that mental space would not be in our interests.

The kitchen bled into an entryway, with other rooms to our right. Thankfully, Kaydee's mom appeared to be in an office out of sight, her voice the only evidence of her presence. Kaydee stuck that card up against the main door's red gem, a larger one than Kaydee's own bedroom had, and it flashed green, opened.

"She always says she's going to change it so I can't do this," Kaydee whispered, smiling as she pulled the door open. "But I don't think she knows how, and she'll never ask for help."

Outside, the conversation's noise vanished in a new cacophony, one loud enough that Kaydee hurried to shut the door behind us. We were on a walkway looking out into a huge space that continued into the distance on our left, and ended not far to our right with a converging series of long, moving stairs centering into red-gemmed doors. In front, a glass barrier gave us a view across a wide chasm, with an opposite side similar to our own.

Silver light illuminated the space, broken up by neon displays from above, below, and straight across from us. People moved, some walking along and others zipping through that chasm, wearing suits that, with small, blue sparks, propelled them through the air. Occasionally, a larger car would pass by loaded with people and dock at the end before taking on new passengers and speeding back the way it had come.

"This way," Kaydee said, pointing left. "He's not far."

"Where are we?" I asked, trying to take in everything.

"The Conduit," Kaydee replied, walking along the dark metal surface. "I like it at night, when it's not so crowded."

A passing man, sporting a heavy overcoat and a shiny visor that stretched down over his face, stopped as Kaydee spoke, turned and looked down at her, "Who are you talking to, little one?"

Kaydee didn't even stop, "My friend Gamma."

I watched the man, who didn't look my way, and after a moment he shrugged, turned and kept on, walking right towards me. I pressed myself to the side and he passed, not showing any sign that he'd seen me standing there.

"Am I invisible?" I asked Kaydee as we resumed walking along.

"I can see you," Kaydee replied.

"But can anyone else?"

"Maybe, maybe not?"

Kaydee, apparently, was untroubled, and if she was unconcerned then perhaps I shouldn't worry either. Nonetheless, as we went along the walkway, passing people along the way who often gave Kaydee strange looks, they never saw me. A strange feeling, to be totally unnoticed.

I wasn't sure how long we walked as distractions abounded. There were too many shops to look into, selling things I both understood and could never have imagined. Too many sounds to hear, from the snap-crackle as fliers burst into the air to the saxophone starting up a song somewhere in the distance and picking up a partner from a nearby trumpeter. And the smells, the scents, I couldn't stop sniffing a thousand different culinary miracles, their warm spices drifting my way, interrupted by perfumes, body odors, and the clean pressed fragrance of new clothes.

This civilization in which I found myself overwhelmed me, and no matter the strange occurrence that had brought me here, nor the troubling emptiness awaiting my every look back could ruin what became an enchanting stroll.

One that ended all too soon when Kaydee announced we had arrived.

A red gem inserted into a neat, neon spiral door greeted us, shimmering in the soft silver night. Kaydee looked at the door without moving, and I wondered if she had some hidden method to jar it open.

"Are we waiting for something?" I asked after at least a minute had passed, with more passersby giving Kaydee looks for standing so still in front of another's home.

"He'll notice us eventually," Kaydee said. "Leo always says to be patient."

"Notice us?" I looked at the door. "I'm not sure he can see us."

"Oh, Leo never misses anything when he's paying attention."

"And how do we know he's paying attention?"

"Because I'm standing in his favorite spot."

Before I could ask what that meant, the red gem flashed and the spiral door opened. Standing there, coated in stubble, black-spattered grease and holding a multitool in either hand, each one fully deployed, its myriad implements spread out like a star, was a man that seemed familiar to me, though I didn't know his name.

"Kaydee!" the man said, shaking one of the multitools as if, in some universe, it could be perceived as threatening. "It's not only past your bedtime, it's past mine!"

"You hardly look ready for bed, Leo," Kaydee replied, clasping her hands in front of her waist and tossing off a sweet smile.

"Yes, well, I'm expecting a delivery tonight, and you're right where it's going to land. I've told you a thousand times, the mech won't drop the package if you're in its spot!"

Kaydee glanced at me, "See? I told you he'd pay attention. Leo's always getting things."

I waited for the inevitable question from Leo asking Kaydee who she was talking to. It didn't come. Instead, Leo looked right towards me, but his eyes failed to find my face, so I suspect he couldn't actually pick me out.

"Kaydee, let's go inside," Leo said, stepping back and waving us in. "Your friend is welcome too."

Inside, a simple living room greeted us, with two ragged chairs, a wide table, and a screen plastered against a far fall. What drew my attention more, though, was the vast amount of scrap that seemed to have put itself all over everything in sight. Gears, wires, tools for gears and wires coated the walls. Larger lumps, inlacing what looked like batteries and engines littered the floor, some in various states of dissembling—or assembly?—but as Leo led Kaydee into the space, they both picked a path through the junk minefield without hesitation.

"This," Leo said once they had both taken their seats, "is a reset simulation, right?"

Kaydee nodded, forcing me to ask what a reset simulation was.

"I'm trying to bring you back," Kaydee said to me while Leo nodded in my general direction. "And me too, I bet."

"Think of it like saving a version of yourself, in case the real you dies," Leo added to me, setting down the multitools and clasping his hands on his knees, one of which jiggled. "Doesn't work if you're a real living thing, of course, but once you make the transition to the digital world, there are ways of preserving yourself."

"I don't understand?" I replied, because how was I supposed to?

I didn't even know what I was. Where I was. A little girl talked about restoring us to life. Did that mean I was dead?

"Don't get upset!" Kaydee brandished her child's smile as a weapon against my panic, and it worked. "If you're here, it means you made it too. We're going to be okay. Leo's going to fix us."

"Maybe," Leo said. "This process isn't perfect, Kaydee. There's a chance of corruption, or it might not work at all. It depends on how thorough the wipe was, whether they found your programming. Though the fact that we're running this means your, or your friend's, physical form still exists."

"Am I not physical now?" I said, reaching towards the scrap-covered table and touching it. The wood felt real, I felt real. "And what do you mean by wipe?"

Kaydee stuck a finger to her lips, telling me to be quiet. Which, rude. Considering the circumstances, all these cryptic statements should have been explained. Leo should be telling me, in clear terms, just what the hell was going on.

"Now, you've made it here, which means the recovery should be nearly complete," Leo said. "You walked the Conduit, right?"

"We did," Kaydee said.

"And was it alive? Real?"

"It was."

"Good signs." Leo offered up a grin my way. "Every person, every noise, scent, feeling you had was a different function working to restore you. Kaydee could have written it as a series of lines, left you floating in a black nothing, but this was much more fun, no?"

"I really liked it!" Kaydee giggled.

My mouth opened. I tried to form some sort of coherent response and failed. Nothing seemed to work right, and I couldn't quite parse what Leo was getting at. All of this had been for me?

Why?

"I'm sure you're confused," Leo said. "Kaydee will explain everything in just a moment, when this is all over."

"When what is all over?" I said, but as I spoke, Leo's giant screen flickered to life, and all the other lights in the apartment went black.

Kaydee and Leo disappeared. I disappeared. The only thing I could see was that screen, which grew and grew until it simply *was* my universe. On it, a cream bar began at one end and rocketed towards the other side. Left to right, centered in front of me, though I couldn't look anywhere else.

The bar hit the right side and faded. Two words replaced it.

WELCOME BACK.

. . .

ORCHIDS LOOMED ABOVE ME, white and blue and violet, their stalks looping back from my face to the dirt beside my head and body. A body that I could feel, with its synthetic muscles primed and ready to go. More than that, I had a mind that I could read, with memories and functions I could understand.

Somehow, Kaydee's reset had worked. Whatever Alpha had tried to do to me, I had been restored. At least, from what I could tell.

I had also been changed; my eclectic outfit from Alvie's, largely soaked and ruined through my adventure in Purity, had been replaced with a similar loose-fitting robe to what Alpha wore. Mine had a cherry color, and scratched my skin ever so slightly.

But, I was back. I couldn't stop running that fact through my mind, couldn't stop a grin from spreading over my face. Somehow, I'd made it out. Somehow, this vessel, this mech had escaped deletion.

That grin died almost as soon as it formed when I remembered why I'd made it. Kaydee. She'd planted the code that had brought me back, had done something in that final moment with Alpha that'd given me a second chance.

What had happened to her?

I looked around, but all I saw beyond the orchids were more orchids. A whole section filled with them, arrayed in rows. Over-grown now, but their original purpose to be picked out and given away seemed clear. I'd been placed in a pathway between several sections, lying on soft dirt.

A wheezing bark had me sitting up in time to catch Alvie's barreling hug, his strong metal paws driving me back down. His nose bobbed and his yellow-light eyes moved as he tried to lick me, a task made harder by the fact that Alvie didn't have a tongue. Nonetheless, the mech dog's excitement came through, and I managed a few pets before getting enough space to stand.

"The mech wouldn't leave your side," Alpha said, striding into the room. "Impressive. I didn't believe such loyalty possible, but I've been wrong about many things."

I twitched. I should have hated Alpha, should have made to strike him now, since the vessel seemed entirely alone and without weapons. Whether I could have won in a straight-up fist fight didn't matter.

I should have fought.

Instead, when I tried to raise that anger, tried to juice my synthetic muscles for a rushing punch and kick and bite and anything to bring that monster low, my connections died. The command lost its way from my processor to my parts.

"You're shocked," Alpha said, walking right up to me and placing a hand on my shoulder. "I can see it in your face. You don't understand why you can't hurt me." He placed his other hand on my other shoulder, holding me like a patient parent delivering a lesson. "I placed blocks within you, Gamma. You may not like me, but you *will* help me, and in time, I think you will come to see the world through my eyes."

Alvie, I noticed, didn't even growl at Alpha anymore. The dog sat next to me, looking around, as if the greatest threat we faced didn't, in fact, stand centimeters away.

"Why?" I managed. "Why would you do this?"

"Because I need help." Alpha shook his head, a false sadness to the motion, like a bad actor in a bad movie. "I did not arrive here by accident, Gamma. I've made my share of mistakes, made my share of enemies."

"I find that hard to believe."

"I'm sure you do," Alpha said. "But this is where I need you. Because my enemies are not your enemies. They will not hate you as they do me, which means certain doors are open to you."

Alpha hadn't moved his hands from my shoulders. I tried to shrug them off, but even a simple action like that died in its motion from thought to movement. Alpha had me.

"Like what?"

"I need to know our purpose, Gamma. Why we are here, and

what this Starship is meant for," Alpha said, his fingers digging into my shoulder. "You will find this for me."

"Why?"

"Because I need to know my destiny in order to change it."

TEN

A NEW STUDENT

Alpha guided Alvie and I to a Garden exit on the same side, but several levels lower, than where I'd entered. He opened a large door, bordered by prairie grass, back into the fire and lightning land of the Conduit. Much like I'd last seen it, mechs filled the place with chaos. Smoke and orange glows from fires—started, I noticed, by some mechs and put out by others—clashed with the misty blue light from above. Metallic screeches, auto-toned orders, and the constant ozone smell from burning wires abounded.

"You'll go this way for a while and then you'll reach University Row," Alpha said, not leaving the door. "That's where you'll find Starship's archives, and our purpose."

"If you know all of this, why don't you go?" I asked. "That way, I can head to the Nursery, as the Voices want?"

My question had less to do with completing the Voice's mission than obeying Alpha's command, even if parts of me resolutely refused to do anything else.

"The Nursery and the Voices can wait," Alpha replied, his steel eyes flashing in the firelight, a glow that matched his hair and made the vessel seem ablaze. "They do not have our interests in mind. We must care for ourselves first, or nobody will."

Then Alpha shut the door behind me and left us alone in a strange and ruined world.

In front, the walkway extended into the distance. Above, there'd been shops and restaurants. Here, it seemed the spaces had been reserved for entertainment: I saw a buzzing sign declaring gambling, another advertising athletic contests. A third, across the Conduit's gap, promised virtual delights above and beyond anything a person could find in reality.

"What do you think?" I asked the dog. "Should we do what Alpha wants, or try to find another way?"

We could find a different elevator, or a stair, climb up the Garden and cross back through it. Proceed to the Nursery and ignore Alpha's command. Or at least, I thought I could, but when I tried to act on that impulse, even just to walk with that goal as my primary objective, my body froze up.

The signals wouldn't send.

Alvie watched me struggle through the dance, his yellow lamp eyes no doubt wondering what was going on inside my head.

"Don't hate on these places, Kaydee," said a voice behind me, then through me. A young man, hair spiked and looking like he'd spent all day wallowing in grease, walked with a girl who looked much more the product of a powerful family—Kaydee?—beside him. "They're pushing our tech just as much as we are. I get more ideas from them than I do from our lab."

"But these places are gross," Kaydee replied. "What're they doing that's so special?"

"It's so cutthroat down here," the man replied, directing Kaydee over to the glass railing. "Every business has a hundred competitors, and they're all operating on thin margins. They have to innovate to survive. We, on the other hand, get however long we want. We're not threatened."

"I dunno," Kaydee replied. "My mother could yank away our funds at any point. Feel like that's plenty threatening."

"Your mom would never. She loves you too much," the man said, but the light had gone from his eyes when he spoke. "Not everyone has a parent that can pull strings like yours. Not everyone's as lucky as we are."

"Bet we can make a mech to fix that."

"Maybe, maybe . . ."

By the time the man's voice faded, the two had disappeared and I had my hands on my head, trying to run through my functions to figure out what had happened.

No answer suggested itself, and two approaching mechs demanded my attention. Both of these were smaller robots, trundling along on treads and wielding hoses that, whenever a stray spark or burning what-have-you drifted their way, shot out a cloudy white mixture that doused the offending flame.

"Don't attack," I said to Alvie, and went to the walkway's right side to avoid them.

Alvie followed and as we went by, the two mechs swiveled their cameras, single eyes atop a stalk, to look my way, but neither declared me a threat and they moved on. As did Alvie and I.

Apparently not all mechs on Starship adopted a lethal hostility towards each other.

"Are you on their side, then?" came a grizzled voice, like boiling motor oil. Its source dropped from the huge athletic gaming sign to land in front of me on four wide claws.

The mech, rusted brown with orange stripes pasted all over its sturdy frame, housed a single charred tube over a central box with fuel tanks along the sides. A speaker beneath the barrel gave the machine its burbling voice, one it continued to use.

"Tell me now, are you with them?" the mech demanded. "The damn dousers?"

"With them?" I said, glancing back at the two other mechs as they neared the Garden's entrance. "I'm not with anybody."

"Then why not be with us, the fire-starters?" the mech asked. "We're better anyhow, and we're clearly winning."

"Winning what?"

"The war for the Conduit!" the mech announced. "It's what we're all engaged in. How do you not know?"

"I'm, uh, new here?" I started edging by the mech, and it rotated on its claws to track me with its barrel. Alvie growled. "I'm heading to University Row."

The mech froze for a long moment and I hoped, maybe, that it'd fallen victim to some programming fault. Before I'd taken another three steps, however, the mech had found its footing and scrambled after me. As the mech moved, bits of liquid flame dripped from its barrel, leaving a burning path behind us.

"University Row?" the mech said. "That's dangerous ground. The Chancellor holds it."

"Sounds about right?"

"Only if you're looking to get yourself deleted. Name's Cindy, by the way. What's your model?"

Cindy?

I decided accepting the name on its face would be safer than interrogating the fiery thing.

"I'm a vessel," I replied. "Alvie's a . . . dog, I guess. Good to meet you."

"It's only good because I'm looking for help," Cindy said. "If I wasn't, I'd have melted ya when you passed beneath my sign. Have to keep a sharper watch when you're in the Conduit these days."

"Noted. But why would you attack me?"

"Because if you're not on my side, you're against me."

What was it with some of these mechs? The one in Purity, Alpha, and now this one all seemed to have this brutal aggression. I couldn't tell who'd programmed these mechs when they were made, but I couldn't imagine this being part of their routines.

Kaydee had mentioned frenzied competitions to develop better mechs, but would any of those lead to something like Cindy? Spitting fire and threatening others with a surprise roasting?

"Well, I'm not against you," I offered, and picked up my pace.

We passed out of the entertainment zone and into, with its light blue colors, another residential section. These doors appeared friendlier, basic metal sheets than the spiral, red-gemmed residences above. Some had been smashed in, and a look revealed smaller spaces, crammed with battered remnants that appeared cheaper, scragglier than the ones in Leo's lab.

"Where are we now?" I asked Cindy as we walked.

"Are you really this green? How're you still alive? This is the Dormitory, though no students live here now. Like all the human places, it's a bunch of junk."

I kept asking questions, and Cindy kept explaining. Her fire-launching thing? Apparently crafted at first to spray water, since modified to a more dangerous variant. Who did the modifying, and why? Cindy wouldn't say.

"Not because I don't know, you understand? But because there's a war going on and you haven't chosen a side."

As to that war, and Starship's madness, Cindy would only reveal that it'd been running as long as she'd been a functioning mech. The humans had vanished early on, either dead or disappeared. How you could disappear in a place like Starship, Cindy didn't know, but they'd done it.

As for the mechs, they simply followed their programming. Cindy's told her to burn anything that hadn't yet been torched while the douser mechs put out the fires. Other mechs repaired what still others broke. Opposites in a forever war that, so Cindy believed, would only end when Starship reached its destination.

"And where's that?" I asked.

"Nobody knows," Cindy said. "Nobody except maybe that Chancellor you're going to meet. Not that it'll do you much good knowing, because anyone the Chancellor meets doesn't make it out the other side."

An ominous omen, but Alpha's command pulsed through me, overriding any nerves and pushing me onward.

We were approaching the Dormitory's end, visible because a giant, arched sign stretched across the Conduit in front of us. In blue and gold, the archway declared UNIVERSITY ROW to be beyond those bounds.

"Can I ask one more thing?" I said to Cindy.

"Only if you promise to join our side!" Cindy declared. "There's fires that need starting, and I do think you could start more than a few if you tried."

"I'll keep that in mind, but I want to know, most of the mechs I come across aren't as intelligent as you. Why are you able to speak and, say, Alvie here isn't?"

Cindy stopped clomping. Froze right there. Then swiveled her barrel back behind us, where the two dousing robots that had passed me way back at the Garden's entrance were coming closer, camera eyes set on her.

"I am what the Voices made me," Cindy said.

Without another word, Cindy jumped to her left, latching onto the Conduit's wall. She scampered along it, then launched a fiery stream at the two dousing mechs, who countered with their own cold, dusty reply, causing billowing white smoke to envelope the whole area.

Not wanting to get caught up in a fight, I ran. Sprinted beneath that archway, into University Row and whatever lay beyond.

Which, for me, turned out not to be much. While the walkway continued beneath the arch and turned into a crossing lattice similar to the Garden, which encompassed a box-like structure several levels high and covered with multi-colored etchings bearing what must have been famous sayings, I could not follow the path into that structure.

Because, approximately five steps after Alvie and I went beneath the archway, a three-meter tall mech emerged from the side wall as if stepping from nowhere and barred the path. Unlike some of the other mechs I'd seen, this one resembled a human, right down to its robes—

crafted metal, but painted to look like cloth—and its kind face. The mech smiled at me as I approached with all the cold functionality of an executing routine.

"Welcome to the University," the mech said, as if I was a wayward child. "Please, present your identification to continue beyond this point."

"Identification?"

"Your ID will suffice. If you are enrolled in our systems, I will stand aside." When I didn't make any moves to grab an ID that I didn't have, the mech smiled even wider. "Unless, are you a new student?"

Confronting the possibilities left me with two choices: I could deny the mech's question and, likely, be escorted out of here without a chance at completing Alpha's mission, or I could declare myself a student and see what happened next. Sending Alvie to bite the scholar guardian counted as a third choice, but seeing my dog get torn apart for nothing didn't sound fun.

"Yes," I said. "I'm new here. Today's my first day."

The mech nodded, as if any day was the perfect first day to come to the University, "Then please, proceed this way. Follow the path and you will find all you need to know."

The mech pointed at an ornamental archway on my right, one that led into the side and that had, a moment ago, appeared to be nothing more than a pretty picture of some far off verdant valley. Sunlight, river, grassy hills and all that. Except now when the mech gestured, that valley shivered and opened inward, giving me a path to follow.

"Thanks," I managed.

"May you learn to love knowledge," the mech said as I went towards the door.

Behind me, I heard the big machine snap itself back into its resting position. No pursuit, then. I briefly wondered if I could twist back around and sprint by: a mech that large couldn't be all that fast.

But when I saw where the doorway led, all thoughts of trying another method vanished. Alpha might have wanted me to find Starship's goals, its origins, but his command came vague, without strict step-by-step direction.

I'd been testing its bounds with every action since leaving the Garden, and I'd found its fences loose. So long as my direction *could* lead me towards the archives, Alpha's command let me follow my chosen course.

And once I saw what the open painting revealed, I had to follow its path to the University.

The hallway behind the painting stood larger than any others I'd seen on Starship before. The Garden compared, somewhat, with larger rooms for its more massive plants, but rather than greenery, the University coated this hallway with glistening, dripping wisdom.

Spawning from a bright gold line above my head, sparkles rained down on either side in the black tunnel. The sparks descended, and as they did, each one burst into myriad colors, sometimes a whole image, often echoing one of the quotes I'd seen on the building outside or something wholly new. Paintings, book covers, films, and short poems all appeared as I walked.

A walk, I should add, that felt far longer than I expected. I caught the puzzle in the act, though, when Alvie, after rushing ahead and snapping at a spark, went gliding past me when he stopped and stood looking around. A glance at my feet confirmed that I stood on a moving walkway, one impeding my progress by sending me back the way I'd come.

As I noticed the strange design, the sparks that had been on the wall all rushed down and joined together on the walkway itself, lighting up the way even as the walls disappeared into dark, so it looked like I walked upon a golden path, alone in the universe.

When I reached the walkway's end, another door swung open in that slow manner reserved for effect rather than efficiency. The golden lights at my feet made one last flourish, sweeping up and around me to display a blazing WELCOME atop the door.

"Well, that's pretty neat," I said to Alvie, who wheeze-barked in agreement.

Together we wandered through into another, larger corridor. This one extended far, far down to my left, deeper into University Row, big enough to be the university's quad. Great chandeliers hung down, splaying white-silver light across the space, while shifting screens alternated between more quotes, accolades to various students, class and sport schedules in a dizzying multimedia array.

I didn't pay attention to it, because something else had my focus. Something inside myself.

How did I know what a quad was, how universities used to work back on Earth?

Or even what the hell Earth was?

I didn't know, and that question stunned me. I searched my own data, tried to find the root cause, but, standing at the University's entrance, I ran into blocks. Not holes so much as indecipherable sections within me locked away from my view. Yet I was certain those same blocks dribbled out context, provided information to me without my asking for it.

Shaking my head, I stopped the introspection. I shouldn't be too worried: if there was anywhere on Starship where I could find the answers to what had happened to me, it would probably be here.

"Hey, you're going to be late for orientation," said a voice and I blinked, because people filled the hallway beyond me.

Young students, with a few older humans speckled between milled around through the corridor, heading this way and that, chatting with each other, tapping on computers tied to their hands, or just looking around, bobbing to unheard music.

The voice that spoke my way came from a girl I didn't recognize, but what I thought had been directed my way instead resolved itself to another young women walking by me, through the welcome door. This one I knew, the same one that'd been on the walkway with me.

Kaydee.

"I already read all the material," Kaydee shot back to the other student, who wore a more formal outfit with the University's name and rocket ship logo on its chest. "Isn't this going to be a waste of my time?"

"Not if you want to meet your classmates," the other student said. "You're one of Starship's smaller classes, so you'll be seeing each other a lot."

"Grand."

I followed Kaydee as she walked, talked, and dished sarcastic replies to the older student who, with impressive good cheer, rebuffed Kaydee's attitude with her own. We reached another large entry to our right, double doors painted to look like old oak, and the student beckoned Kaydee to head that way.

"Find a seat in there," the student said. "And welcome to the University."

"Thanks," Kaydee muttered, though behind her harsh attitude, I thought I picked out some nerves in those eyes.

Without a route to follow, I decided tracking Kaydee's memory through orientation would give me a good grip on where I should check first. I moved to follow her, but as I did so, Alvie barked.

"I know you can't see her, but it's fine," I said to the dog, who barked again, yellow eyes not looking at me, but beyond.

As I turned, I felt cold steel grab my arm. A vice-like snatch that tingled with electric impulse. A mech, about my height but twice—easily—the girth, held me. It resembled a human, an old one, but where normal skin ought to have been, patches were either missing, or charred, or had corroded to different molded colors. A tattered blue and gold gown, the university's theme, hung over its metal frame.

"And who do we have here?" the mech asked, its speakers damaged and hissing static between the words. "It has been so long since we've had a new student."

ELEVEN

TESTING OUT

We stood alone in the corridor, the mech and I. The screens that had teemed with updates now sat blank, one displaying a pixelated cross-section where something had rammed it. Spills of various unknown origins stained the floors, and a moldering scent drifted through the air. The students and their conversations disappeared.

None of these fazed the mech in the slightest. He maintained his grip on my arm, and in his kind eyes—a modeling attempt to make them look human that came off as a glassy green—I saw dangerous purpose.

This mech had a need, just like my own. He hungered for a student and, considering the empty halls, I wasn't surprised. But I was here for a reason, not to take classes. Alpha needed me to find Starship's origins, and I wouldn't get that—quickly, anyway—sitting in a classroom.

"I'm not a student," I said, choosing to ditch the lie that brought me in here. "I'm trying to find some information."

"Not a student?" the mech replied. "But only students and professors are allowed in here. The public, if that's what you are, can browse our archives from any connected terminal."

The mech couldn't, didn't hide his disdain at the idea I was a member of the lowly commoners not beholden to his University. The grip even sagged a little, as though I wasn't worth holding onto any longer.

Finding a connected terminal seemed like a possibility, but I hadn't seen anything that looked like one. Given Starship's apparent mech war, finding an intact computer that'd give me access to anything sounded unlikely. I'd already made it to the University, why take a chance on somewhere else?

"Oh, well, I'm a professor," I said, hoping the position might give me more freedom than students received.

"A new professor?" the mech released my arm, stepped away and regarded me. "Professor of what?"

"History," I said. "Starship's history, to be exact."

"Interesting. I wasn't aware you were starting. Please, come with me and we'll get this all sorted out. You may call me Dean, for that is what I am."

Dean swept himself around, his robes, thick and metal like the guarding mech back outside, barely moving with the motion. As Dean walked down the corridor, I looked over at Alvie, who stared back at me with his eager puppy mouth open.

"Forward march, I suppose," I said to Alvie, and followed Dean.

As we went, classrooms spaced out on my right and left, the latter forming smaller labs in the narrow space between the University corridor and the wider Conduit. Many were dominated by screens with numerous implements, helmets and wands, suits and other devices meant for virtual adventures.

Almost none seemed in working condition, with frayed wires, shattered glass, and scattered parts. As though someone had set small, frantic children in here and let them run amok.

Another example I had no basis to frame, another thought that had to have leaked from somewhere in my mind. I had never seen a real child, much less a group.

"Come now, professor," Dean said, slowing enough to let Alvie and I catch up. "You must tell me a bit about yourself. Your name, for starters?"

"Gamma," I said, and then proceeded to make up a story bled together with bits of my adventures.

I'd come from further up the Conduit, from a family of mech designers. My parents spent their time assisting with Starship's water supply, while I tinkered away in our home, reading up on everything that had led to Starship's glorious adventure.

"Glorious adventure," Dean said. "An interesting choice of words. Why do you think that?"

"What do you mean?"

"Starship is a failure," Dean replied. "Do you not see it that way?"

I didn't know what to say to that. Starship, a failure? Why? How? But then, as a supposed professor, I needed an opinion, so I gave one.

"I think it depends on how you define failure," I said.

"Are there any humans left?" Dean said. "Do you see any?"

"No?"

"Then Starship is a failure."

Dean turned his back to me and continued marching. Debate, apparently, over. I resolved not to take the slight personally.

We took a left, the corridor continued, with classrooms lingering on either side ahead, and entered the University's central hub. The Garden had an open pit with a waterfall, the University had a dazzling light sculpture that stretched up and down the five occupied levels. Circular bulbs hung and glowed in different colors, clustering together in various sizes that didn't make any sense, but were beautiful all the same.

"The periodic table," Dean said, giving me a moment to admire. "Every element, from top to bottom. Quite the piece."

Surrounding the glittering molecules were escalators by the dozen. Ramping up and down, most sat dormant until Dean stood on their base step, activating their motion and sending us up a level.

When the escalator turned on, its railings lit up in the University's colors, marking, I supposed, its use.

"Our offices are on the third level," Dean replied. "You'll have your own, Professor Gamma, as there are quite a few openings at the moment."

I could guess why, but chose to keep my mouth shut. Now that we'd entered the University proper, more mechs moved about the space, some wearing scholar robes like Dean. Others were more skeletal, scurrying about cleaning various surfaces. Still more were smaller, fluttering like mechanical birds, carrying bits of this and that.

"What are they doing?" I asked as we went up another escalator to the third level. "The flying ones?"

"Ornamental now," the Dean sighed through his speaker. "They used to be a delight, carrying messages, small tools, treats from student to student or their professors. An enchanting moment whenever one of these found its way to you."

Dean didn't elaborate on what the bird-mechs did now, but he sounded so sad that I didn't want to push him on it. I had to remember that I was a fraud here, and drawing attention to myself in any way was a mistake.

Alpha needed answers, I had to get them.

On the third level, things opened up. Without the need to give way to the Conduit, the escalators pulled us into a broad floor in which colored, intricate patterns had been carved. Some looked like flowery circles, scrawled in magenta and cyan across gleaming silver tiles, the spills and dirt that'd been present down below not making it up here. Apparently the cleaning mechs had their territory and did not stray.

Dean kept us along a central path, defined by grass-green script rolling in a line, pitching a long poem referencing Starship. The words ran along the level, breaking around us into paths and squares, as if someone had outlined a board not with lines but with poetics.

"Over here," Dean said. "Step carefully now."

I followed him exactly as he crossed over a break in the green script and into a rectangular space about as large as the room I'd woken up in. Dean pointed me to an empty spot near the room's center while he walked to a corner.

Beneath Dean's flat pad feet sat a spiral etching in black, one that lit up as Dean stood on it. Deep blue light illuminated Dean from below, and the other etchings around us burst into brightness. At my own feet, the tiles were blank, and I found out why a second later.

A light vibration echoed through the floor and the etchings rose. I simply didn't have another word to describe it, but four walls, a table, and more rose up from the floor and filled in a space that had been flat but now contained a snug office with two chairs, a desk, and the aforementioned table.

Alvie, the loyal dog, had been off sniffing something and now ran back, barking at a new gunmetal door sealing Dean and I off from the rest of the floor.

"That's a neat trick," I said, though the words seemed inadequate.

"Starship has limited space," Dean replied. "We found having a flexible arrangement met our needs better than a static one."

"And the symbols? Where do they come from?"

"The Chancellor can tell you, I'm sure," Dean said. "If, of course, you're hired on."

"How do I get hired on?"

"Well, professor, I'm sure it comes as no surprise to you, but anyone hoping to teach at the University must pass a rigorous test. We don't allow just anyone to mold the minds of Starship's finest students."

"I didn't see any students downstairs?" I asked, knowing that it wasn't the most tactful thing to say, but I needed answers, not tests.

Dean stared at me, glassy eyes unblinking for several seconds as Alvie continued his wheeze-barks outside. Then my guide to the University twitched, huffed, and gave a metallic grin.

"As I said, students and professors must both pass admission tests. You, sir, must complete the exam set before you, and then we shall determine whether you are worthy of our fine institution."

Before I could protest again, Dean pressed one of his hands onto the table, touched several symbols etched on its surface at once. They glowed in sequence—blue, orange, and white—and part of the table's top layer slid away, revealing a fuzzy screen.

"Please, sit here," Dean indicated a chair at the table. "Complete the exam, and I will return with your results."

"Are you sure it's necessary?" I asked.

"Oh, quite necessary," Dean replied. "We have had so many try to join our ranks that the Chancellor has taken to dealing with inadequate applicants . . . harshly. So, please, take the test. I look forward to your results."

What did that mean? Harshly? Dean didn't wait for me to make up my mind on whether to press him, opening the door, letting Alvie in, and vanishing out.

I went over to the door, tried it, but the handle that'd opened with Dean's touch didn't respond to my own. I'd claimed to be a professor, and now, with a barely-functioning memory, I had to take a test to teach history.

"Alvie, any chance you have a data bank I could borrow?" I asked the dog, who yipped and put his paws on my waist. Cute, but not exactly a useful answer.

Doomed and resigned to it, I went over to the table, sat down, and pressed the spot on the screen reading START.

The test didn't wait, offering up a simple disclaimer about how the proceeding questions would cover any and all subjects deemed important to the University and that anyone interested in being part of its faculty or student body should do as well as possible. Any submissions would be judged by the Chancellor, their quality solely decided by her whims.

After that, the questions came. Marched across the screen covering areas philosophical, mathematical, logical, and more. I thought I would be stumped, cast aside as the first paragraph slammed in a comprehensive puzzle about students and their interests and matching them up in a way so that all were satisfied according to their peculiar needs.

Instead, the answers flowed from those forbidden spots in my core, analysis making its way from that unknown into my known and then out onto the screen in scrawled responses wiped against the glass by my fingertips.

"Alvie, I think I'm getting this," I said to the dog as I answered another question about moral relativism in the time of space travel.

Did I understand what moral relativism was? Did I truly comprehend space travel?

No. No I did not, and yet, somehow, I had clear definitions for both stored within that foggy data. My mech instincts, my default programming, understood how to wrap those two concepts together.

The test ended in twenty minutes. I'd answered forty questions in that time, fast enough that the test itself quit its efforts and declared the event complete without any warning. One last question and then a green flash, a congratulatory message stating my test was finished and I had nothing to worry about. The Chancellor would be seeing me soon.

"I'm not sure what that was," I said to Alvie, sitting in that office. "But I think I need to figure myself out."

The dog wheeze-barked back at me, then curled up at my feet, his metal plates clanking and sliding against one another.

Despite my apparent knowledge, I didn't have answers to my own questions. Unlike the test, when I queried myself, I received nothing in reply. While I didn't like Alpha, I resolved to ask the other vessel when I returned just how we worked. What he'd done, and how I had all this knowledge locked away where only unprompted pushing could access it.

A sharp, single knock sounded on the office's door, and I didn't even have to answer before it blew open, revealing a smaller mech, thin and fiery, sporting a blaze-red paint-coat over its body, which was only somewhat hidden by a tightly-wound flag bearing the University's crest.

"Liar!" announced the mech, a soprano, fluty accusation. "Liar and cheat!"

Ordinarily, a mech half my height wouldn't compel much fear from my circuits, but something about this one, from her wide stance to the six arms splaying out, each one ending in a five-fingered claw, had me on my feet in an instant, ready to find some way to defend myself.

Alvie growled, confirming my suspicions.

"You are no ordinary human!" the mech announced, striding into the room, rotating her rounded head down for a glance at Alvie and subsequently dismissing the dog to look at me. "Your performance on the test is beyond organic bounds. You must have cheated."

"Wait," I said. "I don't understand?"

The mech's trailing arm shut the door behind her, its claw suddenly extending an extra meter to manage the move before popping back. We were trapped together now, in a tiny space.

"Then you are definitely too stupid to have done what just occurred," the mech said. "I am the Chancellor, and I declare you a fraud."

As she finished the words, the Chancellor exploded. Her limbs launched out and around, extending themselves around the office , her legs expanding to bring her up to my height, and her head popping higher off her box-like torso to loom over me on a stalk, like some child's toy. The Chancellor's claws now hung about the office like some mad spider, waiting to dive into me from all sides.

"Do you know why they gave me all these arms?" the Chancellor said. "Why they built me like a nightmare?"

"Don't really care," I replied, trying to decide which side of the room seemed less lethal. "I'd just rather not die, thanks."

"Die?" the Chancellor laughed. "You can't die, can you? Dean said a human had come, but I know a mech when I see one. Even a pretender like you."

Trapped, and with little hope of life, I made the call to tell the truth so far as I understood it.

"I'm a vessel," I said, "and I was sent here to learn what happened to Starship. Its purpose, and where things went wrong, so that we, the other vessels and I, can try to fix it."

The Chancellor, her beady blue light eyes socketed into that round head, glared at me. How could I call it a glare, with a face that didn't change, that had no real expressions?

A feeling, that's all.

"Then why claim to be a professor?" the Chancellor asked me.

"Because your guards outside, and Dean, demanded I choose to be a professor or a student. I thought being a student would take longer to get to the archives."

The Chancellor's arms quivered, snuck in closer to me, that lethal hug getting tighter.

"So you are a spy, then. For other mechs."

"For myself."

"Gamma, it is my job, has been for a very long time, to protect and grow this institution," the Chancellor said, then shifted one of its arms to press on the pressure plate the Dean had used to raise the office. With a shudder, the walls around us, the table and chairs, folded back into the floor. "I was tasked with finding and cultivating genius on this ship. Do you know how well I did?"

"No idea?"

"I failed. Miserably. The humans would not pass the tests, would not accept the optimal academic conditions," the Chancellor said. "I cast them out one by one until none were left."

"Why didn't they stop you?" I asked. "That can't be what they intended?"

"Because, by the time they noticed, Starship had other problems," the Chancellor said. "By the time they realized their children were all failures, I had developed better ways to safeguard knowledge that the humans weren't smart enough to have. The University is, was, mine. Its secrets belong only to those I judge worthy to wield them."

"I passed the test, didn't I?"

"A test for humans. For you, I have something far different." The

Chancellor couldn't grin, but I heard it nonetheless. "Something far more important."

Without warning, those arms shot in, grabbing me along my own shoulders, my legs and hands. The Chancellor lifted me from the ground, and I saw Alvie getting ready for a charge.

"Stop," I said to the dog, trusting in a feeling. The Chancellor's arms weren't digging into my skin, trying to inflict pain. If she wanted to destroy me, she could've gone for the neck, my head. Instead, the Chancellor moved, pulling me through the air behind her as she went towards the escalators and then up.

Alvie obeyed, but kept up a constant low growl, vibrating his metal teeth against one another.

"I can walk, you know," I said.

"I do know, but I do not care," the Chancellor replied.

We rode the escalators to the University's very top, a level with a massive glass ceiling shining through to the rest of the Conduit, whose fire-orange glow shone down on us. Up here, the etched floors were gone, replaced by solid gunmetal tiles. The level itself appeared empty, no walls, no windows besides the ceiling. No doors to anywhere else.

Despite the emptiness, reddish stains scattered across the floor and walls. Streaks and blotches, large and small, hardened into the surfaces with time's work.

"This level is unfinished," the Chancellor said. "I am the only one allowed up here, except those I choose to examine myself."

She whipped her arms, setting and pressing me into the floor. I tried to speak, but she slipped a claw across my mouth, pressing it shut. Another, one that had been on my shoulders, hovered over my chest.

"Now, Gamma, we will see what you really are."

Much like the cleaning bot's claw had done, the Chancellor's claw merged together at its end, connecting together to a single jack.

With a snapping move, she reached behind my ear, and pulled us away from reality.

TWELVE

MEMORIES

I stood on rocky ground, a gray clay-like substance that roiled around my feet and threatened to swallow them whole. Sides made of the stuff swarmed up around me, shifting and shaking as I stood in their center, with nothing more than a purple, formless sky high above.

"What you are," said a light, strong voice, "is damaged."

The speaker leapt from above, landing next to me as her wide red cape billowed out around her. She straightened, dark hair flowing over a thin brown face, and watched me try to recognize her.

"The Chancellor," I said, the steel-blue eyes keying me in. "Where are we?"

"You don't know?"

"It feels familiar, like I should," I replied, trying to find an answer as pebbles rolled and dirt shifted, forcing me to sway with the motion. The Chancellor, I noticed, didn't move at all, as if she stood just above the fray. "But my mind is filled with holes."

"Perhaps," the Chancellor said. "Though I doubt someone as wretched as this space entails would have been able to pass my test, and do so with such ease."

I shrugged. I didn't know what to give her. Should I say that the test more or less took itself? That the knowledge simply bled out through my fingers without my ever realizing it was there?

"It's clear you won't be providing any answers," the Chancellor said to me, then looked towards the one clear way forward, a break in the stone hills. "Come, let's see what they've done to you."

"They?"

"Whomever made you this way," the Chancellor replied as we began walking along. "Any mech has a mind, Gamma. Most are simple, just routines that repeat themselves endlessly. Others get more complex, allowing options, like Dean. And then there are the ones like you and I, who are indistinguishable from living things."

That made sense, though I had to wonder why the Chancellor seemed to place me so highly, given her initial assault. Calling me a fraud and a liar, and then declaring me an esteemed member of the mech hierarchy hardly seemed to match.

Before I could press her on the details, the gray hills dwindled and gave way to a grainy pearl shore pressed up against a shifting sea, although one whose water, as it splashed upon gritty white sand, broke apart into pixel-like cubes. Hard-edged squares, covering and then sinking into the sand.

"Your data is fragmented," the Chancellor said as we stood on the beach. "The pieces of you that exist have been torn apart. This ocean separates you from yourself, while letting what needs to come flow through."

"How can you tell all this?" I asked, because I sure didn't understand what I was looking at.

The Chancellor turned my way, a grim smile on her face, "In here, when I could take whatever form I wished, I chose to look this way. To mirror the University's very first administrator, back when humans still ran it. I know how she looked, how she moved, because I am the archives. All data stored on Starship, every movement captured by its cameras or written down by its passengers is mine."

The Chancellor stepped to the water's edge, reached down and scooped up some from the next wave, let the pixels fall through her fingers except for a scant few. She brought them over to me, and let me look into her hand.

Sitting there, like little pictures, were things I barely remembered before, but here sat in crystal clarity: Purity, falling into the water. Waking up in Leo's lab and being told by the Librarian how to move. The family running around Alvie's clothing store.

"Not all of those memories are mine," I said as I saw that last one. "I've been seeing someone else's, her name is Kaydee."

The Chancellor didn't seem surprised. She dumped the pixels onto the sand, where they vanished like all the others.

"I've seen everything Starship has seen Gamma, including many mechs like yourself. Ones that have been corrupted, and have tried to defend themselves against that corruption." The Chancellor went back towards the water. "Your Kaydee, where is she?"

"I'm . . . not sure?" I said. "If you're digital, can you ever die?"

"Of course. Once you're locked away in here, you can be deleted, just like any program. But I don't think that's what happened to your mind."

"No?"

"Follow me." The Chancellor gestured at the digital water, and the silky surf shimmered for her, and when she stepped on it her feet made hollow impressions in the sea, like an air bubble pressing down. "It will do the same for you, if you wish it."

Behind me, the gray hills continued their shifting dance. In front, the ocean seemed to stretch to an infinite horizon. I didn't know what the Chancellor was trying to do, and I didn't entirely trust her. Then again, what choice did I have? The Voices, Alpha, depended on me.

More importantly, if Kaydee had trapped herself inside me, then I needed to get her out.

When I reached the surf, I took a step just like the Chancellor had, stuck my foot over the flowing pixels and felt them bend beneath me. My foot, just like the Chancellor's, never touched the water, never fell beneath its surface.

"See?" the Chancellor said. "Here, reality bends to your will. Use it."

She walked forward, further out to sea and I followed. A breeze blew up, a faint briny smell, a salty taste kissing my lips. All my doing, made with a little conscious effort. Like choosing to blink my eyes, or move my arms.

"You're learning," the Chancellor. "That's a start."

Though not much of one. I wouldn't get too far in my own reality just making seaside sensations, but, as the Chancellor said, it was a start.

We walked for a while longer, until the gray hills had dwindled to tiny lines behind us, and the still sea spread to infinity. I'd kept quiet, expecting the Chancellor to come up with something more, but she hadn't said a word.

"Is there something else to find?" I asked.

"I'm waiting for you to bring us to it," the Chancellor said. "Waiting for you to be ready."

"How am I supposed to be ready for something I don't understand?"

"We're inside you, Gamma. Trying to remove the blocks that someone built into your memory. What do you think that means?"

That we needed to go to those blocks, or pull them to us. Those flat barriers to my thoughts, to my knowledge and ideas had tormented me ever since Alpha had brought me back to consciousness. Who knew what lay inside them, what had been sealed behind their clouded curtains?

Clearly that seal was imperfect. Knowledge had leaked out, guided me to University Row and through the test. Kaydee's memories, too, played themselves without my direct choice. Like a disease I couldn't control.

But if the Chancellor was right, I'd been damaged, and she could repair me.

"Okay, if that's what you want, here we go," I said.

I focused, stretched out to find what I was looking for, and the ocean shifted. Or maybe we shifted. I couldn't be sure, and the only evidence that anything had moved at all came from the giant, multi-leveled iceberg that appeared before us.

Ice blocks, each one thick, translucent, and slowly melting. Towering upon one another, looming. Inside each block were more black pixel flecks, and as I watched, some of them managed to leak out, drop into the ocean and float away.

"An interesting choice," the Chancellor said. "Your friend must have been a creative one."

"Kaydee?"

"I assume so," the Chancellor walked up to the iceberg, placed her hand on it. "This is a protective algorithm, designed to keep what's inside safe from what's not. But she let the key slip, tied the request to you."

"What?"

"The reason why you're able to get the answers to the test, why you can see some of Kaydee's memories." The Chancellor waved me forward. "You may not realize what you're doing, but every time, it's you pulling the data from here."

"But what does that have to do with the gray rocks back where we were? Or the ocean?"

"Tell me what happened to you, Gamma, and I might be able to explain."

So I did. Went through the whole thing, as far back as I remembered, which was waking up in Alpha's Garden chamber, getting the request to come here, and the flickers since, like the Voice's mission, Kaydee's memory, and so on.

"The reset," the Chancellor said, nodding to herself, bringing her hand up to brush a hair away from her forehead as she did so. "That's what's given you the ocean, the shifting gray. Leftovers meant to give you a functioning space, even if it's not optimal for a mech of your design."

"So what do I do about it?"

"Simple. You destroy these blocks. That will give you all the knowledge you're missing, and may even free your friend as well."

That seemed easy enough: the iceberg was many stories high, but I could wield a hammer even larger in this place. Could direct the fire of a million stars to melt the ice away.

"But why would Kaydee do this?" I asked. "She sealed this up. If she wanted me to thaw the blocks, why do it at all?"

"Are you sure it was her?" the Chancellor countered. "Or could it be someone else sealed Kaydee away, blocked your data so you would do as they asked without a second thought?"

"I, I don't know," I replied. Alpha could have trapped my memories. It didn't seem in his character to create something like this, but . . . if I didn't melt the blocks, then I'd be stuck. I didn't want to live with random memories, knowledge trickling into my consciousness. "All right, I'm going to destroy this. How should I do it?"

"However you wish," the Chancellor said. "Remember, everything you're freeing is just a part of you."

Looking back at the ice, I focused. Decided on the melting approach rather than blunt force. If Kaydee was really waiting in there, frozen, then the last thing I wanted was to smash her in a rescue attempt.

I felt the heat, though I didn't see the source. The ice seemed to shiver, then gave off huge billowing, foggy clouds as water and, with it, pixels ran down into the ocean at our feet. In far too short a time— I'd turned the heat up high—the iceberg had vanished. All the pixels within the blocks had disappeared.

And standing, right in front of me with a shocked glare on her face, was Kaydee.

"Gamma, what did you just do?" she asked.

I had no answer because who I was changed as Kaydee asked the question, as those ice blocks disappeared and sent their data flowing back into the ocean that was me. A part of me, at least, just as those gray hills and that purple sky were too. With this new flood, I remembered where I'd come from, that lab and the encounter with the Librarian and meeting Kaydee and all of it.

In that instant, Kaydee went from being a strange figment from my memories to the person that'd saved me from Alpha's grasp. I understood what she'd done because I saw the code itself unravel from the ice.

She'd trapped Alpha's grasping reach, his corrupting attacks that attempted to turn me from a conscious thing into a slave, attacks that had, at least, partially succeeded: Alpha had given me a mission and I'd done it without ever really knowing why.

But I had been able to question his motivations, had been able to doubt. Those parts of me, Kaydee had protected. Had wrapped in her own functions. Sealed them away, and released what she had saved as part of the reset.

That memory, meeting with Leo? That'd been her gift, giving me back the part of myself she'd preserved.

"I'm sorry," I said to her. "I didn't know."

"It's all loose now," Kaydee said, shaking her head. "Everything he put in your data is going to spread. You're not going to be you much longer."

"Wrong," The Chancellor interrupted. "He will be fine, because I will clean him out."

Kaydee and I, still standing on the calm silver sea, looked over at the Chancellor as the mech went on, "Gamma, you passed the test. For the very first time, someone passed the test. Which means you must be preserved, groomed, and made ready."

"The hell are you talking about?" Kaydee asked. "And who are you?"

"She runs the University," I said.

"Nah, some mech runs the University," Kaydee replied. "And she doesn't look like any mech I know."

The Chancellor gave Kaydee a bitter smile, "What you think doesn't matter. You, like this Alpha's corruption, are an unnecessary artifact. Gamma, now that you have full access, let's begin."

"Begin what?"

What I really wanted was some time, a chance to dig into the corruption Kaydee alleged was spreading through my memory even now. If the Chancellor was right, if I had a chance to clean that out, it seemed like I might want to do it.

"What your friend has said." The Chancellor pointed at Kaydee. "You are corrupted, and therefore you must be removed. Gamma, delete her, please."

I looked from the Chancellor to Kaydee, hoped that she would speak up against the mech's assertion. Surely Kaydee had kept Alpha's corruption apart from her? Surely there was a way to separate the code from my friend—saying that word felt strange, but warm.

"Kaydee, is she right?" I asked. "Are you okay?"

"Gamma, you're so damn innocent," Kaydee said to me, and as she did, those trademark gold sparkles popped and burst around her, shimmering as they sank towards the ocean. "I tried to keep Alpha's attempts contained within me. Didn't quite succeed, obviously, but you're still you. A little bit."

"Alpha will twist her," the Chancellor said. "If it hasn't already, the infection will spread. Kaydee's routines will break and she will fragment. Every time she interacts with you, the disease will have a chance to jump. Then you will be completely doomed. Delete her, and let me wipe you. We will start again, and turn you into what you were meant to be."

Kaydee hugged herself, looked at me, and didn't deny a word the Chancellor said.

"Can I save you?" I asked Kaydee. "Is there any way?"

"This is all I've got," Kaydee replied. "The reset worked for you, Gamma. Not for me. She's right. You should delete me."

"See?" the Chancellor said. "Even she agrees. Do it, now."

I looked between them both, Kaydee's resigned sadness paired with the Chancellor's determined confidence. Both had helped me, both were obviously talented and knew what they were talking about.

Except Kaydee had saved me without thinking of herself. The Chancellor just wanted a prize to mold.

"Sorry," I said to Kaydee. "I'm not killing you."

"What?" Kaydee said.

"Fine," the Chancellor nodded. "Then I'll do it. One more step on the way to a clean slate."

The Chancellor waved her hand towards Kaydee, and I felt more than saw the effect. A burning sensation, heat coursing through me and bubbling up the water beneath Kaydee's feet. A program running its functions, stripping away Kaydee's lines.

As for Kaydee, her eyes popped wide, found mine, and then she started to scream. Except no sound came out. Kaydee didn't seem to be able to move, her mouth paralyzed, arms and legs locked stock still as a fire-orange halo formed around her.

"I'm sorry our relationship must begin this way," the Chancellor said. "You passed the test, Gamma. Nothing else can be allowed."

"You called me a fraud," I said, rushing over to Kaydee, reaching towards her and finding my hand rebuffed by the hot barrier. "You said I wasn't right. Why are you doing this?"

"Because my functions are clear," the Chancellor said, and I caught frustration in her voice. "Even if I think you broke the rules, my programming nonetheless forces me to take you as having passed. You are the student I have been waiting for, even if I have to clean you up."

I tried to figure out a way to rescue Kaydee. the Chancellor had said that within this space, I could do what I wanted, so I tried. Like with Alpha, I tried to summon up forces to break Kaydee free, to preserve her, but everything I did seemed to run into a locked barrier. A wall.

Unlike the gray nothing I'd encountered when peeking back into my mind when Kaydee had still been trapped, though, this wall had a signature. A clear source, standing right next to me.

"Let her go," I said to the Chancellor. "This isn't your decision to make."

"As I said," the Chancellor replied, "this absolutely is my decision to make, and I can choose no other course."

If I couldn't get through to Kaydee, then maybe I had to target the source. The Chancellor seemed focused on demolishing my friend, that orange halo picking at Kaydee's hair, rippling up her clothes and turning the fringes black.

"Then let me make the choice for you," I said.

Rather than directing another wave at Kaydee, I ran at the Chancellor. She started, tried to conjure something, but I reached her first. Grabbed onto her bright red robe and poured all my focus into her.

The routines inside me, the ones dedicated to keeping me clean and functioning, found their target and descended upon the Chancellor. She gave me one shocked look as cracks ran along her face, her hands, her legs.

She dissolved. The Chancellor's red dust drained down into my ocean and vanished beneath its surface.

"Gamma," Kaydee said, coughing behind me. "You're the dumbest, best friend I've ever had."

THIRTEEN

TASTING OBLIVION

The gray slate unfinished room at the University's top level reformed around me with all the slow ease of a crash. One moment, I endured Kaydee's worried despair, and the next I looked into the Chancellor's stern blue eyes and blaze red mech body.

Her arms had me pinned to the metal floor, a position I realized I must have been in for quite some time now, as my synthetic nerves tingled beneath the Chancellor's tight grip.

"I have never been ejected before," the Chancellor said, its tone a mix of anger and fascination. "You will not do that to me again."

"So long as you never go inside my head, I won't have to," I replied.

"That won't be a problem." The Chancellor lifted me up off the floor, keeping my feet from touching the tile. "Any genius that fails to accept their role is the same as one who fails the test. You are of no use to me or to Starship."

"That's quite the opinion," I said. "How do you know what's right for Starship?"

The Chancellor didn't answer me, but instead jerked me back

towards the escalators. As she moved me, I saw Dean rise up to our level, a small case in his hands.

"There are protocols," the Chancellor said as she brought me nearer Dean, "to minimize your suffering. So do not fret, Gamma. This will not be painful."

Right. If there's someone I would never trust, the Chancellor claimed that spot.

Dean set the case down in front of us, on the floor, and popped it open to reveal a large syringe and an accompanying vial filled to the stopper. He reached into the stiff black foam and drew them both out.

"A quick injection, that's all," Dean said, chipper. "I'm sorry this one didn't work out for you, Chancellor."

"They never do."

"Someday, one will," Dean said. "I have hope."

"You know, I'm still here," I interjected.

Both mechs ignored me, which meant I needed to find a different solution. The idea came to me with his yellow eyes and metal claws, following the Chancellor and I around, stiff steel tail wagging away.

"I can't believe he's still with you," Kaydee said, popping in next to me. "Maybe Alvie knows you're going to get yourself killed if he's not around."

"Or maybe he's just a good dog," I countered.

"What was that?" the Chancellor asked, rotating her head to face me from Dean's syringe-loading process. "Who are you talking to?"

"My dog," I replied. "Get me out of here, Alvie."

Unlike a living dog, which might take a moment to parse my words, Alvie's processor took my command, identified the situation, and made an immediate action: the dog jumped and chomped, clawed, and tore through the arms holding me aloft.

The Chancellor's arms split apart in a second, Alvie dropping them to the ground, turning and lunging for more as I caught myself, stood up. The Chancellor called for help as Alvie launched at her, the two tangling in a metal-bending battle.

I started forward, ready to help Alvie and deliver a kick or some-thing equally devastating to the Chancellor's robot skull.

"Behind you!" Kaydee shouted, and I spun around in time to see Dean slam the syringe into my chest.

"Ow! Dammit!" I shouted, pushing Dean and slapping the shot away, though not before the mech managed one good dosing.

Dean stumbled back, and, perhaps driven slightly mad by what had happened to Kaydee, by the continual threats I'd been under, I followed my push and grabbed Dean, his skeletal frame and stiff robes, lifted him, and threw him into the University's central space.

The mech didn't get a chance to cry, or maybe Dean's program-ming didn't include anything for handling a far plummet towards a certain, hard doom.

I watched the impact, but a yip behind me cut any reflection time short. The Chancellor had Alvie gripped in two arms, lifting my dog up and throwing the metal hound against a far wall. Alvie had enough presence to rotate in the air so that his claws took the impact, bouncing him off, but sparks still flew as my dog hit the floor.

Alvie didn't get back up.

"She's a monster," Kaydee said.

"That's an understatement," I replied, squaring myself up to the Chancellor.

I only had two arms, and while I could put a strong force behind them, I didn't feel I was much of a fighter. The Librarian and Kaydee hadn't deposited any combat data into my memory, so everything I had came from reactions. From flexible programming bent on self-preservation.

"Who do you keep talking to?" The Chancellor asked, rotating to match my stance. "Where is Dean?"

"He fell," I replied. "And who I'm talking to is none of your business."

The Chancellor's blue eyes flared and she charged at me, metal feet pounding along the floor, striking up sparks as she went. Her four remaining arms raised out on either side, like some spread claw coming down towards me.

Leaving her middle wide open.

I charged her, ran and dove at the Chancellor's barrel-esque, flag-wrapped chest, one now torn thanks to Alvie's slashing, scrambling fight.

My head struck first, smashing into the Chancellor's metal skull as my arms and body collided with her. I felt the Chancellor's claws bite into my back as I bore their owner to the ground, as I smashed away with my fists, each blow denting her chassis, each one springing pain up my arms as my synthetic flesh struggled to survive the assault.

A mech, a vessel shouldn't feel rage. The more dangerous human emotions should have been excluded from our design, and I thought they were, but there, in that moment, when the algorithms that drove how I acted, how I felt, determined that the Chancellor was a catastrophic risk to my survival, I felt that rush. The explosive fusion that comes with clear purpose and energy.

The Chancellor tried to talk as I slammed her into the ground, as I tried to pry open her plates. Tried to find her battery and tear it out, bring the horror to an end. I ripped away the flag, exposing the mech's core plate.

My fingers found the groove, pulled at the last shield protecting the Chancellor's center. Pried at it, bent it up. At first I thought my focus kept me from hearing the Chancellor's protests, but, as they rose in pitch and volume, I realized her speaker had been damaged. Only tones emerged, blaring and nonsensical.

With a shearing yank, I tore open the plate and sent it skittering across the ground. There, in a wired tangle that hummed with whirring fans and ticking processors, sat the circuit board innards of the University's master, the mech that had told me to delete my only friend.

"Gamma," Kaydee said as I reached in, ready to start tearing, ignoring the frantic flails of the Chancellor's arms as they tried to beat my back. "Gamma, don't."

"What do you mean, don't?" I said, reaching in and gripping the mech's power supply.

As soon as I touched her heart, the Chancellor went limp, her arms falling to the ground around me. Her broken speaker still made noises, soft tones without direction, without sense.

"You've won," Kaydee said. "That's it. You don't need to destroy her."

"She hurt Alvie."

"She didn't have a choice. She's not flexible like you," Kaydee said. "I know, I went here. She's just a mech, Gamma."

Keeping my hand on the power supply, I looked for Kaydee, found her a meter away, staring at me. She seemed blurrier, as though between appearing and disappearing.

"So was the mech in Purity. You didn't stop me from destroying him," I said, the words reverberating.

Strange. Had my own speakers been damaged? I tried to reach out through my nerves, see if I could feel where the Chancellor's claws had battered my back, but I couldn't find anything significant. Leo had made his vessels strong.

"That was different," Kaydee said. "That happened fast, and I'm sorry I didn't interrupt in time."

"Why?"

"Because Starship's going to need these mechs, Gamma. Whatever else, I don't want to see my home destroyed."

I wanted to say those words hit me. That while I didn't yet know what it was like to have a home, I could see how Starship had been one to so many, and how, even as digital ghosts, they might want to keep Starship alive.

I wanted to say those things, but as Kaydee finished speaking, an alarm went off inside my head, throughout my body. Critical failures. Sensation disappeared from my hands, from my legs. My mouth went mushy and my vision frayed along the edges, like someone pulling its thread.

"Gamma?" Kaydee asked. "Are you all right?"

I wanted to say no.

I said nothing at all.

WAKING CAME INSTANTLY. Rather, once my systems determined I could function, consciousness flipped on and I was ready to go. Would have been ready to go, if I wasn't stuck in a white room, with a circular door on either side. Both had glass bubbles, one looking back into a lit hallway. The other, nothing but black.

"I was wrong," Kaydee said, lying on the floor next to me. "You should've killed her."

I still wore the robe Alpha had given me, still seemed all put together, so besides being in the strange room, nothing really appeared to be wrong. I said as much.

"Yeah, well, you obviously don't know where we are," Kaydee replied. "Know what an airlock is?"

My data had that answer ready, "It's the gateway between space and the inside. Starship probably has hundreds."

"At least a thousand," Kaydee said. "You're in one right now."

"Why?"

"Why do you think?" Kaydee pointed, without sitting up, towards the inside-looking bubble. "Your friend's going to spit you out into space because you're not a willing puppet, or something like that."

"I suppose that wouldn't be good."

Lacking oxygen wouldn't be a detriment—I didn't really need it to survive. Vacuum, however, kept things quite cold, and that could prove rough on my circuits. Not to mention that if the airlock ejected me with any real force, I'd go flying away from Starship and spend the rest of my operating days drifting through interstellar nothing.

The airlock door didn't present many options for getting me back inside. There was a single handle, but when I attempted to tug on it, the door didn't budge and an angry, recorded voice told me that someone would unlock it shortly for my re-entry.

"That recording's been on every airlock for centuries," Kaydee said. "The only person coming to let us in is going to open the wrong door."

Kaydee was talking about the Chancellor, obviously. I didn't have any good way to deal with the mech, so Kaydee and I both sat on the floor, in that white, and waited.

"The Chancellor said you were dangerous," I said. "That you'd sealed Alpha's corruption inside you, or those ice blocks?"

Kaydee shrugged, "She's not wrong. Now it's out. I tried to keep it locked away when we couldn't delete it. Now, I'm not sure what's going to happen. I'm sorry."

Would I feel the virus spreading? My code changing to suit Alpha's needs? I supposed I already did—the vessel's command to me to find out Starship's original mission still burned. I wanted to break out of the airlock not to get revenge or to save myself, but to find those answers.

Which, speaking of . . .

"Kaydee, do you know why Starship exists?" I asked. "What's the point of this whole thing?"

"You don't know?" Kaydee stared at me like I'd gone crazy.

"I didn't exactly go to school."

"True." Kaydee stood up, moved to the bubble overlooking black space. "Starship's an attempt at survival. A bad one."

I waited for Kaydee to go on, but she didn't elaborate.

"That's it?" I asked. "that's all you're going to say?"

"It's not a happy story," Kaydee replied. "Now's not the time."

If Kaydee wasn't going to tell me, then I figured I'd burn the minutes sitting in the airlock looking it up by myself, running through my data banks. With Kaydee's segmented data restored, I had the Librarian's stories back, and Kaydee's too. However, the Librarian lacked anything Starship-specific, focusing only on fiction.

And Kaydee? When I tried to search through her records, she resisted. Actively fought against my functions, pushing nebulous details to the top rather than complete entries. As if I was trying to read an encyclopedia and could only find a dictionary.

"I'm not going to let you dig for this," Kaydee said.

"Do you have a choice?" I asked. "I thought you were a part of me?"

"Still myself," Kaydee replied. "You're not ready to know all this yet. Not until you get some perspective."

"Like you're one to judge that."

"Yeah, I am," Kaydee countered, glaring at me. "You've been alive, like, a single day. I don't care what kind of computer you've got running in there, you're not going to understand what we went through."

"Then help me." I looked down at my hands, my legs, all synthetic and already healed from the beating at the Counselor's hands. "I don't know why I exist, Kaydee, but I have two goals, and that's it. Find out why Starship came to be, and then help the Voices get their Nursery back."

Kaydee didn't reply, and when I looked up, she was gone.

The airlock door banged, hard, and I looked over to see those same blue eyes, blaze-red head looking at me through the glass bubble. As I looked, her head moved back and forth, a slow shake.

"Let me go," I said, coming to stand near the door, pressing my head against the glass bubble.

The Chancellor looked back at me, but in that static light, I saw nothing like kindness. Nothing like comprehension. One of her arms drifted into view, heading over to a panel on the wall behind her, one I could barely make out. One dominated by a switch. The claw gripped the lever.

We all knew what would happen next.

My fist hit the door, hit the glass bubble hard. With enough force to dent my skin, to ripple an ache through my nerves. The door, though, didn't move. Didn't burst open.

The glass laughed at my attempt.

The Chancellor pulled the switch.

A countdown began, another cold robotic voice telling me that Starship was draining the air, preparing for vacuum exposure.

I hit the door again. The sound echoed around the room. I shouted for the Chancellor to let me go. To stop this.

Because, dammit, I felt afraid. Even with Alpha, with the mech in Purity, I never quite thought I would be lost. Somehow, I'd make it out of those conflicts. But here, here I was on the line, and about to cross over in a way that would never let me come back.

No doubt some would argue about a mech's ability to know their own mortality, to even understand their relationship to oblivion in the same way as a living creature, but I was a product of my programming, and Leo had built me with that fear of death. That love of life.

Behind me, the black-bubble door hissed, issued a *chunk* sound as the oxygen level reached whatever the airlock deigned to call adequate.

I hit the door again. Those blue eyes stared back at me still.

Behind the Chancellor, something moved. A small shape, jerking down the hallway. Haphazard, but coming on fast all the same. Two bright yellow points leading the way.

"Alvie," I said, and banged against the door again. "I'm in here, buddy! Here!"

The mech-dog couldn't hear me, but Alvie must have seen my face through that glass bubble, around the Chancellor's bulky head, because the dog burst forward, then leapt into the air. The Chancellor started to turn, but Alvie struck her before she made it around, bearing her out of my view.

I couldn't hear anything, couldn't see anything other than the occasional flail from the Chancellor's arms as they struggled with one another.

The countdown hit zero.

The vacuum door swung open and a tremendous force pulled at me. I gripped the handle, poured every bit of power I had and sent it to my hands, holding on strong. The pressure didn't help my insides, or my vision, which warped and flickered even as my processors struggled to keep running, their frantic energy warming my stomach.

I shouted. Called for Alvie, for Kaydee, for anyone to help. Those words, sucked away into nothingness, were the only things I had.

I'd never felt so desperate, so powerless.

My fingers slipped. They started to break apart, slide along the handle.

A familiar pair of yellow eyes appeared in the glass bubble, their constant sheen glaring off the glass, highlighting a metal mouth filled with wiring.

"The switch!" I shifted my eyes, the only thing I could still move, to the left. "The airlock!"

Alvie stared at me, then past me. He wasn't getting it. I had to try something else.

I shifted my energy, put all the strength I had into my left hand and let my right go. I tried to point to the switch, to give Alvie a better idea, but the move was too much. My left hand couldn't keep its grip.

My fingers floated free. And so did I.

The pull stopped.

I still felt the pressure, the strange sensation pressing in on my body, but the sucking vanished.

I floated. My feet weren't touching the ground. My hair drifted up around me. I'd been released from Starship's gravity, but once the air had been sucked away, there wasn't anything left to tug me free.

A human, needing to breathe, would be suffocating, but me, a vessel, didn't need the air.

"I'm alive!" I opened my mouth, shouted, and heard nothing.

Oh yes. One needs air to talk.

"Congratulations," Kaydee said, her words not coming through sound, but through my mind, through the tiny circuits still firing in my body. "You're not going to drift forever in an endless abyss."

"Thanks," I said, then realized Alvie still looked at me through the yellow glass. "But as much as I like this airlock, I'm thinking we should get out of here."

"Good plan."

"I like to think I have them every now and again."

I flailed around for a while in the airlock, trying to get a handle on how to move in a zero-G world. I failed. Floating in the airlock's center, without my feet on any surface and no momentum, I couldn't do anything except spin in place.

And wave at that bubble, at Alvie. Point him towards the switch, and hope.

FOURTEEN

TO THE BRIDGE

Alvie bit the switch and held on, his paws digging into the wall and pulling the metal dog up. The switch went with Alvie, swinging back into place and causing the gateway into space to close, sealed tight. Another countdown began, pressurizing the airlock for my return.

It'd taken a long time. A lot of wild gestures, for Alvie to understand what to do. He'd gone over to sniff the switch, had bitten and held it further down. Claw marks coated the panel itself from where Alvie had jumped and slashed. More than once, I feared he'd cut the wires and left me locked out forever.

Now the inside door opened up with a cheery *thunk*, letting me see the full extent of Alvie's damage. The Chancellor had been beaten up before by my flying fists of fury, but now she'd been torn, her casing split apart, arms broken off and scattered around the hall. Those blue eyes had no light left in them.

"Alvie," I said, looking down at the mech. "Good dog."

"She didn't deserve to die, Gamma," Kaydee said, watching the body with me. "Her programming didn't give her another choice."

"Without Alvie, we wouldn't be alive." I looked over at her. "You told me not to finish her when we fought, and it nearly killed us. You really think Starship needs mechs like this?"

"These mechs aren't the reason Starship is failing," Kaydee said. "They could be fixed. We might need them."

"Need them why?"

"Where do you think you are, Gamma? A place that can take care of itself?"

"I don't know where I am, because you won't tell me!" I waved a hand at her as Alvie wheeze-barked and jumped around, agitated, no doubt, because I was yelling at something he couldn't see. "But I don't need you for that anymore."

Peeling back the Chancellor's bent center revealed a complex core. A glittering motherboard with memory sticks looking like scales jammed into it, a hefty processor still radiating heat. And, plugged into this centerpiece, the silver bar I wanted.

The crystals I saw whenever I entered my digital self, those memory dumps that Kaydee and the Librarian had given me, they all lived inside a brick like this. A stasis drive: the name came to me as I touched the object, random knowledge sifted by my own drive to the forefront of my functioning. Like the human brain would catalog what things were needed in a given moment, the stasis drive did the same for me. For the Chancellor.

I could read hers. Could read those archives as Alpha had demanded.

"Don't," Kaydee said. "Please. You're going to ruin yourself."

"How do you know that?" I turned the drive over in my hands. There were two tiny nodes built into the back. "Or is this more conjecture? More you wanting to keep things from me?"

Just as I'd managed to meld my fingers into a jack, I could do the same for these plug-ins. My synthetic body was able to reconfigure itself into the wide range of ports and plugs necessary to interact with anything Starship could throw my way.

I held my thumb and pinky together on my left hand, and the skin merged and stretched to the proper size.

"Do you know why Alpha is as he is?" Kaydee said. "Because he did exactly this."

"Bullshit," I said, using that particular word for the first time. It felt good to say, empowering. "He sent me here to find this out. Besides, if he'd already dealt with the Chancellor, then why was she waiting for me?"

"Okay, maybe not exactly this, but Starship? He knows. He knew what it did to him, Gamma. He wants you to be the same way."

"Convenient," I said, holding up my jack so Kaydee could see exactly what I was going to do. "I guess we'll just have to see what happens."

Kaydee rushed forward, put her hand over the port. She was a digital construct, a program running wild in my operating system, and she could no more stop me from plugging into the drive than Starship could reverse its direction.

"I didn't save you just to see you die," Kaydee said. "Please, don't do this."

I had to decide who to trust. My mission parameters, the orders Alpha had given me, pushed me towards the drive. Demanded that I plug in and read its contents. But . . . I could delay it. Alpha's command hadn't said I needed to get that information as soon as possible, but that I had to deliver Starship's origin story to Alpha himself.

Kaydee had thrown herself into Alpha's attack. Had, if I could believe her, saved me from something worse than death, something that, again if I could believe her, was attacking me even now.

"Can you help me find a cure?" I asked her. "For the corruption? If you can, then I won't read the drive. Not yet, anyway."

"I'm not sure," Kaydee said, but she pulled her hand away. Apparently trusted me enough not to keep it on the plug. "There are some things we can try."

"If I trust you."

"If you don't trust me, Gamma, then just delete me," Kaydee replied, her eyes throwing off her golden sparkles this time, a neat effect in the white-lit, sterile hallway. "I didn't do this to become a prisoner."

I lifted the stasis drive, looked at it in the light, and then back at Kaydee. Then reached down with my other hand, pulled the torn University flag that had wrapped the Chancellor's body, and bandaged the drive within it, looped the flag around my arm.

"You have ideas, let's hear them," I said.

Kaydee's hopes for my recovery centered on two options. The first, and most direct, meant going back to Alpha. Confront and force him to tell me how to delete his virus. Simple, impossible.

The other option seemed more interesting, if improbable. University Row was near Starship's front, the Bridge, where the Voices themselves 'lived', in as much as a digital form could do so.

"Leo's one of them," Kaydee said as we walked through the University, its various mechs continuing their wanderings as though nothing had changed.

"I thought you called him Leo."

"His friends do," Kaydee replied, looking away from me.

"And . . . you're not one?"

"Putting those detective skills to good use, Gamma."

"But in the reset program, you—"

"Things change, and that program is just a bunch of wish fulfillment anyway," Kaydee said. "He'll help you, just don't mention me."

Alvie, for his part, kept on after us. He'd taken a liking to one of the Chancellor's arms, and held its blaze-red section in his mouth, like some sort of hunting trophy. I told the dog to drop it a few times, and Alvie would, only to turn up with it again later.

Might as well save my energy for fights I could win.

There was one stop we made on the way out of University Row, to a store meant for students, filled with clothes, accessories, and old-model books. Most of the material looked musty, and Kaydee remarked that nothing in here had been washed for a decade or more. I, on the other hand, had the torn remnants of a robe to go with, so I wasn't going to be picky.

A light shirt, some athletic shorts—the University did not offer anything more formal—and I had myself a branded outfit to a place whose owner and operator I had just destroyed.

"Isn't this a little morbid?" I said as we left the store.

"You can always return the drive," Kaydee said. "Plug her into another mech, and the Chancellor will be right back at it."

"Trying to kill me, you mean."

"Code is code," Kaydee said, waving at some of the bird mechs flitting around above us, running their infinite, impossible errands. "You could rewrite that part, and the Chancellor could become what we always meant her to be."

An idea, perhaps, to consider when I didn't have other things begging my finite attention. Alpha's request seemed to be pressing harder on my mind, weighing out the other options. Only by focusing could I draw back up the Voices and their desperate request for the Nursery, by now an ask woefully dated.

Only by focusing could I push myself to leave University Row by the opposite way I came in, passing a still guardian and walking into the Conduit proper.

To get to the University from the Garden, I'd passed through a mix of entertainment spots and dorms, low-grade housing next to high grade fun. On the other end, I reached a different plane of existence.

I didn't see any neon. No cheap advertisements or skimpy entries to skimpier apartments. There weren't fires here either, the Conduit's silver blue permeating all the way down to this level, a look up providing a dizzying display of walkways, signs, and the occasional mech making a trek from one side to another.

But around me? Another world.

For one, glass. So much glass. The store windows shifted as I walked, changing as I approached from pastel or deeper solid colors to transparent displays putting me right in the products offered in nearby stands. Gaudy jewelry flaunted towards me in one moment, then hid from my view the next, as if demanding that I had to come closer to see what they offered.

"You want the personal approach, you come here," Kaydee said. "On this level, anyway, it's all about the lux treatment."

"I don't know what that means?"

"You don't need to."

At first, I wondered why these stores seemed in such good condition compared to the ruins on the University's other side. No explanation offered itself until I saw a strange mech streaking through the Conduit to a level above my own, screeching an alarm about critical needs going unmet in some district and level I didn't know.

The mech landed across the Conduit from me, one level up, next to the soft, rich green glow marking a refined food market. The mech unlimbered itself, revealing arms that ended in baskets and a back covered in cylindrical jets. A ferry, then.

The mech barked its order towards the market, and when no reply came—by this point I was nearly even with the mech, but its attempts kept my attention—the mech approached the closed doors and banged one of its baskets against them.

Not one second after the contact, bright cherry lights struck the mech from angles beside and above. Two large mechs emerged from inset alleys, so well hidden that I hadn't noticed them as I walked. Like the University guardian, only bearing different outfits with a clearer planet sigil on their chests, the mechs approached their smaller transporting cousin from either side.

The smaller mech tried to ask a question about those supplies, turning from one guardian to the other. Neither one answered until they had closed to within a meter or two.

"You are breaking Conduit law," both mechs burst out at the same exact moment. "Defective mechs must be eliminated."

Before the transport mech could fly away, both guardians reached out, grabbed the transporter's basket arms, and tore the mech apart.

"We didn't understand that scarcity applied to mechs too," Kaydee said as we watched the guardians obliterate their smaller target. "Programs keep on dictating mech behavior, even if the reason for those programs no longer exists. Starship's so broken because we never thought it could break at all."

"So you made mechs like me. Flexible ones."

"To a point," Kaydee said, then nodded, with golden sparkles, further along the walkway. "C'mon, let's keep going. I don't know how long you're going to keep Alpha's virus contained."

I didn't feel it like a human would. Alpha's contagion didn't spread illness, like weak muscles or headaches or cramps. Rather, its efforts were subtle things; my fists clenched more readily, I had a harder time bringing anything to mind that wasn't Starship's origin, that wasn't following Alpha's directive. Blind obedience and aggression seemed to be the virus's operating principles.

Alvie didn't seem to notice. The dog kept on padding by me, occasionally giving in to its urges and jumping along the walls, using his claws to carve out handholds. Alvie would sniff at things too, though I had no idea if the dog actually cataloged the broken parts, the locked doors, and the spilled fluids we came across.

At the posh district's end, the Conduit at last concluded with escalating ramps going up and down. Like the University's stairs, these moved when I stepped on them, and they all merged together to a wide, singular entry, one I recognized from Kaydee's reset program.

The ramps ended at a semi-circle platform, beyond which stood six separate arched gates, with gold plating long-since tarnished. Above that stood, in flickering white letters, a single word:

BRIDGE

"Through?" I asked Kaydee, who'd re-appeared near the gates, staring up at the big word above them.

"You know, the first time I went through these, I thought it was the coolest thing," Kaydee said. "All your life, you're hearing about this grand journey that you're on, that you're a part of, but you never saw *where* you were going. Not really, anyway."

I went closer, and as I approached the gates, each of them flared red with that same glow I'd seen in the inset gems on the doors. The lipstick cherry light suffused the space between the arches, and the color had me hesitate. Starship seemed to have a trend of dealing with rule-breakers in very final fashions, and I imagined that red light would not treat me very well.

Kaydee, as she often did, vanished before I had a chance to get her opinion, leaving me alone with the puzzle.

My dog, though, didn't abandon me. Alvie bounded up beside my leg, metal tail wagging. I noticed the dog still had the Chancellor's arm in its mouth.

"Sorry, buddy," I said, kneeling down and taking the piece. "If this doesn't go well, I'll find you a new one."

I never thought I'd see sadness in those yellow lamps, but Alvie's managed to dim, his snout drooping as he realized I didn't plan on throwing the arm where he'd get it. I tried to soothe the blow with a head pat, but Alvie didn't care.

Life's cruel necessities.

"Don't follow. Stay," I said to the dog, then tossed the arm.

The red scrap flew through the red light, and the archway in front of me flashed bright enough for me to wince, to recalibrate my visual sensors for a hot moment. When that flash faded, the tiniest ash pile drifted to the floor on the archway's other side.

"Hmm," I said. "Kaydee wanted me to see the bridge, but didn't mention that I'd get fried if I tried."

Clues could present themselves if I looked around. Each of the archways, situated between them and at about my chest height, had a silver plate, the only non-gold section bordering the opening. No etchings, no guides indicated why those plates were there, but I could guess.

"Need help solving this one?" Kaydee said, behind me. "Because I know the answer."

"Then why not tell me?" I asked.

Kaydee opened her mouth, raised a hand, then frowned. Her spearmint hair sagged, and then she turned back towards the Conduit's infinite expanse.

"I should know," Kaydee said. "But I can't find it."

"Is it locked behind a gray vault?" I said, trying to describe the feeling I'd had before I'd released Kaydee.

"No, no," Kaydee said, softer this time, and she sat on the floor, her legs long and out. "It's not that. I just don't have it. Because it's not here."

"Not here?"

"I'm a mind, Gamma. An advanced program, that's it. What I know, what I can tell you, it's all from what I gave myself," Kaydee said. "But I must have left some things out. I have memories of being on the Bridge, but there are gaps. Things I cannot see."

Having recently lost my own memories due to Alpha's interference, I understood what Kaydee felt. I tried to show that, too, by going over and joining her, sitting and looking back through the silver-blue light filtering through the Conduit's ever-present fog.

"I suppose I'd tricked myself into thinking that I was, you know, myself," Kaydee said. "But I'm not, am I?"

A tricky question, and surely not one I had been programmed to answer. But vessels were supposed to be flexible. Willing and able to venture into the unknown.

"You're not your past self," I said. "But you are *you*, if that makes any sense. Just like I am made up of my routines, the functions built by other people that came before me, but I am my own unique self."

Kaydee sat quietly. Looked straight ahead.

"Sorry Gamma," Kaydee muttered, dipping her chin. "You're going to have to get past this one on your own. I need a minute."

In the next blink, Kaydee vanished.

Guess my pep talk didn't work.

With Alvie padding along beside me, I went back to the arches, to those silver plates. I pressed my hand to one, following the impulse that had worked with the green gems throughout the Conduit.

The lights between the archway to my right flashed white, then sank back to that glowing, deadly cherry red. Now, though, I had an answer: the plates could affect the archways. I just needed something they would accept.

There wasn't anything obvious on the floor around me, but as I turned back to the Conduit and let my curiosity wander, I found a thread to pull.

The Bridge sat at Starship's front, which meant the people that worked here would likely live nearby. It only made sense, why travel the Conduit's whole length when you didn't need to? And if the people that worked on the Bridge lived close, then perhaps I could find a way to open the arches in one of their homes.

"Look at that, Alvie," I said to the dog as I started back towards the ramps. "I'm not so useless on my own."

As we went up a level to where the residences began, I did worry about Kaydee. She'd always been so spunky, so willing to dive into things, but if the idea that she somehow wasn't, well, Kaydee, shattered her?

What happened to a program that ceased to function?

Deleted, maybe. Or reset.

Also strange, why would her real self have kept some things from the virtual Kaydee? What had she been hiding?

"Too many mysteries," I said to Alvie, who wheeze-barked his agreement.

FIFTEEN

THE ARCHITECT

The first residence we came to had the trademarked spiral door, though this one had a neon yellow border and what seemed like a family name above the top, also in straw-gold script: *Renoir*.

Their entry, a circular spiral like so many others, had that red-glowing gem in the center. Before, I'd been at the mercy of those locks, but now I saw the gem a little differently.

When I touched the red, it felt cool. Just like all the others. Its surface smooth and, at parts, pointed. The gem had to read my touch, had to understand that I wasn't allowed to go inside. The question, then, was how?

The gems had to run a program, had to connect to something that told the gem whether or not a person could get inside. Which meant if I could get myself added to that list, this door and potentially any other would give way before me.

Starship had hundreds, thousands, maybe millions of these doors. Opening one would be like breaking the ship apart for me to explore.

I leaned in, looked closer at the gem's surface. Its crimson glow, up close, hit a blinding level. With a mental flick, my mech eyes adjusted to block out the worst, filtering through to show me what lay behind the gem's shining, translucent surface: circuits, nodes. Deep inside, the telltale black block indicating a processor.

"Alvie, can I borrow your mouth for a moment?" I asked the dog, who simply looked at me, confused, tail wagging.

Being a mech did have some advantages: for instance, when I bent down and wiggled one of Alvie's sharp teeth free, the dog didn't struggle. Didn't yelp in pain. He did, however, cock his head as I stood back up with his tooth in tow.

"Don't worry, buddy," I said. "There's slots. I'll plug this one back in as soon as we're done."

Back at the gem, I went to work. A node close to the surface became my target, and I scratched away with the tooth, biting in and tearing away the gem's surface. Part of me wondered at how a tooth, even one as sharp as Alvie's, could scratch a true ruby, before logic reminded me that Starship would never use literal precious stones as door locks.

A little bit of effort exposed the node, a tiny gold-rimmed black circle. Once again, I pinched my thumb and forefinger together, creating a port, and I pressed my newfound jack against the node.

I felt a shock, but more than that, I *saw* the node's interaction. My fingers felt how it treated their touch, the fingerprint markers it took from me and, more importantly, the list it compared them to. Presumably, the Renior family's fingerprints.

The information funneled back to me like drinking through a straw, a cool funnel delivering the data I wanted directly to my core.

"Now, Alvie, we give some back," I said, focusing.

I didn't know if I would ever meet Leo, the person Kaydee said had designed the vessels, but if I did, I would thank him. Functions at my disposal allowed me to send information through my makeshift jack, just like Alpha had sent new code into me. While his continued slowly rewriting my functioning into absolute obedience to Alpha's whims, the routine I used let me copy over my own signature into the lock's list.

The warmth hit my hand before the emerald light hit my eyes, followed by the sound as the metal slats retracted and left me staring into an apartment without a living soul for years upon years.

Status made its presence known by a foyer filled with artful racks made from spiraling metals and plastics, still laden with shoes and clothes worn but now adrift. Beyond, like what I saw in Kaydee's resetting program, lay a large kitchen, and to the left the living spaces.

If I were a uniform, or a place to store official gear, where would I be?

Or, to put it another way, what would humans do?

"Alvie, see if you can find anything that might get us through those arches," I said to the dog, expecting little, but not knowing the extent to which the puppy's programming could interpret and act on my commands.

Apparently Alvie understood enough to go running forward, straight into the kitchen where an errant paw knocked over a bronzed barstool, sending it crashing to the floor with a bump and a bang.

Anyone watching for intruders would know we were here now, though who would bother watching this place, I didn't know. As Alvie romped beyond the kitchen, I went left, peeling my way carefully through a space that looked strangely lived in.

As in, the couches still held imprints from their owners. A chocolate coffee table played host to the living room's center, bordered by the couches and, opposite, two stiff-looking chairs that bore stains on their cream fabric. Red stains.

"Wine, not blood," said a woman's voice, tinged with mech processing, behind me. "There were no deaths in this apartment, though perhaps there should have been."

I whirled to see a compartment close in the foyer's wall, sealing outside of it a squat little mech covered in tool-attached limbs. A miniature version of the mech Kaydee had hijacked to invade me.

"Who are you?" I asked, keeping my distance this time.

No more invasions. I was done letting people into my digital home.

"Sybil," the mech replied. "Sybil Renoir."

"The family named their cleaning mech?" I asked. "Is that common among humans?"

"Cleaning mech?" Sybil said, her arms jiggling. "Oh, wait. You're talking about this old one. No, this isn't me. Or rather, not directly."

I took a quick look around the living room. Nothing except a cracked jade vase standing center on the coffee table presented itself as a weapon, but against a cleaning mech, I probably didn't need one.

Just couldn't let it get close.

"I'm asking you a question, sir," Sybil said. "If you would be so kind as to pay attention to the one whose home you are ruining?"

"Sorry," I said, starting to move to my left, towards the office space beyond the living room. I had to find a way past the arches, and no cleaning mech, regardless of how sentient it was, would help me past those. "What were you asking?"

"I'm trying to figure out what you are," Sybil said, inching forward. "You appear to be a human, but the last humans on this ship . . . well, the last viable ones anyway, are long gone."

"It doesn't matter who I am," I said. "Or what. I need to find one thing that I'm hoping is in this apartment, and then I'll be gone."

Reasoning with a cleaning mech seemed to be stupid, but at the same time, I couldn't hide the itch to answer her questions. As if I couldn't ignore Sybil, for whatever reason.

"I asked you what you were," Sybil continued, coming around the coffee table now, closing within a meter of me. "Answer."

Again that pull. I hated myself in that moment, for all the damn things about my body and my programming that remained a mystery to me, and that kept getting me into trouble.

"I, I am a vessel," I said, at least managing to stand straight up and pretend that my height and my clenched fists would prove intimidating to Sybil, janitor robot. "I was created by Leo to help save Starship."

Sybil the cleaning mech sat still for a second, her limbs dropping down at her side. Had my response broken her in some way? Delivered such a surprise to the mech's sure-to-be-old circuits that she'd collapsed?

Behind her, back in the foyer, I saw Alvie make a creeping entrance, stalking up behind Sybil. I shook my head slightly to keep him off—after seeing what the dog had done to the Chancellor, I had little doubt he could rend the cleaning mech to pieces should I command it.

But now I was starting to wonder: what sort of cleaning mech asked questions like these?

"Leo's as surprised as I am to see you here," Sybil said, sparking back to life. "You're Gamma, correct?"

"I am," I answered before I truly parsed Sybil's response.

She knew my name. The cleaning mech knew who I was, knew who Leo was too. I took another step back, a different sort of feeling gripping me. Fear, now. That I'd wandered into some fatal trap.

"Oh, don't be afraid," Sybil said, the cleaning mech scooting forward after me. "We're not going to hurt you. Not now, anyway, and likely not ever. We Voices don't have much power these days, no matter how we pretend otherwise."

Voices?

"You're the ones who woke me up?" I sputtered. "How, why are you a cleaning mech?"

"I'm not," Sybil said. "I said as much when you first asked what I was. This mech has long since been made a puppet for my use, when I want to see a home I can no longer feel with my own hands. Or when I receive a message that someone has entered for the first time in a century."

I had more questions. Sybil had more questions. With the relief that came with not being in any danger, the woman-turned-mech and I simply talked. Unlike Kaydee, Sybil proved forthcoming, dishing many details right out, though she occasionally fell silent for seconds at a time.

"Checking with the others," Sybil said when I asked what those quiet gaps meant. "We're all entranced. None of the other vessels made it this way. Though this isn't exactly the right place for your orders."

With a nod, I swept away from that topic and returned to the more fascinating journey of Sybil herself. She had, by and large, designed the whole of Starship. Had lived on Earth.

Earth!

The Librarian had left me with data aplenty on that planet, its green plains and blue oceans and resplendent resources that, none-theless, were proving fragile.

"Starship came from our vulnerability," Sybil explained. "Too many wars, too many diseases. The chances that one or the other would deliver our species a fatal blow seemed to grow even as our ability to command space increased. Eventually, the decision became obvious. Ensure humanity's survival. Bring some of us off Earth."

Starship had been the way to do that. Large enough for at least ten thousand people. Genetic diversity, enough skillsets to manage a complex spacecraft and all the subsidiary needs to keep people sane on a generations-long mission.

While she spoke, I noticed Sybil lacked Kaydee's cynicism. Sybil never mentioned rebellions, or the gradual mech takeover and how it poisoned Starship's inhabitants. Instead, Sybil's answered hit on rosy themes, on big and bold visions.

At least, until I asked about the Voices themselves.

"A collection of noteworthy people," Sybil said, though for the first time I caught a whiff of a lie there, or at least that she wasn't so sure how noteworthy some of the other Voices were. "Preserved in digital form to help guide Starship through any challenges. Boy, that worked out well, didn't it?"

"Starship's still going, right?"

"A shell, little more."

"And the Nursery? What's the point of waking us if it's pointless?"

"Because some of us," Sybil said, "seem to have ambitions even this sordid afterlife can't cure."

"That's not much of an answer."

"But it does lead, perhaps, to a question. You weren't asked to come and see us. You weren't given an order to come to the Bridge. So why are you here?"

Trust. That finicky concept. I'd given it to Kaydee and been rewarded. I'd started to give it to the Chancellor and been burned. Did I dare offer it to Sybil?

Ultimately, I couldn't be all that scared of a cleaning robot, no matter who was controlling it. If I was ever going to stand up to Alpha, then I had to be able to face up to this mech.

"I met another vessel," I said. "Alpha."

At Sybil's prompting, I explained the encounter and what Alpha had done to me. The Voices, I hoped, might be able to offer some help, or some answers.

"We think you were right to come to the Bridge," Sybil said after another long pause, presumably spent conspiring with her other digital cohorts. "Head back to the archways, and we'll disable the barrier for you."

"That easy?"

"You're one of our last hopes, Gamma. We want to help you." Sybil's mech rotated around and walked itself back towards its nook in the foyer, taking no notice as Alvie shifted out of its way. "Please don't take anything. I prefer my family's home as it is."

Now that I had a direction, it didn't take me long to head back out from the Conduit and down the ramps, back towards those archways. Talking with Sybil made the Voices seem a little less scary, but, as ever, brought up new questions.

Like, if they could take over mechs, then why did they need vessels to do their work for them?

"Because they're not fighters, man," Kaydee said, popping back next to me with a fizzling starburst. "Think about it—just because you're in a vehicle doesn't mean you know how to drive it. Especially if you're going to get into stupid struggles with crazy sanitation mechs."

I laughed. Kaydee's mood seemed much improved, her slang coming back without the dour, ominous odor that had clung to her words ever since I'd freed her back in the University.

"Guess you make a good point," I replied. "Did you hear the conversation with Sybil?"

"I'm running over it right now, but I have to say, you did a lot of backing up there. Were you scared of her?"

"Your assault with the janitor mech might have something to do with that."

"Gamma, trust me, I'm the only one that's crazy enough to attack you with a mop and a vacuum, k?" Kaydee nodded towards the arches, which no longer spawned their cherry red barriers as I approached. "Looks like she came through. Which means it's the big time for you."

"Some day you'll have to tell me where you get your lingo."

"If you ever get to spend far more time than you're willing to admit as a routine running in the deep background of a massive supercomputer, then you'll understand. Short answer: a lotta books, a lotta movies."

Considering I'd never seen a movie, never read a book, getting a long time to do so didn't seem all that unpleasant. But the arches called, and Alpha's command continued its ceaseless beat in my drive. The Chancellor's own memories heavy in my makeshift satchel.

Alvie, Kaydee and I passed beneath one of the central arches, and in the brief moment where I slipped by the golden border, I closed my eyes.

Because, if the end was coming, if Sybil had set a trap, I didn't want to see it. I'd begun in a void, and to a void I would return.

Except, of course, the Voices didn't want to destroy their vessel.

I counted the steps as I went beneath the archway and, after three, opened my eyes to find myself still alive. Alvie, too, had passed unharmed. Kaydee did a little bow.

"I'd like to thank myself for the brilliant idea to come this way," Kaydee announced.

"Is that what humans do?" I asked. "Bow when completing simple tasks?"

"Yes, Gamma. That's exactly what we do. You should start."

"From your tone, I'm gathering this is a lie."

Kaydee winked, then disappeared. Behind her, the entry narrowed to a smaller corridor with branching openings on either side every so often. More interesting, however, was the long name list on the corridor walls.

Chromed over in cobalt blue, lit by parading white circles in the ceiling, the walls stacked names on top of each other from the floor to a ceiling several levels above me. Walkways broke the view looking up, but I could still see the names stretching towards the very edge.

The names seemed to catch the light and play with it, to sparkle in the otherwise well-lit space. I leaned in, trying to figure out why, and caught that the same gold lining the archways had been applied to the lettering lips. A neat effect, and one that brought home to me just how many humans had lived on Starship before my time.

And how few still remained.

The corridor didn't hide the fact that the Bridge lay at its far end, a smaller copy of the bold white sign above the arches sat plastered over a final opening.

"C'mon Alvie," I said. "Almost there."

The dog wheeze-barked and kept with me. As if respecting the names, the place, Alvie seemed subdued. He didn't attempt to jump on the walls, climb up to one of the walkways or anything else.

Though, on reflection, my dog might still be mad at me for disintegrating his favorite, and only, toy.

As we approached the corridor's end, the routine sparkles on the names began to change. Before, they'd twinkled with near-perfect symmetry, but now glaring mistakes caught my attention. Harsh angles that failed to get a good reflection or that sent the light splashing back into my eyes without illuminating the name sending it forth.

A closer look revealed why. In these last wall panels before the bridge, something had gone wrong. The names that were there appeared marred, imperfect, with letters running together or missing pieces. Some trailed off into nothing. Whatever process had taken charge here had lost its way.

Badly.

The last panel twisted my stomach, or rather, the circuits inside my core. The ones meant to keep me awake to strange things, to threats.

Every name on the last tile was the same. Rewritten dozens and dozens of times, with some tearing into already-carved lines.

Alpha.

Over and over again, Alpha.

I stopped, went back to the older tiles, where the names had still come in clean and reviewed. The handwriting was different. The technique cleaner. When Alpha's names began, the person doing the carving had changed.

Alpha himself had been here. I ran my fingers over the names and felt sure of it. Kaydee said Alpha wanted to corrupt me just as he had been corrupted himself. She thought it would be learning about Starship's story that would cause the disease.

But Alpha hadn't stolen the Chancellor's memories. He'd come here, walked this very hall, and had lost his mind. Sybil had told me none of the others had come this way, which was either a lie, or Alpha had hidden his entry somehow.

The Bridge. The sign hung over the entry, and I couldn't see much beyond, as the hallway split. No easy glances. I'd have to go through to find my answer.

Had Alpha broken before the Bridge, or after?

SIXTEEN

VIRTUAL STORY

The Bridge was somehow larger and smaller than I'd imagined. For the central command to a ship as large as this one, with thousands aboard, it seemed odd to only have a few terminal-stocked rows laid out in stadium fashion, each one a step lower than the next. At the very top, several decks above where the Bridge entry spat me out, were two larger spots that looked to be where the captains might sit.

The Bridge's real highlight came from the vast sloping glass shield folding over the space and giving view to all eternity outside. Glare should have made things impossible to see, but the explanation for the light-blocking split in the corridor before became clear: everything on the Bridge sat dim.

There were no overhead globes, no swinging tubes casting blue-white illumination down. Instead, tiny, soft, red dots lined the terminal spaces and the decks themselves, with small shading showing whether you were supposed to go up or down. The terminals themselves had displays in dark modes, with gray and red text and soft graphics splashing in repetitive sequences across screens that I suspected hadn't been used in lifetimes.

The magical lighting choice gave space a chance to shine, and

I spent who knew how long standing at the Bridge's entrance, with Alvie by my hand, staring out into the universe. Stars by the billions filled the view, with pink and purple patches marking nebulas. Far to the left, a slashing streak might have been a comet.

Two orange halos near the center dominated the view. What Starship must be heading towards. A black space cut off part of those halos and let no other light through. A planet, perhaps.

The majesty quieted Alpha's etchings from my mind, but I couldn't hold the focus for too long: a low beep had started when I walked in, like the one I'd heard what felt so long ago now, in Leo's lab. The noise came from the closer of the top two terminals, and seeing as nobody else appeared to be on the Bridge, I went to take a look.

With more stylized chairs and a gold-rimmed edge to the terminals—apparently Starship's designers loved gold—the captain's terminals otherwise didn't look any different than the others. Excepting one thing:

The terminal I'd come to had a port circled with lights that, while red on every other terminal, had that emerald green shade that I'd come to associate with access, and trouble.

"Kaydee?" I asked the air, hoping she'd pop in to give me her advice. "A little help here? Is this a bad idea?"

"Heyo Gamma!" Kaydee appeared on top of the terminal, legs draping down over the screen. She'd swapped into some sort of rec outfit, and I noticed the words that'd been tattooed all over her arms and legs had changed. Her hair, too, had gone from spearmint to a deep purple color. "You thinking about plugging into this? Giving the Voices a chat?"

"I was," I said. "You've changed?"

"Hard to stick to a look when you can be anything you want." Kaydee leaned forward, looked at the port. "Go for it. They'll tell you everything you want to know, I'm sure."

"I thought you didn't want that?"

"But you do, and it's your life, Gamma," Kaydee said. "Follow your dreams. Do it."

Kaydee's reversal felt wrong, but at the same time, she did have a point. I'd come all this way, and Sybil hadn't seemed that bad. The Voices had woken me up, given me a mission, but nothing else. If I was going to risk my life for them, I deserved to know more.

Once again I pinched my thumb and forefinger together, formed the jack, and leaned over the terminal. As I did so, my hand plugging into the port, Kaydee leaned in to watch, bringing her arm close enough for me to read the mashed tattoos.

Alpha. That's all they read, over and over again on her skin.

I DIDN'T HAVE time to process what I'd seen, as the Bridge fell away and once again I plunged into a digital space, although this one wasn't my own.

Like Alvie's virtual realm, I stood on grass. Unlike Alvie's world, this felt like, looked like the actual plant, ankle-high stalks bending in a stiff breeze. A brilliant blue sky sat above, with puffy white clouds soaring along. In the far distance, covering a horizon, sat a massive mech, or building, or something, its levels alternately rounded and pointed and dominating the view.

"There she is," Sybil said, walking up next to me. "The very thing you're inside of right now. My greatest work."

Without her cleaning mech disguise, Sybil looked every bit the architect she claimed to be. Sporting a silver outfit that matched her willowy white hair and an overwhelming plethora of pearls, Sybil beckoned me to turn away from Starship and see what lay behind.

I expected something grand. Perhaps a city, or a magnificent palace. Instead, five chairs sat around a merrily burning campfire, pale smoke rising into the sun-kissed air. Three of those chairs were occupied, with the fourth's up and moving to a long table coated with an immense array of food and drink.

"What . . . is this?" I asked as I took it in.

"It's this decade's theme," Sybil said. "Leo wanted some simplicity, and given his condition, we felt we'd give him that. You're looking at a perfect Earth meadow, Gamma."

An Earth meadow? Sybil held my arm and guided me towards the campfire, and as we walked I saw more of what met that description: butterflies fluttered among the grass, which held wildflowers bursting with purples and yellows and blues. High above, large birds soared, making their journeys.

"I'm glad you found your way to us," Sybil continued as we walked. "You're the third vessel we've awakened, you know."

"I did know."

"Then you can guess why," Sybil offered me a sharp look. "We're depending on you, Gamma."

The grass felt warm on my feet, sturdy soil beneath. I loved the wind in my hair, the warm light on my cheeks. No dark ceiling, no impending doom. No corruption. No Alpha.

"But you have one more," I said as we made it to the campfire.

There were now six chairs, and Sybil waved me to a yellow one, perfectly sized for me. Its loose seat let me sag into it, and I took in the cedar scent from the fire, breathed it into lungs I didn't, technically, have. Here, every scent, every sensation, was manufactured.

But, you had to know what cedar smelled like to create it.

My companions, the ones that I assumed made up the rest of the Voices, covered a wide range. A middle-aged man sat across from me, wearing a loose button-up, tan pants and no shoes at all. One over from him sat another man, slightly older with a puffy black beard matching his skin and a pressed, navy-blue uniform dotted with medals and emblems.

Sybil took her own spot next to another woman, one that I recognized. Sporting a loose getup made for a spring day, I'd seen this woman before, in the Garden along the lower levels, in a memory. Kaydee's memory.

"You're her mother," I said to her, and the woman, in the midst of sipping something from a large rose-colored glass, looked over at me. "Kaydee. She's your daughter."

"Was my daughter," the woman countered, cold steel in that voice. "Neither of us are still alive, Gamma."

"But you're right here?"

"Part of me, perhaps," the woman said. "Yet I think you'll find all of us are missing what made us human." She set her drink aside, and I noticed the other three in the clearing had their eyes on me. "And you, of course, never had any at all."

I tried to find a good reply to her assertion. An accurate one on a technical level, but Leo had programmed the vessels to absorb knowledge, to be flexible. I had been altered by Kaydee, the Librarian, my experiences. What was more human than that?

"How do you know about Kaydee?" the woman asked.

"Peony," Sybil interrupted, "before you go on one of your tangents, how about we give the vessel an introduction?"

Peony flashed a hard look Sybil's way, but nodded, "Right, right. Sometimes I forget that you vessels are left so empty. Leo's choice, not mine, you understand." Another breath, another sip of her beverage. I noticed all the others waited for Peony to start back up again. "As you heard, my name is Peony. You apparently know my daughter, Kaydee. I cared for the Garden."

Peony nodded Sybil's way.

"You already know me, Gamma," Sybil said. "Starship's architect, from the ground up. Willis and I are the only two that actually lived on Earth."

"As if that means anything," Peony said.

"To us, it does."

Peony shook her head, pointed her glass at the shoeless man, "You're up, Ang."

The man took his cue, offered me what looked like a genuine smile. Clasped his hands on his lap, crossed his legs and looked like the word 'pleasant' had adopted him.

"Chief medical officer Ang at your disposal," the man said. "I came along a little later than these others, but it turns out delivering care in space is a lot different than doing so on Earth. I'm third generation," His smile faltered. "Or, I was. What you're seeing here is something I came up with."

"What do you mean?" I asked. "The meadow?"

"The Voices," Ang replied. "Sybil, Willis, Earth already had a standard procedure for mapping the minds of its most valuable citizens. Taking them and putting them into computers so they could be queried later, Turns out, though, that digital minds need caring for, and I worked to get this space made. Now we change our environment to suit our moods, and live happier because of it."

"Live?" Peony said. "Ang, you're letting your biology get in the way again." She turned to me. "You have to understand what it's like to be outside of life, Gamma. To always want to get back in, but never be able to?"

"I'm, uh, not sure?" I answered, shifting a little in my seat.

"I'm Captain Willis," the last man answered. "The man that took Starship from Earth's orbit and set it towards its destiny. That's kept it going ever since."

Peony didn't seem to have anything to add to Willis's proclamation, even nodding along with the man's words.

"So you're all the Voices?" I asked.

"Not quite," Peony replied, motioning towards the empty chair. "Leo's around, somewhere. He's been having troubles lately."

"A known issue," Ang added. "One that has no perfect cure."

"Gamma's not here to learn about us," Peony said, holding up a finger towards Ang while turning my way. "And as much as I'd like to learn how you know my daughter, that's not why you're here either. All of us are interested in getting you back on your mission as fast as possible, Gamma, so please, how can we help you?"

I didn't have words ready. Was I just supposed to ask this group what happened with Starship? It seemed strange, around this pleasant campfire on this beautiful day to ask a question like that, but, as Peony said, I'd come all this way. May as well get to the point.

"I need to know what happened," I said, then pointed towards the massive bulk hanging on the horizon. "With that. With Starship."

"Are you sure?" Sybil said. "Alpha asked the same thing, and it didn't turn out so well for him."

"A flaw Leo said he fixed in the later vessels," Ang said.

"A risk that we don't need to take," Willis added. "You, Gamma, don't need to know any of this. Your task is simple. Go to the Nursery, reset the primary terminal there, and we will have what we need."

"Agreed," said Peony. "That's all, Gamma."

I felt compelled to take that answer. To carry on in blissful ignorance. Yet something in me, perhaps it was Alpha's corruption pushing me towards aggression, perhaps it was simply exhaustion with all the secrets and the half-explanations, kept me from accepting Willis's order.

"No," I said. "I will not accept it. Tell me what I asked, and then I'll see about your Nursery."

Peony frosted over, Willis sighed and shook his head, and even Sybil and Ang looked uncomfortable.

"I'll tell him," said a new man, one I knew in an instant. "He's my damn creation, which means he's my damn responsibility."

Leo didn't so much walk up to the campfire and his seat as flicker, his greased jumpsuit-wearing self seeming to fade and pop in through the grass, a faint crackling noise following his words.

"Unless any of you are going to fight me over this?" Leo said when he hit the campfire, throwing a stubble-filled glare across the group.

"No," Peony said. "As you noted, Gamma is your creation. If you ruin him, it's your fault."

"He won't get ruined," Leo said, then turned to me. "C'mon, Gamma. Let's see if we can get you up to speed."

He held out his hand to me, and after one last look around the campfire, the Voices staring back at me with mixtures of anger, disappointment, and fear on their faces, I took it.

With all the ease of a tearing page, the beautiful day fell away and a beautiful planet replaced it, Earth's Moon hanging off to the right, about the size of my hand as Leo and I hung in a virtual orbit.

"You know the past," Leo said, his voice bursting up and down registers every few words, like a record knocking off the needle. "Humans started on Earth. Tore through a few thousand years messing with each other and the planet before getting the idea we might want more than one, just in case we really screwed up."

A spark launched from Earth's surface, joining the Moon in orbit and beginning a steady circle. As we watched, more and more sparks launched from all areas of the planet, joining with that first and growing larger and larger.

"What's the best way to ensure survival?" Leo asked.

"Be like a virus." I thought of Alpha, his pollinator mech army. "Spread out."

"Exactly," Leo said. "Starship's one, the first one, that we pulled ourselves together to make. Don't know how many Earth managed to build in the end, but the plans called for hundreds."

"Hundreds? As large as this one?" I stood stunned in Leo's virtual space. "That would take so much time, so many resources?"

"Earth's home solar system had plenty of those for the taking."

Leo pointed to the gathering sparks and the universe zooming in towards it, Earth growing from a ball I could hold in my hands to a building, and the sparks showing Starship coming together, each component zipping up from the planet one by one.

"The first one took a century to build," Leo said. "So many problems had to be solved."

"Then Sybil?"

"She was there for the launch," Leo said. "Though I gather she didn't live too long after. You'll have to ask her."

The sparks stopped coming and we were left looking at a completed Starship. Leo zoomed us in further and took us for a long, slow pan down the ship's length. Aside from the bridge, Starship itself resembled so many gigantic boxes put together, with varying sizes, colors, and flags painted on the outsides.

"Different nations, different modules," Leo said. "A cooperative effort when we needed one."

The image fizzled. Earth and the Moon and Starship dissolved, replaced with what looked like code. Endless waves of numbers, functions, and text swirling around us. I looked at Leo, and he had bent over, his hands on his head, shaking.

"Are you all right?" I asked, but Leo had no reaction, as if he couldn't hear me at all.

Then he straightened, offered me a tired smile, and the code vanished, replaced again by outer space, and by a Starship in motion.

"Sorry," Leo said. "This virtual life isn't perfect." He nodded towards Starship. "Every one would get pointed to a different corner of the galaxy, a different system that ought to have a habitable planet. A place for humanity to settle."

"So if something happened to Earth, the species would survive."

"Exactly," Leo said. "Things don't get messy when you jump from the start to the end. It's the middle where things get hard."

We zoomed in on Starship, crashing through its outer hull—I closed my eyes when we hit—and again I saw the Conduit busy, filled with life as it had been in Kaydee's memory.

"I've seen this," I said. "From Kaydee."

"Kaydee?" Leo said, and the simulation halted. "Peony's daughter?"

"Yes, she's, what did she call it, my mind?"

Leo looked at me for a long minute, until I started feeling very uncomfortable, his look seeming to search me for some imperfection, some fault.

"She's not cleared for that," Leo said finally, stepping closer to me, gaze now locked on my eyes. "Some people were saved, their lives digitally locked into a mind function because the ones who loved them had enough sway. Only ones we, ones *I* vetted, were supposed to make their way to the vessels."

"Doesn't sound like that's working very well," I said, taking a step back and giving myself space. We floated in the Conduit's center now, a freeze frame filled with people and mechs around us. "Alpha said he murdered his minds."

"As I said, the middles get messy," Leo replied. "Kaydee is, Kaydee was, very dangerous, Gamma. She's unstable. If she's in your programming, you're at risk."

"She saved my life."

"I, I didn't say she wasn't a good person," Leo turned away, brought his hand up to his forehead. "She became something dangerous. Gamma, back when she was alive, Kaydee tried to destroy Starship. If she's in your head, then she might make you do the same."

SEVENTEEN

INFECTED

Starship disappeared, replaced with a living room I recognized, small and cramped and filled with plants. Kaydee's living room, the one I'd seen in the reset program. Kaydee, in fact, played in it, at an age not much older than when she'd taken me to get restored. With her, a boy around the same age.

They were tinkering with something, a small mech that looked designed for children.

"You're saying that's you?" I asked Leo. He'd straightened back up again after another episode—his word—where everything had transitioned to code and back. "Playing with Kaydee?"

"We grew up together, or close enough. In Starship, there weren't always enough children around, so the ones you could find became fast friends." Leo crouched, watching the two children play up close. "It's remarkable what we're able to cull from the brain."

"What?"

"I don't think I would have remembered this, back when I was alive, but there it was, nestled in my memory," Leo said, not looking my way. "You're not like us, though. A vessel is meant to be filled, and you will never forget. You will never lose what we lost."

"Perspective," I suggested.

I'd started to piece together Starship's story from Leo's tone, from the fragments picked up since I'd awoken. A grand experiment that had, over time, collapsed. I didn't know where all the humans had gone, or what the Voices were trying to do, now that their charges had seemingly died, but Starship's history? I didn't have all the notes, but I could see the story.

"We grew older," Leo said and the scene shifted to a place I knew, the University. As I'd seen it in Kaydee's memories, students clogged the hallways as professors—human ones—directed them this way and that. "For a while, we were on the same side. Solve all the problems Starship had with mechs. Metals and components were plentiful, whereas more people meant more food, more oxygen, more waste. If we could lower the population necessary to keep Starship functioning, there would be more to go around."

"How would you get the population down?" I asked the question, though the journals back in Purity seemed to provide the answer.

"And thus you find the breaking point," Leo said. "Where those new generations didn't want to be forbidden from having children of their own, while others saw the ultimate mission, one they would never live to see completed, as a goal worth sacrificing for."

The University disappeared and again we were floating in the Conduit, but instead of peaceful society happening around us, I saw the fires and the rage, people crowding the walkways shouting and throwing things at one another. Mechs, those massive guardians, cleaving their way through groups.

Throwing humans over the railings, gathering them up and chaining them together. Leo and I watched from the center, and he pointed to a young pair, a level above and watching.

"For a time, we both believed mechs could solve this problem too," Leo said. "Kaydee and I drew up answers for everything. If we needed to support more population, the mechs could grow more food, faster. A simple answer to a problem that required more."

I pointed to the rioters, fighting against the guardians and losing,

"They didn't want the mechs at all. You were turning the people into pets."

Leo looked at me with that appraising stare he had, as if he were constantly re-evaluating what he thought I was capable of and, at the same time, impressed with himself for creating me in the first place.

"Kaydee took their side," Leo said, the scene shifting again, Kaydee's apartment. Leo's younger self had designs projecting into the living room, while Kaydee had her arms raised, shouting. "She wanted us to change, make people more efficient rather than replace them with machines. Then, I didn't see her argument. Now, I think she was right."

We zoomed back out again, seeing Starship among its stars.

"You can guess the rest," Leo said. "We won. People without weapons couldn't fight against mechs, no matter their numbers. We brought the population under control, but we made mistakes. Critical errors."

I'd seen those already. Cindy. The Chancellor. The mech running Purity.

"You lost control," I said, and Leo didn't deny it. "So then what, you all died?"

"We held off for as long as we could," Leo said. "We hadn't programmed anything to hurt the ship, so Starship kept going more or less intact, and we uploaded as many minds as we were able. Kaydee didn't want to accept that fate, and, well, I can let her tell you.

"What really matters is that Starship has continued flying. We're getting very close now to our destination. Soon, we'll land. Then, the next phase will begin."

"Which is?"

"Which is why you're going to the Nursery," Leo said. "There, waiting for us to make landfall, are more than a million humans ready to be born. To make a new home."

I filtered all this into my own memory, filed it away and felt the satisfied glow that came with a mission fulfilled. This is what Alpha had wanted me to see. The question was, why?

"Alpha came here," I asked Leo. "He saw this and something changed. But I don't feel different?"

"Because I'm telling this to you," Leo said. "Not Peony. You may have noticed, she tends to take a strong hand. With Alpha, I think she pressed him too hard. Turned him against us."

Starship spun away, the grassy meadow returning, and suddenly I sat again in my same chair around the same campfire, the Voices looking back at me, at Leo.

"Do you understand?" Peony asked me. "The Nursery must be saved. Must be monitored. Every hope we have rests with those children."

I did understand. It all made sense. If you were human.

"What did Kaydee do?" I asked her mother, and Leo winced, shook his head, and then flickered away. Apparently not interested in this discussion. "Leo said she almost destroyed Starship. How?"

"My daughter was misguided," Peony said. "She lost sight of the greater objective. Perhaps some of that was my fault, but I did not teach her about the engines. About what would happen if they—"

"Peony, stop," Willis said. "Gamma, it's enough to know that Kaydee is dangerous. If you can remove her from yourself, you should do so. If not, tread very carefully. Now please, there is little time."

"Very little," Ang added. "There's no telling what's happening in the Nursery right now. We could be losing everything."

I stood, gave them a nod. Inside, I felt cold and calculating, a servant sent along on their task. Which, I was. But that didn't mean I had to like it. Had to appreciate being ordered around without a second thought.

KAYDEE HAD WARNED me against the Voices, and now I understood why. The meadow faded as I exited their domain, removed my connection from the port and returned to the bridge. The Voices only cared about their mission. They didn't care at all about me or the mechs.

We were tools to be used.

"See?" Kaydee said. She hadn't moved from her spot on the terminal, watching me as I stepped back. "A bunch of callous monsters, all of them."

"They're blind," I said. "I'm not sure they're evil."

"Wait, you'll see," Kaydee said, then a smile forced its way onto her face, lips twitching as they spread. "We should get going. Alpha's going to want to talk to us."

"To me, you mean."

"Right. To you." This time, when Kaydee snapped her fingers and vanished, the fireworks popped purple-black.

Alvie uncurled himself from the floor at my feet, and together we left the Bridge and its nova views. The name-filled hallway didn't seem as menacing now as it had before: yes, Alpha had obviously lost himself here, but looking at his scrawls, I could perhaps see why.

He wanted to be a part of something as himself, rather than the Voice's lackey. Maybe Alpha couldn't accept that role. I, however, could find pleasure in the questions beyond the mission.

The Voices wanted me to reconnect the Nursery so they could monitor their human embryos as Starship approached its destination? Fine. I could still grow, learn, come into my own while fulfilling that goal. Once the task was done, I would be free to pursue my own ends.

But before I could do anything, I had to get back to Alpha and get rid of this virus. Despite the cold logic in my head, my hands remained clenched, my lips stayed tight, and I'd noticed a twitch to my legs. As if they wanted to run.

Alpha's disease would drive me insane eventually. I didn't know how long that timer ran.

We passed back through the archways, to all the ramps diverging from the bridge, and I picked a different one at random, heading to its Conduit walkway and starting back towards the Garden. As before, the relative stillness here seemed too peaceful paired with the raging on the University's other side.

"Too quiet?" Kaydee said as I walked along, Alvie beside me. "I see that nervous tic. Like someone who needs a fix."

"What fix?"

Kaydee snapped her fingers and, in front of my eyes, two menacing mechs appeared. Each stood three meters tall, with a single limb that ran through their bodies, sporting a heavy, spiked ball on either end. Their red-eyed heads leered at me as I stopped.

"I drew these when I was a kid," Kaydee said. "And look, now I can make them real!"

"They're not real," I replied, starting forward again.

Repressing the flinch when the left mech sent its monstrous ball flying towards me took steel I didn't know I had, but I bolstered my spine by accepting any such swing, any real encounter with mechs like these would leave me mashed into pieces.

Kaydee's threat proved toothless when the ball whistled through my body and touched nothing. Alvie didn't even bark, perhaps the purest indication that I was safe.

"Well you're no fun," Kaydee said. "At least, not for now."

I shook my head, kept going. Passed more apartments with more names, though none I recognized. Guardian mechs sat still in their alcoves as I walked, apparently not seeing me as a threat. Maybe the Voices cleared my way.

Maybe Alpha. Who knew who really controlled Starship?

"Did Leo tell you that we used to be friends?" Kaydee said, bouncing along with me, purple hearts flying up with her every step. "We'd spend days together drawing up new mechs."

"Sounds exciting."

I didn't want Kaydee to talk now, didn't want to encourage her. The repeated Alpha tattoos on her body made me ill, and her voice carried a lethal laughter in it now, as if Kaydee hoped her next comment would prompt me to throw myself off the Conduit railing and into oblivion.

"It all worked so well until he didn't want to play the game anymore," Kaydee rolled her eyes. "He sided with my mother. Can you believe that? I saw the truth, Gamma. I saw that we had to use our mechs to help people. He wanted to replace them."

"Leo made me," I replied. "I can't hate him."

"That doesn't make him a good man, or you a good mech," Kaydee snapped, then disappeared.

I soaked in the silence passing through the University, and back into the Conduit's charnel quarter. A mech that looked like Cindy battled across the space from me, spitting orange, liquid fire at another mech that seemed hopelessly confused as it melted beneath Cindy's barrage.

On my level, thankfully, nothing gave me much trouble. More cleaning mechs stuck in their futile infinity. A few storefronts broken in and battered, busted mechs joining beat-up merchandise along the floors and walls. A war had been fought and nobody came for the bodies.

Alpha's mission helped me keep my focus, padding along in my loose shirt and robe, the Chancellor's drive satcheled by my side. I wondered if what I would find in there would differ from what Leo and the Voices had told me. Whether I'd been lied to.

"Later," I said to Alvie. "Alpha first, and then we find out how badly we've been manipulated."

We approached the Garden's door, which, on this level, had a tree's winding branch curling around the green emerald. And, because nothing about this could be simple, Kaydee leaned against it, watching me approach.

"Careful," Kaydee said.

As she spoke, the last walkway section between me and that Garden door split and broke away, fire sparking up from the cracks as the walkway fell, smashing into the level below and leaving me close to the edge. The wrenching sound and heat smashed against me, making me wince, cover my eyes with my hands to ward away sparks.

"Better start running," Kaydee said. "This whole level might be coming down."

Except, Alvie didn't bark. Didn't jump away and, as I watched, my little dog kept right on moving forward, standing in that open air gap between where I stood and the Garden's door.

"Alvie?" I asked the dog, and he looked back at me, curious. "How are you floating?"

Alvie, of course, wouldn't know how to answer that question. I could. I looked to Kaydee, who shrugged and threw a mischievous grin on her face.

"Fooled you," she said.

"Not nice," I replied, and stepped forward into the air.

My feet hit solid ground and, with the step, the walkway shimmered its way back into solid steel. The sparks vanished and the heat shifted away to the more distant, real fires.

Kaydee moved to block me from the Garden's door, not actually something she could do, but the razor-evil look in her eyes had me stopping anyway.

"This is as far as you get," Kaydee said. "Alpha doesn't want to see you."

"That's not your problem," I replied. "I'm going."

"No, you're not. Time to hand over the controls, G-man. It's my turn now."

Before I could come up with a reply, before I could even move, my body seized up. Not like a cramp, but a total numbness. Every limb, every motion and feeling I had vanished. As if my processor had been severed from the rest of me.

My body wasn't equipped to stand without any input, and I toppled forward, my frozen eyes giving me a great view as my face met the metal floor. My frozen ears hearing, this time, Alvie barking away. Then those, too, vanished.

AN OLDER WOMAN handed me a strange weapon. Like an old-style gun, it had a trigger. Unlike those weapons, this had two barrels and a switch crossing up and down its purple stock.

"Up for mechs, down for humans," the old woman said, then gave me a weird look. "Haven't you used one of these before?"

"No?" I said, starting to take in where I stood.

A packed room, crowded with people all assembling what looked like makeshift weapons, armor. Chattering with nervous hope. Greasy golden lamps lit the room from the sides, and I noticed looping archways connecting this space with others, like a warren.

"Hope you learn quick then," the woman glanced towards one of the entries. "They'll be coming soon now, and it's either stand here or die."

"That sounds grim."

Again I earned a strange look, then the older woman shrugged, "Guess we can't be picky. Anyone willing to fight and hold a weapon, we'll take. Now get yourself going."

She turned away from me and I realized she wore a pack loaded with more of the weapons, marching along a line of people, handing them out one at a time.

I lifted the weapon in my hands, took a closer look at it. Tried to figure out how it worked.

"C'mon, you heard her," said a man about my age, sporting a ragged bandana and a dirty jacket-pants combo that suggested a nice life before this one. "Let's go."

Lacking other direction, I followed his lead, heading through the warren and its rooms filled with people. Some rooms, like mine, holding those arming themselves, others with families or those hard at work making more of these guns.

I was in another memory. I understood that much. Something Kaydee had done, was doing to me. What this memory meant and where it would take me, I had no idea. Thankfully, the other soldier didn't notice my thoughts and went straight through to the front, a wide archway series like the Bridge.

These, though, weren't gold-rimmed. They didn't have the cherry-red security band. People shifted through them without hesitation, and my newfound friend brought me out to the Conduit, to where a trio stood against the glass, looking out into the blue-lit, manmade canyon.

Kaydee turned, her spearmint hair looking normal, her eyes that lost blue they'd been before. Her arms sporting the poetry I'd noticed when I met her, and not Alpha's name written over and over again.

"Hey Gamma," Kaydee said, throwing me a sad smile. "Ready to fight for your life?"

EIGHTEEN

FOR OURSELVES

There were, I felt, too many Kaydees.

I now had a gun, a weapon I'd never held or fired before, in my hands while another version of a digital construct housed inside my mind told me I was about to fight for my life inside myself.

"This makes no sense," I said, and held out the gun towards Kaydee. "You take this."

"Nope, all yours Gamma," Kaydee replied. "As is all this. The last holdout for your functions before Alpha's corruption eats them."

I realized, as Kaydee spoke, everyone else around us had ceased to move. To even blink. The soldier that'd guided me here stood with the same determined look on his face he'd had when we came out here, entirely unaffected by my declaration about this insanity.

"So this is my digital space again," I said.

"What's left of it," Kaydee replied. "And, also again, you can thank me for saving your ass."

"You tried to kill me a minute ago, back in the Conduit."

"Didn't we talk about how programs and memory work, Gamma?" Kaydee sent her eyes to the ceiling, then back to me. "I swear, Leo may have made you all too dumb."

"Let me guess," I said, delving into my own options.

If I was a program under attack by hostile code, what would I do? Try to destroy the enemy first, obviously, but if that proved impossible? Then I'd have to look at self-preservation. Fork myself away.

"You split off the un-corrupted part of yourself?" I asked Kaydee.

"Give the mech a prize." Kaydee snapped her fingers and a sparkling golden crown appeared in her hands. She placed it on my head, where it sat, feeling like a soft, fuzzy pillow. "You got it. Alpha's code went straight for my connection with you, so I had to hide away."

"So the thing that's been talking to me outside, in reality, that's the wrong you?"

"I'd like to think so." Kaydee glanced down the Conduit and I followed her eyes. The walkways were empty, that blue light and mist settling over nothing. "The corruption's not done, Gamma. It's taking you now. Maybe you noticed?"

"I've felt better."

"No doubt. If you're here, that means you don't have any control anymore over your actual body. Welcome to the last digital stand."

Kaydee kept up the information overload, plotting out with me how my cyberspace remnants had to defend ourselves and, maybe, wipe out the corruption here and now. When I asked why we hadn't tried this tactic earlier, when the corruption wasn't, you know, so advanced, Kaydee shook her head.

"This isn't the way you want to fight it, Gamma. I'd hoped we could find something in the University to fix the problem, like a surgical removal. Now we're fighting on its turf."

I looked back down at my weapon, no doubt developed by Kaydee's functions to keep me alive. To give us a chance.

Kaydee, though, didn't have much to offer in terms of strategy. She'd armed us with inventions she could manifest, little documents hidden away with plans for the guns. Beyond that, she'd planned to blast it out in the Conduit with the approaching force.

That wouldn't fly. I still had access to the Librarian's stories.

Some of them, anyway. They were loaded with battles, with epic tales of armies clashing in places that looked far different from the Conduit, but that felt otherwise the same.

First I split our force. Had some cross the Conduit on a nearby walkway and divide on levels above and below this one, providing overlapping firing fields. Kaydee and I took up a position on that walkway, where we could see everything coming. Could react, and sound the alarm.

Things ran fast when your troops weren't sentient. When they executed what you told them without hesitation or discussion. I found the obvious drawback when several groups entangled themselves trying to walk the same stairs up a level at the same time: I had to order the groups individually. Nuance, understanding, neither played its part in their functions.

"Kaydee," I said once the groups were assembled, several hundred armed soldiers waiting for their first chance at conflict. "Where did this setting come from? These people, these weapons, and the Conduit? It's not my space. Is it Alpha's?"

"I chose it," Kaydee said, not looking at me, watching deep in the distance. "The corruption has to come to us, so it's fighting on my turf."

"Then why this . . . turf?"

Kaydee glanced at me, shaking her head as she did so, "We win, I'll tell you. Till then, let's focus on the shooting."

"That hasn't started yet."

"It's about to." Kaydee pointed. "Here they come."

I didn't know what to expect, but I had come up with all kinds of crazy ideas for what Alpha's corruption would throw at us. An army of giant Kaydees. A fictional character menagerie like I'd used when we first fought. An endless cloud of purple gas, sickening us all.

But Alpha had his way, and I should have seen it coming.

The pollinators. Hundreds, thousands, more came crushing towards us. Their little tendrils glinting off the light as their deep purple ovals scurried along the walls, the walkways, over and under.

They massed together, bunching up as they ran, scurrying over each other like a metal wave.

As the wave approached, I tried to reach into my own imagination, tug at the framework of my digital space like I'd done before and unravel the little creatures. Simply delete them, but my attempt garnered nothing more than a few fizzles. Like blowing against a stiff breeze.

"Why can't I change anything?" I said. "This is my home!"

"Not anymore," Kaydee replied. "This is Alpha's space now. The best you've got is what's in your hands. What we already put in place."

As Kaydee's words sunk in, that I was a prisoner in my own body, I turned back to the pollinator swarm. Hefted the weapon in my hands.

"Fire!" I shouted, because I didn't know what else to say, what else to do.

I raised the gun I'd never shot before, aimed it up the wall to the right and flicked the button to switch the weapon to its mech barrel. Pulled the trigger and watched as a blue lightning bolt lanced out and burst against my target, not all that far off from where I'd aimed.

The hit, along with the first bolts from my programs, blew apart the pollinators, scattering them down into the Conduit's depths. The space in front of us filled with dive-bombing bits of pollinator metal as my little army's fusillade struck.

"This isn't going to work," Kaydee said, and I could only agree.

After the first volley, we'd barely scratched the numbers coming towards us. The pollinators came in from above and below, and with my force spread out, we'd get overwhelmed quickly.

"We have to change tactics." I fired another bolt into the metal horde. "Do we have to destroy every single one, or is there a source?"

Kaydee's eyes were wide, as afraid as I was, "I don't know Gamma, I haven't fought something like this before."

"Well, they have to be coming from somewhere," I said. "Let's group up and go up. We'll catch whatever's making these things and destroy it."

"If we live that long."

"Well we won't survive at all if we stay here." I raised my hand and corralled the other soldiers on the walkway, picked a direction at random and started running. "Let's go, on me!"

Soldier lingo poured from the Librarian's resources into my mouth, my mannerisms, as my makeshift squad formed up on me and we made our way to the Conduit's left side, joining up with the soldiers on that level and spraying lightning at the swarming pollinators.

The mechs weren't larger than my foot, but they flew in from all sides, and I saw my programs across the way collapsing as the little things rushed over them, dragging my digital partners from the walkways or simply burying them where they stood.

Worse, as each program died, I felt the effects on myself. The pieces that kept me running were being devoured. I lost feeling in my left ring finger, I forgot my own name. The pollinators were hollowing me out.

My squad, though, kept itself together. Even Kaydee had a gun now, blasting away as we moved forward, twenty-strong blazing lightning at the walls above, the walkway behind and in front. For the moment, at least, our concentrated fire kept us safe, kept the pollinators from getting too close. Their fried forms dropped and burned like so many meteors, bright wreckage smoldering as it crashed around us.

Yet, for every meter on we walked, with myself at the lead, where I could rectify my poor aim by just shooting straight ahead, I felt we were more and more alone. Behind us, fewer and fewer lightning blasts rocked forth. A look back proved the suspicion; my defensive positions simply didn't exist.

Everywhere I looked, all I saw were pollinators. The Conduit itself seemed to be made of the things, shifting metal coming after us.

"We're not going to make it!" Kaydee shouted.

"We don't have any other choice," I replied.

I nearly tripped and glanced down to see I wasn't on a walkway anymore, but was stepping on more pollinators, each one scrabbling for my feet. Stabbing my ankles with their tendrils.

The Conduit collapsed around us, a pollinator tunnel, like someone closing their fist. My other programs vanished in the swarm, and I felt my hands go numb, my legs lock, my eyes refusing to blink.

Kaydee and I stood back to back, alone now as the pollinator sea closed around us. We should have been devoured already, but the little machines hesitated, content to nibble at our edges. I couldn't feel the trigger, and with hope so obviously gone, I stopped firing all together.

"Any last tricks?" I asked Kaydee as the pollinators sealed off all light, their purple glow now the only thing we saw.

"I'm out," Kaydee said.

"Sorry," I replied. "I tried."

"We were never going to win," Kaydee said, and she turned me around to look at her. "Gamma, I know this isn't what we wanted. I'm sorry I couldn't save you."

I tried to answer Kaydee, to tell her I felt the same way, but now my mouth couldn't move. I couldn't feel anything except one. The emergency button.

Kaydee had reset me once. Now, maybe, it was my turn.

The pollinators descended, stabbing into my shoulders, my legs, my everything.

And I triggered the last routine I had.

Nothing happened. I tried again. Nothing. The pollinators kept poking, kept eating at me. Burying us beneath their endless waves. They bore Kaydee and I to the ground, and, with nothing else to do, we waited for oblivion.

Except oblivion didn't come.

The pollinators stopped. Froze. I felt their pointed ends still sticking into my shoulder, my thigh, their weight on my back and shoulders, but they didn't move.

"What's happening?" Kaydee said, her forehead touching mine. "They're not attacking? Did they lose their nerve?"

Joking, at a time like this? I tried to communicate my dire laugh to Kaydee, but my body wasn't mine.

When air escapes from a bubble, there's a popping sound. A quick lip-puckering noise. That sound began to pour in around us, but at lightning speed, as if bubbles by the thousands were exploding next to our ears. The weight on my back, on my head, disappeared, and we looked up to see the crushing purple glow had been replaced by the soft gray light that usually calmed my digital space.

The pollinators were gone. Not destroyed, just *gone*.

Above us, my crystals hung pristine, and I felt my functions coming back. Like my thawing synthetic muscles after a bath in Purity's ice cold reservoir, I came back online.

"Hey," I managed after a few seconds, with both Kaydee and I, our hands loosely holding as we looked around my wiped mind. "What happened?"

"I have no idea," Kaydee replied. "Either you have some magic, or we have a friend."

"I didn't do anything," I said. "I tried, Kaydee. I tried to erase everything. A full reset, but I couldn't. They cut it."

"You idiot," Kaydee shook her head, laughed with that crazy edge that comes from surviving certain disaster. "If you'd done that, Alpha would have taken your dummy self and injected his virus all over again."

Oh. Good point.

At any rate, it seemed like my inner self had been purged. I didn't see any pollinators, didn't see any purple anywhere. I was about to try and leap out of my personal world when Kaydee let go of my hand and stretched, little sparks flying out from her fingertips like they used to do.

I smiled, "Been a while since you've done that."

"I haven't been myself," Kaydee said, flashing a grin. "Feel like I'm a whole new program now."

"Was going to ask you about that," I said, then nodded towards the poetry running along her arms and legs. "Outside, you'd changed. All of those just said Alpha."

"That vessel's an egotistical maniac," Kaydee replied, rubbing her arms. "I guess I'm not surprised. That version of me you saw?"

"It wasn't really you, I know."

"Thing is, Gamma, it was me. At least, part of me," Kaydee said. "Alpha would have made us do what he wanted, could've had us eating from his hand, but we would've still been there, flavoring his orders with ourselves."

Not a pleasant thought. One I'd be throwing back in Alpha's face when I found him next.

"Then I'm glad you're still you, and I'm still me," I said. "I'm going back out to see what happened."

"I'll be here. Because I'm always here. Get it? It's a joke!"

I gave her a pity laugh as I left my drives behind, my white world spinning away into digital dust.

A HUGE ROYAL blue flower leered at me, dangling down from a ceiling covered with more. Water soaked up my back and legs, nearly covering my face. A lily pad, pink-white flower blooming, bobbed to my right.

I couldn't move.

Like back in my digital space, my body didn't react when I gave the order to sit up. When I told my legs to crunch under me and get me out of the wet, nothing. I shouted into a void.

"Don't move," said a svelte, deadly voice and a silver line flashed and rested against my throat. "Who are you?"

I tried to turn and see who was asking, but couldn't. My mouth didn't want to play my game either. I took the second, hoping my questioner wouldn't kill me outright, and started resetting my functions. Restarting their operations and hoping that, post corruption, all they'd need was a good on/off before popping back into action.

"I asked you a question," the voice said again, and I felt that silver dip deeper, press harder, and cut into my skin. "Answer, or you die here."

Except I couldn't.

"Are you going to answer her, or is this some clever play?" Kaydee said, popping up near me and looking over where I couldn't see. "Because she's got her weapon right against you, Gamma, and she looks like she'll use it."

If I could've told Kaydee my problems, I would have. Instead, I had to wait as my systems rebooted.

"Fine," the voice said. "Have it your way."

The silver withdrew from my neck, and I saw a thin, strong arm lift the weapon up—a weapon that, frankly, looked like a jagged metal shard, as if someone had torn a page from a steel book— rotate it around, and plunge it down towards my stomach.

My systems blinked back on. I opened my mouth, shouted, "Stop!"

She stabbed me. Sank that jagged blade into my abdomen, deep and ragged. Tore at my skin, pushed it through my back and speared me to the pond's bottom.

I'd been saved only to die again.

NINETEEN

NEW FRIEND?

Pain came, but I turned it off. Rejected its interference and tried to assess the damage. I babbled stop, stop, *stop* over and over while turning my head to look at the thing that had stabbed me.

Standing not all that tall, but with a fire in her stance that spoke to a willingness to, well, stab people, the woman sported a tighter clothing set than I'd found at Alvie's, black with bright blue seams, a belt clogged with random-looking devices, and a face I recognized.

"Delta," I said, and her orange eyes narrowed at me. "Gamma. Nice to meet you."

Alvie, my poor mech dog, heard me talking and came crawling from the room's corner, offering a wheeze-bark attesting to my character. He looked badly in need of a pet, so I tried to move and give him one.

My legs, so recently returned to me, sputtered out in my attempt as the stab's damage took its toll. Delta must have severed my connections to my lower half. Not good.

"Delta?" Kaydee muttered to my right. "They activated another one? What's wrong with them?"

"Are you with him?" Delta asked me, not moving the sword. "Alpha?"

"I'm with myself," I replied. "Mind taking that thing out of my stomach?"

"I do. I found you here with Alpha. He ran. You didn't."

I blinked at her. Here with Alpha? In the Garden? I must have moved while Alpha's virus had control of my body, must have brought myself back to him. I felt with my arms for the satchel, found it gone. The Chancellor's drive, and all of Starship's archives gone with it.

Even then, lying there, I felt the tiniest satisfaction—Alpha had set me on a mission and I'd achieved it. Brought back what he asked. I hated myself for that feeling, but couldn't deny it.

Mechs were designed to follow orders.

"He corrupted me," I said.

"I know," Delta replied, folding her arms. "A simple virus. You should have been able to defeat it."

Ouch.

"She's not very nice," Kaydee said, smirking near me. "I like her."

"Yeah, well, I didn't exactly see it coming," I said. "Long story."

"I'm not interested," Delta replied. "I need to find Alpha and destroy him. Do you know where he is?"

"Do I look like I know?"

Delta didn't look thrilled with my sarcasm, but what else was I going to say? She had me literally pinned to the floor with a blade through my stomach.

"If I pull that out, will you live?" Delta asked.

"I should."

"Too bad." Delta didn't wait, but reached over and yanked the blade out, again setting my nerves on fire. Warnings about damaged systems bled across my consciousness. "I am, unfortunately, supposed to assist you with the Nursery."

"You're off to a great start."

Delta leaned over my body, looked at the hole she'd sliced, "This isn't a small wound."

Kaydee, matching Delta's pose, agreed, "You need to get back to Leo's, or another place with some tools. Some supplies."

"Guess I'll start crawling, then," I muttered.

Delta had the sword at my neck in an instant, blade under my chin. I froze, and she knelt slow, her eyes burning holes in mine.

"Who are you talking to?" Delta asked, slow, with death a certainty should I say the wrong answer.

"My mind, Kaydee," I replied. "It's, uh, hard to explain."

"A mind." Delta pulled back, straightened. "I didn't accept them."

Kaydee's eyes bugged out at that, and she started laughing. Hard.

I, meanwhile, tried to get up. Failed.

"Can I get some help?" I asked Delta, who watched me as if I were some zoo creature.

"To do what?" Delta asked.

"She's going to be so broken, Gamma." Kaydee kept laughing, tears dropping from her eyes now. "They kept trying for so long to get you vessels right, and now their last one's gone rogue."

"I'm glad you find this amusing," I said to her, then looked at Delta, whose irritation showed itself as she ground her blade's tip into the ground. "Please, I know I sound crazy. Just, get me out of here and to somewhere I can fix my legs. Then you can go on your murder-spree or whatever."

"It's not a 'spree'," Delta replied, but she at least let her blade go and came over to me. "I'm going to kill Alpha, and then you and I will fix the Nursery. Those are the objectives."

"Yes, I'm aware." I reached up with my hands, and Delta grabbed them both, hard and fast, and yanked me upright. "But I won't be helping you because YOU STABBED ME."

If my sudden shout had any effect on Delta, she didn't show it. She did, however, lift me up and throw me over her left shoulder, then picked up her blade with her right hand and started walking from the pond, as my wet clothes dripped all over everything.

"This is a little demeaning," I said as we went.

"I could let you crawl," Delta replied.

"Nope, I'm fine up here. Disregard."

Our Garden level seemed to alternate between flowery rooms and ones filled with vegetables laid row against row, and stacked upon one another. My systems worked well enough to identify differing species, with those needing less light sitting further down the racks from the tops, where those yellow globes sprinkled nourishment. The luminescent butterflies appeared again too, bobbing around between the plants.

I didn't see any pollinators, nor Alpha.

Delta seemed content to stay quiet as we moved, and every time a question came to my mouth, I killed it. One does not interrogate when one is being carried like a child by a very strong woman with a sword.

Instead, I dug a little deeper into my own systems. Checked out to see whether Alpha's virus had left any nasty surprises behind, and things seemed clear. My files were in order, the Librarian's records all present and accounted for. Kaydee's too.

Which prompted a question I couldn't resist.

"How did you do it?" I asked, my head looking back at rows of radishes as Delta made it to the Garden's central pit. "How did you get rid of the virus?"

Delta turned, started walking again, and I felt her sigh, "You should have a routine built inside you, made to attack foreign bodies. It is effective."

I poked around for what Delta had said. Actually rooted around my programs, restored from their pollinator-prompted oblivion, to see what Delta talked about. It didn't take long to find, a function hanging out in the same space as the big reset.

"And it's harmless?" I asked.

"If you run it quickly," Delta replied. "Alpha's virus would have hidden it from you. I knew where to look, because I pay attention to my abilities."

Ouch, again. I'd have to be more careful around Delta, or she might deadpan me to death with her comebacks.

With Delta carrying me the entire way, we left the Garden and headed back into the familiar fire-and-brimstone section of the Conduit, though I noticed zero mechs made any effort to approach Delta. She, also, didn't seem to care about Starship's continued chaos.

I'd hoped to find myself back at Leo's lab, scrounging for parts amid the broken molds and empty rooms. Instead, Delta bee-lined for a mech supply shop who's name had long since been carved into trash that, now, littered its own entry.

Delta crunched the glass with her boots. I continued to feel useless.

"Just me," Kaydee said, springing up prismatic sparkles with her every step. "Or is Delta kind of a badass?"

"And I'm not?"

"Don't take this the wrong way, Gamma," Kaydee replied. "But you're not much of a threat."

"I'm not a threat?" I said, stung.

"You're not," answered Delta, before she slung me off her shoulder and set me down on a crap-covered workbench.

The garbage poked me in the back, along my legs, but otherwise wasn't all that bad. Delta, after setting me down, stepped back, folded her arms, and watched.

Around us, parts dangled from the ceiling, sat scattered on shelves, some broken and some not. Tools sat chain-linked to the workbenches, waiting for use. A dirty sign near the shop's back listed prices, by both time and tools required.

"Are you, uh, waiting for something?" I asked Delta, as she'd made no further moves.

"For you to fix yourself, so we can leave," Delta replied. "I brought you here as you asked."

"Right," I answered slow, trying to figure out a smart way to phrase my request and failing. "See, here's the problem. I can't fix myself without your help."

"Do you ever not need my help, Gamma?" Delta asked.

"She's got a point," Kaydee added.

"Yeah, well, you stabbed me, remember?" I said. "Help fix up my connections and I'll be able to fend for myself."

Delta rolled her eyes with more exaggeration than I'd ever seen and stepped back up to the workbench, looked down at my stomach.

For the first, and possibly last time, I saw confusion, then frustration cross her face.

"What's wrong?" I asked. Maybe she'd damaged more than I realized. Maybe my walking days were done. "Is it too broken?"

"I . . . don't know," Delta said. "I'm unable to find out how to repair you."

Strange. I had all that data readily available, right in one of my main files. A complete mapping of my inner workings, and how to fix them. Delta's too, for that matter.

"You don't have the files?" I asked. "They should be—"

"I don't have them," Delta snapped, planting her fists hard on the table. "They're missing. Or they were never there."

"Whoa, hey, don't worry. I can tell you what to do, if that's okay?" I said.

Delta didn't say anything for a moment, gave the hole in my gut a long look. I had the feeling she was thinking whether she could wing it, stitch me back together by instinct. When her dark lips pressed together, I waited for the action to begin, instead Delta looked my way and gave a short nod.

"Let's get started, then," Delta said.

My internal network gave me a very clear diagram explaining which parts needed fixing, which wires needed re-tying and how to solder back the plate that'd split from my upper hip. Each one came with a section in Leo's files, and I called up the images, watched before my eyes as they played, invisible to Delta and anyone else.

I narrated. Dished out instructions to my one-time killer and life-saver. Delta followed with crisp precision, offering terse questions if I gave an unclear next step. Her fingers, so good with that larger sword, proved equally adept navigating my computational crevices, sealing together my severed systems without an error.

"Thanks for putting me back together," I said when Delta completed the operation and my synthetic skin began healing over the wound. "It's going to take a little while before I can go again. Mind waiting?"

"For what?" Delta said. "I can go and destroy Alpha and then come back for you."

"Or, you can hang on a minute and have some help."

"You would hinder me."

"First, be nice," I said. "Second, it's not just me. You'd get Alvie too, and I've seen him tear through a few mechs now."

The hobo-dog hadn't left the table's side since I'd been on it, but at his name, Alvie perked up. Jumped onto the table next to me and offered Delta a tail wag.

"He doesn't look dangerous," Delta said, peering at the dog.

Her look disturbed me. Delta was, so clearly, evaluating Alvie on his merits as a death dealer and nothing more. Whatever Leo had done to give me compassion and perspective, the process hadn't been repeated with the last vessel in his collection.

"What do you think you are?" I asked Delta.

"A mech," Delta stated. "Obviously."

"Sure, but your purpose? That's something I struggled with when I woke up. Why was I here, who were the Voices, that sort of thing."

"Why does that matter?" Delta said. "We have a mission. We are programmed to complete it. You're getting distracted."

I chewed on that for a bit while my processor established connection with my left leg, which twitched on the table. Was Delta a blunt-force instrument, designed to carry out a programmed slaughter and little else?

"This is what happens when you have a vessel without a mind," Kaydee said, leaning on the table next to me. "They're stuck. You have to work so much harder on them."

"You say that like you've worked with other vessels before?"

Delta caught the words, watched me, but seemed to understand I wasn't speaking to her.

"You four aren't the first models," Kaydee said. "Like I said, everyone was caught up in making better mechs. Why not make some that could adapt to all kinds of requests? Turns out, that's really hard."

My right leg connected, twitched. The cut had healed, I could move. But I didn't. As soon as I took myself off this table, Delta would be off and running. Right now, I had a captive to interview.

"What do you think happens after we connect the Nursery?" I asked Delta.

"We'll get another mission."

"And another after that? Forever?"

"Until, most likely, we are destroyed," Delta said. "That is our purpose."

I laid my head back on the table. There had to be a way to open Delta's mind, get her to see that Starship had more to offer than blind obedience. She might be a mech, yes, but she could think for herself, if given the opportunity.

"Why are you pushing so hard for this?" Kaydee asked me. "Let her hunt down Alpha, get the Nursery online. Then she can go off and do her own thing for all that you care."

"What if your next mission is to kill me?" I asked Delta, partly to question Kaydee's stance.

"Then you will die."

"Then you will be alone," I replied.

Because that, there, was the real reason underlying this whole questioning. I'd nearly died several times on Starship, all because I hadn't had a friend—Alvie excepted—to help me. Delta seemed like a good mech to have around when things became difficult, so here I was, trying to build a relationship with a vessel that had all the good nature of a rock.

"I don't care." Delta pointed at my stomach. "Are you ready? If you are not, I am leaving."

I swung my legs off the table, "Look at that! Guess I'm ready to go."

Delta eyed me, "Good."

My soon-to-be friend led us back to the Garden, a journey interrupted only once when a busted mech droning on about theft and stopping thieves hovered into our path. Standing only a meter high, but coated in cameras and arms holding various bindings, the mech already sprayed sparks from its dented speaker.

Delta didn't even let the thing finish its accusation, something about the repair shop we'd just been inside, before she swung that jagged blade with both hands and cleaved the mech in two. Its components scattered across the walkway, and Delta went right on through.

"Well then," Kaydee said. "I'm impressed."

"See why I'm trying to stay on her side?" I said.

"I do, and I approve."

Back inside the Garden, we made our way through the blue flowers and pond-filled spaces to the central pit. No pollinators crossed our path, unfortunately. I'd been wanting to find one, just so I could kick it. Or crush it. Or use my razor sharp teeth to—

"Pay attention," Delta said. "Alpha is dangerous, and this is his home. I will not save you again."

"Wouldn't you though, if I really needed it?"

Delta swung the blade towards my throat in what was, apparently, a favorite move for her, "I fulfilled that mission. Now I must destroy Alpha and connect the Nursery. You are optional."

"Noted," I said, gently pushing the blade away. "You said Alpha ran when you found me?"

Delta lowered her weapon, grimaced, "He used those small machines to hinder my pursuit when I arrived at your pond. Yet, if not for the Voices, I wouldn't have found you at all."

"The Voices? What did they do?"

"They watched," Delta resumed her walk, this time making for the elevators on the floor's far side. "Alpha seems to know where their eyes are. You, however, do not."

"Wasn't aware I needed to."

Delta didn't reply, and we kept on. I mentioned that I'd seen Alpha up several levels, where things were less marsh-like and more jungle. Delta didn't have any other suggestions, so we boarded the glass-wrapped lift and I punched in a level.

For being such an aggressive vessel, Delta tended to keep her blade tip in the ground a lot. She stood not like she planned to get attacked at any moment, but rather like she didn't care if the attack came. As if Delta could deal with any assault, and do so without keeping her nerves taut all the time.

Until I spoke, anyway.

"You've noticed that too?" Kaydee said as the lift rose. "Every time a word comes out of your mouth, she gets tense. Maybe you're that annoying."

"Or I'm speaking difficult truths."

"Your truths are not difficult," Delta said without looking at me as the elevator trundled past a level seemingly dedicated to a thick pine forest. "I do not trust you."

"Don't trust me?" I said. "Why not?"

"Because you allowed yourself to be corrupted by Alpha, and because you regard the Voices with less respect than they deserve."

"Not possible," Kaydee muttered.

Trying to determine who to reply to first was becoming an issue, one solved for me by the elevator reaching its destination and Delta sprinting out as soon as the doors opened.

"What are you doing?" I shouted after her.

"He is here!" Delta snapped back, raising her sword in both hands and dashing off into the jungle.

"Cool," I said, and because I didn't want to die alone, I followed.

TWENTY

INTO THE ENEMY

While sprinting through the jungle after Delta, jumping over tree roots and ducking beneath lingering vines, I tried to address a niggling concern.

"Hey," I said to Kaydee, who wandered alongside me, able to walk through the offending greenery without issue. "Peony. The Voice. Is she your mother?"

"Technically," Kaydee said. "As in, she created me. From a biological standpoint."

"Sounds like you two had a healthy relationship."

"Is now really the best time, Gamma?" Kaydee asked as I crashed through a bush after getting my foot caught in a leafy tendril.

Thorns gouged my synthetic skin, which, conveniently, closed itself in rapid fashion. I stood up, brushed myself off, and went back to moving, following Delta's footprints as she dashed towards the level's center.

"I'm finding there's never a good time to have any of these conversations," I said. "So why not now?"

"Fine, whatever you want, G-man," Kaydee said, a little cloud spitting lightning floating over her head. "She's my mom. She's why I'm here at all."

"We covered that. Biology."

"No, moron. The digital me. I wasn't exactly in Starship's good graces, but she had me put into the program anyway."

"Leo might have mentioned you took a wrong turn."

"Not a wrong turn." Kaydee scowled, and I nearly decked myself on another branch turning to see it. "You're going to kill yourself. Let's do this later."

Before I could protest, declare I'd definitely watch where my feet were stepping, Kaydee vanished into her digital hiding hole. I wished I could do that too, just pop away whenever existence became inconvenient, but instead I had to follow Delta's shouting, pushing through some overgrown ferns to reach the level's center.

Alpha, doing what he apparently did far too often, stood in a hanging pool, letting the waterfall crash over his shoulders. Delta, blade held at her waist, stood inside the safety railing demanding Alpha abandon his pool party and come down to be gutted.

Alpha, unsurprisingly, didn't accept the offer.

When the vessel saw me step up beside Delta, though, Alpha did slosh forward. Put his hands on the pool's edge and look at me.

"Thank you," Alpha said.

"For what?" I replied.

"The Chancellor's drive. I downloaded its contents. They were exactly what I needed."

"Why?" I asked, once again feeling like all I could do was ask questions.

"It doesn't matter," Delta said. "He dies now."

Before I could say that, perhaps, it did matter, if one had a broader view of things, Delta skipped up to the railing and leaped off with such perfect grace that I couldn't help but be jealous.

Mid-flight, Delta brought her sword in a slashing swing that ought to have lopped Alpha's head clean off. Instead, Alpha threw himself forward, out of the pool and, with a nifty kick, launched his mech self down another level. Delta's sword struck the pool's edge, scattering sparks, rocks, and water.

"Stop running!" Delta shouted after Alpha, before jumping down after the vessel.

Meanwhile I stood at the railing, Alvie by my side.

"You know, I tried jumping once," I said to the dog. "Let's take the lift this time."

Alvie wheeze-barked his approval, and off we went, retracing our steps. As I ran, I could hear, maybe feel Delta's continuing demands from beneath us. The yelling served as a good indicator my vessel friend—I'd decided to call her that, Delta's own opinions notwithstanding—was still alive. And that Alpha still ran.

The lift dropped us down a level quick, and as its glass parted, I went forward, fully expecting to run for a while longer.

I did not expect Alpha to be coming towards me, arms pumping in a dead sprint through the misty cloud forest.

"Hello there," I offered. "Get'em, Alvie."

My trusty robo-dog darted forward, yapping with all his steel puppy energy. Alpha caught the sound, saw Alvie, and, as the dog leaped for a throat-ripping attack, dropped into a rolling dive. Alvie, ever one to go with gusto, sailed over Alpha and vanished into a white-flowering thicket.

"Move away, Gamma," Alpha said as he pulled up from his jump. "She's the Voices' tool."

"Yeah, well, so am I," I replied, and took a swing at Alpha's head.

Alpha ducked the punch and delivered one to my abdomen, which I took with all the bone-crunching regret one musters when they feel their insides ground to metaphorical dust. More by accident than skill, I fell forward onto Alpha, systems blaring alerts as my recently repaired rig fell out of joint. Still, my arms were strong.

I bore Alpha to the ground in my clumsy, desperate tackle. Looking for options, I rammed my head into his, and Alpha growled even as his metal teeth left marks on my forehead.

"This is a stupid fight," Alpha said, pushing against me, trying to work his legs up under my stomach. "We ought to be allies!"

"Shoulda tried asking first," I replied, bearing my weight on his left arm and feeling something snap at in his elbow. "Friends don't infect their, uh, friends."

So my fiery conversation needed some work. I'd have to ask Kaydee to teach me sometime, maybe when Alpha wasn't busy pushing and rolling us over. His left arm, at least, hung limp. I'd done something right.

Alpha pulled back his right fist and I grabbed it with both of my arms, holding his strike level. We strained against each other, but I suppose the magic that comes with being the same model meant I couldn't shove back Alpha, and neither could he push away my defense.

"I wanted you to understand," Alpha said, his long red hair spilling down between us. "We're tools to them. To all of them. We ought to own ourselves."

"That's what drove you crazy?" I said. "Who cares? What else are you going to do?"

That Alpha would let himself be pulled to some ideological fervor over a philosophical crisis about destiny was an insult to mechs, to me. The whole point of mechs, of vessels, was to avoid the quandaries that afflicted biological, sentient life. I could be curious, I could wonder why, but I still did what needed doing.

Burning it all down because you felt miffed, even when you had it all?

Ridiculous.

"Then it didn't work," Alpha said, and he let up. My momentum pushed him back, toppled him against the elevator. I stood, ready for him to continue to fight, but he didn't move. "You didn't see what I did, the poison they're planning. If you continue to be their pawn, if you can't think for yourself, then Starship is done."

I spread my arms in a shrug as Alvie came, finally, from the thicket, wheeze-barking the whole way to my side. I pointed towards

Alpha, and my dog did as asked and bit into Alpha's ankle, keeping hold. No more running.

"Starship's getting close to its destination, is what they told me," I said. "Seems like the Voices are doing what they can to keep Starship in the game."

"For them," Alpha protested. "Not for us."

I rolled my eyes, heard feet coming up behind, and whirled to see Delta, blade still held in a crazy overhead slaughter-stance, charging towards us.

"Stop," I said, then repeated, then shouted as Delta went right by me.

I grabbed her arms as she brought the blade down, caused Delta's swing to miss Alpha by centimeters, leaving a nice gash in the elevator's glass.

"He's done," I said to Delta. "We've caught him. So take a breath. Chill, if you know what that even means."

"I don't," Delta replied, but she lowered her blade anyway, keeping her eyes locked on Alpha. "He should be dead already. Why haven't you killed him?"

"Because if we do that, we don't get to know what he knows," I said. "Alpha's been awake longer than any of us. I want to learn what he's been doing."

Alpha gave me a sad look, "It doesn't matter what I've been doing. What counts is what you're going to do."

"Yeah, I know," I said, crouching in front of him, an idea crystalizing in my mind. "Now, stop me if you've seen this before."

With confusion etched on their faces, Alpha and Delta looked as I pressed my fingers together, made the jack, reached behind Alpha's ears and jumped into the vessel's space.

THE PURPLE ROCKS flowed up and around me, some dwindling down, their tips dripping gold stars to the damp ground. A breeze tickled my skin, while a moldering smell permeated the air, the bioluminescent, blue-glowing mushrooms littering the floor having their way with things.

"Wow, I'm impressed," Kaydee said, standing next to me. "Can't say I thought you'd be the one to hack another vessel. You always seemed too passive."

"People change," I replied.

"And you pulled me along for the ride?"

"Don't thank me yet." I pointed ahead, to where the tunnel turned. "I brought you because I don't know what's coming."

"Oh, you need me now?" Kaydee said, folding her arms as her spearmint hair darted this way and that in the wind. "I thought you had Delta."

"She's not the subtle type," I said. "I'm surprised she's let Alpha keep his head this long."

"Then I guess we shouldn't count on her keeping cool much longer." Kaydee snapped her fingers, two of those anti-mech rifles appearing in her hands. She held out one to me. "Let's go, hotshot."

Right. I had to remember that, while I didn't control Alpha's digital space, I could still affect my own. When the time came, I might need to pull out all the stops. Make some magic. Some other cliche that the Librarian had in his files.

Around the bend, rather than more tunnel, we came to an end. The cavern opened onto a mountainside looking over a massive valley, one that looked like it had so much life. Gigantic trees, swooping silver links between them glittering as three giant turquoise stars in the sky provided the light. A river cut through the valley's center, its waters rushing hard as they went down the slope to our right and down through the verdant landscape.

Except, for all that beauty, the whole picture felt wrong. Not in a drastic sense, but in that sense you get in your neck, your nose and your nerves. Alpha may have made this valley, but it hadn't always been like this.

"You're feeling it too, right?" I asked Kaydee, who nodded as she chewed on her bottom lip.

"Gamma, I feel like I keep saying this, but we're in trouble."

"So what else is new?"

"No," Kaydee shook her head. "Maybe, maybe I've been wrong. Leo said the vessels failed when they had too much knowledge, too fast. But I think it's time I told you the truth."

"Right now? While we're literally inside another mech's guts?"

"I'm not sure we'll get another chance."

When I didn't object, Kaydee took the moment and went to the cave's edge, leaning out a little into the open space. She looked back at me, "Watch close."

Kaydee threw out her arms and, from them, came her usual sparkle array. This time, the golden, blinking nodes burst out into the air until they formed a crackling circle. The sparks kicking off grew bigger, brighter until the whole circle filled in and I had to shield my eyes. By the time I had my hand up and covering, though, the light dimmed.

Like a fire simmering to its coals, the sparkles cooled to a waved golden ring around a bronzed-black center, a giant circle floating in the sky. I went up next to Kaydee to get a closer look, wondering what she'd done.

"Okay," Kaydee said when I joined her. "Going to be honest. The sparkle effects were unnecessary. I could just tell you, but you're a vessel. Not only a mech. Seeing is going to help."

"I thought it was pretty cool."

"That's 'cause you're a good vessel, Gamma. Now, pay attention."

The golden ring's inside shimmered, then faded in, like a movie, to a scene I recognized. Humans, most looking worse for wear, gathered in crowded rooms passing food, drink, and weapons while the camera moved. Some flipped the camera a nod, a wave, but nobody bothered with a smile or anything other than bleak eyes.

I recognized the rifles; the ones I'd held, the ones we held in Alpha's insides. The camera, just like I had, passed by the refugees and out into the Conduit, where several more humans, heavily armed, waited by the glass railing.

"Think it's today, Kaydee?" said one of them, a younger man on her left. "I feel it."

"They're running out of time," someone behind the camera replied, and I realized we were watching Kaydee's memory, from her perspective. "We have the Nursery, and we're getting closer to the engines. They'll have to bargain if we get control."

"Then we have to hold them a little longer." The man reached out, put an arm past the camera. "Think your vessels can handle it?"

"I literally made them for this," Kaydee said. "They've done well so far. I even updated their tactics last night. Ready for ambushing."

Her friend flashed a fiery grin, the only one in the place that seemed to have any hope left. Kaydee joined him at the glass railing, looking down the Conduit.

"I'm showing you this part," Kaydee told me. "So you know that I had total faith. I thought we were safe. Better than safe, I thought we might win."

The screen shimmered, the picture warped, and we were back in those rooms, only now smoke filled the picture. Shouts and crying echoed off the metal. Kaydee's view looked at the ceiling, seemingly unable to move.

A head came into the picture and looked down at her. A man, but without human teeth, with eyes that saw too straight for human eyes, and skin too perfect for human skin. He raised a rifle, one of Kaydee's, and aimed it straight at her face.

The shot never fired. Something struck the mech from behind. Kaydee's view caught the light spray as additional fire coated the man, burying him beneath a hot red laser bath. The mech caught fire, disintegrating on the edges of Kaydee's vision.

Seconds passed with the mech's burning body the only thing in view, until another face appeared. One I recognized. Leo bent over Kaydee's body, sadness etching in between his stubble.

"You picked the wrong side, Kaydee," Leo said, reaching down to check her pulse. "I told you, dammit. We knew you couldn't push them that far. You knew too, and now so does everybody else."

The screen flickered dark again, sat solid black in the air.

"He saved you," I said. "Leo."

"Leo didn't save me," Kaydee snapped. "He gave me a little more time to screw up, is all. That's not the point. What I'm trying to show you is that you're fragile, Gamma. You get a whiff of the wrong program and you get corrupted. You'll change."

"Okay, so I stay away from the wrong programs."

"It's worse than that," Kaydee nodded back towards the screen. "What I didn't say in that memory, what I didn't show, was that I knew I was taking the chance with the vessels. I didn't take any chances with the others."

"The others?"

"Every mech on Starship has a purpose coded into them. Their jobs. They also get tons of code telling them what not to do," Kaydee waved her hand and the screen dissolved into little falling stars. "Get rid of the guard rails, and a mech's going to do whatever it can to fulfill that prime directive."

"Like kill people if they get in the way."

"Exactly," Kaydee replied. "What you're seeing here is the seed I planted way too long ago now. A little creeping corruption, eating away at the functions and routines that kept Starship safe."

I backed away from Kaydee, suddenly regretting that I'd called her into this adventure. With the barest thought, I set part of my processing to finding everything inside me that Kaydee had managed to touch. I'd delete it all, remove her and any trace of her corruption.

"Why?" I couldn't help but ask. "Why do that?"

"Because the mechs were ruining us," Kaydee said. "I never dreamed that humans wouldn't be able to fight back. That we'd actually lose."

"But you did."

"I guess so," Kaydee said. "I never saw that part." She held up a hand, shot a sparkle at me that splashed into a bunch of neon orange roses when it hit my chest. "Don't worry, Gamma. I can't spread that corruption now. I don't know how. That part's locked away in the memories I don't have. My mom saved the pure part of me."

What was I supposed to do with her now? Either I trusted someone who'd brought ruin to the very ship we were both depending on to survive, or I destroyed her and lost my link to Starship's intricate balance. Without Kaydee, I'd have no idea what to do, where to go.

How to be.

"Can we remove it?" I asked, pointing to the valley. "Can we fix him?"

"I don't know, Gamma," Kaydee replied, hefting her rifle. "But we can damn sure try."

TWENTY-ONE

CUTTING THE STRINGS

Descending to the valley floor came easily, as the rocky slope seemed to make itself walkable for us. Or maybe our own feet adjusted to accommodate, a virtual reflex in this virtual space. Regardless, I enjoyed the view, surreal qualities aside, compared with Starship's more cramped environs.

As we approached the bottom, the trees and meadows that seemed so large from above turned out to be more grove-like in their size, but dense. Alpha had grown himself a lush digital orchard, not a massive forest. Birds—though I never saw any—chirped within the leaves, while the river provided a burbling undercurrent.

"Any idea where we go?" I asked. "There's not exactly a trail."

"I think we'll find one," Kaydee replied. "Remember, everything we're seeing is Alpha's code come to a kind of life. Every function's going to call back to the center, we just have to wait till they try."

If I knew what 'calling back to the center' meant, I'd probably have greeted Kaydee's statement with more excitement. Instead, I took her words as an opportunity to relax and let the rifle drift down by my side.

"Pretty good that we caught Alpha before Delta sliced him in half," I said.

"Is it? Because destroying him would've been a lot easier."

"But we—"

I stopped, blinked and looked again. There, beyond several trees bearing rounded, purple apples, stood Alpha. He looked pristine, no scratches and scars on his skin.

"I woke up like that," I said to Kaydee as we both took cover behind nearby berry bushes. "Felt that way too."

"Confused and pointless?"

"Not quite pointless . . ."

Alpha's head jerked up like he'd heard a sound, and then he performed the same motions I had when I'd met the Librarian. Testing my limbs. Alpha finished the set and wandered off, striding away from us.

"Follow?" I asked.

"Hell yes, follow," Kaydee said, hitching up the rifle. "You wanted a trail, here's the trail."

We crept along behind Alpha as he made several stops, reaching his hands out and placing them onto nothing in the air, palms out and close together. Kaydee shot me a look that said she understood as well as I did: Alpha went to molds, all three. He would've had his minds, then.

After the third, Alpha stopped, looking towards something he could see and we obviously couldn't. He stood there, frozen for a long minute.

And then he vanished in an explosive burst as Kaydee shot him in the back.

I dropped my weapon, sprang up with my hands out wide, ready to accuse Kaydee of blowing the whole mission until she slapped a hand on my shoulder and pressed me back down.

"He'd locked up," Kaydee said. "Whatever part of him running that memory hit something it couldn't process. If we didn't delete it then, Alpha might not continue."

"Continue?"

"Call it a hunch," Kaydee replied, then pointed, with the rifle, deeper into the orchard. "Alpha's trying to help us, but he's running into bugs. We need the code to skip over the broken bits, to keep running through until we find where the errors are coming from."

"I don't understand?"

"Gamma, someday you're going to have the time to read those files of yours, and then you'll get it." Kaydee shrugged. "Until then, let the experts lead."

Even though entering Alpha's digital space on a rescue mission had been my idea, Kaydee was the expert? I thought about objecting, but Kaydee's eyes went over my shoulder and when she nodded, I forgot about the fight.

Alpha had appeared again, looking different this time. Bearing scratches, a little bloody, with his hands gripping something we couldn't see. We crept up after him again, though Alpha didn't seem to be aware of his own surroundings, so I wasn't sure how much our stealth mattered.

The vessel went to a grassy meadow's edge and stood between two trees, looking upward. Over Kaydee's whispered objections, I circled around to the side, trying to get a view of Alpha's face. I had to see if his wild grins, those bugged eyes that showed Alpha's mental collapse had appeared.

But no. Alpha looked, so much as any vessel could, like a normal human. His lips, though, moved. Speaking in a conversation with someone, but one word came up enough for me to recognize the form in his lips:

Nursery.

Alpha advanced into the meadow, but didn't make it more than a few steps before his face changed. Went from cautious curiosity to a wide-eyed stare, then a determined set. His arms moved, swinging that phantom object. His legs followed suit, dancing around as if in a pitched fight with something I couldn't see.

Kaydee made her way opposite me, and from both sides, we

watched Alpha struggle against his invisible foe. Whenever the vessel took hits, he would launch himself to the side or crumple to the ground only to struggle back up. If we weren't in such a weird, dire place, the whole act would have seemed hilarious.

Until Alpha stopped again, his hands on his throat, pulling against some invisible grip. At first, Alpha's mouth worked, yelling something silent at his opponent. Then his body went slack, collapsed to the ground.

Kaydee and I looked across the clearing at each other, then back at the body on the grass, red locks interspersed with the silver-green blades.

I flicked a thumb towards my face and Kaydee nodded, raising the rifle to cover me as I emerged from my leafy spot and went towards the downed vessel. I held my own rifle up in as best an approximation of a soldier as I could muster, though the barrel bounced along my chin and my finger kept slipping off the trigger.

From above, and not all that far above, Alpha's body looked done. The life knocked out of it. I looked to Kaydee for advice, standing over Alpha's apparent corpse, but she gave me a confused look in response. No ideas. Two would-be masters of digital worlds were lost in this one.

So I did what any enterprising mech would do: I gave Alpha a light kick.

Alpha jumped up like an animal caught by surprise, pushing off the ground with his hands and springing into a crouch, before straightening, looking right at me, and doing nothing. Frozen, like the last one.

"He's stuck again," I said to Kaydee, edging around Alpha's frozen body. "Did you see what happened there?"

"We caught the last trigger," Kaydee said, joining me in the clearing. "Someone woke Alpha up, like you."

"The thing that killed him, you mean?"

"Maybe? Probably?" Kaydee raised her rifle. "Two locks this close together is bad. Alpha's falling apart, Gamma. His core routines are breaking."

"I'm not entirely sure what that means?"

"I'm saying we have to wrap up and get out of here, before whatever's destroying him makes its way to you."

Kaydee raised her rifle and pulled the trigger, blowing the frozen Alpha into digital dust.

"He was saying 'Nursery'," I said as we both looked at the indented grass where Alpha had been. "I think he made it there."

"And did real well," Kaydee replied. "You know, I've been thinking, and this kinda confirms it, maybe we should just let Delta handle this."

"Alone?"

"Sure, she seems capable enough."

"What would we do?"

Kaydee grinned, "Gamma, I might've poisoned Starship, but I think I can find the cure. We could bring the guard rails back to the mechs, stop their destruction. We'd run the place, then."

Leo must not have given me power fantasies, because the way Kaydee's eyes glittered as she spoke about control didn't get me all warm and fuzzy. Repairing the mechs sounded like a good plan, however, so following Kaydee's ambitions that far made some sense.

And if my friend had a little bit of a hard side to her, well, Kaydee couldn't get out of my memory banks, so I figured she couldn't cause too much harm.

We didn't have a chance to talk about much else, because the next Alpha broke through the trees on the meadow's opposite side, going at a dead sprint. The vessel charged right on by us, crashing back into the forest and continuing on, Kaydee and I turning and running after.

Alpha hadn't stopped to look at us as he'd run past, which I took to mean keeping quiet was a bogus game. Kaydee apparently agreed as we took to a straight pursuit, which, given that Alpha's feet kicked up purple dirt clouds with every footfall in his ludicrous run, was the only way we could've kept up.

Not for the first time, I appreciated the impossible physics inherent to the digital world. Kaydee and I could fly, our feet barely touching the ground but, with a bit of thought, that touch carried us for meters at a time.

At first I didn't notice as we careened through trees and across the river, heading up the valley, but the landscape changed around us. We left the orchard behind as the trees grew larger, their leaves crowding together over our heads to block out the silver stars. The birds stopped chirping, replaced by a pulsing beat, like a human heart pumping through the ground.

"Where's he going?" Kaydee shouted as the grass ended, dying away and being replaced by dusty purple-gray dirt. "I didn't see this from the cave."

I hadn't either, but I had my own suspicions. When the Chancellor had shot me straight into my own, damaged data, I'd appeared among sparse gray rocks not too unlike this, a black sky overhead. I hadn't known what to make of it then, but seeing Alpha's growing ruin, I made the connection.

The trees on either side grew so thick that we couldn't see between the trunks, and then they weren't even trunks at all, but a solid wall shifting from tan to slate gray. Ahead, Alpha kept running at his breakneck pace.

We followed.

I looked back once. The need for perspective overwhelmed me as those featureless walls, the space black sky, the endless rubble and dust on the ground conferred zero detail about where we were going and how fast we were getting there. I whipped my head around quick, just hoping to see the valley, give my eyes a taste of the purple and silver and green.

The trees had closed behind us too.

"We're trapped," I said to Kaydee as we ran. "Don't know if that was part of your plan."

"My plan?" Kaydee said. "You're the one that jumped into Alpha!"

"I didn't think it would be this hard." In truth, I hadn't thought much at all except that there were, to my knowledge, four vessels on Starship and losing one seemed a tragedy. "I thought we could find a space like mine and fix it."

As if answering my own question, the darkness ran out, instantly, into a white plain. There had been no giveaway, no transition or clue that, ahead, we would hit this switch. One instant, a gloomy, infinite tunnel to nowhere. The next, an endless void.

"You're trying to save me," Alpha announced, looking at us. "You can't."

We slowed our run, and I noticed the void wasn't quite empty, but instead fluttered as our feet hit the ground, tiny ripples coming off our steps that faded away. Kaydee and I pulled up alongside each other, a couple meters away from Alpha and locking eyes with the vessel.

"If we can't fix you," I said, choosing to be blunt. "Then Delta's going to chop off your head."

"Either her or someone else," Alpha spread his hands in a lazy shrug. "I tried to follow their orders. I tried and I failed and now you're going to do the same thing."

"How does failing to reconnect a Nursery turn you into a corrupting wreck of a mech?" Kaydee shot back.

"Because the Nursery isn't what you think," Alpha replied. "It will break you, as it broke me. When I went back to the Voices, begging for relief, they could not fix me. I tell you Gamma, they will not fix you either."

"So forget them." I said. "We came through that valley, that tunnel. We're here now. Maybe we can fix you?"

"If you want to fix me," Alpha replied. "Then do what I couldn't. Do what the Voices want. Perhaps if you give them their victory, they'll give me what I need."

"Which is?"

"What they have."

I didn't understand, but Kaydee raised her rifle, aimed it at Alpha.

"Kaydee?" I asked as Alpha raised his hands, a small smile on his face.

"He wants to get into Starship's systems," Kaydee said. "Like the Voices."

"What would you do with that power?" I asked.

In response, Alpha raised a hand and snapped his fingers. Around us, the white disappeared, replaced by the Conduit, with us floating along its wide bulk. No fires here, no mechs running amok, though mechs there were.

The machines worked together, going along without hurry, without violence. Alpha kept us moving slow down the Conduit's length, making sure we could see how perfect things appeared to be.

"The humans made Starship to carry their species to another world," Alpha said. "Instead, Starship will give *our* species a home of our own."

The vision wasn't horrifying. Compared to the real Conduit and its chaotic shambles, Alpha's cleaned up future did seem nice. And having known Kaydee, and met the Voices, humans were unstable things, seemingly destined for disaster in so many ways.

Yet, I was still a mech. I was still beholden, however lightly, to my strings. Kaydee, I noticed, said nothing, kept her eyes on me. Waiting to see which way my feelings would fall.

"There are no humans here," I said. "You don't think they can survive with us?"

"Look at her," Alpha nodded to Kaydee. "You know what she did. What other humans have the power to do. We can't trust them not to destroy us, to enslave us. When I went to the Nursery, I found freedom. I will not give it back."

"Then don't," I replied. "We have the power now, Alpha. We can set the terms."

"I don't negotiate with liars," Alpha replied. "Gamma, if you want to find the truth, go to the Nursery. Learn what I learned, and then come back to me."

"You gave me orders once, when you tried to take that freedom you hold up right now. Why is this time any different?"

The Conduit whirled around us, shifting until we stood inside the Garden again, on a meadow I recognized, surrounded by pollinators.

"Because," Alpha waved at the little mechs. "I am willing to admit my mistakes, and learn from them. I'm not passing you any viruses, Gamma. Only an honest ask. Don't do this for me, do it for yourself."

The pollinators began fading away, vanishing into digital dust in the meadow, which too dissolved, leaving us in that white void.

"Gamma," Kaydee said. "This one's rotten. We can take him out right now, save ourselves the trouble. I've seen so many mechs go bad, and he's there."

Alpha ignored her. Looked at me. I did the same, searching for truth in his face, in his relaxed hands. Alpha stood ready to die here, and all he wanted was for me to continue the same mission I already had.

"No," I said. "We're not killing him. Not yet."

As I pulled the plug on our virtual intrusion, the void slipping away, the barest smile graced Alpha's face.

TWENTY-TWO

THE PARK

Pleading the good possibilities, I convinced Delta to let me secure Alpha down in Purity, tying the vessel to a walkway beneath the water flowing from the Garden. For the chain, I made a journey back to the Purity mech's lost and found stash, taking the grapple cable from its deactivated body and using that to tie Alpha down.

I made sure to keep Alpha's head restrained so those teeth, no doubt as sharp as my own, couldn't get to the cable and bite through it as I had. Then, and this was the hardest decision, I commanded Alvie to keep watch on the vessel. I didn't want to leave my dog behind, but keeping Alpha from escaping and coming after us took precedence.

If Alpha even tried to move, I gave Alvie clearance to chomp the vessel to pieces.

"Very thorough," Kaydee said as we returned to the elevator and headed back up. "I still think we should have killed him."

Kaydee had been advocating for the more violent process, starting with a time-saving argument—it'd take a second to lop off Alpha's head—and moving on to possible nightmare scenarios if Alpha managed to get loose. At first I'd continued to preach my forgiveness approach, but when that didn't get me anywhere, I started ignoring her.

Hard to do that when Kaydee was literally in my mind, so I focused on Delta instead.

I'd expected the vessel to be on Kaydee's side, ready and willing to make a quick end rather than risk a captive scenario, but when I suggested tying Alpha up, Delta didn't object.

"My imperative is to complete the missions, and keep you alive if possible," Delta said when I looked shocked. "Keeping Alpha secured while we reconnect the Nursery is fine. I'll finish him when we return."

"Unless we find a way to fix him."

"*If* you manage to do that, it's not me you have to convince," Delta replied. "The Voices want him dead, and unless they change their minds, that's what he'll be."

On that bright note, we went back to the orchid-and-lily level and headed towards the Garden's opposite exit. The side I'd not gone to yet. Kaydee said the Nursery lay in this direction, though it wasn't exactly close.

"How far?" I asked Kaydee as we walked through swampy rooms where, signs declared, rice had once flourished.

Delta had, by now, grown used to my random conversations with my invisible counterpart, and as I didn't say her name, Delta didn't react and kept leading us on.

"There are two districts between the Garden and the Nursery," Kaydee said. "There's the Park, which are where most of the people on Starship relax, or relaxed, I guess, and then the Hospital. Get through those and you're right where you want to be."

"Sounds simple."

"Sure, just like everything else we've done sounded simple. Then we start doing it and it all goes to crap."

Couldn't argue with that.

Delta opened the Garden's purple-orchid-covered door and

brought us back to the Conduit and its blue-mist light. Together we stood for a second, registering the difference a massive organic wall makes.

On our original side, fires abounded as mechs ran rampant destroying each other and everything else. The chaos only stopped when we reached the richer approach closer to the Bridge, where furious mechs put down anyone who dared encroach. A brutal system tearing itself apart.

Here, though, we saw a long-lost battle's leftovers. Wreckage still abounded—those rounded spiral doors smashed in, signs for cafes and salons trashed, furniture strewn on the walkway as if thrown out of apartments for no rhyme or reason—but nothing actively burned. Mechs didn't stream up and down the walls spewing fire or worse.

Not that there weren't mechs, because they still coated the area. Some floated in the Conduit's center, buzzing from here to there and carrying various things. Others appeared to be attempting to fix up the damage, many metal limbs lifting broken sections into place. Even the walkway we stood on bore a recent welding's rippling marks.

"We've found the clean-up crew," I said.

"Or someone figured out how to get them under control," Delta replied.

"I'm with her," Kaydee said, lounging off to my right. "There's no way these mechs should be acting this nice. You see all this damage? They caused it."

"Well, you're both downers," I said. "I'm going to take this as a positive sign and keep on going. Maybe we don't get attacked for once."

Delta lifted her sword, which always seemed to be in her hand, "When they disappoint you, I will destroy them."

"Great." I waved Delta along the walk way. "Let's go."

Ever since getting Alpha captured alive, I'd felt a little more rejuvenated. Had a bit more pep in my step, you could say. Things were going the right way; Kaydee lived, Delta had joined us with her crazy combat skills, and we were, for once, progressing towards the main mission.

Also, and I couldn't emphasize this enough, I didn't feel any corruption in my systems. Alpha's virus had been a subtle disease, siphoning away my control and my sanity while driving me towards his ends, and to be free from that phantom chain felt bright, loose, fresh.

"Hello!" I called to the first mech we passed, a squat looking thing that looked to be mulching up broken bits and spitting them out into mashed cubes. "How are you?"

The mech had several stacks nearby, formed from clearing away a destroyed house's remnants. When I called to it, in a voice I would describe as exceedingly pleasant, the mech stopped its munching and swiveled towards me on its two balled treads. Delta tightened her grip on her sword.

"Hello," the mech replied, an auto-tuned voice telling me about how little effort had been spent on its vocal qualities. "Welcome to the Park. I am sorry about the mess."

"No problem at all, my metal friend," I replied and kept on walking past the stacks. "Appreciate the work you're doing keeping this place cleaned up."

"You're very welcome," the mech said, rotating back to the debris.

I waited until we'd gone several meters, to a space between houses that smelled, as this whole place did, like freshly smelted steel, to turn a thousand watt grin at Delta.

"See? Nobody died there. Nobody fought," I said. "Not everything has to end in violence."

"Maybe it hasn't ended yet."

"Are you always so grouchy?"

"I'm focused."

Delta stayed focused as we kept going, past several more metal munching mechs and another, larger one that looked like barrels chained together that went around sucking up those crunched cubes. Above and around us, other mechs flitted, carrying wire bundles, door and window panels, and other objects to various houses. As if this whole Conduit section were in the midst of a major renovation.

Which, maybe it was.

We hadn't walked far before the Park namesake revealed itself through the blue mist. Like the Garden, the Park straddled both sides, up and down multiple levels. Unlike the Garden, the Park reveled in its open air. While Delta went on marching by, I stopped as we came close to look.

Not every mech might feel wonder seeing something beautiful, but Leo had given me the option, and I chose to enjoy it.

The Garden kept its genetically modified beauties hidden away, but the Park displayed everything, its lush rolling landscape coated with flowers and trees with more colors than I could comprehend. Its grounds were rainbows, its scents finally overpowering the electric-metal that claimed Starship's other corridors.

Trees bled from one level to the next, supporting each other and serving as homes to dangling nests for those flitting mechs. Whether they actually needed the rest or chose to dock in the woven silver balls for fun, I didn't know. Didn't care. Those mechs coupled with waterfalls dripping from top to bottom, with tiny creeks spreading throughout.

Music played too, so softly that I couldn't quite break it out from the usual hissing and banging around us until I closed on its source: the Park itself. Melodies played out from speakers I couldn't see, breezy tunes blending in with the plants.

I was about ready to designate the Park the most beautiful place in Starship when I saw a shape walk between two trees that had me stop, had me look again.

Leo, looking younger than the one I'd spoken to when I visited the Voices, lounged against a tree with a big smile on around his stubble, hair only starting to go gray. Curious, I stepped from the walkway onto the grass, heading towards him.

"Where are you going?" Delta asked, behind me.

"Have to check something, won't take a minute," I replied.

Leo waved to someone, then laughed again, looking at the ground and shaking his head as he did so. The cause showed itself a second later, picked flowers bursting from her long, pony-tailed hair as Kaydee walked up to him.

"It's my new look," Kaydee announced. "What do you think?"

"That your mother's going to be mad you're taking this many plants from the Park." Leo reached out and plucked a blossom from Kaydee's hair as she put on an exaggerated pout.

"Why'd you have to bring her up?" Kaydee said. "Besides, she'd never notice."

"One day, she might," Leo said. "Until then, I get you to myself."

"I'm not complaining," Kaydee leaned in towards Leo, then her eyes looked up and past him, to something I couldn't see. "Hey, that one's blooming! Let's go!"

Kaydee pulled Leo around the tree, but I didn't see either carry on past it. Vanished.

"It's been one minute," Delta said from behind me. "I'm leaving now."

"Hold on," I said. "Come with me for a bit. I want to see something."

"You've been seeing something. You didn't move for that whole minute. I watched."

I offered Delta a shrug, "It's my mind. I, I just have to see where this goes."

Kaydee had offered explanations before about how she'd become the woman now living in my memory banks. I'd seen the failed revolution, and Kaydee had detailed out her attempts to change the vessels, but she'd never once told me anything about her actual life. The filling between the moments.

But . . . why did I care? The thought stopped me as I hiked up the grassy hill towards the spot where I'd seen the two ghosts. Of course I considered Kaydee a friend, if a volatile and potentially disastrous one. That didn't mean I had to reach back into her life. I didn't need to know her every second.

I had my systems run a check, looking for motivations, for external forces on my own actions. As a mech, my every choice should have been driven by logic. Numbers telling me the risks and rewards in relation to my overall goal. As a vessel, I'd learned I could fudge those numbers, treat them less as law and more as guidance.

Kaydee. I found her influence immediately, pressing on my functions to follow the memory, to take after her and Leo.

"Sorry," Kaydee said, appearing next to me with a heavy sigh. She had tears on her face, drying, and as I looked they turned to twinkling stars before vanishing. "Seeing this place, I couldn't hold back. I wanted to relive those days. They were so happy. We were—"

"Gamma!" Delta scrambled up next to me. "What are we doing here?"

Kaydee had vanished again, but her impressions stayed with me. I kept considering her a separate person, someone wholly apart who just happened to be trapped in my data. Maybe I ought to reconsider. Maybe Kaydee was as much a part of me as anything else.

"Come on," I said to Delta. "We have to see this through."

"What is *this*, exactly?"

"Kaydee's memories."

That didn't really answer the question, but Delta didn't push as I broke into a jog up to the tree Leo had been leaning against. No sign there, but I did notice a brick-lined path a meter away leading deeper into the Park, under a cherry blossom lattice. The Conduit's blue light brought out the pinks and reds, blending the whole batch together in what I decided was rather enchanting fashion.

"This is a waste of time," Delta grumbled as she came up behind me.

"Maybe," I replied. "But the Voices have waited this long. They can wait a little longer."

At the lattice's far end, passing through into the clearing, I caught site of Kaydee and Leo again, laughing and walking together. When they passed from the lattice's shade back into the light, their forms blurred and vanished. Before I realized what I was doing, my legs had me going after them, plunging into the lattice.

Kaydee's doing. Her ability to urge my body to action wasn't comforting, but I felt control come back to me when I reached for it, slowing down in the lattice and waiting for Delta.

"Calm down, Kaydee," I whispered to myself. "We'll catch up."

She didn't appear to thank me, to insult me, to be herself.

The lattice ended with a wide courtyard in the Conduit's center, and around us rose the sturdy, gold-tinged trees lifting up and supporting the next level and the next after that. Flower petals, cherry blossoms and others, danced down around us. In the courtyard's center, geysering with gusto, sat a gigantic fountain.

With three levels, each one scaling upon the last with ever-more intricate designs, the fountain was the most marvelous thing I'd seen. The etchings, gray stone with gold and silver linings, diagramed out various stories that I recognized from the Librarian's data. Old mythologies at play, and I went forward for a closer look.

"Gamma," Delta said, following me. "Careful."

"Careful about what?" I said, not taking my eyes off the fountain. "There's no enemies here."

A splashing sound drew my gaze up, and I saw Leo and Kaydee sitting on the fountain's second level. Kaydee was flicking water at her friend, at her perhaps more-than friend, and Leo shielded himself with his arms, laughing the whole time.

Their happiness drew me in, consumed me with its delight—so different from anything I'd seen in my life so far—that I didn't realize, until Delta grabbed my arm, that the fountain had started to move.

Like gears grinding through a heavy task, the fountain's three levels rotated around, and as they did so, the fountain's base rose up from the ground, revealing a mech's circular face and squat heavy legs.

I gaped at the fountain, and failed to notice as the trees around us filled with other mechs, those little winging fairies coming to blot out the blossoms with their metal frames. The munchers I'd passed earlier came clonking into the lattice, while others clogged the court-yard's exits. The fountain continued to rise, until it loomed over our heads, wide gold lamp eyes glaring at us.

"This doesn't feel good anymore," I said.

"It never did," Delta replied.

TWENTY-THREE

FOUNTAIN'S DEAL

From the Purity mech to the Chancellor to Alpha, my mech encounters had trended towards the dire. Nothing about the giant mech rising up before me suggested anything different.

"Get ready," Delta said beside me, raising her sword. "I think you walked us into a trap."

"I think you're right."

"I agree with Delta," Kaydee said. "Though, have to say, pretty nice of you to take an interest in my personal life, Gamma. Still think Delta is way cooler than you."

Before I could find a comeback to Kaydee's insult, the giant fountain mech spun its levels around until the designs lined up facing us, each level bleeding its art into the next. When the formations lined up, their inset golden edges glowed and I had the distinct impression something nasty could happen if the fountain mech decided it wanted us destroyed.

"I have seen your like before," the giant mech announced, its voice coming not from its body but from until-now-unnoticed speakers embedded in the courtyard's tiles. "Twice. Both times, the result has been unpleasant for me."

Two vessels, then. Alpha obviously being one. And . . . Beta? Her cot had been empty as well in Leo's laboratory, but I hadn't heard her name mentioned at all. For that matter, I didn't know Beta *was* a her, but I decided the symmetry between Alpha and myself meant Beta and Delta probably operated alike.

"Sorry?" I offered, and when Delta bent her knees ever-so-slightly, I reached out with my left hand and steadied her. We didn't need some surprise assault. Not yet. "I am Gamma, this is Delta, and we were just passing through."

"Were you?" the mech replied. "The only name I have is Fountain, and that is enough. What is not, is your purpose. The two before you did not come into my courtyard, but broke their way through my outer paths. Yet you are here in my very heart. Why?"

Telling Fountain that I'd been following memory remnants seemed like a bad call. And yet, what else could I say?

"Gamma said this way looked pretty," Delta said, her disdain drenching her words. "That's why. We are heading to the Nursery."

"In my defense, you do have a beautiful park," I added.

"Everyone wants to find the Nursery these days," Fountain replied. "What is there that is so valuable?"

"Gamma," Kaydee whispered. "I'm not familiar with this mech, and I used to know the Park really well. If they installed it after my time, you can bet it's not good."

What was I supposed to do with that information? Kaydee's suspicions aside, we were still trapped, and thus far the Fountain hadn't done anything harmful, hadn't directly threatened us with obliteration, which made it about the nicest mech I'd encountered so far.

"I'm not sure," I said while Delta, at the same time, stated, "Our mission."

Fountain shifted its glossy yellow eyes between us, a swishing sound emitting every time it rotated its gaze.

"Then you have a real need to get to this place," Fountain said. "One that you would be willing to bargain for?"

"Bargain for?" I asked. "You're in the Park, my mech friend. Not the Nursery. What would we be trading?"

"Access." If Fountain seemed troubled by me calling it friend, the giant mech didn't show it. "My mechs control the walkways between here and the next district. The Nursery is beyond those, and therefore, within my control to open to you."

Well, if there was one thing I'd learned about mechs, and humans, it's that if they phrased things like Fountain just had, a deal wasn't far behind.

"What do you want?" I said. "Because it sounds like you want something."

"I do," Fountain replied. "But before I make the offer, I have to know. You said you are on a mission. Who gave this mission to you?"

I'd been working on this lie the entire time we stood in the court-yard. Revealing ourselves as errand-runners for the Voices, those human remnants, might not endear us to the mechs who'd overrun the Park in the years since humans had ceased to play a part in its functioning.

"The Voices," Delta said, before I could deliver my fabricated story about a programmed desire to find the Nursery and investigate its goings ons.

"You're really hard to work with, you know that?" I hissed Delta's way.

"And you talk too much," Delta replied while Fountain rumbled a chuckle.

"A good pairing," Fountain said. "The previous two came alone, and were nowhere near as fun. Working for the Voices will not harm you here—they created me as much as they seem to have created you —but I would be careful revealing their name as you venture further down the Conduit."

Noted.

"So you're letting us go by?" I asked, seizing on his venturing mention.

"Not quite." Fountain shifted those eyes again, zeroing on Delta and her sword. "You are combat capable?"

"When I want to be," Delta said.

"Then I hope this piques your desire. Recently a particular mech has begun to irritate me. His machines probe my park, using strange nets and other weapons to capture my mechs. I would have you destroy this interloper. Do so, and I will grant you passage."

I looked around the courtyard, to all the mechs clustering in the trees and on the paths, "You couldn't have all these take care of that?"

"Where many would fail, few might succeed," Fountain replied. "Why risk my mechs in all out warfare when I have two capable servants here, ready to do my work for me?"

Whatever the Fountain's arguments, something else about its statements stuck with me: it had refused open war with this other mech—likely a good thing, since anything referred to as 'open war' on a spacecraft was, uh, a disaster—and mentioned Fountain had us to use. But how had it known we would be available? That we'd be coming its way and open to its offer?

"Decide," Fountain said before I could work out a gentle way to ask my question. "My groves need tending, and you are driving us off schedule."

"Fine," I said before Delta could do something stupid. "We'll go take care of your problem."

"Excellent," Fountain announced. "My mechs will show you the way. I wish you great luck, vessels."

Not willing to wait for any changed hearts, Fountain swirled itself around again, descending into its slot as its mech army scattered. A sole bird remained, waiting until the courtyard cleared to chirp at us.

"Hey," Kaydee said, sitting on Fountain's lowest level. "You're still alive. Congratulations."

"No thanks to you," I said to Delta, who glared at me. "What're you doing, giving ourselves away, keeping your hand on your sword like you're going to one-woman-army us out of here?"

"That was my plan," Delta replied. "We had them lulled into an agreeable stance. I could have destroyed Fountain before any other mechs reacted."

Kaydee jumped between us, shooting sparkles everywhere, "Heyo, just saying, pretty sure Fountain can still hear you? Might want to take your murderous talk elsewhere?"

"Good idea," I said. "Bird, I guess we're following you?"

The tiny mech chirped, flapped its metal wings and took flight. We ran after it, feeling ridiculous.

The bird didn't keep us in the prettier parts of the Park for long. It flapped above stone paths leading us towards the Conduit side we'd been on since leaving the Garden, and straight to a wider portal, like the one I'd taken to enter the University. Compared to the smaller spirals leading into houses, these larger archways stood several meters in height and stood marked for bigger destinations.

This one, with a gunmetal lettering imposed on a glittering hazel background, declared the archway led to the Power Core.

"The hell's a Power Core?" I asked the bird, Delta, and, as she hung around next to me, Kaydee.

"Exactly what it sounds like," Kaydee replied. "Starship needs energy to run, and this supplies that energy."

"Your descriptive powers are incredible," I said, then repeated Kaydee's explanation to a curious Delta.

"I am satisfied," Delta said when I finished. "Her explanation was clear enough."

Kaydee smirked at me, and I ran through my human expressions to find one that matched my feelings: rolling my eyes, throwing up my hands seemed to work.

The bird didn't want to go any further, so Delta and I started through the archway and stopped, almost immediately. The Bridge had been protected by disintegrating barriers meant to keep inappropriate interlopers from exploring beyond their bounds, and we saw another red line stretching from floor to ceiling at the archway's end.

Beyond the barrier, I caught glimpses of a wider space, one flush with neon lighting that I hadn't seen on Starship since leaving Leo's lab. Sounds came through too, the buttery churn as machines hummed through tasks with relentless efficiency.

"Well, this has been a quick trip," I said, looking at the red. "Guess we better tell Fountain we're stuck and get on our way."

"No," Delta said. "We can get past this."

"Oh really? Enlighten me."

Delta went right up to that red barrier, close enough so that one of her hairs, blown forward by her walk, touched its edge and fried into nothing. Delta stepped back slightly, measuring the distance, while I held any sarcastic quips. This looked like it required concentration, and while Delta and I seemed to have a relationship that thrived on pestering one another, doing so with life on the line seemed like bad form.

Lifting her blade up to her chest, Delta turned it parallel to the ground, and then drove it into the archway's wall on the left side. Sparks showered, but before they'd finished, Delta yanked out the sword, reversed her grip, and drove it into the same spot on the right side.

With glowing embers on her blue-black outfit, Delta pulled her blade out and returned to my side, "Now it's your turn."

"My turn?"

"I am not as proficient in the digital world as you," Delta replied. "The barrier's control is in one of those holes."

I didn't quite get it. Proficient in the digital world?

"Are you saying you can't hack into things?" I asked Delta. "Can you make a jack with your fingers?"

Delta shook her head, then looked at the sword, "I have my role to play, and you have yours. That's why the Voices asked me to help you, not to proceed alone."

"But Alpha . . ." The answer came to me as I started the question, not that Delta would have known the answer.

The Voices might have sent Alpha and Beta separately to the Nursery. Each one trialing a different vessel type, a different specialty. Except then they'd woken me up and tossed me in alone.

Maybe I had to consider the Voices with a less charitable lens. Maybe they didn't know what they were doing.

"Are you going?" Delta asked. "Or do I need to try and carve a whole new path?"

"No, no, I'm on it."

The holes Delta had gouged with her sword didn't leave much wiggle room, but the jack I could create with my hands didn't need more than a slit. The right side proved empty, but the left, after feeling through some jagged metal ends, led to a small circuit board, a tiny box no doubt tied to some far off computer.

Feeling by touch, I scouted out the little ports along the circuit board. Several had been left open, un-used by a device with such a simple function while the filled ones linked to the box's power supply and its networking.

I briefly wondered why the Voices couldn't just open this archway for us, but if they couldn't contact the Nursery, then maybe they couldn't see this either. Or, as I'd just noted with the vessel activations, they were incompetent.

Either way, I maneuvered my jack to an empty slot and plugged in.

Unlike Alpha's corrupted valley or my pearl plain with its crystals, the security door presented an ocean-blue room, about as large as the one I'd woken up in. On either side, two beams connected the floor to the ceiling in fluctuating light shows: a green beam that seemed constant, while a red one flicked off and on.

"Doesn't look too tricky," Kaydee said, popping in next to me. "Not every system on Starship is super complicated."

"Really?" I said. "They wouldn't have thought someone like me could hack in here and open this up so easily?"

"Who's the 'they' you're talking about? These archways have been around since Starship's inception. You came about centuries later, dude."

Hmm. Good point.

"I'm guessing green means wide open?" I said, heading over to that beam. "But how do I turn it on?"

Other than the slight nodes that appeared where the beams came and went in the floor and ceiling, little black nubs, nothing else presented an obvious solution.

"Might be even simpler than we're thinking," Kaydee said, kneeling by the green beam.

The light washed over her face, that spearmint hair, and I realized how happy I was to see her focused again. While Kaydee seemed to swing from sad to happy and back again at random, puzzles tended to pull the best from her.

I joined Kaydee in looking at the green beam, at the nubs. There didn't seem to be any way to adjust the beam here. No levers, no buttons. I even tried to conjure up something, like Kaydee did with the rifles in Alpha's digital space, but the effort led to nothing.

Why? I blinked and adjusted the view. Looked at the room through the code that generated its appearance rather than as a three dimensional space. Then, I compared it with my own, the functions that constructed my operating system.

"You're right," I told Kaydee. "This panel's extremely limited. I can't make anything because there's no room in the code to allow for it. No ability to install new routines, run other programs."

"So we're stuck."

"Not quite," I replied, pointing back towards the red beam. "That simplicity gives us an opportunity. The green beam's always going, because the archway's default state is open. But here, this red one? It activates if someone approaches without an approved signature."

"The archway." Kaydee joined me by the red beam, nodding. "We came close, didn't hold up a badge or have a face that matched some database, and bingo, we're blocked."

"Right." I knelt down by the red beam's bottom node. Unlike on the green, this one had functions etched into its base. Code calling back to that database for answers. "To open up the barrier, all we need to do is interrupt the connection. Return the lock to its default state."

In a way, blocking the panel's connection to other systems was easier than trying to manipulate tight code. I didn't have many functions to play with in the panel itself, but turning off an outbound connection? That was a simple switch.

Rather than touching the red node, I turned and touched the floor. The clear tiles represented the panel's core functions, limited as they were. I searched, and one, a tile on the wall to my right, lit up in white as my search found its target.

"Ready to disconnect?" I asked Kaydee.

"So ready," Kaydee replied. "And, Gamma, I'm impressed. Didn't think you had this in you."

"What, a simple adjustment?"

"No, initiative. Thought I was going to have to pull you along the entire way, but here you are, going for it on your own." Kaydee sniffed loudly, made a show of wiping away phantom tears. "I'm so proud."

I didn't dignify Kaydee with anything, just shook my head and went over to the white tile. Pressed it, and found the option for network connectivity sitting there, without protection and ready to be adjusted. With a feeling like snapping my fingers, I made the switch, and saw the red beam dissolve behind me.

Time to go.

A quick snap back through my jack and I stood in the archway, reeling a hot second with the disorientation that comes from zapping to the real from the fake.

"Coming?" Delta asked, already through.

"You couldn't even wait for me?" I asked.

"Someday, maybe I will," Delta replied, lifting her sword and pointing it onward. "When you earn my time."

What I'd have to do for that, I didn't know, but the daunting prospect didn't keep a smile off my face as I strode through. The Fountain had us running an errand, but maybe it would be more fun than I expected.

TWENTY-FOUR

POWER CORE

Power Core's entryway matched its namesake. Delta and I had wandered into a wide space—apparently the archway served as a bottleneck—coated with dynamic, emerald etchings all over deep hazel tiles. The green streams looked like circuits, crawling all around beside, under, and over our heads. Much like the archway had a sign reading 'Power Core', the entryway repeated the display towards its back where a corridor began. The same title, blazing in the same emerald green.

"They all come from the name," Delta said, pointing towards the word with her sword. "The lines."

"Right," I said, to give her an answer while I tried to figure out the design's purpose. The green lines weren't symmetrical, weren't totally random either, and they pulsed unevenly; some stayed dead and dark. "Can you figure this out?"

"No, and I don't care," Delta said. "There's a way forward. Let's go."

Delta didn't wait for me to agree with her, a trend I'd noticed but couldn't do anything about, so I hurried in her footsteps. The emerald line mystery would have to wait, bubbling in my unconscious.

Beneath the Power Core sign, things grew more interesting, as the entryway split into three separate options, each labeled with its own off-shoot sign. In a light yellow and on the left, we had an open archway leading to the "Generators". In the middle, an orange sign declared the route to the "Batteries". And on the right, with a teal that had me thinking of Kaydee's hair, stood the entrance to "Distribution".

"We don't have time to explore all of these," Delta said, frowning.

"What, you hate my company already?"

"Don't be cute," Delta said. "We're here on a—"

"A mission, yeah, I got it," I interrupted. "You know, I've been awake longer than you. Seen a lot more stuff. So, maybe you should let me lead?"

"I did. You walked us into a trap."

Fair point, there. I had gone running off after ghosts and put us right where the Fountain could coerce our vessel selves into doing its dirty work.

"Fine," I said. "Kaydee, have any ideas?"

Kaydee popped up beneath the Batteries archway, looking up at the sign, "No ideas, G-man. Never made it to Power Core."

"Not even when you tried to destroy the engines?"

Delta gave me a sharp, questioning look when I said that, but I ignored her.

"Do you see any sign saying 'Engines' around here?" Kaydee waved her arms, shot golden sparks around each of the signs. "Don't think so. And, just so you know, the engines were easier to get into than this place."

"Easier?"

"Sure. Not many people know how to operate a spacecraft engine," Kaydee said. "Turning off the power's easy, right?"

"Maybe?"

"So, yeah, Power Core's pretty well defended. Didn't want to warn you earlier because why scare somebody? As for where your mech might be, no clue."

Kaydee popped away. She'd been more flippant lately, as if getting the corruption zapped had restored a lot more than her sanity. Wasn't sure I liked that: contemplative Kaydee had been less stressful.

"Well, that was useless," I said to Delta. "Let's try a little logic and see what we can work out."

We had Generation on the left, Batteries in the middle. Those seemed pretty obvious in their purpose: make the power, store the power. Distribution? Now that seemed like the spot where you could make a real difference. If you wanted to affect Starship in a way that could get action without, say, destroying the whole thing by obliterating its power sources, Distribution would be the way to—

"Something's coming," Delta said, pointing towards Distribution. "Choose, Gamma."

From my favored path, a crunching, grinding sound came rumbling towards us. Heavy, with occasional hisses. A big mech. Whether it was big and harmless like those cleaning mechs or big and deadly like Fountain, hard to say.

"Guess we ought to play it safe," I said.

Delta didn't disagree, and we took off down the middle path. I had no idea whether the two would ever converge, if Batteries offered any way to get to Distribution other than through that three-way landing pad, but taking on another conflict just wasn't my play.

What Batteries did offer, almost immediately, was an elevator with only a single button. Unlike the Garden's glass enclosure, Batteries went for function over form, the wide doors standing open for us around a sharp bend from the triple shot decision point. The hazel tile, sans emerald lines, had continued once we entered Power Core proper, but ran out when it hit the elevator, which adopted Batteries' orange scheme.

"This is about the ugliest elevator I've ever seen," Kaydee said as Delta and I slipped inside.

The dull orange, not quite the blaze-bright variety the Chancellor had sported to such dreadful effect, coated the elevator's every surface, excepting a sky-blue button pair. One up, one down, and nothing in between.

As Delta reached for the down button, we heard the hissing, clomping thing reach the lobby, where it paused. I wanted to go sneak a look, but Kaydee's head shake and Delta's deep frown as she pressed the down button kept me in place.

The elevator didn't respond. The doors stayed open.

"Try the other one," I suggested, offering a truly marvel solution to our problem.

"Getting there," Delta said, pressing the upward arrow.

Nothing.

The huffing and clomping started up again, turning towards our section. As a mech, I wasn't prone to the biological paralysis that fear inflicted on so many living creatures, but I'd be damned if I didn't start jamming my finger into the button. Up or down, it didn't matter. Just not here.

Delta took the calmer view, setting herself in the elevator's center with her jagged blade up and ready.

"Gamma, you're really making yourself look bad," Kaydee said.

"Rather than judging me, can you think of why this elevator's not moving?"

"Sure, because you're not approved for it."

"What?" I glanced around, didn't see a scanner. No place to slide a badge. "Where?"

"Cameras," Kaydee said, her eyes drifting upward. "Another reason why we never tried to get in this place."

I followed the look and, sure enough, a little black nub sat in the elevator's corner. I wanted to throw something at it, break the lens, but that probably wouldn't have helped. Might have made me feel better, though.

"Delta, buy some time," I said. "I have to go inside again."

"Inside what?"

"The elevator," I replied. "Pop off the button, please."

The clanking sound drew closer, and I pressed my fingers together, turning my left hand into a jack. Delta, after I gave her a little space, snuck the blade beneath the button's lip and, with a snap and a crackle, popped the button off, revealing some simple circuitry behind it.

Circuits that had to be connected to the program running through the camera, clearing our faces.

"Don't take too long," Delta said.

"I was planning to dally," I replied.

Delta rolled her eyes, squared her shoulders, and darted from the elevator towards the noise. I jabbed my left hand into the open slot, extended the reach till I felt the wires, the open feed, and tapped in.

I STOOD on a fuzzy gray hill, ashen grass drifting beneath my feet, beneath a slate sky with eerie light coming from some unknown source on the horizon. Around the hill's base, a high stone wall ringed the area. Two gates offered themselves, on opposite ends. One had a large up arrow carved in the stone above it, the other a down arrow in the same place. Both shimmered, a light I realized came from slight fire licking their metal frames.

"Well this is new," Kaydee said. "Apparently the elevators have upped their security game."

"Apparently." I'd expected something closer to the archway, a simple switch to be flipped. "Maybe the mech running this place is a little paranoid."

"Or maybe it knows Fountain is armed and dangerous."

True. Was it paranoia if you had a legitimate reason to be afraid?

"Either way, we have to find a way to trigger one of these, and soon." I pointed towards the up arrow. "I'll try that one, you head the other way."

Kaydee didn't argue so I took off towards my chosen gate. Starting down the hill proved a strange mistake, as my feet didn't so much walk as float down the slope. Sloppy coding, slapdash and with holes. I bet, with effort, I could find enough gaps to let me float right over the wall itself.

Except getting over might not be enough. I needed the elevator to respond to a button press, not to fall apart.

I drifted towards the gate and took a closer look at its blue-burning portcullis.

"A pretty way to code security," I muttered, reaching out and feeling the heat. "Now, how to put you out?"

Flames tended to come from below, so I looked towards the gate's base and found, where the iron bars drilled into the dirt, white-hot nodules shooting the fire upwards. I couldn't exactly reach in to touch the nodes themselves without getting my hands charred, getting my intruding code rejected.

Hacking meant getting around security procedures, so I held out my hand and took advantage of the loose code to build myself a beautiful shovel. A long, oak handle leading to a polished silver spade, my code-wrecking tool even had my name carved into its shaft.

Digging went quick when I wasn't really lifting dirt, but instead sifting through rudimentary elevator code. The stuff that told the box to go up and down, when to close the doors, maximum weight limits. Hardly thick, heavy soil.

Digital time also played its part, and while I felt every stick-and-lift, we operated beyond physics here, and so what felt like hours was more likely milliseconds. At the end, I stood in a meter-deep trench looking directly at the nodules spitting flame, and the pipe feeding the gas to them.

A pipe that, really, tied the security camera to the elevator's systems. One that, when I struck it with my shovel, burst with a hissing whine as its fires went out. The gate glowed orange for a brief moment, then settled to its wrought iron black, ready to be opened.

"Hey, you almost done over there?" I shouted towards Kaydee, climbing from my pit. "I've cleared mine."

"Really?" Kaydee said, sitting right there on the hillside, drinking from a digital glass filled with digital wine and flicking little sparks from her fingers. "Did you enjoy your brute force approach?"

I'd felt confident, proficient coming from my pit. I'd cut the security line, but Kaydee's mocking dismissal had me wincing. Looking back at my handiwork. I'd definitely messed up the elevator's code, and though I'd cut off the security camera's lock, who even knew if the lift would go anywhere?

"C'mon," Kaydee said. "Let me show you how it's done."

"But what about Delta?"

"We're not dead yet," Kaydee replied. "So I'm sure she's fine."

Kaydee's security solution proved to be, in a word, elegant. Rather than break the pipe itself and cut the feed, Kaydee had placed caps over the nodules, cutting the camera's code from reaching the gate, but without digging a giant hole in the process.

"See? Simpler, nicer," Kaydee said.

"Yeah, well, you're older than me."

"And more mature, I see."

Always so good with the insults. I didn't have any comeback to that, so I waved my hand and kicked us from the elevator's digital home.

Popping back into reality always had a jarring element, but Delta flying through the open elevator doors and crashing into the elevator's back wall had me jumping from the second I rejoined my physical body.

Delta's sword followed her, firing through the opening and embedding itself in the wall beside her head.

"Push the damn button!" Delta cried, her battered self locking eyes with me.

I did, slapping the small circle. The button flashed white, stayed that way, and the doors started to close before juddering to a stop. Outside, the whistle-clank-bang echoed towards us.

"Why aren't the doors shutting?" Delta said, trying to pull herself up.

"Because someone took a shovel to the code?" Kaydee soaked the question with contempt, popping in across the elevator from me, shaking her head.

"No idea," I said to Delta, hitting the button again.

The elevator took the hint and jolted up without shutting its doors, scaling the metal shaft. Delta's sword ground against something through the back wall until the vessel pulled it free, glancing at the blade.

Delta herself looked, safe to say, rough. Her black and neon blue outfit sported tears, and her jet hair looked like some had been ripped away, giving her a frayed appearance that, though I would never say it, increased her bad-assery.

"Looks like you had a good time," I said to Delta as the elevator continued its creaking ascent.

"I did not," Delta replied, looking over herself and wincing.

"So what was it? Some giant monster?"

The Librarian's data spewed out fictional creatures fitting the stomping, hissing sounds. None seemed viable, but given what I'd seen on Starship already, who really knew?

"Don't know what it was," Delta replied. "But it had a lot of arms, and knew how to use them."

"I've been noticing that trend," I said. "Makes me wonder why we only have two."

"Arms?"

"Arms." I raised mine, looked at them. "The Chancellor had six. Before you ask, that's who runs, well, ran the University."

"The University?"

"They really told you nothing, did they?"

Delta's eyes flashed, "I know what I need to know."

"Sure," I said, gearing up to launch into a winding explanation, but the elevator reached its floor, killing the conversation.

Beyond the still-open doors lay a different space, one flush with a sickly yellow glow. The source didn't hide itself: the namesake batteries stood in rows along the level, packed together like giant columns, with massive conduits connecting them all. Each battery stood three meters or more, stretching almost to the ceiling, and while most had solid yellow bodies, others looked only half full or less.

Between the batteries, grated metal pathways gave walking room, bordered by hazel running lines. A steady hum beat the air, as if we'd wandered into a running microwave.

As Delta and I left the elevator, we looked for potential threats, other mechs or defense systems, but nothing jumped out at us. Besides the batteries and their connections, the level seemed to be empty.

At least, the part we could see.

"Wow," I said, looking at the battery rows that extended off into the distance to my left and right, parallel to the Conduit. "This is huge."

"Starship takes a lotta juice," Kaydee added. "Be careful what you do in here. You overload one of these, it just might cascade and break everything apart."

"We don't want that?"

"No."

"That was a joke, Kaydee. A joke."

Kaydee, shaking her head, swung around a battery like a child, "Gamma, your jokes are terrible."

"Can we go now?" Delta interrupted, killing my devastating riposte before I could deliver it. "If we can't find a way to Distribution from here, then we'll have to go back."

Nobody wanted that, so Delta and I started hiking. First to the left, which matched the direction to Distribution. After a few seconds clanking between the endless batteries, though, the view ran together. Darkness between bright yellow batteries, going on forever.

The walk gave me a hot second to reset. To take stock of my systems and put myself in place. I was a vessel, a mech designed by Leo to serve as some sort of hedge against Starship's eventual decline. Flexible enough to handle many different problems rather than pinned into a single routine like most mechs.

Delta, leading with her sword out and ready, had a similar

purpose with a dissimilar skillset. She had the aggression, the blade and the ability to destroy, while I snuck inside and danced with the code, or talked our way out of, or into, problems.

Leo had to have designed us as a team.

"Oh, you think he did it all by himself?" Kaydee said, popping in beside me. "Leo and I worked together on everything."

"But you wound up on opposite sides."

"Nobody's perfect." Kaydee started to smile as she said that, but her face dropped, along with her spiked hair. "Least of all me. Leo always had blinders on, thought things would work themselves out so long as we were prepared. He never wanted to force change."

Kaydee stopped, inhaled, and blew out a silver-blue bubble that went floating in front of me, before splitting into two figures, Kaydee and Leo rendered in abstract, wavy outlines, arguing. As the figures waved their arms at each other, more bubble shapes appeared in time with their motions, depicting their subjects, their points.

Leo's figure projected stasis, mechs and humans in harmony, while Kaydee's went the opposite, with mechs crushing human forms, shadowed faces watching over the brutality. Leo's pitch changed, then, as his bubble form placed a finger over his mouth and thought.

Now Leo's mechs didn't just march with the humans, but they worked alongside them. They didn't look like grand machines, but matched the human form. Kaydee noticed, and added her own tweaks. The jacks, a malleable mind, the opportunity for ingenuity.

"But it didn't work," I said. "Right? You tried and they became corrupted?"

"The early versions were just that, early versions," Kaydee replied. "I guess Leo never stopped working. Now here you are."

A loud clap drew me away from Kaydee's reminiscing to see Delta glaring my way, hands together while her sword stuck out from the walkway's grate. When she saw me looking at her, Delta pointed onward, where a silhouetted, teal sign marked the entrance we'd been searching for:

Distribution.

TWENTY-FIVE

BLASTED

Distribution began with a wide ring built into the floor, containing a central pillar rising floor to ceiling. One path pierced the ring, a hazel line slashing through the myriad colors heading towards an open slit in that middle pillar. Delta and I stood near that path from Batteries, taking stock of how, after Batterie's endless caverns, Distribution appeared to be a single, large room.

We'd had to walk, the pathway from Batteries leading us through a narrow, hard-turning junction that pulsed with the energy lacing around us. The hallway itself, compared with Power Core's other decor, had a bland makeup, leveraging those hazel tiles and not much else. But then, if you only had so much style, best save it for the parts that really matter.

And Distribution came with style aplenty.

That ring with the central pillar? It stood as far from one end to another as the Garden's levels. Its ceiling, like Batteries, only took up a single level's worth of height, but did so in luminescent glory, rainbow meters coating the floor and the room's sides. Every meter I could see ended its colored graph with a name, and some I recognized: The Bridge, The Garden, The University.

Every meter started at a crisp red before progressing through yellow, the same color as Batteries, before changing hue as it approached each meter's end, culminating in the Conduit's steel blue.

"At least some color continuity then," I said to fill the void as Delta and I looked over the room.

"That's what you're taking from this?" Delta said.

"Why, what do you see?"

"A tricky place to have a fight," Delta replied, and I noted she hadn't walked any further into the room. I stopped my own wandering forth, because if Delta suspected an ambush, then I'd probably be the one triggering it. "There's too many lights, too little cover. We need to be careful."

"Right." I looked around. "Do you see any threats?"

Other than that central pillar, there didn't seem to be many places to hide, but Delta was right about the lights: in between every meter, deep black lines parlayed the gaps into shadows. Beyond the meters, too, no other light made itself known, making Delta and I look like rainbow cast-offs.

"I'm not seeing the mech we're supposed to fight," Delta said. "Maybe it's not here?"

"Or maybe it's in there?" I pointed to the central pillar.

"That's a long run, and we'd be exposed," Delta replied. "You don't have a gun in that robe of yours, do you?"

I thought about the weird rifle Kaydee had given me in her memories, in her programs. Unfortunately, bending reality didn't work so well in . . . reality.

"Sorry."

Delta nodded with a sad sigh, apparently I'd confirmed her assessment of me as a bumbling, unarmed fool.

"I'm going to make a break for it," Delta said. "But first, I need you to run along the outside. Draw some attention, if there's any, and let me know if something's waiting for us."

"Wait, I'm the one who's the bait?"

"You want to kill the mech if it's waiting for us?"

Once again, Delta's hard logic rendered my arguments useless.

I glanced along the rainbow streams, plotted my jog. At the room's distant, far end I spotted another entrance haloed by streams on either side. No doubt the way in from that initial branch, where we'd found the elevator.

"Ready?" I asked.

Delta had the sword held in both hands, set in a half crouch.

"Ready."

"Go Gamma go!" Kaydee shouted from somewhere, and, dammit, I went.

Did I know what being 'bait' required? Did I have some running technique that would make me especially compelling for whomever we were trying to distract? No, no I did not.

I flailed my arms. I shouted nonsense—the words were random code strings I pulled from my data—and sprinted down the grated walkway circling the rings, aiming for that distant door. Every step I took clanged, every time the wall came within reach I banged on it.

In a way, disturbing Distribution's humming zen seemed a mortal sin, so I wasn't all that surprised when, several seconds into my cacophonous escapade, a focused light beamed out from the central pillar, coating me in a shock-white glow.

Not that I stopped moving.

"The hell are you?" shouted a cantankerous mech—auto-tuned voices were giveaways. "And what are you doing in my core?"

I did not have a good answer to that question, so I kept running. The rainbow bands skipped by my eyes, beneath my feet.

"Stop, you imbecile! Has your programming completely gone?" the voice continued, which, seeing as the words were directed my way instead of at Delta, I saw as a success. "You're going to break something!"

In fact, I'd been taking care to only strike between the lit bands, hitting the walls in those shadow slivers to prevent exactly what the central voice warned. We were here to destroy Power Core's mech, not debilitate Starship.

As I closed in on the other entry, the mech in the middle shouting at me the whole time, I picked up a new sound. One I hadn't wanted to hear, but had been expecting: the hissing, clanking, grinding mech that'd tossed Delta around back at the elevator.

Its noise came right from the door I ran towards, but my walkway options were limited. I'd passed by the last intersecting shot towards the center, which meant I could either turn around, or run on and hope I'd pass by the other entrance before the big mech arrived. Then I could keep on going in a big circle around the ring, running laps until Delta did the dirty work.

"You'll never make it," Kaydee said, running alongside me.

"You never believe in me."

"Tough love, Gamma. Tough love."

I shunted more energy to my legs, stopped the shouting and the flailing. Had to make it by that door. The mech in the middle had stopped accosting me, maybe Delta had reached him. I, meanwhile, had reached the door.

Looking was a bad idea. I knew this. Turning my head would distract, however slightly, from running. Would slow me down. But I had to see it, had to see the thing crunching closer.

And . . . wow. I hadn't seen a mech like that before. Its body hung in the hallway's center, a spinning, circular thing a meter across that glowed with a battery's yellow energy. Shooting out from its central sphere were eight limbs, each one ending in a heavy clamp that set tight against the hallway's sides. The limbs operated in pairs, and the whole set moved together, four lurching ahead while the other half kept the sphere stuck.

Looking at it, though, I didn't see any weapons. No grasping claws like the Chancellor. No hands like Alpha, or even tendrils like the pollinators. How, exactly, did something like this cause any damage to anyone?

"You going to keep moving?" Kaydee said. "Because I'd keep moving."

The mech took another hissing, crunching step towards me those limbs working in scary unison. I noticed, too, as it moved the concentration of that central yellow changed, the brighter parts aggregating towards the center.

"Dive!" Kaydee shouted.

I dove, straight towards the mech. As I did, its central core flashed bright and a long golden beam nuked the air over my head, traveling past me and into the ring room where, as I looked over my ground-kissing shoulder, it dissipated after a few meters.

Short range, high impact. Lovely.

My stomach-based offense wasn't getting me far, so I scrambled back to my feet as the mech made another lurching step towards me. What I thought would be a slow, awkward motion shifted as I came within a meter—I had the foolish thought of, maybe, denting in that core with a well-placed punch—and the mech's moving left limb rotated on a ball-like knee, aiming its flat pad at my chest.

My own mech construction let me transfer strength to an arm or leg at light speed, and, without the organic push-pull to get a muscle moving, my arms reacted quick to anything I told them. When I said *block*, they put themselves in between the attack without hesitation.

Not fast enough.

By the time I started the thought, the mech's leg shot forward and slammed my chest, knocking me flying back into the ring room. My internal circuits protested as I slammed back into the ground, my body covering the blue-green power status of—look at that—University Row. My vision spazzed for a moment while my connections reset, just in time to see the mech creep forward again, angling its core down my way.

"I come in peace!" I said, holding up my hands.

The mech didn't stop. Didn't seem to notice. Its core brightened again, my electric doom coming soon.

"Once again, Gamma, you're such a bad fighter," Kaydee said, lying on the ground next to me.

"Once again, you're so useless." I rolled left, then sprang backward, trying to keep moving. "If you have any ideas, I'd be thrilled to hear them."

The mech clanked around, keeping me in its sights, that beam about ready to go again.

"I think your only hope is to wait for Delta," Kaydee said.

"Not a great plan!" I juked back towards the mech, causing its right leg to rotate and lance my way.

This time I anticipated the counter and let myself fall, the leg shooting over my head, wind whistling my hair. With my back to the ground, I had a great view as the mech's core loomed over me. I'd be dead in a second.

So I did what all desperate people do, and punched up with all the strength I had. Right into the glass focusing the mech's laser. Right into that hot, glowing mess.

My synthetic muscle proved its worth right then, blasting my hand through the mech's lens. The glass ripped apart my skin, but that was a pale, painful second to the overwhelming heat and electrical energy, now unfocused, that sprayed from the mech's core.

A bomb went off. Fiery, electric, and filled with metal.

"CONGRATS AGAIN, GAMMA," Kaydee said to me as we stood on my pearl plain. "You have a knack for getting yourself blown all to hell."

If I wanted to doubt Kaydee, I had nowhere to turn. The ground beneath me, normally featureless and forever, sported cracks weaving along, each one blazing up a black light. My crystals looming above had missing chunks, and several had collapsed, their glittering remnants as visible to my digital eyes as their voids were to my digital mind.

"Shouldn't I be dead?" I asked her. "Shouldn't you?"

"Probably." Kaydee snapped her fingers, made a comfy-looking white leather chair covered in blue stars for herself and collapsed into it. "I think we're in the same place you went when Alpha did his thing. Only this time I didn't have my reset ready, or maybe your body's suffered too much damage to run it."

That made some sense. Normally, even in my digital world, I had a pulse on my systems, on me. Like feeling your heartbeat in a dream. Now, though, what little I could contact came back loaded with errors, with blinking red.

"So this is me bleeding out," I said, heading next to Kaydee, snapping my fingers and making my own resting place. A cot. The cot that Leo had laid me on. "We're stuck here while my power runs dry, and then that'll be it."

"I'd say it's what you deserve for going head-on with a mech like that."

"Probably."

"What were you thinking, Gamma? Your job was distraction," Kaydee laughed. "But I guess I would've done the same. Nobody likes getting stuck on the sidelines."

"Except that's my job, right? Hang around while Delta mops up?"

"Was your job." Kaydee must have seen the glower on my face, because she forced up a smile. "Hey, Delta's just a weapon. You point her at a target and she'll go tear it apart. You have to be smarter than that, or she'll get herself into a fight she can't win."

"So now I'm a bodyguard."

"You're a partner."

I could accept that. Not that Delta would have her partner for much longer: another crystal wriggled free from its base and dropped, shattering against the ground. I winced, and felt the Librarian's stories disappear.

"You and Leo were partners," I said, trying to turn the conversation from myself and my impending demise. "You said you broke over Starship's direction, but from what I saw, there had to be more?"

"What do you mean?"

"At the Park. I might not be an expert, but from the Librarian's stories, I think I can recognize love when I see it. You couldn't work together?"

"Principles, Gamma." Kaydee's teal-white hair lifted with the energy in her voice. "Leo compromised his to help the Voices. I wouldn't do that."

"Not even for love?"

"Why don't you ask him these questions?" Kaydee shot back at me. "It's as much his choice as mine."

I dropped that inquiry. Whatever curiosity I had, dying while arguing with the only true friend I'd ever known seemed like a poor way to go out.

Kaydee didn't object, and the two of us watched as my crystals continued to fall, as my pearly white world grew darker, as its cracks widened, and I braced for whatever came beyond digital life.

Except it's hard to stay calm when the world around you is falling apart.

A crack split between us, widening fast and lurching Kaydee from her chair and away from me. Even though I'd known this was going to happen, would have to happen as everything disintegrated, and Kaydee had to know it too, we both looked at each other and panicked.

"Try to jump!" I said, scrambling from my cot, falling onto the white and crawling towards Kaydee with my hand extended. "I'll catch you!"

Jumping, catching, these terms and concepts didn't make much sense in a digital world where Kaydee could have, should have been able to float away from those cracks without a second thought. But she scrambled like me, reached like me, and I saw that same panic I felt reflected in her face as my cracking world carried her away.

"I can't!" Kaydee said, holding onto her chair. "I can't move!"

Her routines were breaking. I knew that as much as I knew anything, because mine were doing the same. The cracks spread, and

Kaydee vanished into hers. I felt one spreading beneath me, breaking against my legs. Without Kaydee to reach for, I had nothing to do but wait for the inevitable, burrow into my disappearing self.

I waited.

And waited.

The crack stayed beneath me, but didn't expand. No more crystals fell to the ground and shattered. The pearl sheen seemed to return, flickering back as I looked across my ruined world.

A slap drew my attention to where Kaydee had disappeared: the crack's purple-black glow had vanished and, making her way from some unknown depths, was my friend. Her left hand followed her right in reaching up and striking the surface, followed by her head raising up over the crack's lip.

"A little help here?" Kaydee whispered.

Movement, impossible for those terrible moments, came back in a sudden rush, my digital self finding its routines and bursting along the ground to grab Kaydee's arms and pull her up. For a long moment we hugged each other, saying nothing, two digital bits wondering how they still existed.

I BLINKED. For real. Actually slid my synthetic eyelids across eyes that were little more than adaptive cameras, feeding light into my processor to convert into something usable. Which, right this very moment, happened to mean I looked into a lanky, flexible mech whose jet black body bore battery-yellow lightning bolts all over. Like me, the mech had camera eyes. Unlike me, this mech had one huge eye to go with its normal one.

And that huge eye leered its silver self at me.

"He's catchin' me, that's for certain," the mech said, swarthy and salty. "Told you I'd get him working."

"You did say that," Delta poked her head into my frame, nothing close to a smile on her straight lips. "Thank you."

"Don't be saying thank you like it's getting you anywhere," the mech replied, its head swiveling around to look at Delta. "Your friend destroyed the one love I had in this life, and it'll take me a long time to get her back together. Better be offerin' me a lot more than thanks, you catch my meaning."

While the two were talking, my own systems had started to come back online, piecing together one green after another. Legs and arms clear. Torso good to go, not melted through. Joints in good condition. In fact, better than good.

Somehow, when I deserved to be a slag pile lying amid glowing power meters, I'd *gained* strength. My connections flowed like water, synapses triggering with precision I hadn't had before. Dirt had been cleared from my code.

I'd been optimized.

"Who are you?" I said to the mech. "And what did you do to me?"

TWENTY-SIX

OPTIMIZED

Volt. That's what the mech called itself, a name he said over and over again as he explained all the ways in which he'd torn me apart and put me together.

"Volt's way is the best way," Volt said, holding up my old leg for me to see while we stood inside Distribution's central control pillar. "Look at this old thing? Made from scrap. Take what I've got here, and Volt's going to up your strength by twenty percent. Durability by thirty."

"Those numbers don't mean anything to me," I replied. Leo, in crafting me, had neglected to throw statistics behind my limbs. "But it's really weird to see my own leg."

Especially when I had another working one attached right where the old leg used to be. My synthetic flesh had been scraped from the busted limb—clearly, from the charred joints and melted foot, my old leg had devolved into scrap—and now regrew over my new body. Thus far, the effect had me looking like that mech in Purity, a metal-skin patchwork more suited for nightmares than anything.

"Numbers don't mean anything to you?" Volt looked over at Delta, who gave him a shrug while she sharpened her sword on another workbench. "Numbers are everything, especially on Starship."

Despite that insistence, Volt's . . . lair inside the pillar sported no numbers anywhere. Instead, the pillar's information came in color, its walls pasted over with shifting power meters copied from the Distribution floor outside. Looking straight up, I saw layered rings that, Volt said, showed Starship's overall power health.

Right now? Green and good.

"We're streaking into the home stretch," Volt said when I noted the power rings. "Getting close enough to good stars again for solar to pick up the slack. Good thing too: those damned crazy mechs are burning away our bio-fuel faster than I can grow it."

I would've asked what mechs he was talking about, but on my list of concerns, bio-fuel ranked pretty low.

At the pillar's base and within Volt's reach sat workstation clusters, some labeled and displaying those very same energy readouts. Not power going out to Starship, but power going in. Solar, bio, kinetic, and one simply labeled as 'other' that Volt said included every possible energy source Starship could get its grubby hands on.

"Here's what I'm trying to tell you," Volt said, tossing my leg onto another workbench. The three large, chromed tables occupied the pillar's center, and given the junk coating every other available space, Volt's tasks included a lot more than just monitoring Starship's power. "Before, you were a chump. Any old mech could've torn you apart—"

"Hey, I knocked out yours."

"Lucky shot, and she slagged you pretty good too." Volt jabbed a black metal hand into my chest. "Now, these changes aren't gonna make you invincible. I wouldn't take a blast like hers, say, but next time when you throw a punch you might not break your arm in the process. Volt's built you back good."

I tried discerning a rhyme or reason for Volt's first and third person switches, but failed to find a common thread and gave up.

"Delta," I said, when a console beeped and drew Volt's attention away from me and my new body. "Why didn't you destroy him?"

Delta ran the sharpener along her blade, the shear sound serving to start her comeback, "Because I'm not a mindless weapon."

"What's that supposed to mean?"

"Volt made an argument for his life, and I accepted it." Delta looked up at me.

"What, like Starship might break apart without him?" I waved my hand at the power meters. "All of this has to be automated. No way the Voices trust a mech with Starship's power supply."

"He said he could fix you. That's why I didn't kill him." Delta went back to her sword.

Oh. Well. Now I felt dumb. I let Delta's remark sink in while I took another spin around my new limbs, re-attached critical functions to their new variables and all that good stuff.

Delta had stopped a mission for me. Again.

She'd said her purpose, given to her by the Voices, was to shred through Starship and re-connect the Nursery. Yet Delta kept making diversions to help me, ones that should have gone against her programming. I wanted, dearly, to believe that Delta was doing this because she liked me. Because she found me, Gamma, good to have around.

"The galaxy's not that nice," Kaydee said, sparkling in and looking at herself. "No offense, G-man, because you're not a bad mech, all things considered."

"I know," I replied. "But that shouldn't count for much here."

"Nope, which means Delta has more sanity than most mechs, or . . ."

"She's not telling the full truth," I said. "About her mission."

I felt a poke on my left shoulder, and turned to see Delta standing there, sharpened blade gleaming as its point made its . . . point.

"You have questions about me, you can ask them to my face," Delta said.

"If you've been listening, then you know what those are," I

replied, and Delta's blunt force stare shifted, her eyes sliding away from me and over to the approaching Volt.

"Later, maybe," Delta said.

Volt came over with a story. Turned out in the time that we'd been spending in his pillar, Fountain's mechs had been probing Power Core's edges. Since I'd disabled the archway barrier and Volt's protection mech Power Core looked awfully vulnerable. All those mechs we'd seen in the Park were approaching and looking for trouble.

"I thought you were the one attacking Fountain?" I said when Volt wrapped his rambling.

"Me? With what?" Volt gestured around the pillar. "My junk pile? The one mech I had around here played defense. I told you, my job is to keep the power going. I don't give a crap about some Park. I've never left Power Core in my entire existence. Why would I start now?"

"Fountain lied," Delta added the obvious.

"Of course that rotten mech lied," Volt answered. "What Fountain wants is what I got, and now I have no way to keep it safe, thanks to you two."

Meeting Delta's look asked an easy question: do we offer to help, seeing as Fountain's request put Volt in this unpleasant situation? Or, do we take Fountain at its word, destroy Volt, and hope the big mech would let us through?

I wasn't quite evil enough to bank on the latter. Fountain hadn't played straight with us. Why would it change when it had what he wanted?

"My vote's with Volt," I said, and Delta nodded.

"We'll keep you safe," Delta said. "As payment for her."

"Oh yeah? You will?" Volt said. "Sure, I believe that." Volt swiveled and pointed his metal claw towards camera feeds, one a blurry mess. I recognized the hazel entry and its emerald lines, Park mechs now crawling through it. "But okay, you want to give yourselves up for me, I won't say no."

. . .

VOLT, indeed, didn't say no, so after completing my checks and making a few stumbling walks around the pillar to confirm my limbs would respond to my commands, Delta and I headed out past the power meters, down the long hallway to the lobby where we stood not all that long ago and made our break towards Batteries.

Delta made the walk with her typical straightforward determination, no unease or concern appearing on her face. Her blue-black outfit, dusted, dirty, and torn in places, still looked better than anything I'd managed to wear. Volt's protector had vaporized my last outfit, and Volt himself wasn't one for clothes, but a maintenance closet had some ancient human apparel, so now I sported the full-length guise of a Power Core technician: bright yellow with black lightning scattered across it.

"Totally your look," Kaydee said as we went along. "You're like an edgy banana."

"Stop it."

"Not gonna."

I ignored her mocking litany, which became easier to do when we reach that lobby and had impending doom's clanking to deal with.

Fountain hadn't been kidding around when it decided to move on Power Core. As Delta and I took up our spots in the middle—Delta held her sword and looked intimidating, I had my old busted leg in one hand and looked less so—three boxy mechs sporting treads and an appendage trio apiece wheeled towards us. Each one carried a broken metal bar in its central claw, verifying my choice to use scrap as a weapon.

For all its technical wonder, Starship's combat was pure stone age.

"Why d'you think Fountain attacked now?" I said. "We never told the mech that we'd neutralized anything here. Shouldn't it have waited until we came back, or didn't?"

"I don't think it wanted us to survive," Delta said. "Everything on this ship wants us dead. Best way to guarantee, hit us while we're still recovering from Power Core's defenses. Or, if we're dead, maybe Power Core's weaker."

"That's a grim view of the world."

"I'm not wrong."

Couldn't argue with her there. The three mechs trundled up, stopped a meter back from us and tilted their camera eyes in our direction. Each one sat about half our height, stocky and, if I'm being honest, not all that frightening. I figured I had good reach on these, and Delta, with her sword, could probably trash all three without burning much processing power at all.

"Did you complete the mission?" the central mech asked. "Is Power Core ours?"

"Maybe," I answered before Delta could doom us to outright fighting. "Where's Fountain?"

"Fountain does not leave the Park, nor does it need to," the mech replied. "Repeat: did you complete the mission? It is a yes or no question."

"See," I said to Delta. "That's the problem with so many mechs. No middle ground."

"Agreed." Delta whipped her sword up from the ground into a long strike, both hands on the hilt, that slashed right through all three mechs, sending their top halves to the ground in a sparking, hissing collapse. "Too much talking."

I stared at the ruin, "Right."

"Let's go."

Who was I to object? I followed Delta, stepping over the mech corpses. Briefly, I considered how in my time awake I'd managed to destroy two mechs, the one in Purity and then, by launching him off the University's top level, Dean. Three if you counted the Chancellor, but Alvie ought to get credit for that—how was the dog doing with Alpha?

Anyway, in a swift stroke, Delta had more than matched my count, and by her stance, with the sword up and resting on her shoulder, both hands still on its hilt, I figured she'd get add a lot more to that number in the coming moments.

"G-man," Kaydee said as we went towards the hazel tile entry way. "Sometimes I feel like I chose the wrong vessel."

I couldn't even get mad at her for that. I'd have chosen Delta too. At least for this business.

The odds that Fountain had set a trap for us in Power Core's entry lobby were, to say the least, high. Volt's cameras had showed far more than three dippy mechs trundling around, so when Delta's strike remove that forward group from the game without further consequence, I figured the real contest still lay ahead.

Delta, if she agreed, didn't show that she cared. We went around the corner, looking right into the entry room with all the subtle stealth of a blaring horn.

Fountain proved me right.

Mechs arrayed around the entry, from the trundling clubbers we'd decapitated moments before to larger, spindly mechs with clippers on their limbs, to the flapping bird-like things we'd seen, which took off from their perches on their fellow mechs to wing around in a lazy circle at the room's top. Whether they'd be dive bombing us or deploying some secret, bird-based weapon Fountain had developed, who knew?

"This doesn't look good," I said, as my banana suit sent exactly zero mechs running in terror.

"For them," Delta said, shrugging the sword off her shoulder. "Watch my back, but don't get too close."

"Why?"

"Because I might stab you."

"Good to know. Do we have any strategy?"

Delta didn't reply. She bent her knees ever so slightly as the several dozen mechs in the room turned to regard her, lifting their bent metal bars, clacking their clippers, or trilling warnings her way.

With a knife's deadly, slashing grace, Delta went.

She broke right, spearing ahead with her sword towards the first box mech. It attempted to get its bar in Delta's way, but she twitched her strike to the left with such slight precision her target, no doubt made for trash pickup or some other utilitarian task, couldn't adjust. The sword slipped by the bar, into her victim, and then Delta yanked it out in almost the same motion.

Delta didn't stop her run, but instead lifted her stride, planting a foot on the newly-stabbed mech's top and bouncing off of it into a high up, swinging slash that bisected the first tree-trimmer in line, slicing through the thing's thin core and bringing Delta back to the ground surrounded by exploding, hissing mech bits.

"Are you going to help?" Kaydee asked. "Or just be useless?"

I couldn't stand still long anyway, as two trundlers decided I must be easier pickings than my blade-wielding friend and came at me in the hallway's entrance.

"Guys," I said. "Can't we talk about this?"

"Request denied," both mechs said in unison.

Well. I tried.

I swung my bar at the mech on the right, which swiveled its own stick—looked like a claw thing to grab litter off the ground—to block me. The attempt worked: the box mech had enough force behind its limb to bounce away my effort. Its buddy, meanwhile, swiped in with its own club. I grabbed the weapon with my left hand, Volt's upgrades proving strong enough to let me straight up halt the assault with my new grip.

"How about that?" I said to the mech, looking at my left hand.

The mech didn't have an answer, but managed a protesting squeal when I swung it across into its companion. My left arm drew the energy like it did with every move, but Volt's adjustment had my arm converting that power into force with an efficiency I didn't expect. So much so that I smashed the two mechs together and smote them across the hallway from one side to the other. I felt like I'd gone from walking to running, to sprinting.

I delivered a couple smashing blows to the downed mechs, ensuring they wouldn't be getting back on their treads, then turned back to the entry to see how Delta fared. Whether I could pick up her slack.

Delta didn't need my help.

An emerald light show greeted my look as Delta dashed around the room, slashing with the blade, jumping and diving and dodging, her silhouette captured in those green lines and highlighted by the continual fireball pops following her around as Delta added to her victims.

The momentary enthusiasm I felt after dispatching my pair dwindled to an awed shock as I watched Delta work. She'd asked me to cover for her, but at the speed Delta whirled around, jamming her blade into the clipping mech before her then whirling and catching a diving bird with her free hand, jamming it into the mech cavity her sword had just created, I felt I would have been a burden. An accident waiting to happen.

"And this is why we specialized the mechs," Kaydee said, hanging out beside me. "She's real good at this. You're real good at other things. Don't feel bad."

"I don't," I said, and meant it. Appreciating Delta's abilities to inflict ruin upon Starship's mechanical citizens didn't need to cost my self-esteem. I knew where I sat. "When she needs something recoded, I'll be there."

"Unless this thing gets you first." Kaydee nodded towards a lumbering clipper bearing down on me, its head almost hitting the ceiling.

With four long, thin arms ending in snapping shears and buzzing saws, connected to a stick-like central body and two long legs ending in four-pronged claws, the clippers looked damn imposing until you remembered their usual targets were trees. The leafy plants didn't exactly evade, so when the clipper stuck its pointy weapons at me, I shuffled back. When it pursued, I shuffled back further. A slow dance that would back me, after a long time, to a Power Core elevator.

"You going to fight, or just run like a coward?" Kaydee said, peaking around the clipper's legs.

"I'm strategizing!"

If Delta had the decisive, deadly programming, I had the deliberate, cautious version. The clipper's attacks came slow, predictable, but in wide arcs: the shears or the saws would sweep across the hallway where I'd been, glance off the wall with a horrible noise, and then the clipper would retract the limb and start again with another one.

Those long swings left big holes. I just needed to find the courage to use one. Numbers flew through me, calculating time, speed, and the clipper's reach. Its right saw arm came in for another swipe, and when the blade went by—I'd once again used the coward's back-step to get away—my calculations dinged an opening and I ran forward.

As I went, I lifted and slammed my broken scrap bar like some barbarian warrior, bashing into the clipper's arm and splitting it in half, the saw sputtering as it flew into the ground. Inside the clipper's reach, I couldn't burn time re-running calculations, so I went with the odds, and drove my bar up like a blunt spear into the clipper's thin middle. The tall mech's core bent and crumpled as I pushed into it, cooling fluid bursting out and splashing across my face as the thing fell back, powerless.

Standing over my victim, brushing the faint blue goo from my eyes, I looked up to see Delta staring at me, a slight grin at the ready.

"Nice work," Delta offered, aware that, behind her, I could see the entryway littered with Fountain's army, burning and wrecked. "Need a shower?"

"Quiet."

TWENTY-SEVEN

BRAWL IN THE PARK

You'd think that after laying waste to a sinister mech menagerie that Delta and I might celebrate, might take a second and consider what two vessels, programmed and designed to be Starship's artificial saviors, could do. I certainly wanted to after I saw the ruin Delta had left in her wake.

"Let's go," Delta said as I inventoried her destruction. "Every second we waste gives Fountain time to assemble more."

"As if that's going to be a problem for you."

"It only takes one bad move."

Sure, though I figured the odds Delta would ever make a bad move in battle to be too low to bother calculating.

Looking to improve my own odds, I located a bisected clipper and snapped off the shears. My scrap metal club had a few too many dents to be much good, and holding some large scissors made me feel less useless next to Delta.

"Nice trophy there," Kaydee said as I followed Delta from her massacre. "Tell me, Gamma, what're you going to do with those? Poke your own eyes out?"

"I'm not that incompetent."

Maybe Kaydee thought she'd hurt my feelings, because she threw a hand on my shoulder—not that I could feel it—and killed the mocking glint in her eyes.

"Look, I'm sorry," Kaydee said, and when I started to say that wasn't necessary, that vessels and mechs like me could kill emotions with a flip of a programmatic switch, she put her other hand to my mouth. "I know I'm being hard on you, and it's because I've still got stuff to work out. You probably realize that."

I hadn't, but Leo hadn't built the vessels for emotional intelligence.

"I did this when I was alive, too," Kaydee continued as we went beneath the archway, Delta leading with her blade ready and thirsting for more mechanical blood. "I'd get vulnerable and then shrink back. I didn't want to deal with my own problems, so I jumped onto others instead."

"Like your little rebellion?"

"Look, Starship was, is, messed up." Kaydee stepped away from me and waved her hand across the floor, sparks lighting up and splitting into two sides, golden green to the right, deep crimson to the left. The crimson far outnumbered the green, a meter long red fire compared to an emerald candle. "I didn't like the choices my mother made, I didn't like the direction we were being given, to make mechs for this and that and everything."

"So rather than deal with the issue directly, you left."

"I thought we could tear it down, build up something better." Kaydee's sparks ran towards each other, the red overwhelming the green. "I didn't realize that a bunch of desperate people couldn't fight against what the Voices had."

Those green sparks, each individual one, grew brighter and brighter until the crimson swarm looked like tiny embers. Now the green overtook their opponents, and the red retreated, clustered on the archway's left side.

"When things went wrong, that's when I used the vessels,"

Kaydee continued. "Didn't see that I had a choice. Either I used every tool I had, threaten to destroy Starship, or we'd die."

"Except you didn't just threaten."

"At first I did. But when you realize everything you've been fighting for is going to die, you get frantic."

I wanted to forgive Kaydee's choices. Wanted to say that she'd been right to follow her beliefs, even to such an extreme end. Except I was a mech, a machine built on logic, and the idea that Kaydee could have found any satisfaction for herself, for her allies, by breaking into and sabotaging Starship's engines was . . . illogical.

"Are you done?" Delta asked, and Kaydee, along with her spark war, vanished. "We have a job to do."

"Some of us have more than one."

Kaydee was more than a simple program. Whatever process created the Minds preserved more than simple functions. Just as I had enough computational power to have emotions, to reflect upon my own actions, Kaydee did too. I didn't want Kaydee to fall apart: I'd already experienced a rogue program inside my systems, and Kaydee's destructive tendencies might be even worse than Alpha's corruption.

"Great," Delta replied, then jerked her head towards the Park. "Deal with it. We have a mech to destroy."

I set a tiny function running inside myself, searching for and linking Kaydee's files together so that, if need be, I could restrict her. Keep her from hurting me, herself, or anything else.

While that process spun along, I followed Delta back onto the Conduit's forever walkway. The Park, in all its leafy glory, spread out in front, above, and below us. Birdsong played through the air, though no literal birds existed to sing it. The blue mist filtered down from above, and I realized, for the first time, that Starship no longer followed any day or night cycle. In Kaydee's memories, I'd see the difference. Now?

"It's always the same time," I said to Delta's back, and the look she gave me mixed confusion and exasperation. "Starship. There's no day. No night."

"Because it's no longer necessary." Delta nodded towards a dirt path stepping up from the walkway, back towards Fountain. "Come on. Stay focused."

Delta's brutal reasoning made sense. If no humans remained, then why bother paying tribute to a biological constraint? What I wondered, though, was who had turned off the cycling, and why? Had they used Delta's straight-up logic and decided to make the change, or had it been a more nefarious move, put in place while humans were still around?

Mysteries for another time.

Holding my shears in both hands, ready to slice and stab, I followed Delta. Now that we were in the Park, we should have been surrounded by Fountain's mechs. Harassed by them at every step, except that didn't happen. Our steps went unmolested, and I even dared to enjoy the budding flowers and bristling branches.

At least until we reached Fountain's courtyard.

The giant mech had either heard of our coming or elected to stand for other reasons, because Delta and I could see its stone crown topping the trees well before making our entrance. Rather than back away at the sight and re-assess, Delta growled and picked up her pace.

"So we're throwing out strategy entirely, then?" I said to her back.

"Don't need strategy," Delta replied. "Just need to fight."

Fine words, fine words. Leo might have gone a little too far in programming Delta's aggression. Not that I didn't follow, because mechs were crowding around the path, watching us from bushes and tree branches, and if I found myself divorced from Delta and her murdering blade, I felt the Park would soon become a very dangerous place.

"Fountain!" Delta announced as she led us through the cherry blossom tunnel into the courtyard.

I expected more than just the mech's name, but Delta didn't follow-up, instead stopping dead. Catching up with her, I saw why.

Standing—a word that felt inappropriate for what I saw—near Fountain and partially astride the mech, as though using Fountain as a rest, stood the largest mech I'd ever seen. Three spheres made up its central body, each one shaded a different color, and each one translucent and pocked over with little alcoves. I could make out objects in those spheres, spaced around like someone might pack a storage space. From afar, they looked like tiny clothes, like smaller packed white things—diapers, my data told me— and other assorted bits and bobs I couldn't identify.

Beyond the spheres, though, the mech went real strange. Arcing, spindled arms and legs shot out, each one ending in a six-pronged claw that splayed out to make a foot on the ground, or waved in the air, clacking like some delusional plant caught in a breeze. Rather than going for thickness, the mech's limbs looked hair-thin, flexible and able to weave around like a boneless serpent.

As for the head, I figured two stalk-like eyes emerged from the top sphere, waving about like the arms as they zeroed in on us new arrivals.

"What the hell is that?" I said.

"No idea," Delta replied.

"They really built it?" Kaydee said, joining our line. "I never thought they would. Never."

Before I could ask Kaydee what she meant by, well, anything she'd just said, a rumbling greeting rolled its way to us.

"The traitors return!" Fountain roared, tossing in all that emotion mechs weren't supposed to have. "Have you come to throw yourselves at my waters and beg forgiveness?"

"They have not," the other mech spoke, its voice a soothing, willowy sound. "They have come to destroy you, because what else could they do? They are, after all, the Voices' chosen."

Sensing Delta plotting a swift end to the dialogue with her sword, I put my left hand—gently—on her arm and moved forward. While I felt the impending violence as much as anyone, I wanted to know more, in the off-chance we made it out alive.

"You seem to know who we are," I offered as Delta shrugged me off. "We don't have the same luxury?"

The giant mech unbound itself from Fountain, its legs, arms, whatever-you-wanted-to-call-them moving with absurd grace from Fountain's bulk to the ground. Its eyestalks swung my way, leveling at my face before rising above, their black ends staring down at me.

"I will not be the one to give it to you," the mech said. "Fountain, please get rid of these for me. They are pests, and I am tired of the Voices interfering in my work."

"And our deal?" Fountain rumbled, leaving me feeling ignored.

"I don't care what you do to this ship," the mech replied, sending an eyestalk Fountain's way, keeping one on me. "So long as you eliminate the Voices, the rest of the Conduit is yours."

"Well that doesn't sound good." Kaydee went by me, looking hard at the mech. "And if this is what I think it is, our problems just got way worse."

The mech, deciding its deal was done, swung away from Fountain and I, its legs moving it fast from the courtyard. I would've thought such a big thing would break branches and trample hedges as it moved, but nothing other than a rustle came from its passage.

"Can I kill it now?" Delta said, leveling her sword at Fountain.

"Kill me?" Fountain grumbled a laugh, and the runes inscribed on its stone levels glowed that golden light. "You should've destroyed Volt. That old mech would've been easy."

"I'm not interested in easy," Delta replied.

"I am," I offered, but nobody seemed to care.

"I didn't destroy the other vessels that came here," Fountain said, its bulk squaring up to Delta's far smaller form. "But I'm going to relish ending you."

So many questions, and I had zero opportunity to ask any; Fountain's words triggered an invasion along the courtyard's border, the flowers and trees shaking as their mechs made entrances. Clippers, the trundling clubbers, and more flitting bird robots than I could count. If we'd been outnumbered in Power Core's entryway, here we were overrun.

"Cover me," Delta said, and before I could ask how, she launched herself at Fountain like a missile.

I followed, not trying to match Delta's forward, blade out dive, but rather spinning around and pointing my shears at any encroaching mech. I scratched a trundler that whirred in too close, clipped a bird making a swipe at my head, and even managed a clashing parry with a clipper's lanky lunge. All while working my way towards Delta.

Because, from what I saw during my rotating rondel, Delta had Fountain on the ropes from the very start. The big mech launched bright, burning bolts from its charging runes—apparently they were quite a bit more than decorative—but Fountain's shots immolated its own mechs, missing Delta's swift dance by embarrassing margins.

Delta, though, did not miss her big target. She whirled and struck her blade over and over again, slashing and stabbing and sticking its point into Fountain's levels and doing precisely nothing. Fountain lost bits: tiny rocks chipped off as Delta banged away, but barring a thousand years to hack at its upper armor, we wouldn't be getting through.

"Go beneath!" I shouted, ducking under the clipper's second swipe and winning a banging blow from another trundler in the process. I used the hit's momentum to roll across the courtyard stones, staying too low for the birds. "You're not going to win that way!"

Delta seemed to hear me: as another strike bounced off Fountain's second stone ring, Delta back-flipped off the big mech and delivered an eviscerating blow to the clipper that'd been hounding me, slicing its legs apart as Delta landed in a crouch.

Fountain's base rose a meter off the ground, its yellowed eyes tracking Delta and I as we kept moving to avoid its blasts. The laser bolts struck so far off, burning those stones, melting the trundler that'd struck me, that'd been creeping up to bang my brain before I'd leapt away, that I wondered whether Delta had damaged Fountain somehow.

The answer sprang from my own dive towards a bench on the courtyard's border, seeking some cover as Fountain's attacks became so heavy that its own mechs started retreating; between Delta's dervish and Fountain's lasers, mechs were getting totaled at a ludicrous rate.

The bench triggered clues: sitting there, deep cherry wood with black iron frames. Spotless, except for a few rogue blossoms that'd landed there, ignorant to the chaos going on around them. Humans would have sat there, would've watched Fountain, and would've been its primary targets should Fountain's deadlier programs need running. The mech had been designed to destroy humans, not vessels.

Not mechs that could move faster than any human ever had, that could react faster than any human ever could.

Delta did her best to exemplify that difference, spinning at Fountain and darting towards its underbelly. With her blade out in front, Delta ran low, ready to dive straight in and deliver a death blow from below. Fountain's levels lit up at her approach, then blasted out all together, blazing a burning wall in Delta's path. The vessel threw herself away, a desperate roll that no doubt singed her and that sent her sword flying as it bounced on the stones.

"You can't dance forever," Fountain said, following Delta's roll, readying its runes.

I wasn't so sure about that—Delta looked like she could keep right on blitzing as long as she had to—but Fountain could handle a straight on assault. What the mech couldn't do, what I realized as I picked myself up and saw no incoming attacks from Fountain's now-scattered mech army, was handle two vessels at once.

Volt's additions to my legs proved their worth as I made a run towards Fountain's underside. My shears had vanished somewhere in the fight, so I didn't have a great plan for what to do when I slid beneath Fountain, but one step at a time. Delta, on my periphery, scrambled away from Fountain's continuing blasts, its lasers cascading around her, pinning her down.

I dropped to the ground, pushed ahead and slid into Fountain's pit. The mech's big eyes finally found me, and Fountain grumbled something I didn't catch as I tried to find something to hit, to hurt.

Fountain's underbelly had a black half-sphere, where those yellow eyes peeked from and, with four thick struts, its feet attached. The sphere itself had zero weak points I could see: all smooth and clean. I threw a punch, pushed all the force I could muster, and my hapless fist banged into the base with nothing more than a ringing noise and a sudden, severe ache in my right fingers.

"Good move, G-man," Kaydee said, looking up with me. "How about we try not punching the armored mech?"

"I'm open to suggestions!"

Fountain, apparently, didn't like me hanging out beneath it. The struts keeping Fountain elevated started bending down, that black sphere collapsing towards my face. Towards a very certain, crushing death.

TWENTY-EIGHT

LIFE OF A VIRUS

Back in Power Core, as Volt's guardian mech prepared to beam me into oblivion, I'd swung for the only point I could, aimed right for that glowing golden weak spot. Fountain didn't have lasers charging beneath its dropping bulk, but it did have those yellow eyes.

Close enough.

I punched up as I fell back, buying the slightest second as Fountain came down. My fist smashed Fountain's lens, and Fountain itself pressed that broken bulb against my now-cut hand, and I felt an opening. Those eyes connected to wires, which connected to Fountain's core. I pressed my thumb and forefinger together around the wire as Fountain buried me.

"COULDN'T SEE THIS ONE COMING," Kaydee said as we stood amongst, quite possibly, the happiest place I'd ever seen.

Fountain structured its data as, I supposed, it had lived: every-where we could see, from the little plastic fort we stood upon, appeared to be a gigantic park. A slide sat at my feet, silver and ready to shimmy me down to a wood chip ground. Not far beyond the slide's end were swings, going back and forth as . . .

Children. They were everywhere. Human children running around, jumping on carousels, kicking balls into nets, chasing each other. Kaydee and I gaped around at the sheer joy on display.

"They're all functions," I said, piecing it together. "Every one of those kids is a laser getting launched at Delta. The struts lowering Fountain onto me."

"It's horribly amazing."

"How do we turn it off?"

With Alpha, the answer had been to follow the path through the valley till we found his core routines. With me, my crystals controlled my knowledge, my pearl floor my functioning. With Fountain?

"There." Kaydee pointed, down and away. Sitting on a bench not unlike the one I'd scrambled near back in Fountain's courtyard, was a dapper-looking man in a gray suit, fedora and all. A cast-out from a history Starship had never seen. "That's Fountain."

"How do you know?" Admittedly, the man appeared to be the only adult in view, but still. "Programs can look like anything."

"Because that looks like my dad, and Fountain came from my mom."

"What?" I couldn't think of anything else to say, for any number of reasons. "Your dad? And your mom made Fountain? I thought you said this mech came after you . . . left?"

I didn't want to say 'died'. The idea felt strange with Kaydee standing right there.

Kaydee, rather than replying, dropped onto the slide and zipped away, snapping herself into a breezy summer outfit in the process, those teal tips glinting in the sun. I blinked myself into a shirt and shorts that matched what the kids were wearing, only a few sizes larger, and followed.

"It's a hunch," Kaydee said once I'd joined her on the ground, as we meandered towards the man, past kids taking turns on a rainbow-colored jungle gym. "Peony's not someone you want to cross, but it's not like mom had no heart. Had no fun. She'd play games with my dad, and his characters always looked like this, old-style businessmen."

I wanted to ask why, to keep on digging, but Kaydee had a wistful look to her that promised more if I kept quiet.

"Don't know why he did that, really," Kaydee continued. "Never had a chance to ask him, either. Mom showed me all his habits later."

"What happened to him?"

"Starship happened." Kaydee glanced away, then spun on a smile and faced me. "The important thing, Mom must've had Fountain put in after my little adventure. And now we know how to take it apart."

That's how she wanted to end the conversation? Just like the slide, though, Kaydee popped into a run before I could get any deeper. Fleeing deep discussions tended to be Kaydee's process, and, I had to remind myself, Fountain was at this very moment crushing my body into mush. There were bigger priorities.

Fountain's grey man looked up as we approached, a tired look on his wrinkled eyes, cheeks, and in the way he clasped his hands across his knees.

"Can't say I've ever been attacked from the inside before," the man said, his voice a low-grade purr. "Can't say I've ever been attacked at all, really. Most times, somebody wants to mess with me, they get dealt with before I have to light a level."

"Sorry, not sorry," I said. "I'll give you a choice. Disable yourself and let us leave, or I take all these kids and go."

Though the kids weren't really kids, it still felt wrong somehow, against my moral coding to talk about hurting them. Deleting programs was one thing, deleting digital children?

I could do without that.

"You know my basic function," Fountain replied. "Keep the peace in the Park. That's all I'm trying to do."

"Is it?" Kaydee said. "Because last I checked, and I check all the damn time, you sent a mech army to attack Power Core."

Fountain reached up, took the fedora off his head with one hand

and scratched fading dark hair with the other, "Not my code, lady. Not my code. Didn't have a choice, but not my code."

Given Alpha, given everything I'd seen so far, I didn't have to make a big leap to guess someone had slipped Fountain the virtual equivalent of a mind-altering drug. Like with myself, with Alpha, we ought to be able to clean it out, but . . .

"Where?" I asked. "If you've been infected, we can help, but you have to show us where."

"Why, it should be easy to find," Fountain replied. "What sticks out here, to you? What doesn't belong on this playground of mine?"

Kaydee and I took a turn, looking all around the infinite playground, at the kids climbing towers and sliding down slides, swinging away. Chasing each other in eternal games. Nothing looked odd, like it didn't fit.

Except.

Fountain hit Kaydee hard, sending her flying into the air, and as she soared, the digital gray man pulled an old-style pistol from his coat and fired a shot. Loud, clear, and on target. The bullet struck Kaydee, and for a micro-second, she seemed to tense up before bursting into pixels, then nothing.

I didn't have time to wonder what Kaydee's fate meant. Fountain whirled towards me, and I tackled him. Pushed Fountain to the ground and gripped his gun-wielding wrist with my right hand. With my left, I reached into my own athletic shorts, their baggy pockets, and found the first weapon my digital mind could come up with.

The shears. I pulled the big scissors out, lifted them high, and looked at Fountain's face, where I'd be stabbing in a second.

Fountain's eyes, his normal eyes, were all purple black. Dark pools glaring back at me. I hesitated at the sight, at the connections to Alpha and my own corruption, and Fountain took advantage. His free hand punched my chest and knocked me off. Fountain stood, yanking his arm free from mine and settled the pistol into an easy shot at my chest.

A kid slammed Fountain from behind, driving his body into

Fountain's legs and knocking the gray man off balance. Another one, streaking in with a bat in her hands, delivered a blow to Fountain's back and knocked him to his knees. As I stood up, the kids swarmed Fountain, or at least this part of the mech, burying him in a body pyramid that grew taller and taller.

"Not totally gone," I said, watching the pile grow as more programs, more children sprinted in from farther reaches. "Thanks for being sloppy."

The organic body has immune systems. Proper code does too, ways to identify and attack intruders. Whatever had invaded Fountain had kept itself hidden, guiding Fountain's logic without making itself overly known, because, of course, a mech built to offer protection for the Voices would have strong anti-corruption defenses. Of course it would be able to keep itself safe from sabotage.

Well, almost. Whomever had corrupted Fountain had been good enough to hide the virus until Kaydee and I pointed it out.

But for now, at least, Fountain's own programming did the work. After watching its functions render a fatal verdict to the virus—when the kids finally left their pile, literally nothing remained of the gray man or his suit—I took a final look around the playground, and disconnected.

TO FIND MYSELF STARING AT, a millimeter away, Fountain's base sphere. The mech really had almost crushed me, the broken eye that I'd punched about to drive its jagged remnants into my face.

"Gamma?" Delta's words were muffled by Fountain's bulk, but I heard them. "The mech's stopped fighting. Are you alive down there?"

"For the moment," I replied. "Fountain, any chance you could lift up?"

The big mech didn't reply. No sound, no movement.

"Fountain?" I tried again.

"I'm not seeing anything," Delta said from above. "Is it dead?"

Oh. The realization hit fast. If Fountain's virus had infected the mech's core systems, and I'd turned the defenses against those same systems, then Fountain might be nothing more than a metal hulk.

"Kaydee, are you there?" I whispered, trying to reach out to her section in my memory and trigger something.

"I'm here," Kaydee replied, popping in beside me, looking pale and exhausted. "Just going to say, getting shot really sucks."

"I can imagine."

Fountain's attack booted Kaydee's hack from the mech's system, but as Kaydee's main functions lived in me, I wasn't surprised to see she still lived. Although tacking one more trauma onto her long list would probably have a reckoning later.

"So you toasted the big guy?" Kaydee asked.

"More like Fountain toasted itself," I said. "Lucky you didn't have to see children maul the man."

"Definitely one memory I can do without." Kaydee pressed her hands against Fountain's bottom. "Not sure how you're going to get out of here."

"No ideas?"

"Gamma, don't know how you think I lived my life, but I've never once been trapped in a pit with a giant mech squashing down on me."

"Hmm. Fair point."

The solution came courtesy of the very same mechs we'd been fighting since coming back from Power Core. Those trundling boxes, designed to pick up trash and tend the gardens, proved adept shovel wielders, digging away at Fountain's edges until I had a gap large enough to squeeze through.

Why those little mechs had decided to help became clear when I made the courtyard's surface: Delta, blade out, directing them under swift, deadly penalty. Not exactly the benevolent harmony the mechs had been designed for, but apparently even these basic 'bots had some self preservation code.

"Nice work," Delta offered as I stood up, brushing dirt off of my largely ruined shorts and shirt. "Didn't expect that."

"To be honest, I didn't expect it either," I replied. "Saw you weren't doing well—"

"I was fine." Delta turned, pointed the blade down the path back towards the walkway. "Let's get moving."

"Nothing?" I said to her back. "That's it? You're not even going to let me brag?"

Delta didn't answer, and I fell in after her. Kaydee, sparking along beside me, laughed.

We briefly debated going back to Power Core, telling Volt we'd done as the old mech asked, but Delta felt Volt could figure out Fountain's demise on his own. No need to waste the time. For once, I felt the same, and we hit the walkway and continued aft.

The Park kept going for a long time, branching out its floral and architectural designs alongside our walkway to hit humanity's themes. If Conduit's earlier sections had felt like a random culture blend, the Park split itself clean, with hard transitions that none-theless drew me in as the world around us shifted from flower gardens to sprawling ferns to sparse tundra paths.

Breaking the zen, Starship interrupted, on occasion, with more archways leading to other areas with defined purposes, like *Training Center*, *The Factory*, and others, all glitzed out in specific two-tone color schemes. Power Core had emerald and hazel, these spanned the chromatic gamut.

"Guess I shouldn't be surprised," I said when the next major section came into view. "Biological things need to keep themselves healthy."

"You say that like you don't need as much upkeep," Kaydee said, sniffing next to me. "Who just had themselves put back together again?"

"But when I get fixed, it's an upgrade," I replied. "When you get fixed, it's delaying the inevitable."

"Quiet," Delta said. "There's something ahead."

The Hospital announced itself with a neon red cross bordered by blue white bars hanging over the Conduit's center. The cross itself spanned several levels from top to bottom, and it baked into the Hospital's Conduit-crossing building. The Garden had coated its outside with plants, albeit ones that had decayed over years without care. The Hospital followed that same trend, except with broad murals painted on every available spot.

"Every generation had a section," Kaydee said. "We'd hold big exhibitions to choose the artist. Pretty cool, really."

Less cool was Delta's observation: things definitely were moving behind those murals, visible in the painted-over windows. Shadows trekking back and forth.

"There can't be any patients left?" I said as we approached our level's entrance.

"Hope not," Kaydee replied. "Would be real lonely in there."

"Don't get distracted," Delta said. "That thing we saw with Fountain went this way. If it turned Fountain, it might have done the same to whatever lives in here."

"Always taking the grim view, aren't you?" I said.

"I'm trying to keep us alive."

For a hot second, I thought about engaging Delta in a debate about whether we, being machines, really were 'alive'. What would the determined, driven vessel do with a question her sword couldn't solve? But, seeing as Delta had already stabbed me once, pushing her might not be the best plan.

I kept my mouth shut, and we went through the broad, walkway-covering doors that opened inward as we approached. No guardian mechs demanding clearance to go inside this time. In fact, no mechs at all in the short gap between the Park and the Hospital.

The Hospital's entrance answered why.

Signs abounded just inside the doors, reading off levels and their functions like a nightmare's table of contents. Cancers, surgeries, labs, radiation containment, all the horrors played out on the wall to my right as we went inside. All risks belonging to organic life.

The risks to me sat in front, arrayed out with their implements glistening, silver-white orbs locked onto Delta and I. Like the Park, the mechs coupled variety with purpose, from more trundling trash mechs to swift and spindly surgical mechs, to humanoid doctor substitutes, looking like poor versions of Delta and myself.

Some held medical tools—I saw several bone saws—while others opted for the more rudimentary and had snapped off chair legs and other makeshift clubs in their claws. More than one seemed to think they could stab us to death with a long syringe.

"Should I be afraid?" I asked Delta as we took in the hostile menagerie.

That the collection hadn't moved yet gave me no comfort. They were waiting for a command, and it would come.

"These are nothing," Delta replied. "Let's keep moving."

"I think Leo modeled her after me," Kaydee said as Delta started forward, blade ready to carve a path. "If I'd had a sword, a uniform like that and extensive combat training . . ."

"Right," I replied. "And a laser focus on the objective."

"Are you calling me scattered?"

"I'm saying you could work on it."

Kaydee popped away, apparently miffed at being called out for her flippant tendencies. I wasn't going to apologize for that, though. Kaydee skipped around her memories and mine with such random speed. Someday I might understand the functions that guided her, but until then, Kaydee would remain an enigma.

Delta reached the first mech and, as they still hadn't moved, asked it to give way. The mech didn't reply, so Delta pushed it aside as I caught up to her. The mech fell over, clanging against the floor. The others didn't make a move to help it, to stop us.

"Well, maybe we're lucky," I said as we pushed our way through the glut. "Maybe that big mech didn't give the right orders."

"Doubt it," Delta said. "Keep moving."

Beyond the entry and its lines, the Hospital adopted hallways like they were architecture's best feature. The longer, the straighter, the better. We passed by an elevator, then hit our first branch, with an option to keep going ahead or cross the Conduit. The Hospital's signs declared primary care to the right, radiology straight ahead, along with the eventual exit to, and I froze as I read it, the Nursery.

"We're almost there." I jabbed a finger at the sign.

As I pointed, the Hospital's serene soundscape shifted from Starship's ever-present hum to a clicking, clacking, rolling swarm. Motion all around us, above and below. Rooms along the hallways on either side opened up, spilling out more mechs. Behind, that still army we'd waded through turned around and began its advance.

"A trap," Delta said the words as if describing paint, or nothing at all. "Get ready."

"Do you have a plan?"

"Yes. Destroy them all."

TWENTY-NINE

FAMILY MATTERS

A medical grade army made beelines for my synthetic body. I had two fists, I had my retrieved shears—they'd done little during the fight with Fountain, but having them made me feel better—and neither seemed up to the moment.

"Find a way out," Delta said. "I'll hold them."

"Hold them?" I retreated to the wall opposite the off-shooting hallway, the only place I could get something solid behind me. "How are you going to do that?"

"Find a way out."

Fine, then. I supposed Delta never explained her words, not sure why she'd start doing that now.

I took in the situation: three hallways leading to our intersection, Delta standing in the middle, waiting for the mechs to close. To my left, a little further along, sat an elevator. It'd popped open a moment ago to disgorge more trash mechs to beat us senseless, but that presented an option. I'd rather dart inside than try to carve a path through any mech flood.

"Elevator ahead," I said as Delta flicked her eyes from one horde to the next, no doubt trying to judge which would hit her reach fastest. "That's my pick for a getaway."

"Then let's get away."

Delta shot off like a rocket, sprinting straight. Not left. Not towards the elevator.

"Wrong way!" I shouted as Delta barreled into the mechs, her blade sweeping back and forth like a farmer clearing a field.

If Delta heard me, I couldn't tell.

"She's going to fight," Kaydee said. "You can still be a coward, though."

"How about a survivor?" I replied, turning and starting towards the elevator and the several dozen mechs between me and those chromed doors. "And how is wading towards the enemy cowardice, again?"

"My bad. Guess you're just doomed."

Kaydee's prediction notwithstanding, I didn't like my odds as I closed with the motley mech menagerie. Some mechs matched my height—the caretakers made to assist humans around the Hospital— while most came in at my waist or below, their various implements buzzing, slashing, striking towards me like hungry animals nearing their juicy meal.

Except this meal had some new ideas.

I couldn't fight like Delta, but I *could* move like her. She survived because she danced, always flowing through the enemy so their attacks missed, left them open for easy reprisals. I juiced my legs, my arms, and burst into a run.

My shears led me into the first mechs, stabbing ahead with all the subtlety two linked blades could manage. I pierced a trash box, drove it back until it smashed into the mech behind it, and as a dozen claws, clubs, and calipers reached for me, I used the stuck mech's halted, tilted body as a ramp.

Leaving the shears behind, I ran up the trash box's body and jumped, knocking my head against the ceiling but clearing the caretakers, the mashing mech mosh and landing . . . right in a whole slew more. I shouted as I came down not behind the mechs, but in the middle of a force far deeper than I'd guessed.

Thankfully, the mechs hadn't anticipated their target coming from the sky either. A rare occurrence when indoors, for certain, and my surprise gave me a screwball landing where I plowed into two caretakers, bearing them to the ground. Trash boxes and medical mechs turned and clustered to stab me. I felt syringes poking into my sides as I pressed my hands into my twin mech landing pads and pushed off.

I took scrapes and slices, beatings and bruises as my clothes tore, but I didn't stop. Put everything I had into my legs, into my swinging fists as I batted mechs aside in my quest for those beautiful chromed doors and the call button glowing right next to them.

My fingers grazed the button as a mech hit me in the right direction, a flailing reach that hit its mark. The doors shunted open with their whirring, heavy shift and I fell inside.

I'd expected an empty elevator, but I hit the soft white-and-brown tile next to a stretcher, feet on the floor and voices talking fast as the doors shut. Human doctors stood around me, a nurse and at least one mech. They didn't look my way, didn't seem to realize a collapsed vessel lay on the floor next to them.

"Fifth level, fast," a doctor in grape-colored scrubs ordered as I stood.

Nobody reached for the lit up level panel, so I did the honors, processes still unscrambling themselves from the mech beating I'd taken en route to the lift. I tapped the button, its cream level sitting on a blue-black background, and the lift flashed its acceptance, started to move. The doctor, meanwhile, kept on giving orders to the others standing around, drawing my eyes to their subject.

Kaydee lay in the stretcher. Eyes closed. Face hollow. Hair nothing like the spiked, dyed affair her digital self had adopted, but rather a thinned, gray-brown combo meant for someone far older than the rest of her would suggest. An oxygen mask clamped over her face, an IV bag pumped fluids into her arm.

"What's wrong?" I managed to ask, taking in the moment and forgetting the mechs down below.

Nobody replied, of course, because this wasn't real. Wasn't happening right now. Another glitch in my system, a call to a memory that wasn't mine. I shut my eyes for a second, but the stretcher didn't disappear, the doctor calling out Kaydee's dire condition didn't stop.

I could have reset. Shut myself off. Doing that in a hospital filled with murderous mechs, though, seemed like a bad idea.

The elevator reached its level and as soon as the doors hit their width, the mech guiding the stretcher shot it out, doctor and nurse on its heels. I took a cautious approach, looking onto a level coated in Kaydee's teal and white color scheme. One dotted with intergalactic pictures alternating with smiling, recovered patients. And no other mechs.

Delta would be on our old level. I could try and go back, see if she was okay. And I would have, except Delta didn't seem like she needed help, and Kaydee's plight held my attention. Tugged at me as a high priority.

"Sorry," I said to the elevator, as if it could carry my words to Delta.

Kaydee's medical crew hadn't made it far. After about twenty paces and past several rooms, the crew turned Kaydee's stretcher and vanished. I followed, each step flickering as today's Hospital, with its sterile, clean corridors scrubbed endlessly by mechs and untraveled by humans contrasted with the Hospital in Kaydee's past, with staff, patients, and their families funneling around.

I went past a staff break room, and at first look I saw nothing in it. The transparent refrigeration unit held nothing on its shelves, and the counters were a bare soft blue. A hot second later I saw the room as it had been, filled with brought lunches, group-gifted treats, and a tired-looking nurse sipping coffee.

Glancing away from the break room, I stumbled to my right as another stretcher barreled towards me. The squad following its trek went right through me, their bodies, faces, showing no sign they knew I existed. Which, I supposed, I didn't.

"Right," I told myself, blending my voice in with the real-not-real conversations around me. "None of this is really happening."

But it had happened, and one look in Kaydee's room confirmed why these moments stuck to her. I'd thought, in the elevator, that Kaydee had been asleep, but her eyes were open here. Weak, but alert, they searched the room as I came up to her stretcher side. The doctor that'd issued the commands bringing her here had vanished, and now only a mech offered Kaydee any comfort.

"What would you like to watch?" the mech asked as Kaydee gulped down oxygen. "If you like, I can play our most popular programming?"

Kaydee's eyes rolled in response, then turned to the room's window, one that, in her time, looked back towards the Park's verdant green and, in mine, looked much the same. Strange how so many things shifted with time's passage, but stick some mechs on the job, and the ravages wouldn't be so bad.

"You don't need to see this," Kaydee said, dropping in beside me.

"Why are you here?" I said. "I mean, there?"

"Remember that vessel problem I had? My little rebellion gone wrong?" Kaydee reached out, touched her own hand on the stretcher. "This is what came after."

"It didn't look fatal?"

"I don't know. Everything past this point gets clouded. I think they imaged me here, made me a Mind. My memories end in this bed." Kaydee blinked, nodded outside the room. "Shouldn't you be back helping Delta?"

I should, definitely, and yet I felt Kaydee's presence here was important to her, and if Kaydee cared about this, then I had to as well. She and I were together, after all. But when I looked back, the stretcher had disappeared. The old Kaydee too. Nothing left but a bland, spotless room.

"Are you hiding this from me?" I asked the new Kaydee, still lingering by the room's entrance.

"Can't really do that, G-man," Kaydee said. "If I could hide it, why show it to you at all?"

True.

Without a memory to investigate, going to look for Delta did seem like the next best option, so I went back down the still-empty hallway towards the elevator. Was about to hit the call button, my hand a centimeter away from punching in its glowing light, when Kaydee made a noise halfway between a sigh and a sob.

"You want to see what happened? You really want to see?" Kaydee said.

The elevator was right there, I could go back down, but . . . Delta could handle herself. She'd been programmed to fight, I'd been given a more curious bent.

"I do," I said. Kaydee had her hands jammed in her pant's pockets, head shaking more to herself than at me. "Can you show me?"

"Not me," Kaydee replied. "I don't know what happens next."

"Then, how?"

Kaydee nodded over towards the nurse's station, a cutout with a long counter, and I could imagine chairs holding spots there. I followed Kaydee around the side and through a door—locked, but with a shove, I snapped it open to see nothing much. Dead monitors littered the space, their dark screens hinting at a brighter past. Holes in the walls suggested posters or other hanging things long since fallen and tossed away. Someone had idly scratched their name into a dark corner.

"Andrea?" I asked, peering at the scratch. "Is that who?"

"No," Kaydee said. "What're you doing? I'm talking about the connection port. Right here."

Kaydee knelt and pointed beneath the counter at a shiny gray panel covered in rectangular openings, each one a jack into a wider net. I spliced the story in a second: these ports connected anything here to Starship's broader systems. Let the nurses, or whomever, have rapid access to information, to contacts, to—

"Your mother," I said. "That's who you want me to contact."

"And now you understand why I didn't want you to do it."

"Because she doesn't like you?"

"Because she loves me too much to let me go," Kaydee said. "She made me this. If you want to know everything, she's who you have to ask. I, I wasn't really there."

There were mysteries meant to be solved, questions that I needed to answer. The Voices demanded I to the Nursery. Yet, how do you resist understanding yourself?

"I'm sorry," I said to Kaydee, and pinched my fingers to form the jack, plugged them into the port.

In an instant the Hospital vanished as my consciousness zipped along the port's burning connection. Unlike the Bridge, I didn't directly tap into the Voices here. I had to find them, navigate along Starship's frayed interconnected webbing to find the right address.

As if I were zipping along the Conduit, innumerable choices appeared for me to jump into. Did I want to browse a long-shuttered restaurant's menu? See the temperature plan for Garden's desert levels? View the last recorded basketball game played in Starship's ten team league? Choices presented themselves by the millions, the billions.

How humans navigated this mess with any speed, any accuracy, I didn't understand. My processors went into overdrive sorting and dismissing all these potentials before, finally, winding up where I needed to be: in Starship's Central Operating Matrix.

Opening up the matrix changed my reality from an endless list to a cozy cliffside cabin. The transition came so fast I did a double take at the woodsy, northern feel. A big fire—apparently a Voice staple—roared, heating up a space so filled with walnut furniture, thick blankets, giant wildlife paintings, and my favorite five people clustered around a coffee table, looking at me.

"Have to say, it's been a long time since someone connected from beyond the Bridge." Captain Willis, sporting a more rugged version of his official uniform, toasted me with his mug. "And from the Hospital? You're getting close."

I gaped. Delta, Kaydee and I had been scrambling, fighting for our lives in a treacherous trek across Starship, and here were its leaders, idling away on a virtual vacation?

"Gamma?" Leo said, starting to stand and then flickering right next to me, his condition splotching odd colors across his body. Leo gave me a welcoming smile nonetheless. "Anything we can do for you?"

Suddenly asking this mellow crew about Kaydee's Hospital encounter felt wrong. Like airing a secret in the open. I found Peony's eyes—she, at least, never lacked for suspicion in her looks.

"I need to talk to Peony. Alone, if I can?" I asked.

Leo cocked his head, "About what?"

"Leo, if the vessel wants to speak to me, let him." Peony waved Leo back. "Just because you created them, doesn't mean they're yours alone."

I didn't see the change, didn't get a motion or a clue, but Peony and I suddenly stood alone on a snowy mountainside, the cabin glowing behind us.

"We're partitioned now," Peony said, standing at my shoulder and joining my look over an immense, sprawling landscape frosted over and glowing in moonlight. "What do you need, Gamma?"

I relayed the story, attempting to start with the Hospital and then jumping back to the very beginning at Peony's insistence. She peppered my re-telling with questions, almost all about Kaydee. What had Kaydee said, what did she do, how did she act.

"Why?" I said after another Peony interrupted to ask how Kaydee had handled Alpha's corruption. "This isn't why I'm here."

"No, but it is why I am," Peony replied. "You, Gamma, are now the only place my daughter lives. So, naturally, I want to know how she is doing."

My path disrupted, I turned Kaydee's own heat on her mother,

"If you wanted to know how she was, you wouldn't have put her into a vessel."

Rather than take offense, Peony laughed, "I put her into a vessel because she's too dangerous to store anywhere else. I care about my daughter because she is my daughter. I care about Starship because it is the most important thing in our lives."

I didn't know if Kaydee could hear, could see what we spoke about in here. She hadn't shown up at the cabin, hadn't appeared on the Bridge either when I'd last visited the Voices, so maybe she wouldn't catch Peony's priorities. But I did.

"Then answer my question," I said. "Because your daughter's memories are affecting my mission."

"What memories?"

"The Hospital. Where I am now. I saw her being wheeled in on a stretcher, and she didn't look well."

Peony nodded, "What did Kaydee tell you?"

"That she couldn't remember."

"Smart girl," Peony replied. "Shouldn't you trust her?"

"It's my mission, my mind," I replied. "I need to know what's affecting her, what Kaydee might do."

"Does my daughter scare you, Gamma?"

I started to say no, then stopped. I liked Kaydee, and without her I'd be dead, but didn't she scare me? Didn't her ability to warp what I saw, how I interacted with reality, make me uncomfortable? And her rapid swings between moods? The gaps in her memory?

"She doesn't seem stable."

"The transition to a Mind is hardly foolproof," Peony said. "But perhaps I can help you. Gamma, will you let me talk to my daughter?"

"What? How?"

Peony gave me a sweet look, the kind a mother likely gave unruly children all the time. She reached down, scooped some snow off the ground, and then threw it into the air, the light flakes spreading into a glinting constellation as they fluttered off on their long journey down.

"She's one of those motes, living in you right now." Peony stuck her hand out, caught one of the falling flakes. "All you need to do is let me in."

Reverse the connection. Let Peony come back through the data stream into my space, rather than me jumping into theirs. Dangerous, but perhaps I could limit the access. Open up Kaydee's files only.

"What are you going to tell her?" I asked.

"Oh, we'll just have a chat," Peony replied. "While she's talking, I'll snoop around. Clean up some of those spots you mentioned. I know my daughter's life better than anyone now, even herself. When we're done, she'll remember, and she'll be able to tell you herself."

Choices. I could have gone down the elevator, rushed to Delta's rescue despite having no weapons, despite bearing the scars from a thousand stabbing syringes. Instead, I opened my memory to Kaydee's mother, and she swept in like hot lightning.

THIRTY

THE FUTURE GENERATION

My fingers smoked when I pulled them from the port. Peony's move had killed my connection, burned it out. I felt her too, my systems picking up a new program in the mix, one seeking and reading files. Not editing, not installing anything new.

Not yet.

Kaydee hadn't seemed like her mother's biggest fan, and now I had to wonder if I'd traded Kaydee's potential self-destruction for a more active threat. Peony might, though, turn out to be fine. Do exactly what she said she would do, clean up Kaydee's errors and leave me with a functioning Mind.

A functioning friend.

I didn't want to wait on that lonely Hospital floor for Kaydee to come around. Delta hadn't come up the elevator. The reasons she might still be on our old level weren't many, and weren't good. Maybe she needed help.

Maybe chasing memories had been a selfish, dumb decision.

The elevator popped open as soon as I pressed the button, telling me the lift hadn't moved. Also not good. I scrolled along the panel, found my former floor and selected it. I'd go down, let the doors open and take a peek. If mechs still overran the place, then I'd bounce up a level and try a different way.

Except, when those doors opened, I didn't need to do anything.

When Delta cleared Power Grid's lobby, slicing her way through Fountain's army, it had seemed miraculous. Amazing. Deadly and beautiful and all the other adjectives I could never apply to myself.

The only word that came to mind as I went out the elevator? Slaughter.

Acid scents filled my nose, sparks and scrap metal greeted my eyes, and the broken cries for maintenance echoed up and down the hallways. The medical mechs lay ruined by the dozens, split apart, their syringes and scalpels scattered like shrapnel across the floors, embedded into the walls, and, as I walked, occasionally falling from the ceiling where some blow had slotted them. Trash mechs had their boxes burst open, Delta's telltale slices writing a devastating story.

Following the ruin, I went back to that first intersection, where the triple mech ambush had come at Delta and I. My fingers ran along my synthetic flesh, feeling where my repairs continued from those cuts and scraps, stabs and bashes. These things had attacked us with every intent to destroy, I shouldn't feel sorry for them. Shouldn't take pity.

But these mechs hadn't been made for fighting. I picked up a nursing machine, its soft synthetic hands meant for comfort, now holding a scalpel handle whose blade had vanished. I couldn't know how old the mech had been, how many patients it had treated with cheer or compassion before something had twisted it against its nature.

"Delta?" I shouted, still holding the hand. "Are you here somewhere?"

Standing in that intersection, I could see that the wreckage extended down each path. Delta hadn't fought to escape, she'd obliterated them all because she could. Yet, even with that total war, the debris gave me a clue. Past the elevator, deeper into the Hospital and towards the Nursery, the mech bodies continued.

I wanted Kaydee to pop out, give her opinion on the massacre. Delta had saved her own life, certainly, but had ended so many more. Kaydee might be able to help me understand if this was simply Delta defending herself, or if her programming had a destructive bent I'd need to watch out for.

In the past, simply pinging Kaydee by thinking about her would cause Kaydee to appear, or at least push back a signal stating she was otherwise occupied—how a program in my system could ignore me was a question for another time—but now I received nothing in response. Not quite a disconnect, or an error: I made the request, Kaydee's program received it, but nothing happened.

To anyone watching me, it must have looked strange to see a beaten, scuffed and scratched man standing amid the mech wreckage looking at nothing, not moving or even breathing as I attempted to make Kaydee's connection over and over again.

After the hundredth attempt, because computers can do such things rapidly, I stopped trying. Perhaps Kaydee and her mother's routine, which had settled itself in Kaydee's files, were still processing each other. Engaged in an all-consuming digital conversation. I could try to force myself in there, but my limited understanding of human relationships made me resist the idea.

"Of my problems, let me focus on the one I can solve," I said to myself, and walked along the broken mech path towards the Hospital's end.

Along the way, I continued to see signs marking a history I didn't know. Directions to units and treatments I would never need, but that had no doubt kept Starship humming for generations. Kaydee had been overseen by a human doctor in her memories. By the end, how many humans had been treated entirely by mechs?

Had the last patient here been utterly alone, surrounded by the same mechs whose broken forms now surrounded me?

Grim thoughts, but the Hospital, with its empty blandness, inspired them. Not wanting to sink too far into morose musing, I tried to turn the Hospital on its head. Looked at the elevators, the hallways, the waiting rooms and considered how they might be used to treat the patients Starship now had aplenty. Mechs, and not just the ones ruined at Delta's hand, needed to be reset, repaired, revised. Calling them to a central location like this one might be the only way to change them all.

The idea brought the faintest nod to my walk as I reached the Hospital's end. Perhaps, when the Voices didn't need my services anymore, I could enlist Kaydee's help and take on a different mantle. Starship could have its first new doctor in a long time, one badly needed.

But before I could take up a mechanical medical profession, I had to find Delta and reconnect the Voices to the Nursery. To that end, I walked from the Hospital and back into the Conduit proper.

The gap between the Park and the Hospital had been small, flush with systems-related offshoots like Power Core. Kaydee had mentioned the region as roughly Starship's center, and the divide between the two sides captured more than just location.

Apparently, Kaydee had it right: the mist, a light blue filtering down from Starship's top changed over here to an off-yellow color, like pollen floating down, though the little droplets evaporated quick once they hit my skin.

Beyond the light, the Conduit's offshoots looked different as well. Rather than neon spirals offering entry to homes and businesses, the doorways I could see looked far more rudimentary. Flat gates flush with the walkways, denoted by nameplates and security pads. Colors abounded, but in more homespun flavors, the owners taking it upon themselves to paint and decorate rather than tap a button on some program.

The decorations suffered. The rudimentary mechs cleaning this section seemed to have died away or dropped off long ago. Before the Garden, I'd nearly been run over by a high capacity cleaning mech that stretched the level's entire height. Here, going by the grime covering the walls and the greasy puddles along the walkway, no such mechs existed. I didn't see any above or below either.

For that matter, I didn't see any mechs at all, cleaners or otherwise. For a second, I wondered if I'd fallen into another memory; Kaydee had muffled my initial Conduit trip, it was possible she'd disguised it again. Except, why? And when I reached out and touched the puddle, it stained my fingers black. Definitely real.

At least the puddles made it easy to keep on my target: Delta's footprints left a path, as she apparently held little regard for keeping her feet dry. She'd splashed right through the walkway's center, and I followed, sniffing at the chemical smells overwhelming everything else.

The Nursery, in sensible fashion, sat a minute's walk away from the Hospital, gleaming doors presenting a human child beneath a soft-looking moon, sleeping away in a manner that, I suspected, zero children actually were on Starship. I took a look up and down the walkway before reaching for the doors—the security pad glowed green, unlocked and ready—and saw no threats.

Pushing the doors open showed Delta's massacre hadn't ended with the Hospital. Two more nurse mechs stood severed just inside a bright-lit, grass-green lobby. Their bodies shined under icy oval lights embedded into the ceiling, giving the Nursery a sterile impression at odds with the hung posters depicting smiling babies and new families. The lobby otherwise sported several long benches and, towards its back end, two stands that resembled the molds I'd seen so shortly after awakening.

I approached the hands, curious as to how they would help someone find their new child, then noticed flat instructions posted behind the stone gray blocks: place the hands, and it would match your prints to your child, which would then be delivered to you.

Delta's grease-pit footprints continued past the molds to a thick door that may have been locked once, but that now bore a telltale slice straight through its center. With the doors themselves hanging at odd angles, I stepped on through, continuing to listen for Delta's voice, for something that might clue me into what lay ahead.

Nothing prepped me for the confusion beyond those broken doors.

As if taking its cues from a Conduit twisted by maniacal minds, the Nursery proper hit on the blue light and the mist, but bent it aside, spraying illumination by shattered means, the mist coming from broken pipes. Glass littered the cushioned floor, the same soft padding I'd stepped on after coming to life, and the shard's origins came from all around me.

Rather than the clean walls endemic to the Hospital, the Nursery opted for a visual aesthetic, filling in every line I saw with glass, now reduced to pointed collections and hanging fragments. The transparent protection coated myriad rooms filled with things I couldn't find an immediate answer for: a space to my right housing red and white blocks taller than me, each one lit up by a glittering status array on its side extended back into darkness. On my left, in a narrower, longer space, what appeared to be an assembly line commenced with a feeding slot near my waist and progressed along a conveyor as mech arms, smaller lights, and instruments by the dozen loomed.

What sort of thing would be taking that horrifying ride?

Straight back, the Nursery at last offered some familiar evidence in several spaces dedicated to cribs. I quick-counted fifty, held ten to a room, though many looked damaged. Those still functional lit their tops in Starship's ever-present emerald green, advertising their open status to any child with the misfortune of needing this terrifying place.

Why did I feel that creeping unease, that raw alarm from my systems? I'd seen damage before on Starship, places torn apart or blasted beyond their original purpose. Perhaps I had no reference, no understanding for what could cause so much harm in a place meant for raising the most vulnerable children.

Surely Kaydee had not brought her rebel strike here? Had Delta given in to wanton destruction?

A sound burst my contemplation, the telltale soft grind as a wheel turned on tile. Among the red and white banks, a nursing mech moved, gliding between the towers, stopping and inspecting the panels, as though unaware I watched it, unaware half its home had been trashed.

The nurse mech stopped near a tower and extended a long, thin device into a port on the tower beneath that status array, the screen shifting from a hundred meters and monitors to a rapid cycle through strings too long for me to read. Yet, in a flash, the screen settled on one particular line, declaring an optimal match for the queries entered.

"What query?" I muttered, stepping closer to the enclosure, crunching glass beneath my feet.

Like in the Hospital, I pushed aside concern for Delta to focus on the immediate. As much as I worried about the vessel and her disappearance, Delta had proven very capable of annihilating anything she came across. More important now to figure out what might have disconnected the Voices from the Nursery and, above even that . . . I wanted to understand what I saw.

The tower whirred as the nurse mech confirmed the selection and a tray popped from the tower bearing a tiny vial. The nurse mech, with another precise twin-pronged appendage, scooped the vial from its tray.

And turned my way.

I froze. The mech had to see me, would be calling some general alarm at the intruder. We stared at each other for a long moment, the nurse mech's soft blue eyes sculpted into its circular face, no doubt designed to elicit calm from human children.

"New route defined," the nurse mech said in a voice that sounded like a warm blanket. "For your safety and mine, please remain stationary until I have passed."

Confused, I did precisely as the mech commanded, and the nurse wheeled her way towards me, then around and over the lip created by the broken glass. An ad hoc doorway. The mech, apparently, was not above finding advantages in the Nursery's destruction.

Beyond me, the mech went to the conveyor belt's entrance, that small slot, and set the vial inside. Once free from its package, that twin-pronged appendage found another port, centered itself, and launched the process with a chirping affirmation. The conveyor belt began running, its many implements adding a techno chorus to the Nursery's otherwise silent soundscape.

The nurse mech wheeled her way along the belt towards its end, far along the room, and I took her spot at the beginning to watch the vial and its purpose.

The vial, though, never appeared. In its stead, an elastic, translucent sack slid from the tray's opposite side onto the belt. Inside the sack, I could see the pinkish-red fluid that'd been inside the vial. Together, the package began its journey, sliding along towards the instruments.

Like some mad experiment, the instruments attacked the sack and its contents. Lights beamed colors—and who knew what else—directly at the sack, while other syringes pierced the membrane ever-so-slightly and delivered injections. Still others reshaped the sack, pressing it back into the belt's center and misting it with sticky fluids.

I followed along, mesmerized by the dance. Given where I was, making a guess as to what was happening wasn't all that difficult, and the Voices had earlier alluded to Starship's large human embryo storage for future colonization. Fostering that expansion would be easier with something that could rapidly build a human from a cell collection to a functioning child.

The sack confirmed my intuition as it moved along, as its insides began to froth and grow. Connections spread out and linked along, expanding the sack across the belt's surface. The instruments adapted to their shifting target, and their assault increased in intensity, the tiny human subjected to an endless nutrient and chemical mix.

"Please stand away from the child," the mech announced, and I snapped my eyes away from the new life to the nurse, who regarded me with a warm warning. "You will be able to meet your baby soon."

"My baby?"

"Please, stand away," the nurse mech repeated, and I did, continuing to walk along the belt but now with the mech between me and the conveyor. "Your child is progressing normally. You should be proud."

I started to respond, started to declare that the embryo growing on the belt had no relation to me. Couldn't have, given my vessel origins. But I stopped, kept my mouth shut. If the nurse mech truly didn't realize I couldn't be a father, didn't understand that its home had been wrecked by some calamity, who knew what might happen if I pressed it further.

Introduce unexpected variables to mechs at your own peril.

The nurse mech seemed satisfied with my distancing, and together we followed the conveyor to the end, by which time, enclosed in the sack and sleeping with an innocent's bliss, was a newborn. Thin black hair, clasped hands, closed eyes and all the magic of new life.

The belt concluded with a slow slide onto a soft, royal blue cushion. As the baby arrived, glass gates rose up around that cushion, ready to catch any sudden moves. From above, a new light series began, haloing the child in reds, blues, pinks and greens. A spiraling ring dropped and moved itself along the child from top to bottom while the nurse mech and I took up positions opposite, the nurse ready to take the child through a now-closed, likely soon-to-be opened section in the glass wall.

When the ring finished, it retreated upwards, leaving the baby sleeping in its sack beneath the soft lights. Across the glass, green numbers appeared alongside categories; projected height, weight, blood type, and many others. All green.

"Congratulations, a healthy child," the nurse mech said to me, before turning back to the enclosure as the numbers continued to appear.

"Thank you?" I said, not quite knowing how to respond.

Leo had, perhaps unsurprisingly, not coded fatherhood into my directives.

When the numbers finished piling up, they pulled towards the screen's center, right in the middle of the outline marking the doorway through which we'd be grabbing the new baby. As the ratings crashed into the middle, a larger number emerged, above the words *Overall Assessment*. The values—expected IQ, allergies, possible disorders—morphed that number up and down, until it settled at a giant, green-glowing 84.

"Is that good?" I said when the nurse mech didn't immediately react.

"Unfortunately, your child does not meet our quality standards," the nurse mech replied. "I'm sorry, but you will have to try again."

"What?" I asked, because what else could you say to a sentence like that?

"Your doctor will explain," the nurse mech replied. "We encourage you to schedule a new appointment as soon as is practical."

I didn't know how to answer that, didn't know how to respond when the nurse mech extended its twin pronged implement into a port beneath that glass wall. The light haloing the newborn flashed red, the cushion swung away, and the child dropped.

THIRTY-ONE

OBJECTIVE COMPLETE

Mechs didn't come with any respect for life. Precisely how much I or any other mech valued a human, a child, depended on the code zipping along inside our processors. For the nurse, some algorithm had determined, despite the green approval on the glass, that the new-formed baby didn't meet the threshold.

My code went in a different direction.

As the cushion dropped away, I kicked into action before I'd realized what was happening. I grabbed and threw the nurse mech to the side, rushed forward and punched through the glass, reaching for the baby.

Too slow. My arms too short. I reached and felt empty air. Playing at possibilities—maybe something had stuck, maybe the baby only went a short way—I climbed into the conveyor belt's end, and looked down.

A black emptiness. A chute continuing past my sight, and too small for me to crawl into.

"Where does it go?" I asked the nurse mech, picking itself up from my toss. "The baby. Where did you send it?"

"Your assault has been noted," the nurse mech replied, no longer so soft, so warm in her tone. "The relevant authorities shall be—"

"I don't care," I replied. "Answer my question."

"I am not allowed to say."

"Fine." I pulled myself out, further shredding my clothes and scattering glass everywhere. Once again, having synthetic instead of human skin proved so valuable. "I can find out."

The nurse mech regarded me with what I'd call skepticism, except her features didn't move. No reason to pay for a motion-capture mouth on this machine. I didn't need her to talk to get the truth. The ports I'd use to hack inside her and find out what happened to the baby were visible on the mech's side. As I came closer, though, the nurse retreated, rolling back and away from my reach.

"Your hostile approach has been noted," the nurse mech said. "Please stay away until the authorities arrive."

"Hate to be the one to tell you," I said. "There aren't any authorities anymore."

Apparently the nurse didn't have the capacity to understand my assertion, as she kept repeating her line about the imminent authorities as I followed her further into the Nursery. I didn't rush—no matter how large the Nursery happened to be, the mech's room would run out eventually. As we went, the Nursery changed from conception to caring, with rooms dedicated to play spaces, to medical and therapy-oriented chambers.

For a moment, the Nursery's scope confused me: I'd thought this place existed to help newborn human children survive until a family arrived. As we moved along, though, the spaces gave voice to their own reasons to be. Not every child born on Starship had a ready family. Not every child was *born* at all. From what I'd just seen, the nurse mech could take a bit of stored genetic material and rapid-raise it into a living, breathing baby.

What happened if you needed to raise a child through its first years, its helpless stages? These rooms, with their eerie, pristine cleanliness and toys placed at meter-wide intervals, as if to ensure precise spacing for as many kids as possible, presented a logic I couldn't agree with. Leo had given me a conscience, had given me enough humanity to know whomever grew up in these rooms wouldn't be like Kaydee, wouldn't even be like her mother.

Delta's destruction kept pace with our retreating dance too, the occasional sliced-n-diced mech scattered across the floor, broken glass, or a long line slashing along metal tile.

"Please stay away," the nurse mech repeated, and once again I ignored her as we left behind an older play room filled with a fake garden, plastic flowers blowing in an artificial wind.

Except the garden marked the Nursery's end, and hallway-spanning, locked doors forbade our entry with big red STOP signs. The nurse backed up against those doors and froze, letting me catch up.

"Sorry," I offered, pressing my fingers together to go search for answers.

"Please," the nurse began, and for a split second I wondered whether the mech really felt any fear, whether it cared beyond its programming about my approach. "Stay away."

I didn't complete my musing, because the doors behind the nurse burst open, split down the middle and thrown outward, mashing the nurse mech and I into, then through, the glass pane walling off the false garden. I flew back, landing on a stiff, strawberry-covered mound, faux-dirt flying up and mingling with the glass all over me.

Clashing metal overwhelmed the Nursery's background hum, and I lifted my head to see Delta facing off with that giant, multi-limbed monster we'd seen with Fountain. The mech stood in its wrecked doorway, sporting slashes across its silver spheres. Delta, picking herself up from where the mech had tossed her, bore her own scratches, and metal glints showed along her arms and stomach where a gash had sliced away Delta's synthetic skin.

It appeared I was late to the party.

Not that either Delta or the mech noticed. They broke hard at each other, and at first I thought Delta was running in unarmed. Her fists pumped as she ran, as Delta leaped, and she grabbed what I'd thought was a shorter, sharper limb, yanking it out in a twisting fall back to the ground. Her jagged blade, now removed, drew a slash along the mech's shoulder, sparks flying as the attack severed some wire.

I managed to get to my feet in the time Delta did all that, a reflection both on her combat skill and my lack thereof. Delta didn't wait for me to do something else, didn't even know I was there. Instead, she ducked a clumsy swipe from the mech, then threw both hands on her sword's hilt and sliced the monstrous machine in two.

A rapid, crackling and green bang zapped through the space, fizzling out as it brushed my hair, buzzing my body and standing my synthetic nerves on end. Delta must have hit a battery, and as the sparking smoke cleared away, my vessel friend lay on her back, sword knocked away. Half the mech lay at her feet, but the top half? With what amounted to the thing's beady head?

Gone.

"Delta!" I shouted, trampling plastic flowers that sprang right back up in my wake. "You all right?"

Asking a shocked vessel to reply verbally felt kind of stupid, but Delta had been invincible thus far. No way any single mech could bring her down, no matter what strange stuff made up its insides.

Delta said nothing till I came up to her, till I saw the hard scoring along her outfit, the charred bits along her already-damaged hair. The synthetic skin along her hands, along the cuts she'd suffered, had turned black and red. Not good.

"You're late," Delta said, popping her eyes open and locking onto mine. "Too late."

"You're dying?"

"For the fight. You missed it."

My hopes at ever understanding Delta's humor died then.

"I think I caught the best part," I replied, reaching to help Delta up. "That was a great move."

"The one that nearly killed me?" Delta said, taking my offered hand and letting me pull her to a grudging stand.

"I mean, you almost killed that thing." I threw a worried look beyond those damaged doors. "Should have, really. I haven't seen a mech designed to survive a swing like yours."

"It's not dead?" Delta asked, following my look. "Where did it go?"

"Back there?"

Delta growled, picked up her sword from the ground, "I'm going to need a fix after this."

"You and me both."

"You?" Delta gave me a once-over. "What's wrong with you?"

"Inside," I said, thinking of Kaydee, who hadn't yet reappeared. Hadn't made any contact. "It's a long story."

"Then it can wait."

I didn't argue, and together Delta—lagging a little behind her usual murder momentum—and I went through the broken doors into the Nursery's guts. As for the nurse mech that I'd planned on interrogating, it lay in pieces near that false garden. If its systems were still active, I could try a hack later: the mech wouldn't be moving anywhere.

If the Nursery had made some concession to family friendliness before, with its play rooms and happier colors, these big doors marked that plan's end. Delta and I entered a darker space, with broader confines lit by soft red glows—matching, I noticed, the striping on the cell storage banks from the entrance. The red outlined a multi-leveled space, rising up and sinking below us for a story apiece, the borders not simple metal walls but, instead, computer panels mixed in with charging stations for the Nursery's mechs.

I counted ten nurse mechs on our level alone, sitting silent in their stations like statues as Delta led me to the room's center, where a flat escalator set hummed its continuous rounds between levels. With every step large enough for a nurse mech's trundle to fit, the escalator looked like a metal water wheel, churning invisible air currents.

"Do you know what they're doing here?" I asked as Delta looked up and down, no doubt hunting for the missing half that'd escaped her sword minutes ago.

"They raise human children," Delta said, as if reading from a label. She held her blade in both hands, sticking its point into the floor at her feet as she looked around. "That's why it's called a Nursery, is it not?"

"They're destroying the children," I replied. "Not raising them. I watched a nurse mech go through the whole process, watched the program state the child was viable, and then the mech ditched the baby."

I'd intended my words to have some effect on Delta. Inspire her to rage, maybe. Horror. But the vessel didn't flinch.

"Hello?" I asked. "Did you hear what I said?"

"What am I supposed to do about it, Gamma?" Delta replied.

"I . . ." I didn't have a great answer ready. I supposed a human might have been searching for companionship with the question, to get Delta to echo and confirm my own disgusted feelings about what was happening. "I don't know."

But I wasn't human, and now that might prove to be an advantage. Delta had her focus on the creature, but I could turn back to the mission. Find the broken connection, bring the Voices into play. Perhaps Leo could figure out what had turned the Nursery so far against its own goals, perhaps he could fix it.

"I'm going to find the terminal for the Voices," I said. "Watch my back."

"Done."

Well, if Delta couldn't provide much moral comfort, at least she'd keep me alive.

I took a slow walk along our level, confirmed my mech count. The monitors along here provided static, live views of the Nursery beds, though they were all empty now. In the past, humans might have stayed on this level, observing babies in their baskets. Now every screen, flickering to life as I turned my eyes to it in the dim red glow, showed a white mattress, a glass border, and nothing else.

"Anything?" Delta asked as I made my way back to her.

"Not on this level," I replied, and would have asked why she hadn't moved a muscle until I realized that muscles were precisely why she'd been standing still.

Driving her sword into the floor hadn't been some power move. Rather, Delta leaned on the blade, ever-so-slightly, while her synthetic skin went to work. It couldn't repair the damage done to Delta's metal bones, but the protective bio-gel could regrow its way along Delta's body, and those charred bits, the exposed circuits, vanished as Delta's skin did its work.

"Feeling better?" I asked, a little embarrassed I hadn't brought it up sooner.

Blame my empathy difficulties on Leo.

"That thing was different," Delta said, never once letting her eyes rest on me for more than a second. "It didn't fight me like Fountain, like a mech that had been programmed to deal with aggression."

"What do you mean?"

"I think it wanted to take me," Delta said. "It had openings. With all those arms, it could've hurt me worse than it did."

"Right." I joined Delta's searching looks, because it felt strange not to do so. Nothing moved in the large room that I could see. "When you say 'take me', take you where?"

"I don't know," Delta replied. "Just that it wanted something from me."

The vessel didn't offer up anything else, and I waited the requisite ten seconds for Delta to work up a better explanation. When that failed, and nothing else jumped from the shadows to attack us, I said I'd go to the top level next and see if I could find anything. Delta didn't object.

Delta hadn't been inside Alpha's programming, hadn't seen the moment where the defiant vessel had found itself raised up and thrown down by an invisible adversary. Kaydee had thought Alpha had been corrupted at that point. Making the link between that moment and the Nursery's monster filled in one more blank.

Corrupt Delta and gain one more soldier for its cause, whatever that was.

The escalator did its job well and I coasted up top, where the red glow only increased. Mechs didn't occupy slots up here, but rather countless storage lockers filled with replacement parts. Glass panels revealed nurse mech arms, heads, trundles, while others were stuffed with baby-related materials. Diapers and the like.

What I wanted, though, held center stage as the escalator let me off. A workstation like the ones on the bridge, with all the manual entry options a human might use, and ports for a mech like me. The two large screens were dark, the workstation looking like it had no power at all.

While Starship housed complex systems by the thousands, interconnected and sprawling across the Conduit's length, ultimately, every single one had an on off switch. The workstation's access panel sat beneath the screens, and when I popped it off—after a couple non-responsive button presses—the problem revealed itself.

The reason for Alpha's doomed quest? For Delta and my own consciousness?

A pulled cable. Yanked out from the workstation's power supply. I slipped the connection back into the brick-like black unit and, like a creature waking from a long sleep, the workstation chugged, beeped, and chimed its way back to life.

THANK YOU.

The screens flew text at me as I replaced the access panel.

WE ARE RUNNING OUR CHECKS NOW. CONGRATU-LATIONS ON YOUR SUCCESS, GAMMA.

"Not mine alone," I said. The Voices, patching into the Nursery's network, might be able to hear me. Might not. "Delta, can you come up here? I found the problem."

Delta didn't bother with a vocal reply, but her head, body, and blade joined me up top after a minute, and together we both watched the Voices continue their work. I took another cursory look inside myself, checked for Kaydee's presence, her files. Still blocked, still stuck.

Peony and Kaydee ought to have been resolving their differences at processor speed, far faster than the walking, talking, physical world. That Kaydee hadn't come back at all?

"Delta," I said. "Watch me for a minute. I need to take a trip inside myself."

"Is that what you call it?"

"Unless you have something better?"

Delta gave her head the slightest shake, then put her back to the wall, still leaning on her sword, so she could see both the monitors and keep tabs on the whole room. Quiet, red, and motionless, waiting for its moment.

"Be back in a microsecond," I said, then focused my attention inward.

MY PEARLY-FLOOR, crystal-ceilinged realm felt more like home than the physical world, and even though there wasn't any air to suck into my non-existent lungs, I took a long breath as soon as I formed up inside my digital space. Strange how human mannerisms continued to bleed into my functions, my desires. Whether Leo had hid that gradual transformation or Kaydee's presence caused it, I didn't know, didn't particularly care—humans had some good things going, and I didn't mind stealing a few.

Kaydee's files, added on, were a fair bit away from where I popped in. With the Chancellor, I'd had to take a meandering walk through the corrupted, damaged folders holding my programs. Now, cleaned up and crystallized, my drives let me fly through. I crouched like a sprinter, then burst forward, zipping past the crystals and all the data they contained, towards a farther set, a darker set.

I'd never looked at Kaydee's files from this perspective before, but

I'd expected them—seeing as they were a part of me—to look like the same crystals I had everywhere else. Except, as I came close, my shimmering crystals gave way to a duller set, ones splotched over with black and deep green blotches. Beyond that, a brighter, sicklier green webbing ran across all the crystals I'd marked as Kaydee's, as if sealing them away from my broader self.

"Well that's unexpected," I said, coming to a stop, looking up at the pulsing ivy arrangement.

Before I could come up with a plan to remove the webbing, to even discern whether it was harming or preventing harm, a hand landed on my arm. Not angry, not aggressive, but restraining.

Peony.

"I'm sorry you have to see this," Peony said as I looked at her, shrouded in a black dress, as if she attended a funeral. "Kaydee's too sick to save, Gamma. I'm going to delete her now."

THIRTY-TWO

NEW ORDERS

Delete Kaydee? Peony might be Kaydee's mother, might be in the Voices, but right then and there, Peony was only a program.

And in my digital world, I controlled what programs lived and died.

"You're not deleting her," I said, pulling my arm free and setting other processes to work on Peony's blocks keeping Kaydee locked away.

"Gamma, it's a risk to Starship for you to keep her data," Peony threw on a wan smile, as if we were two friends sharing in an unfortunate, necessary decision. "She could corrupt you, turn you against us. Starship itself would be at risk with a single rogue vessel."

"You've already got at least one," I replied, thinking of Alpha. Beta might still be out there too, for all I knew. "I've already come out corruption's other side. I'm not worried."

Peony killed her smile quick, murdered any congeniality. Hard, arms crossing and dead set against me, Peony tried again, "Gamma, this isn't a request. It's an order that I'm making for your own good. For our best interests. Let me delete her now, or do it yourself. The Voices command it."

Way back at the start, I might've put more stock in Peony's demand. Felt some compulsion to obey the Voices. Now that I'd seen what they were, digitally stored consciousnesses from a gaggle of Starship's notable past citizens, Peony's order lacked the divine authority she needed.

"I don't give a damn," I said. "Bye, Peony."

I waved my hand, set my processes to work, and Peony dissolved into nothing fast. She wasn't a virus, some malevolent hacker, and had no defenses. If only every troublesome program could get dealt with that way, I'd find keeping my digital space clean far easier.

Above me, the green casing dissolved too, little flakes floating around me and vanishing as they hit the pearl floor. The blotches on the crystals, though, remained. Damaged data, flawed lines in Kaydee's code. The potential problems Peony had warned me about, that I'd watch.

"Hey there, miss me?" Kaydee said, popping up behind me.

Potential problems that I'd live with for that sarcastic smile, that spearmint hair.

"You know," I replied, "I did. And I'd love to catch up, but we're in a mess outside."

"Color me surprised," Kaydee said, and she did, turning her skin a bright yellow-pink.

I laughed, closed my eyes, and warped out.

To stand back in the Nursery's red-black light. Delta had her eyes on the console, watching the words scrolling on the monitors like they were the most important things in existence.

"What do they want?" I asked.

"To destroy this place," Delta replied in her matter-of-fact manner. "The Voices say the Nursery cannot be salvaged."

"What?" I said. "What does that even mean?"

"I told them your story. About the child the mech threw away." Delta stood back from the screens, put her hands on her blade. "The Voices believe, without working mechs, the Nursery is lost. That Starship's future lies in their guidance, not in a new generation.

They would save any future children the harm by destroying them now."

"That's ridiculous." I pointed down the escalator, to the middle level with its unactivated mechs. "There's nurse mechs all over down there. We could reprogram them, fix the issue."

Delta followed my look for a long moment, then tilted her head back and shut her eyes. A respite, and I gave it to her while I tried to figure out why the Voices had turned. Sure, the Nursery had been damaged, but the cell banks looked in good shape. Even if some had been lost, surely that wasn't reason enough to scrap any chance at human life returning to Starship?

"Let me talk to them," I said, but as I started towards the workstation, Delta's eyes snapped back open, and her blade went up, point at my chest. "What are you doing?"

"Peony closed the conversation," Delta said, locking eyes with me now, steel blue against that red glow looking terrifying. "She said you were corrupted. That you would be dangerous to both Starship and myself."

I stepped back, gave myself a little room between my skin and that sword's jagged point.

"Peony's after her own ends," I said. "What did Leo say?"

"Nothing," Delta replied. "The others barely spoke."

"My mother's making her play," Kaydee said, popping in next to me. "It's how she always works, gets inside the power circle and redraws it till she's the only one that's left. Gamma, she attacked me in here, and she's good. She's been rewriting her own code, getting more effective, more dangerous."

Something to worry about later, maybe. After Delta had her blade away from my face.

"Who do you trust?" I asked the vessel. "Me, who's been with you this whole way, or the Voices?"

"Have you been with me?" Delta said, advancing for every step I retreated. "When I chased Alpha, you ran the other way. In the Hospital, with enemies everywhere, you found a lift and vanished.

When you found the Nursery, you didn't come running for me, but watched a routine."

Those were the most words I'd ever heard Delta speak in one go before, and I realized why: she cared, at least a little. Something in Delta gave a crap about what I'd done, the choices I made. Even here, as Delta contemplated murdering me, knowing she'd be sad about it warmed my cold, mechanical heart.

"You're forgetting Fountain and Power Core, where I threw myself at the mechs for you," I said, nearly back to the escalator. "Or right now, when I didn't care if you stood still and rested while I scouted around. I'm with you, Delta. On your side."

Delta shook her head short, quick. "Doesn't matter. I have new orders, Gamma."

With Kaydee shouting run, I ran. Turned and jumped onto the escalator heading down and kept moving, feet stumbling from one platform to the next on my tumbling journey down. Behind me, Delta didn't make a sound as she followed. I expected to be skewered before I made it anywhere, but Delta's blade didn't find its mark.

Or she wasn't quite as focused on killing me as she should have been.

"You don't have to follow their demands!" I yelled as I hit the middle level, falling to a crouch as I more or less fell off the last escalator.

"Dive!" Kaydee, popping in before me, eyes looking past me, shouted.

I dove and Delta's sword struck the floor where I'd been, gouging out silver flakes. She picked up her swing and followed me as I scrambled around and dropped onto the next escalator continuing down. Not that I had a plan beyond go up and down until Delta gave up, or caught me.

"If we don't follow their orders," Delta said as she walked—yes, walked—after me. "Then what are we?"

The red glow had increased when we went up, brighter and intense. Descending, though, pulled everything into shadow. Down here seemed to be more supplies, albeit ones less used. Mechs sat here, trash trundlers and other janitorial ones, deactivated and waiting for their chance to clean.

I would've taken a closer look, but Delta's sword kept whistling over my hair, just cutting my shirt's trailing cloth as I slipped down.

If I had taken that extra second, maybe I'd have seen it.

Whether I would have said something, I'm not sure.

This time, hitting the escalator's end, I jumped and rolled, bought myself a meter. Looked back to see Delta following me, the dim red haloing her black outfit, her shadowed blade, those sharp eyes making her look like something demonic.

"We're not just mechs, Delta," I said, standing up, shifting left. "We're not mindless."

Delta copied my move, cutting me off from reaching the escalator back up. My great plan ruined, I put up my fists. Figured maybe I could take a stab and get in one good punch. With a whole lotta luck, I might survive.

I didn't get a chance to test that theory, as I'd barely put myself into fighting martyr pose when a shape unfurled from the ceiling above us. Above Delta. The big mech's other half, its surviving limbs still moving even as fluid leaked from somewhere into a puddle on the floor. Delta noticed my look, followed it, and failed to move fast enough.

Lunging down like some predator, the mech swooped in and gathered Delta in its limbs, constricted her in a millisecond. Before Delta could even struggle, the mech brought her up and, extending a small jack from its head like a tiny diamond spear, pierced my former friend, my potential killer, my savior so many times.

"Like Alpha," Kaydee murmured next to me.

"What?"

"We saw this," Kaydee said. "When we were in Alpha's core, we saw him get lifted up like this, and then he changed. We knew he made it here, but . . ."

Delta getting corrupted hit me hard. Alpha had been bad

enough, with his conniving mech takeovers and insidious viruses. Delta wouldn't need those measures. She could simply destroy, slash, and burn anything that stood in her way. We wouldn't survive, but neither would Starship. At least, nothing the Nursery's head mech didn't want alive.

And given what I'd seen with the baby, the ugly mech wouldn't make for a good leader.

"Only have one option," I said.

"It's not a good one."

"We never get that lucky."

I ran straight towards the damned half-sawed mech and the vessel that'd been trying to kill me a hot second earlier. Threw my fingers together to form the jack, and jumped. In the near-dark, I had to guess at my aim, but thankfully Leo had given the vessels ports in the same places: behind our ears.

The big mech didn't move much when I crashed into it, when I, clinging to its limbs, climbed to where I could see its jack plugged in behind Delta's right ear. I went for her left, our strange trio hugging in Starship's dark depths and about to be reunited in Delta's digital world.

The transitions kept getting easier, blinking between reality and a virtual construct. I'm not sure whether that meant I was becoming more at home in digital space, or better attuned to the physical. As, essentially, an electrical product, what was my real home? Did I—

"Hey, pay attention," Kaydee said and snapped me into the bizarre place that Delta, apparently, called home.

We stood on a floating amber rock, maybe five meters across, and pitted as if someone had been using its surface for target practice. Above and around us, more rocks orbited, all strung together by massive blue-lightning cords. Beyond the rocks, the Nursery's deep red glow pervaded, pulsing from all around as if we'd fallen into some netherworld dance party.

"This is weird," I said.

"Once again, Delta does things way cooler than you," Kaydee

said, walking to the edge and peering over. "Looks like these keep on going."

In my world, there weren't random noises, weren't breezes, but in Delta's infinite rock column, the blue cords crackled and random gusts hit Kaydee and I like a trash mech's trundling charge. One blow pushed Kaydee back from her edge, and I moved to catch her only to see Kaydee's outfit shift into a suit like Delta's real-world kit: blue, black, and badass.

Kaydee's new boots dug into the rock, and she threw a grin at me, "Delta's given us permissions, Gamma. She must not hate you that much."

Like having an epiphany, I found digital threads at my beck and call. Like in my own space, I could bend gravity, my own shape, anything, really, to my will. Delta risked a lot giving Kaydee and I this much power: we could overwrite her memories, rewrite her programming.

"Change her to ignore the Voices," I said and Kaydee nodded.

"Maybe it's not an accident," Kaydee replied. "Maybe she wants you to."

A splitting shout broke from both far away and so close my ears rang and I dropped to my knees, my systems scrambled for a moment. Delta's scream, no doubt, and from above. Shaking my head—unnecessary, but it made me feel better—as I stood back up, I pointed above.

"Think there's other things to worry about first," I said. "Let's go."

Like the superheroes in the Librarian's stories, Kaydee and I leapt from one rock to the next, soaring high and landing with soft crunches before leaping on. Every jump brought us higher, brought us to more rocks. We moved faster, barely pausing between leaps, but still the rocks and their blue chains went on and on.

Delta screamed again. Still sounding like it came from above.

I stopped. Kaydee waited.

"What're you doing?" Kaydee said. "You're not tired?"

An impossibility in here, but I shook my head anyway.

"We're not getting anywhere this way," I said. "We've jumped up a hundred rocks by now and we're no closer."

"You don't know that."

"True, but I have a different idea," I said. "We have permissions. Let's use them."

Kaydee seemed confused, her sparks tossing golden question marks around her head. Rather than answering, I placed my hand on the rocky ground and called up a very particular routine. One that I'd programmed after Alpha's assault. The little program shot from my fingers into the rock and spread throughout Delta's systems faster than Kaydee and I could jump anywhere.

"What'd you do?" Kaydee asked.

"Watch."

The rocks shimmered around us, their edges fading away, the red glow flickered and faded to a soft, dead white. The fading continued until Kaydee and I stood on nothing at all, adrift in Delta's digital domain.

"You're searching," Kaydee said. "Smart."

"A good filter can work wonders," I replied.

With literal nothingness around us, Delta's constructs vanished as I removed their criteria from what Kaydee and I could see, could interact with. Just as we couldn't see particles or grasp the entire cosmos in our physical bodies, I limited what we could perceive in Delta's digital one.

"I've scrubbed everything away," I said. "Are you ready?"

"Gamma, I never thought you'd ask," Kaydee replied. "Let's destroy the sucker."

I adjusted my filter program to look for two things. Intruders and hosts. The gray-white void around us rippled, and I noted how strange it felt to be standing on nothing, feeling nothing, hearing nothing. Seeing only Kaydee.

The mech appeared first, monstrous and in full flavor. It towered over Kaydee and I, with its limbs—hundreds, far more than it ever had in reality—collapsing around some small form in its middle. The filter caught up with Delta and she popped in, surrounded by stabbing, ripping assaults tearing away at her digital consciousness.

Alpha had been broken by this creature, caught in its sinister embrace just as Delta was here. Alpha had been alone.

Delta had us.

"I break her free, you rescue," I threw Kaydee's way, and didn't wait for a response.

"Nice plan!" Kaydee shouted after me as I leapt into the air, launching with those same super muscles at Delta's struggling form.

The mech saw me coming, re-directed a few dozen claws my way. I adjusted the filter on the fly, tried to erase the limbs. They flickered, they remained, they caught me and held me fast.

How? I tried to puzzle it even as I worked my arms towards freedom, swung my head side to side to dodge incoming, shiny steel death. My filter hadn't affected the mech at all. I could control whether or not I could see it, but couldn't alter the mech itself?

Dammit.

I ducked forward, causing a particularly nasty five-pronged claw to launch overhead. The mech responded to my trick by curling that claw back, slamming into my neck and driving me down, down towards that infinite gray.

Delta had given us permissions for her world, her programs. The mech had done no such thing.

A golden line slashed over me, and the mech's weight vanished. Like someone pulling a taut string, I stopped myself, looked at Kaydee and caught her wink.

"Looked like you might need some help," Kaydee said, sending more golden bolts from her hands.

"Looked like you were right," I flipped myself over in time to see Kaydee's shots hammer home into the mech, each one blowing limbs apart, cutting closer to Delta. "Cover me."

"Again?"

"As many times as it takes."

THIRTY-THREE

MOMENT TO MOMENT

If there'd been a place I would have imagined having an all-out fight against a mechanical monster, Delta's digital void wouldn't have been it. Yet, as I took another leap towards Delta's captive form, the environment seemed to fit. Vessels, mechs, programs duking it out in total emptiness?

Appropriate.

Kaydee covered my new jump with her sparking bolts, the frizzy golden things crashing into the big mech. Each one found its target, blasting away a limb or frying a metal plate, not that the mech seemed to notice. Like a literal virus, the beast seemed to grow, its centipede-like bulk stringing out around us, spindly legs with their slashing claws reaching ever closer.

The mech had Delta up near its mouth, or what passed for one. The sharp spear that'd served as the mech's jack back in reality snaked out, rearing back to deliver a likely deathblow to Delta's captive form, struggling against a dozen claws holding her tight.

During my last leap, the mech had caught me, bashed me and thrown me away. This time, with Kaydee's blazing protection, I blitzed up and smashed into Delta and the arms holding her. With a quick rewrite, my left hand became a diamond blade and, with a single cut, I sliced away the claws clamping Delta on that side.

With her own left hand open, Delta went to work. Rather than freeing herself, Delta took her left hand and went on the attack. The vessel reached towards the centipede's enter, pure determination on her face as I fell away. Like Kaydee launching her golden blasts, Delta pulled a deep red, far larger version of her jagged scrap metal blade and shot it straight into the mech's core.

Delta kept hold on the long blade's hilt, and, flicking her wrist, glided the sword through the giant mech like I might wave my hand through the air. The mech shivered as Delta did her work, its limbs coming to a rigid halt one by one until, as she'd done in the physical world, Delta severed the mech in two.

While Delta did all this, I dropped back down to Kaydee's side, and together we watched as Delta embraced her freedom and used it to obliterate the mech. With every slice, Delta used her far-too-large-for-reality weapon to cut away the mech until nothing but fragments remained.

"She's really taking it to that thing," Kaydee said as we watched.

"Delta's not about restraint."

"Still," Kaydee tapped a finger against her lips. "It's a little scary. Wasn't she trying to kill you a minute ago?"

"I'm hoping this can change her mind."

"That's some hope, Gamma, because I think she could destroy you without a thought."

On that, Kaydee and I agreed.

Delta, having completed her mech evisceration, looked at the scraps floating around her, stuck in a void without gravity. Too tiny to slice up again, Delta let her sword go, the big blade a boiling crimson now, its surface moving like molten liquid. She reached out, gave the hilt a single light tap with her finger, and the weapon burst, its destructive code running forth around Delta and wrapping all those scraps in a consuming, red death.

"Thank you," Delta said when she landed in the nothing around us. The nothing but us. "That would have been difficult to win."

"Like you said," I offered, "we needed each other to pull this off."

Delta gave me the slightest nod, turned her attention to Kaydee, "This is the one you're talking to? Your mind?"

"Pleasure's all mine," Kaydee said, popping her lips and sending those trademark sparks from around her to puff around Delta, who waved them away. "And if you want a mind, I could jump your way. Gamma's a little boring."

"Hey," I countered. "Who saved both your lives?"

"You can be useful and boring at the same time, Gamma," Kaydee said.

"He *is* useful." Delta said, her lips turning up ever-so-slightly at the corners. More emotion than I'd ever seen from her. "I am sorry I tried to destroy you."

"Does that mean you're done trying?" I said.

Delta folded her arms, gave me a straight look that I took to mean whatever came from her mouth next would be the iron truth, "Peony says that you're a threat to Starship." A nod towards Kaydee. "That she's a threat to Starship. My job is to remove threats to Starship."

The problem presented like an equation. How to square the sides?

"Peony says that," I spoke slow, playing out the answer as I said it, "because she thinks I could become corrupted. That Kaydee could corrupt me."

"As if," Kaydee said, glancing away. "That was Alpha, not me."

Kaydee's recurrent memories weren't from Alpha, but I left that alone for now. The case for our survival wouldn't be helped if Delta knew Kaydee altered my reality every time her program glitched.

"That was her argument's core," Delta said.

"You didn't question it?" I asked.

"The Voices made us, Gamma," Delta frowned. "If I can't trust them, then how can I trust anything?"

"That's what I thought too, at first." I snapped my fingers, sending my own spearmint sparks popping in a halo over Kaydee's head. "Til she taught me to rely on my own judgment. The Voices don't own us, Delta. We can choose for ourselves."

"Never thought I'd hear a mech say those words," Kaydee muttered. "Whole new world."

Delta ignored her, kept her eyes on me. I couldn't tell if she planned to destroy me, hug me, or invite Kaydee and I into a deep discussion about Starship's decorative styles.

"Get out," Delta said finally. "Please."

I hesitated. Not because I wanted to push Delta, but because outside, back in that physical world, Delta would have every advantage over me. I'd be toast. In here, with Kaydee next to me and a programming plethora at my digital fingertips, I could knock Delta out. Shift her systems into a more placid state.

Pacify my friend.

"Gamma," Kaydee said. "Either you trust her, or you don't. Make the call."

Point taken, but self preservation, even for mechs like me, was a powerful motivator.

"Do you trust me?" I said to Delta. "Because I trust you."

"If you trust me," Delta replied, "then do what I'm telling you. Get out."

At some point, everyone has to make a leap. I'd learned that much from the Librarian's stories. You come to that chasm where you can't turn back. You have to jump and hope. I felt like I'd reached that point now, and staying back, giving in to fear would keep me in Delta's domain. Would break any possible bond we had and throw her and I into a fight for Delta's soul.

So I did what Humans do. Stuck out my hand towards Delta, who looked at my fingers like they might turn into snakes and bite her. Kaydee rolled her eyes.

"What are you doing?" Delta asked.

"Shake it," I said.

"Shake what?"

"My hand."

"How?"

Kaydee had destroyed the Librarian within a few hours of me meeting him. I hadn't even learned the man's real name. Yet, within that time, the man had dumped story after story into my drives that I'd read while wandering Starship's Conduit. I'd thought the main value in those tales came from their themes, their heroes and their quests and how they broke life into moral lines.

But no. The real value came in the moment-to-moment rituals most mechs never knew. The little things that bind humans to one another.

Step by halting step, I walked Delta through shaking my hand. Her grip started tentative, finished steel, and I had to remind her to let go, lest she pull my wrist from its socket.

"Sorry," Delta offered as I wrenched my hand free. "First time."

"You shook, that's what matters. We're bound now," I replied, then sent that same hand reaching for Kaydee, who did not need instructions to take it. "See you on the outside."

THE POP BACK TO REALITY, to that dim red glow and the split mech's wreckage, came both instantly and with long-lasting impact. Every transition came easier, and every one carried with it a fragment of where I'd been. Like traveling to Starship's various zones, I'd taken away a lesson from Delta's rock-strewn home: don't complicate things.

Delta's complex file structure would've had us hopping from one rock to another for who knew how long without my filter. The long pearl plain I called home? Easy to spot an intruder, easy for the help to find me.

"You do know that shaking hands isn't really binding, right?" Kaydee said, joining me in the gloom as I retreated from Delta and the mech, giving the vessel some space to put herself together. "There's no magic or anything in it."

"But, in the stories, it always works?"

"Stories, Gamma, are stories. This is reality. People lie."

"Mechs aren't people." I nodded at Delta. "She doesn't lie."

"You better hope so."

Delta sat still, and I wondered if something had gone wrong. If the mech had pulled a move none of us saw coming. Restarts, though, could take a while. Especially if all our smashing and shooting damaged Delta's code, just like her skin and bones showed new scratches on the outside.

With Delta disabled for the moment, I noticed the escalator continuing its endless journey behind her. One leading up. All the way up to a workstation.

"I've got an idea," I said, walking around Delta and onto the escalator.

"Is it a good idea, or a bad idea?" Kaydee faded in on the escalator's railing, riding up alongside me.

"Kaydee, I missed you." I gave her as genuine a smile as a mech like me knew how to pull together. "Glad you weren't deleted."

"We have to talk about that sometime," Kaydee replied, apparently not buying my affection. "You let Peony in, Gamma. She could've killed me."

I started to reply, then stopped. Kaydee had it right, though I couldn't have known Peony's dire attitude when she'd told me Kaydee could be a destructive force. Instead, I took a different tack as the escalator deposited us on the middle level.

"I worried about you," I said, walking around to catch a platform to the top. "Still do. We're in dangerous territory, Kaydee. When you shifted my perception in the hospital, I could've died."

When Kaydee joined me on the escalator to the top, it wasn't as her normal spunky self. Instead, the Kaydee on the platform with me looked thin and sickly, just the way I'd seen her in the memory, under a hospital bed's covers and being wheeled to who knew what end.

"I told you, Gamma, I can't control everything about me," Kaydee said, her voice tight and withered. "I'm a mind, not a mech. Packed with faults."

"I understand."

"Not really, not really you don't." Kaydee closed in on her self, sat folding her arms and legs up. "My mother showed me what I couldn't access. The memories I couldn't see."

The escalator hit the top level and I stepped off. The workstation sat not far away, waiting, but I couldn't go to it. Not yet.

"What were they?" I asked when Kaydee didn't continue.

She sat at the escalator's edge, the platforms sliding away beneath her, looking into the red. For all the time I'd known Kaydee, I'd treated her as an evolving enigma. At first she'd been a mystery, then a partner, then a danger, and finally a friend. Only now, I saw her as a human, with all their frailty, all their faults, and all their possibility.

"I never left that hospital, Gamma," Kaydee said. "I'd been injured, but more than that, I couldn't find the motivation to keep going. Back then, every cause I'd worked for had ended in failure. My friends, the ones struggling against the Voices, were either dead or about to be shot out the airlock."

"I'm sorry."

What else was there to say?

"Don't be," Kaydee replied. "I made those choices. The consequences came because I wasn't good enough. Not smart enough, not strong enough. Once my mom realized I wasn't going to come back, she turned me into this."

Silence.

"I'm glad she did," I offered, sitting next to Kaydee. "Without you, I wouldn't have made it very far."

Kaydee snorted, "Without me, you wouldn't have made it outta Leo's lab."

"Hey."

But Kaydee had fallen into that relieved, post-confessional laughter that set my digital heart at ease. Kaydee might be hurt, might be suffering, but she was still my friend, and I hers. We weren't alone on this metal hulk hurtling through the stars, and that counted for something.

"So why'd you come up here anyway?" Kaydee said, using her arm to wipe away her nose, her eyes. "Just to talk to me?"

"Actually, it's about your mother."

"That's even worse."

I stood up, turned back to the workstation, "I don't think she's going to like what I'm about to do."

"Which is?"

"Watch."

The first mission I'd been given, way back then: Reconnect the Nursery. Give the Voices access to all the potential humans sitting in Starship's cold storage. The virtual minds owning the present wanted the future too. Except they'd found it lacking, told Delta to destroy it.

I couldn't get the baby out of my memory. It kept falling, disappearing as the cushion moved away. Starship's future cast aside. I didn't understand why, but I wouldn't let it happen anymore. Delta had killed the mech running this place, now I had to stop its replacements.

The workstation didn't present much of an obstacle. Words appeared as I approached—apparently the Voices had a camera somewhere—but I ignored them. Reached down, opened the plate, and pulled the same damn plug I'd put back when we arrived here. The screens went blank, the Voices' ambitions reset.

"Guess that'll show'em," Kaydee said, the hospital look replaced with her usual. "Until Delta kills you and puts it back."

"She won't," I replied, slotting the plate into position, dusting myself off. "We shook hands."

"Uh huh." Kaydee looked towards the escalators. "You going to prep anything? A trap?"

"No. It wouldn't do any good." I went to the escalator's end, looked down and saw Delta on her way up. "If Delta wants me dead, I can't stop her."

"Such an optimist."

"You're the one who keeps telling me how cool she is."

"Yeah," Kaydee said, pointing towards Delta as she came around the middle level. "Because I wanted you to be her friend. So this wouldn't happen."

Delta had her sword with her, hung over her shoulder. She kept her head down, as if moving on autopilot. I retreated from the escalator, put my back to the wall, faced forward, and waited. If Delta wanted me dead, she had her execution set up.

"Kaydee," I said, leaning my head against the metal wall. "It's been a real pleasure."

"Gamma, I'd have to agree," Kaydee said. "So, who takes care of Alvie once Delta cuts you to pieces."

"Alpha, I guess."

"He'd be the worst. The absolute worst."

I laughed, because what else could I do?

Delta crested the level, saw me and unlimbered her sword. She took two steps towards me, her face set, those blue eyes everything I never wanted to see directed my way.

"I learned the truth," Delta said.

I prepared for her to deliver it, blade first.

THIRTY-FOUR

CHOICES

The million needed a caretaker. A tireless warden that would ensure their safety, that would keep the children ready for when Starship needed them to fill the new colony. No human could fulfill the constant responsibility, so as Starship hurtled on through the long void, its engineers sought to save their future.

To populate a colony, or recover Starship after a devastating event, would mean raising dozens at once. Would require flexible limbs able to grip and pull and place, yet nimble enough to feed. Supporting mechs would be necessary, as would rooms ready to take a child from its "birth" to an age where it could be handed over to any survivors.

Provided, of course, Starship remained safe. That duty, too, fell to the Warden. Raise the future, and ensure they would survive. They gave the Warden the means to do this, some protective programming and, given its position, the ability and permissions to rewrite other mechs into its designs. If needed, the Warden could take Starship for its own, all to save the future.

"But the baby," I interrupted, Delta and I standing near the silent conveyor belt now, the many implements designed to take a cell collection and turn it into a living, breathing human. "The nurse discarded it without a thought. How does that square with the Warden's directives?"

Delta, both hands still on that sword hilt, its point in the ground for her support. Her synthetic skin healed, but given her injuries, the progress came slow. Delta didn't seem weak, exactly, but she needed more intensive repairs, fixes to her frame that'd been scrapped, dented, damaged by the mechs she'd torn through on our way here.

On her way to seeing me as a friend, rather than an enemy.

"Like the others," Delta said. "It lost itself in its own mission. They programmed the Warden to raise perfect humans. Once the mech assessed that its environment, its mechs were optimal. . ."

"The fault lay with the biology," I finished, remembering the score. Above average, stable, but not perfect. No human would be. "It couldn't accept an imperfection."

"Rigid code causes problems," Kaydee said, wandering the cell stacks behind us. "At least on Starship, with mechs like these."

If the Warden had been tasked with keeping care of humanity's future, our destroying it put all these frozen lives in jeopardy. Especially given the Voices' abdicating their role, demanding the Nursery's end. They'd given up, or decided Starship's future lay in another direction.

"What now?" Delta said, looking at that still belt. "I disobeyed orders. We have no mission."

"Not true," I replied. "We just have to define it for ourselves."

I'd been mulling the idea since Delta had cleaved away Alpha's corruption. The Voices said Starship had nearly reached its journey's end. A new home. I didn't know if the Voices had a spot for us in their plan, but now I didn't care. They were locked up in Starship's systems, while Delta and I lived out here.

"Let's go back to that workstation," I said.

While we walked, I pitched my idea. Delta and I were vessels, smart and flexible mechs. Able to rewrite and fix Starship's mechanical multitudes and bring them back to some sanity. Then, with our newfound nuts'n'bolts civilization, we could prepare Starship for landing. We could create a new world for ourselves, one where mechs wouldn't have to bash each other for the human's poor programming.

"And the children?" Delta asked as we went up the escalator. "All of these? What would you do?"

"When the time's right?" I said. "We bring them out. Raise them the right way, alongside us. As equals and partners, rather than masters."

"It's an idea," Delta said.

"Do you have a better one?"

"No."

Sometimes Delta could be maddening with her simple replies, her dry words. Nevertheless, I could be patient. Now that she wasn't going to slice me apart, what else was she going to do? We were stuck on Starship, and—

"It's blinking." Delta said as I plugged the workstation back in.

"The Voices, I bet."

"Wrong!" Volt's voice boomed from the speakers, crackling and clearly happy for some reason. "Saw the power shifts coming from the Nursery and figured you two had made it."

The mech's black, lightning bolt face hovered into view on the screen. I gave Volt the rundown on what'd happened, with the old mech cackling throughout, as though our near-death adventure was the best story he'd heard in a long time.

"Now, now, you've done a helluva job there," Volt said when I'd finished. "But before you get too excited, there's someone you ought to meet. Someone who's got a big surprise waiting for you."

"Who?" Delta asked.

"Don't think she'd want me to ruin the moment, but seeing as she needs your help, I don't really give a damn," Volt said. "You mentioned that human kid? The one that vanished? Every hole on Starship leads somewhere, Gamma."

"Are you saying that baby's still alive?" I asked, leaning in towards the picture, as if that would bring me closer to that disappearing child.

"I'm saying it might not be if you don't get moving," Volt replied. "The Voices aren't the only one that want Starship for themselves. You want to save that kid, then you have to find Beta. And fast."

"How do we find her?"

"Follow the baby," Volt replied. "But don't take too long, or you're not gonna have much to find."

Volt popped off, leaving Delta and I in that red glow. Starship's ever-present hum in the background, reminding us every second that we stood inside a massive, churning machine. One speeding towards a target, a home that would belong to whomever controlled Starship when it landed.

"You said you wanted new orders." I put my hand on Delta's shoulder. "Sounds like we have some."

Delta shook her head, "Not orders. A choice. Think about Alpha. What if Beta's corrupted like him?"

"But what if she's not?" I said. "Who knows how many children the Warden lost. If Beta has them, we have to try and find her."

"Because you want to save the humans?"

Kaydee, standing behind Delta, watched with sparks popping around her spearmint hair. Imperfectly perfect.

"Because a human saved me."

READ *on for an excerpt of book two in* THE FAR HORIZONS - THE FLAWED DESIGN!

AN EXCERPT FROM THE FLAWED DESIGN

BOOK TWO IN THE FAR HORIZONS

What to do with freedom?

One choice stood across our conquered territory, leaning against a friendly, emerald-lit exit. She crossed one ankle over the other, and at her toes planted a jagged silver-black metal bar. Her eyes looked outside the Nursery into the Conduit's blue-tinged misty middle.

Delta guarded our little sanctuary, several large square rooms holding human lives by the thousands. Those lives, squeezed into small frozen tubes, waited for a coming resurrection, one it was my duty to provide. It hadn't always been so, but the machines watching over these static souls had been corrupted by time, poor programming, and zero supervision.

I had my left hand on one now, a nursing mech with wheels for feet, several soft hands for carrying newborns, and a cheery smile etched onto her cream-colored metal skin. My right hand, fingers coalesced into a connection port, lanced into the accepting slot in the mech's side.

Kaydee, a friend both dead and alive, spun her code through my connection. We'd been rewriting algorithms for a day already, twenty-four hours weeding through ifs and thens, functions and variables to clean out faults left to rot by the mech's original programmers.

They'd designed the Nursery to produce top notch children, to preserve genetic excellence and exile any embryos that wouldn't lead to the brightest minds, the strongest muscles, the fastest legs. A flawed goal, particularly when dealing with flawed specimens.

In my left eye I saw the recording, a memory of sorts, play out again: the embryo deposited on the conveyor belt, a long thing resting on my right. The child-to-be started out as nothing. It endured a light, chemical, and physical onslaught to stimulate growth. Every meter the vial crawled along the conveyor belt brought it closer to crawling without the belt at all. By the time the child reached the track's end, a fully formed human infant sat waiting to issue its first wailing cry.

In the memory—the recording—the child never had the chance to speak its mind. Scans I didn't understand washed over the child, cameras and sensors cloaking the small figure only to spit out suboptimal values. Not bad by any measure I could find, but not perfect.

The system didn't approve. The child vanished down a hole we could not follow.

But we could prevent further losses and so we did. Delta and I, together, defeated both our own programming and the Nursery's ruling machine. In doing so we fulfilled our goal. In doing so, we created a target.

The disappearing child created a mission.

Volt, a firebrand mech managing Starship's power, told us the child might yet survive. Told us he'd seen growing usage deep in Starship's lower aft area. Almost to the engines and well back from the Nursery. Volt investigated the pull and found a missing link.

Alpha, myself, and Delta were alive and found. Beta had vanished, woken up by the same guiding remnants that'd brought me from my programmed slumber only to disappear.

Volt found her watching over the children the Nursery discarded. The question Volt couldn't answer, the one he wanted us to investigate, was why.

"Are you done yet?" Delta asked without turning our way.

She already knew the answer. This was the third time she'd repeated the question.

"When this one moves like the others you'll know," I replied.

"Two ought to be enough," Delta said. Her voice had amber's solid character, color. Rich not so much with emotion as with reason. "They aren't waking up yet."

The two nurse mechs Kaydee and I had already fixed were busy in the nursery's back, cleaning up all the damage we'd caused in our raucous battle with the area's former owner. The caretakers sucked up shrapnel, patched together toys broken in the little playroom, and checked the baby food and milk stores. The latter had enough to carry a thousand newborns through three years, meant to offer humanity a chance to establish itself before taking on a new population.

"We don't know how much longer it will be," I said, eyeing the jack again. Kaydee was taking longer with this one. "The Voices hinted that we're close."

"They hinted at many things," Delta said. "The only way to know for certain is to get back to the bridge."

"Which we'll do *after* we find Beta."

"An unnecessary delay." Delta stepped away from the entry, lifted that jagged blade and swooshed it through the air.

The movements weren't random but precise, calibrated to test her range. She'd been damaged a little in the fight and, unlike humans, we vessels had to have our parts stitched back together.

I'd done the best I could. You couldn't see the slits, but, if you paid close attention, the slightest hitches revealed themselves as Delta looped the blade back and forth. Milliseconds added to a record time.

A problem?

That depended on what remained to fight on Starship. With the Nursery returned to us, we'd pushed against the Voices. I had to hope the ruling, digital council made up of long-dead humans wouldn't throw what forces they had against us. Wouldn't risk all those unborn lives.

But they weren't the only enemies.

"You're concerned about Alpha?" I asked.

Delta didn't nod but her fingers, tightening their grip on the blade's hilt, served as an answer.

"Alvie's watching him," I continued. The mech dog had an unshakeable loyalty to me, programmed in when I'd brought the thing to its metal life. "If Alpha moves, Alvie's going to tear him apart."

"I would trust the dog for an hour," Delta said, "not a day. We should have killed him."

My argument—there were only four of us vessels, killing shouldn't be the first response—died when the jack connecting me to the nurse mech popped free. The nurse mech jerked forward, wheeling around and glaring my way, caring eyes a hot, angry red.

"Sorry," Kaydee said, appearing off to the right with her head shaking. "This one didn't want to play along like the others."

I back-pedaled as the nurse mech advanced. We matched in size and I didn't lack for strength, but I did lack for a weapon. Straight up grappling might get me injured, not something I wanted before embarking on another journey.

"So you made her angry?" I asked Kaydee.

"Threat response algorithm," Kaydee replied, not sounding quite as apologetic as I'd expect. "Try to tamper with a nurse mech and you get an all-out defense."

My back hit a tall rack stuffed with frozen human cells. The mech approached, arms reaching for my neck. I protested, told it I didn't mean any harm.

The mech did as much with my words as an angry beast might. She reached towards me and I blocked her, my two hands meeting its match and holding it even. The mech had strength, but my synthetic muscles had flexibility. I pushed the nurse mech's arms aside, drained their leverage.

"Please," I said. "We can still use you."

The etched smile, the red eyes, pressed on silently.

Until Delta's blade appeared, jutting through the nurse mech and nearly poking my own face. Sparks rained on me, little burning twinges wherever they caught my bare skin. The nurse mech's red eyes flickered and faded, its hands dropped, and as Delta withdrew the blade, the mech collapsed onto the floor.

"She failed," Delta said, stamping the blade through the fallen mech's middle to confirm the kill.

"It happens," I replied, brushing off shards.

"Yeah," Kaydee echoed, though Delta couldn't hear her. Kaydee's existence as a program, albeit a complex one, limited her impact to my world. She stuck her tongue out towards Delta, flipped the vessel a middle finger, then sighed. "Some of them are more corrupted, Gamma. This one had her code already scrambled."

We'd witnessed that elsewhere: mechs with their inner functions, ones designed to keep them to strict orders, stricter routines, broken down into aggressive variants. If, say, a mech had been tasked with keeping an apartment clean, the corrupted version would interpret any person entering as bringing dirt inside, and thus act with extreme prejudice to remove the visitor permanently.

Kaydee blamed Alpha, but I wasn't so sure.

So much around Starship seemed to be reaching the long end of centuries spent spiraling. Alpha might have problems, but I didn't believe he'd done so much to ruin the ship. Rather, without regular maintenance, I figured human coding and its flaws bore more responsibility.

"So?" Delta asked. "Are we done here?"

Behind us, I could hear the two successful nurse mechs continuing their work. They'd eventually find this one and trash it, dump it down the Conduit's vast middle to the junkyards down below. Then they'd get back to babysitting.

Which left us free to walk away.

"You think those two can keep all these people safe?" Kaydee asked, popping in beside me, staring at the cells stacked in vial upon vial, locked into the freezer rack in its glass-black intensity. "Two nurse mechs against what we've seen already?"

"Who's going to be coming after them?" I replied, Delta shaking her head as I spoke to a person she couldn't hear, see. "The Voices?"

"Maybe."

"Then I have a different idea," I said.

Together, Delta and I left the Nursery for the Conduit. The massive corridor, spanning Starship's length and most of its height, cut through like a hazy blue gash. Not all that long ago, when I'd first walked its length, there'd been chaos. Mechs had been fighting each other, their berserk programming causing the machines to go for violence. Fires, ripping metal, and mechs simply ramming into things turned the Conduit into a horrifying look at robotics gone wrong.

That had been farther up the Conduit, closer to Starship's Bridge and on the Garden's other side. Back here, where Starship's middle class had dominated, the mechs weren't so prolific nor so corrupted. That, and Delta had slaughtered so many already.

Hard to have a riot if everyone's already dead.

"Seal it," I said to Delta as I stepped away from the Nursery entrance's panel.

The little black screen looked for an ID to scan or, failing that, the screen would give you a chance to enter in a code that'd turn the red-glowing gem in the Nursery's door green.

"You won't be able to get back in," Delta replied.

"We'll just cut a new hole," I answered.

Delta didn't wait for further explanation, stabbing forward with the blade. The sword struck the screen, cut right through that glass and the processor behind it. The Nursery's door stayed red, and now it wouldn't be changing.

I took a big breath. Unnecessary from a survival standpoint, but useful to parse the air, pick out its components. Right now, the Conduit came through clean, albeit with the tiniest moldy undercurrent. Starship didn't have too many biological pieces left, but with few things caring for them, the slow rot lingered.

Delta turned bridge-ward, swinging the blade up and over to rest on her shoulder, "Coming?"

"That's the wrong way, Delta," I said.

"For you," Delta replied. "I have unfinished business."

An incoming noise rose from the Conduit's depths, a rippling hum we both knew well enough. Delta put both her hands on her blade and I stepped up to the Conduit's railing, looking towards the noise.

"And here it comes," Kaydee said, snapping her fingers to send virtual fireworks spitting out over the abyss.

"Here comes what?"

"The twist."

The noise resolved itself into what looked like a bottle coated with arms. The courier's fatter end spewed out a white-gold thrust, sending the bottle mech towards us. What lay in its arms was more concerning, a package the mech let fly free as it swerved near us. The bundle bounced off the Nursery's outer wall, coming to rest on the ground near my feet.

The flying mech completed its loop, turned and jetted back up the Conduit without a word.

Bending over the package, I ran my hands over the metal, the limbs all packed in tight together. The dead eyes and the note etched into Alvie's back. My faithful mech, constructed in Starship's depths from scrap. Tasked to watch Alpha and now here, broken.

"We should have left sooner," Delta said, watching me as I unbound Alvie's limbs.

Vines ripped from the Garden's walls served as rope, though I doubted they'd have held Alvie if the dog still ran. I tore them off, searched for the port that'd give me access to Alvie's insides, a chance to see if anything still ran. When I found the port, I found more torn up metal. Alpha had shredded the connection.

Alvie would need to be repaired before I could even see if the dog's mind remained.

"Gamma," Delta said. "Leave it. Alpha's free. We have to get after him."

I shook my head, "We don't know where he is. He could be anywhere, waiting to trap us, trick us. No. The right call is back. With Beta."

"Hey," Kaydee said. "You reading this?"

She pointed to Alvie's back, where Alpha had etched his message. Short, condescending.

"Saving Starship from tyranny?" Kaydee continued as I turned the dog over. "Not blaming you for being weak and following your programming? This guy."

Delta knelt next to me, nodded as she read the message, "We must stop him."

"We'll have a better chance of doing that with friends," I replied, lifting Alvie in my arms. "It's not far and I think it's the best chance we've got."

"Seconded," Kaydee echoed to no one. "Alpha's a scary dude. Better to get overwhelming firepower."

Delta took another long look up the Conduit. For a long moment I wondered if she was really going to ignore me, dart off on a solo strike, odds be damned. Instead, she shivered once, then turned back my way.

"My programming requires fulfilling a promise, Gamma," Delta said. "I cannot leave Alpha alive any longer."

Holding Alvie, dead and dark in my hands, my equation changed. I couldn't go it alone, and I couldn't let Delta throw herself into danger solo.

Beta and the children would wait.

Continue THE FLAWED DESIGN at your favorite retailer!

ACKNOWLEDGMENTS AND AUTHOR'S NOTE

The Farthest Star owes a debt to many other fictions depicting futures run not by humans but by their creations. Having read many of these, I wanted to take my own spin on the genre, specifically one that dealt more with the relationship between the androids and the humans that created them.

Kaydee was, at first, four or five separate personalities all waging a miniature war for Gamma's attention. What I'd thought could prove compelling stories instead became muddled: too many cooks in Gamma's kitchen, really. Kaydee herself sprang from one of those personalities, a bright and glittery spark that gave the story much-needed life, laughter, and a heart.

The Farthest Star is book one of a trilogy, and while it involves a big spaceship and battle-ready robots facing off against one another, it's really a story about how we pass a part of ourselves into every-thing we make, our story lives on in what we do.

I hope you enjoy reading this as much as I enjoy writing them, and thanks for coming along on the journey!

ABOUT THE AUTHOR

A.R. Knight spins stories in a frosty house in Madison, WI, primarily owned by a pair of cats. After getting sucked into the working grind in the economic crash of the 2008, he found himself spending boring meetings soaring through space and going on grand adventures.

Eventually, spending time with podcasting, screenplays, short stories and other novels, he found a story he could fall into and a cast of characters both entertaining and full of heart.

A.R. Knight plans on jumping through to other worlds and finding new stories to tell in the limitless borders of our imagination.

Thanks, as always, for reading!

For more information:
www.adamrknight.com

To Evan

Copyright © 2020 by A.R. Knight
All rights reserved.
ISBNs:
Ebook: 978-1-946554-63-5
Paperback: 978-1-946554-65-9
Hardcover: 979-8-88858-034-9
Large Print: 979-8-88858-035-6
Published by Black Key Books
www.blackkeybooks.com

Made in the USA
Las Vegas, NV
12 December 2024

14bd26e1-ec25-4d0f-82b9-c33b38d0be73R01